RUNNING IN THE RAIN

Ronda Burke

For my daughters, Emma and Lily;

may they never find the need to run.

"Life can only be understood backwards;

but it must be lived forwards."

Soren Kierkegaard

1

I FIND HIM IN THE MEADOW

Summer in Manhattan and the only outlet I find from the never-ending lack of fresh air is Central Park. During the day, I ride my agent's rickety, pea green ten-speed in the streets of the city to avoid the costly subway fare. For all the places I need to go each day, the bike seems like the most practical idea. Riding the bike in the streets of New York is a dangerous and death-defying rush of pure energy, not to mention a welcome physical workout and test of endurance. It is a test, a challenge, a break from all that I'd ever known; and for this reason, I am nearly pleased with the craziness of it all.

I endure the noise, the traffic, the dirt, and the smells every day, and then realize quite suddenly I am alone in my race down Broadway each morning. Where are all the others interested in saving a buck or shedding a pound? I look around only to find a few muscular messenger boys racing here or there with a package. A couple call out to me, pointing to their heads and their hands. It takes me awhile to figure out what they are trying to say, and then I decide to look at what they are seeing: a skinny, young, mid-western girl in a short black skirt with a backpack on her back. They shake their heads at my reddening face as I speed through red lights, my long brown hair flying free in back of me.

They see a fool without gloves or helmet, glasses, proper shoes, or kneepads. They see an accident waiting to happen, I suppose. I smile at them, agree with them, and pray to the Lord for the third time that day to bring me home alive.

My insurance must be invisible, unrestrained. I don't have time for all the gear and prevention. I ride on faith. Is it my fault I finally feel invincible, free, even liberated? I ride to celebrate a long-awaited departure from the confines of a place to which I will not return. Such a ride should not be so planned or premeditated. It would take away the joy and sensation of escape.

Michael tends to disagree with my preferred mode of transportation even though I've argued my case on several points. His first concern is my safety, but only because it affects my beauty, my skin, my marketability. He begs me to ride the subway and insists upon it on days I have bookings, which are becoming more and more frequent. God forbid I get something in my eye on the way to a shoot. I acquiesce because Michael has taken the place of caretaker, father figure, or favorite uncle for me. Not that I ever had a favorite uncle, or even a father figure, for that matter. But if I had someone like this, I would want him to be like Michael. After all, he let me use his bike on the very second day he knew me.

I am completely caught up in the current mess in which I find myself, as I tread lightly upon it and stand as an opposite to it, for that is what I came here to be: quiet, clean, desired, fresh—all the things the city isn't and is willing to pay for to get.

But if it weren't for the park, the one place that stands along side me in contrast, the garden amidst the garbage, the sanctuary amidst the savage, I would find it much more difficult to keep up with the race. I go there as often as possible and always on the weekends. I ride the pea green ten-speed to Sheep Meadow with my backpack full of park necessities: my yellow Sony walkman that no longer rewinds; my tattered, cotton quilt I've had with me since I can't remember; pumpernickel bagels; plain yogurt: and whatever Margaret Atwood novel I might be reading at the time. I lie there in the green, soaking in the weirdness around me: homeless, old hippie men picking at their hangnails; young lawyers and stock brokers strutting through, walking their bikes in their short, white shorts, losing themselves like me or looking for girls like me.

I went out with one of them once. He was a lawyer who seemed quite taken with himself. I dressed up in black and heels and we met at a play that was showing Off-Broadway. I feigned a small, serious interest in the production, trying to fit in with the crowd, and afterwards he suggested we stop for a bite to eat at a quaint, underground restaurant he knew of near his apartment. I consented drowsily and dragged my uncomfortable shoes five blocks to watch him eat a hamburger and home fries while I sipped my mineral water and chewed on some sesame breadsticks. It just didn't seem like the occasion to let on that I was really a hungry tomboy wannabe who had been raised to enjoy big steaks and buttered potatoes with ice cream and hot fudge for desert. Instead, I pretended to be the pristine princess these kinds of guys seemed to be looking for. Why? I had blood running through my body that desired to please, which needed to please to feel worthwhile.

"Would you like to see some of my art?" Apparently, my young lawyer was an aspiring artist on the side. How impressive.

"Sure," I said, with just a slight inflection at the end to show how interested I was. Certainly an artist has no naughty intentions of seducing a young girl he barely knows. So I followed him up to his small apartment where everything was in its proper place, and all the towels hung evenly when I visited his bathroom, which seemed to house more beauty products than any woman could have found good use for. There were gels and conditioners, tweezers, clippers, two blow dryers, hair dyes and shampoos for dyed hair. On the sink sat antiseptics, astringents, mouthwashes with plaque fighters, flavored dental floss, and a dental rinse. The electric toothbrush hung on the wall in its own plastic case.

I couldn't help myself. I opened the medicine cabinet. I heard that if left alone in someone's bathroom, over 40 percent of people give in to their curiosity to find themselves examining other people's prescription medications. They said looking into someone's medicine cabinet was one of the best ways to get to know them. Of course, I am not sure who "they" are, but I trust them anyway.

Bingo. More stuff. Facial masks! Green ones and brown ones, and a clear one that can be peeled off in one piece after it dries. That looked like fun, and for a moment I had a disturbing vision of the two of us in matching masks sitting on his bed making prank phone calls or something. Not that I would do that. I mean, I have, but I wouldn't again.

I stood staring at a bottle of Prozac until I realized I had been in there too long. And I hadn't even used the facilities. Oh well.

When I opened the door he was standing there smiling, holding his framed canvas of red, green, and yellow triangles that were geometrically connected by black circles.

"I just finished this yesterday."

Bravo. I raised my eyebrows and nodded my head, looking from him to the painting, and back to him.

I let him show me around his place, feigned fatigue, and accepted the ten spot he offered me for my cab ride home. I took the subway instead and made nine bucks.

My only regret was that I said he could call me. Now I would have to ask Susan to answer the phone for the next week or so, which meant I would then owe her a favor. I don't work that way, but I was noticing that more people did than I was comfortable with. These favor traders are as nice as pie when I first meet them. They even seem to go out of their way for me—let me wear their clothes, lend me a dollar, offer me some of their food. But then watch out! Not hours later sometimes, the favor traders want compensation for their generosity, as if they feel depleted in some way after giving. Like an empty stomach, they grumble and groan and demand to be fed. And they know they have you. Because didn't they just let you make that long distance phone call on their line, recommend you for that job to their friend, or have you over to dinner more times that you had them over? The favor traders keep score, and to do so, they need quick and full payment on their favor lest they lose track and do something without getting something back.

Susan is a favor trader. If she lets me borrow a shirt one day, it is almost a guarantee that I'll find her moaning about having nothing to wear the next day, even though her wardrobe is twice the size of mine. She wants me to offer her something of mine. She wants me to play the favor game.

I don't like to play the favor game, but I also don't like conflict or contention. And so I often find myself in a predicament after the fact. I could have easily told the lawyer I would rather not have him call me. But how? How do I politely decline without feeling the air thicken? Easier to take the money and run; for now anyway, until I figure things out.

The spot I pick each time in the Meadow is the same, and I rotate slightly as the sun makes its curve in the sky. I adore the sun in my face. It makes me feel whole and blessed. I watch everyone from where I sit and I try to avoid them all. And yet it was my own flirtation that Sunday in the park after church that attracted his attention and made him call me over to him. I was there that day with an aspiring journalist I had met running in the park. I was wearing my Green Bay Packer sweatshirt, which gave him his first line.

"You from Wisconsin?" he asked, as he huffed and puffed and sweated next to me. I kept my gaze straight ahead.

"Yeah."

"Where from?"

"Sun Prairie."

"Oh, yeah. Right outside of Madison. I went there a couple semesters. What a party. I'm from La Crosse myself."

Did he want me to stop and shake his hand?

"La Crosse."

"Yeah." I continued my lap, but quicker. He stayed right with me. I glanced over. No going back now.

"Hey, you wanna go to dinner some time or something?" No wasting time here.

With La Crosse, I was much more able to be myself, but he wasn't that cute. I found it difficult to hang out with someone I wasn't much attracted to. His nose was too long, and his hair was already thinning on top. If it's one thing I love, it is hair. Lots of hair; thick, curly, long, whatever. As long as there is hair. At nineteen, I just can't settle for balding. But I went out with him anyway, to avoid the conflict of having to turn him down. He took me to his favorite Italian restaurant in the city and stuffed me with pasta and garlic bread until I felt I had grown two sizes right there in my chair. I didn't let my fellow Wisconsinite down, not even for dessert. He was impressed with my appetite as he complained about how most girls these days are either on some sort of fad starvation diet or are throwing up in the bathroom before the bill is paid for.

I was pleased with his acceptance of me while I stared down at the empty bread basket and butter bowl and plate in front of me that a half an hour ago held a heaping serving of Fettuccini Alfredo in a creamy, white cheese sauce. I pictured myself moving back to Wisconsin and wearing my mother's hand-me-downs while La Crosse and I gorged ourselves on pizzas and beer as we waddled through the state fair year after year.

I hung out with La Crosse for the next couple weeks because I had nothing else to do and because he didn't pressure me sexually. I told him I was a religious girl, and it was all he seemed to need to respect me physically. So of course this bored me to no end.

It was just last Sunday that we were in the park together so he could show me his manly side while he threw a football back and forth with a friend. The wind blew his thinning hair straight up in the air, exposing his baldness. Did I want to throw the ball around with them? No thanks. Do your man thing. I'll just take a walk. Run away from this, I told myself. If it's not right now, it won't be later. I knew I was right. I should listen to myself. But I just stood there and watched the footballs and the frisbees, the hackeysacks and the kites fly all around me in a great cycle of confusion. I was lost and free at the same time as my backpack slouched off my right shoulder. I took it off and put it on the ground, ready to unpack my things when I saw him.

He sat in the midst of his friends, in the midst of the grass, with a guitar in his lap and black curls falling onto his shoulders. The sun spotted him as well, shining down upon his face and chest, browning them both to provide a sweet contrast to the loose, white muslin shirt he wore. I stood there and forgot my name.

I did all I thought I could at the time to celebrate the vision, to attract attention, to mark the moment. Three cartwheels in a row in his direction—a talent left over from those Monday nights in my grade school gymnasium where I learned tap, ballet, and gymnastics. I loved the sound my little black tap shoes made on the hard, wood floor; heel, toe, heel, toe, clomp, clomp, clomp. There was nothing like that silver metal piece hitting the polished surface below me. It was like saying, Here I am, see me, hear me!

Through the little cartoon stars my brain invented for my eyes to see, I caught him looking up at me in between chords. I casually walked back to where I had left my backpack when I lost my head, thanked God it was still there, and decided to make my way over to my intentioned spot on the grass.

"Hey."

Hey? Was he talking to me? Should I look over? Should I be acting as if I'd purposely turned cartwheels to attract a stranger? I walked past them just a couple feet and offhandedly turned my face in their direction as I focused on a hackeysack that had gotten away from a group of kids and was rolling in my direction.

"Hey!"

Is that the only word he knew? Who was I going to settle for now? The cheap imitation of some rocker hippie dude whose vocabulary is limited to one-syllable words? Wasn't I already involved with one guy I couldn't stand? I looked back just one more time, to remember what I was making myself miss. His guitar was down. He was standing. Walking to me. I stopped.

"Excuse me. My friends and I couldn't help but notice you."

"You mean…" And I pointed.

"Yeah. The cartwheels. Pretty impressive. Three in a row."

He had counted them?

"Sometimes I just can't help myself."

"Hey, I know what you mean." He does? "Anyway, we were wondering…would you like to join us?"

Join them and do what? Join them and appear tramp-like when La Crosse comes to find me?

"It's okay if… I mean, we'd just thought we'd ask."

I glanced over at the rest of "we."

"Sure, yeah. Okay." And I walked next to him back to his friends on the grass with their hair and guitars and drumsticks and sun shining in their eyes.

"So what's your name?" Once we were all sitting and all eyes were on me.

"Rachel."

"Rachel." He repeated my name. It was as if no one had ever said it before.

"And you are…"

"Dylan, John…" I didn't even hear the rest of his introductions as he pointed to each in turn. I had never experienced such instantaneous lust. Did he realize through his rumblings that I wanted to place the palm of my hand firmly on his tanned chest and run it up around his neck to allow my fingers access to those curls?

"We thought your cartwheels were fantastic." It was the guy sitting next to him. John.

"Thanks."

"So what do you do, Rachel?" It was John. His eyes seemed to pierce my own as he grinned a rosy grin. Dylan picked up his guitar and began strumming, hypnotizing me with every movement.

"Um. Well, not much, really. I ride my bike all over the city, smile on cue, do my best to stay as thin as possible." How could I say that I was a model? It seemed like such a shallow, conceited occupation.

"So you're a model?" Dylan looked up with the sun and question in his eyes. Did he want me to be a model? I could be something else. I'm not stuck on this model thing.

"Yeah, for now. I guess." I unfolded my legs from the Indian style position I was sitting in and brought them out in front of me as attractively as I could manage.

"What do you want to be later?" When he spoke to me, he ceased everything else, his strumming, his breathing, it seemed. Or was that my breathing that stopped?

"A *National Geographic* photographer. I'd like to photograph wild animals and wild people. Fly all over the world. Be paid handsomely." Where did that come from?

"Wow."

I was trying to impress them. I knew I was.

"What about you?" If I could be so bold.

"John and I, and the band…" His hand swooped towards his silent, sunlit friends. "Well, we're getting a band together, have a band, actually. We're working on our first album."

Wow.

"Really?" I raised my eyebrows in sincere awe. Rockers. I have always been terribly intrigued by people who think they can make music. "Do you guys have a name?"

"Well, yeah." He looked over at John. "Not really. We're working on one, though."

"Oh." I was suddenly at a loss for words. His beauty was blinding me; his deep, brown eyes penetrated my own with his luscious stare. That was the first time.

* * *

It was the first time I really wanted someone, wanted them from the depth of my being, from the bottom of my soul. It frightened me that day the way I felt, the way I wanted to feel. It made it easier, though, to escape the balding one from Wisconsin. Stop reminding me of where I come from, I wanted to shout, as he walked past me on the grass that day in the park. Maybe he realized that I had never really liked him when I decided not to get into it, decided not to answer his request to join him and his friend for dinner. I'd had enough dinner.

What I was shopping for was lunch. Lunch with Dylan in the park with his friends and my one. Susan had agreed to come along for an early Fourth of July celebration. The score was two to zero with Susan in the lead. He said he'd bring the wine if we'd bring the sandwiches and chips. If *I'd* bring the sandwiches and chips. Susan was no help in matters of hospitality and food preparation. She was too self-consumed, as far as I could tell. But who was I to judge? Dylan had asked if I could bring along any of my friends.

Friends and sandwiches and chips would have been a tall order for the lawyer or La Crosse. But I would have hunted down a wild pig to roast, had Dylan asked. I entertained this vision while I stood in line at the deli waiting for my turn to order thinly sliced Virginia baked ham, smoked turkey, and baby Swiss cheese while my little red basket dangled domestically from my left forearm.

I decided to stand patiently in the cool store and not sigh deeply when the young, pimpled boy in the dirty white apron and plastic gloves took forever to help three customers ahead of me. I could have sighed. I could have sighed for the two people standing behind me, and they would have nodded in silent agreement and wiped their brow or shifted their weight from one foot to the other. But happiness of this sort tasted so good I didn't want to spoil it by giving into the impatience of society. The rule in New York is impatience. Move faster, is its motto; speed, its slogan. It is not rude to scoff or fidget or sigh if something isn't moving fast enough. It is the requirement. But today I wasn't interested in keeping up the pace. I had met someone who in moments had filled me with a patient tolerance that fed my lungs with plenty of sweet oxygen. No need to sigh today.

After my stint at the deli, I figured I might as well fetch my personal groceries for the week. My budget for myself is tight. I try not to buy anything over $2.00 no matter what. It is the $2.00 rule. Anything over that is just too expensive. Raw oats, brown rice, fresh vegetables, fruit, nuts, seeds, plain yogurt, pumpernickel bagels. Well, the pumpernickel bagels I purchase from the bakery on 72nd street. They are large, dark, and chewy, and they are my main sustenance. Each time I visit the warm aroma of the crowded bakery I am tempted by the muffins and varieties of bagels. Not so much by the frosted things or chocolate delights, but by the breads and buns that seem healthy and really aren't. Bran muffins, to the average Flo Shmo, might appear as a weight watcher's wonder. Who could go wrong with bran? Ever read the fat content on a package of bran muffins?

My shopping goals are simple: healthy, low fat, cheap, and easy to prepare. The down side of these objectives is I often eat the same thing day after day, week after week. Fruit and oats for breakfast, bagels for a snack, brown rice and vegetables for dinner. I am a model. I'm not supposed to enjoy food anyway. But it's not that I don't enjoy variety or relish a home cooked meal. I had partaken of a few. I just can't deal with the cooking ritual. It is probably the one thing I inherited from my mother. Her idea of dinner was a package of hotdogs and a box of generic macaroni and cheese with a can of pears for desert, prepared by yours truly. That was after they got divorced, after Mom didn't have to be in the kitchen with Dad screaming at her to make his fried eggs without breaking the yokes. Maybe she rebelled because she was allowed to. After the divorce, I was the one who got yelled at to make the meals for the kids. Maybe that's why we ate hotdogs so often. It was the only dinner an eight-year-old could manage by herself.

Before the divorce, the meals were the typical Mid-western fattening array of beef, cheese, milk, eggs, and more beef. About a year before my parents parted, my father purchased half a cow and stored it in our basement freezer along with the leftover chocolate bars from the vending machines at the gas stations he owned. My brother and I would creep down there in the summer while my dad was still asleep on the couch and grab Almond Joys, Hershey bars, and Reese's peanut butter cups to share with our neighborhood friends. After feasting on chocolate all day, Mom would send me down to the freezer to fetch three white packages of beef for the grill. A-1 steak sauce and a potato with butter and sour cream. A cold glass of milk. Neapolitan ice cream with hot fudge for dessert. It's wild to think now that I thought nothing of it then.

If I haven't learned to cook since then, at least I've educated myself on health foods, fat content, calories, and the colon. Some items move through with ease; some like to stay a lifetime. I'd rather not hang onto any leftovers. I figure knowledge of health takes precedence over the thankless, never-ending ability to prepare what will only be eaten in a fraction of the time it takes to make. Figure at least an hour or more to cook a decent dinner. Clean up time is going to be a half hour or more, especially if it's done by hand. Of course, there's the packaging of food not eaten into plastic bags and Tupperware for which covers can never be found. The time a person spends actually eating such a meal might be fifteen minutes, twenty if you count the after dinner yawn and belly rub, which is supposed to communicate some sort of gratification. I don't know, but to me the math just doesn't add up. And it's not as if this ritual is a once a month activity or something, because then I could rationalize the preparation time and buy into the hype of creative cooking and all, but this is a thrice daily necessity! Slowly, slowly, the once happy, recipe-finding maiden of the kitchen becomes slave of the stove and sink, victim of veracious appetites that clamor for more. And it never ends—the thawing, wiping, pre-heating, baking, boiling, scrubbing, mixing, blending, spreading, cleaning, washing, fixing, setting, arranging, shopping, reading, pouring, figuring, scouring, measuring, counting, frying, greasing, slicing, dicing, cutting, and freezing until what? Until hell freezes over, most likely. It could make a young girl dizzy and a grown woman insane.

I recently vowed never to begin this female ritual. Never would I wake up at 5:30 AM, as my great-grandmother did, to begin dinner preparations for the homemade soups, breads, and roasts. After the ingredients were mixed and refrigerated, the breakfast could begin. Coffee and eggs, French toast, pancakes, sausages. Almost everything was made from scratch and whatever the family wanted, the family received, from great-grandchild to great-grandfather. It drove me crazy to watch him sit in his lazy boy with his pipe and *Reader's Digest* while my grandma stood on her feet and fixed dinner after dinner, bound by her apron and her sex. And then after supper, he would sit in his lazy boy with his pipe and watch television while his stomach grew fat and his quiet wife washed every dish by hand and scoured the counters so that they would be ready for the next morning at 5:30 AM. Around and around, cemented by tradition and expectation and routine.

The fact is, when I'm hungry I simply want to eat. I don't want to stand over stoves and counters and duck into refrigerators for hours before I can have my meal. If I do decide, one day a year or so, to cook a well-planned feast, I find that by the time everything is finished I have lost my initial hunger, which drove me to preparation in the first place. And then what do I have? A pretty, edible picture I end up eating in fifteen minutes or less so it doesn't get cold.

I walk the New York cement home, vowing again never to become one whose life revolves around food. Sandwiches and chips were perfectly acceptable. A dinner to impress every now and then. Fine. But that's the limit.

My bags weigh each of my arms down equally as the humidity pulls the curls out of women's hair and invites tiny beads of perspiration to form inside the collars and around the necks of men in ties. I try not to breathe the air around me, try to keep my gaze straight ahead to avoid the looks of those living in their boxes on the curbs. I really tried with the homeless until I realized they are just as rude and picky as people with money and homes. When I first entered the city, I offered them anything from my shopping bags. A bagel? An apple perhaps? And I would hold the items up for them as they shopped through my things. But they wanted pizza. They pointed to the pizzeria across the street. They wanted my money. And I don't blame them, really. I mean, I want to choose my own food when I'm hungry, too. That's why I work.

At home I find Susan sprawled across Danny's semi-circular black leather couch eating what appears to be a chocolate éclair as the last bit is stuffed into her mouth. *Elle* magazines and Helmut Newton picture books decorate the shiny glass table in front of her. I walk past her without a hello and begin putting my food into my part of the refrigerator and cupboards. We all have our specified places so no one can give the excuse of not knowing whose last piece of bread it was, last glass of milk, slice of cheese. Food is a precious commodity, but not because of what it costs necessarily. It's a touchy subject. Every bit is a number of calories, planned out, put aside as a reward, counted, avoided, dreamt of. It's true. I often dream of eating. One grape, two grapes. I can taste them in my sleep. It's actually quite pleasurable. Anyway, food is a tough topic in a model's apartment.

When I first arrived in New York, there was a skinny, young blonde who was actually trying to gain weight and was always accidentally eating other people's food. The rest of us, who sat in awe of someone who could wolf down an entire pizza and then get sent home from an appointment because she was too scrawny, didn't find her amusing. And female tension coupled with competition and weight watching isn't a pleasant atmosphere. During the fight of the female, the air thickens and gossip lurks around every corner. Facetiously they face one another with sarcasm and sardonic grins masked by wicked nonchalance.

Women are proud. They must stand aside from the rest and be admired for their individual beauty. They need attention and security. The attention females give to one another is healthy and good and necessary, but each one knows they restrain themselves from unleashing the bitter truths they possess about one another. They hold it back, like a loaded weapon, knowing the hurt they could cause. All this tension is released like a powerful rush of water when the levee breaks if one party even suspects another of disloyalty of any kind. And then it's as if disloyalty breeds disloyalty. The gossip begins, rumors spread. There are long phone calls to be made, tears to be wept, ice cream to be eaten. There are whispers and notes. Sides are chosen.

I try my best not to involve myself in the game of womanhood. The rules are too intricate. I get confused as to whom I'm supposed to be loyal. I prefer guys, men, my brothers, Michael. Men are easy. They want to win and they want women. I feel I can be of greater assistance to men.

When I'm finished unpacking my things and neatly placing them in my areas of the cupboard and refrigerator, I wander casually into the living room and slouch into the black leather waiting to do my time with Susan. I notice a new *Elle*, flip through it, appreciate Rachel Hunter in all her glory, and toss it back onto the table.

"You know when Michael's supposed to be back?" Silence broken.

"I don't know. A week or two, I think Louise said."

"Jeez. You think I could lose what I need to lose by then?" Her hand finds itself on the naked, soft part of her belly. She pulls at her flab and sighs.

"You look fine." I'm too tired to get up and take a shower.

"No, I don't."

"Yes, you do."

"Why did *Cosmo* turn me down today then?" She sits up a little straighter now and gives me a look. I'm supposed to say something quick to make her feel skinny, wanted, and secure all in one breath.

"What did they say?"

"Nothing."

"What do you mean?"

"Louise told me they went with someone else from our agency."

"Jeez, I'm sorry."

"I know. I was really counting on this, though. Rachel, I haven't worked since that thing with the perfume."

"How long ago was…"

"A month. More. Shit. I don't know. Too fucking long."

I stand up. Profanity makes me uncomfortable. She stands up. I sit down. Turning around in her faded Levi's and black, cropped tee-shirt that makes her look even bigger on top than she really is, Susan begins inspecting herself from all possible directions. Her small, white, bare feet pad softly on the wooden floor as she turns in circles like a cat chasing its tail.

"Do you think I'm fat?" She looks down at me and then at her behind waiting for some sort of response. But her backside is not what she needs to be concerned with. Perhaps this is why she is drawing attention there, because Susan is an apple if I am a pear. Her excess weight accumulates around her mid-section, her stomach. I gain mine in my butt and thighs. Do I think she's fat? Fat for what? For modeling? Probably. Would I tell her? No. I would never tell her that she looked fat, and I would expect the same from her. It's an unspoken rule that must be followed so our egos can at least be fed at home. God knows it's tough enough seeing clients and photographers all day who like to get out their measuring tapes without a moment's notice so they can check our stats with their own means. They never pull tight enough around my hips and seem to get a smaller breast measurement than I do. It's terribly frustrating and embarrassing, like the first time a boy put his hand up my shirt expecting something more than I could provide.

"No."

"Are you sure?"

"Sure I'm sure." I was. From the standards set at home in Wisconsin, Susan was thin, beautifully thin, gorgeously perfect. "You're a beautiful girl, Susan."

"Rachel, you're just the sweetest thing, honey."

Her southern drawl becomes very pronounced when she is pleased. Susan comes from Savannah, Georgia where her mother cooks fried chicken and corn bread and her father spoils her. Susan's assets are her flawless skin and her breasts. Her faults are her laziness and her insecurity. Not that I'm totally secure. On the contrary. It's just that I'm completely aware of my insecurity. I'm in touch with it. Sometimes I even bask in it, relishing the fact that I am on the run with no place to go or call home. It's what keeps me alive and aware and working, this insecurity of mine.

Susan looks at me now with her perfectly straight nose, dreamy, hazel eyes, and lips like tiny pink pillows. "You want anything, sugar-pie?" My latest compliment has earned me perks. She's on her way to the kitchen for another mini feast.

"No. Thanks. I think I'll get in the shower." The house feels empty without Michael. I miss him more than she does. She treats his absence as a time to get away with stuff she's not supposed to be doing or eating. I feel abandoned, lonely. I feel as if I am supposed to be the one to "hold down the fort," as my mother used to say. Sometimes I don't feel up to the task.

* * *

"Don't move. If you move, if you fight me…"

"Oh God, no." She whispers this silently, under her breath.

"Come on, baby. Don't fight me now. Ah, look at these thighs. Hmmm. There, it's not so bad now, is it?" He takes her legs and spreads them, and works his hands up and down her chilled flesh. He hurts her, but she feels too weak or numb to notice. Something has dulled her brain and body. She's prevented somehow from fighting or screaming out loud. But she's screaming inside. Down inside she's yelling for him to get out of her room and leave her alone. Instead her body lies there like a rag doll being torn apart by the seams. She can see the outline of his face, his nose, his chin. All his features are distinct and abrupt.

"Damn it! Get this off!" He has his arms around her trying to unfasten her bra. She lies listless, not caring to assist him. She knows he could really hurt her if he wanted to. His anger doesn't affect her. She will try to ignore him until it is over.

His large hands rip at it from the middle. A pleasant look drifts across his chiseled face. Immediately he grabs at the mounds of flesh and begins kneading at them with his greedy fingers. To her this is more annoying than anything, and she quietly wonders why she can't lift her arms to smack his hands away.

A minute or two later as she regains consciousness, she can feel his short nails scrape against her skin. Her entire body tightens and stands erect under his touch without her consent. His wet mouth finds its way in the shadowy dark to each breast. She worries that he will leave bite marks again. Involuntarily a sharp scream escapes from her throat, but this is quickly punctuated by a slap that leaves a warm sting on her cool cheek.

She stays still then, as his hands and mouth work their way down to the broad stomach and in between her thighs. Then for a moment there is nothing. She opens her eyes to him gently pulling at the sash on his silk robe. She cannot bear the thought of him as she feels warm tears running down the sides of her face.

* * *

I sit straight up in my bed and snap the light on.

"Susan, what is it?"

"Rachel?" Her voice cracks.

"Susan, you were crying in your sleep again."

"Did I wake you?"

"Yes. Yes you woke me." My voice sounds irritated. I don't care.

"Christ. I'm sorry." Her sandy blonde curls stick like glue to the sides of her face. There are tiny beads of sweat dripping from her forehead and mixing with her tears. She slowly pulls her legs up from under the sheet and wraps her arms around them as she lowers her head to her knees. I sigh a sigh that means I'm not happy about this, but now that I am up we may as well talk. The several times this happened before she whispered she was fine and I should go back to bed.

"Susan, you've got to tell me what's going on." I look at the clock, 2:36. Prime sleeping time. If I don't get eight to ten hours of sleep each night, I cannot function normally during the day. She knows this. I am hoping this will count as a favor trade.

"Rachel, you don't have to do this. Just go back to sleep, okay?"

Yeah right.

"I'm gonna get some water. Want anything?" This is so out of character for me. I am hoping she is taking notice of my middle of the night hospitality.

"Um… Michael's got some brandy in the cupboard above the sink. Could you be a doll and bring me a small glass?" So timid in her tone. I can't believe I am serving drinks at 2:30 in the morning.

I don't answer her. I just plod into the kitchen, turn on the light above the stove, pour our drinks through half open eyes, and plod back to the room where I find Susan sitting comfortably against her headboard looking surprisingly serene. The flush from her cheeks has vanished. Her face has resumed its normal, pale translucence.

I sprawl out at the end of her bed with my water. We both hold our glasses steady while we get comfortable.

For a moment or two I just let her sip her drink and don't say anything. And then I do.

"Susan, what's going on with you?" I say it with concern.

"I don't know. Nothing."

"It's not nothing."

"It's just dreams, honey."

"Well, what is it that you're dreaming about?"

"I don't know." She drops her eyelids and sips at her brandy innocently.

"Yes, you do."

"I don't remember them completely when I'm awake."

"What do you remember?" Let's get this over with so I can get back to bed.

"Him."

"Who?" If I'd been a cat my ears would have perked up.

"No one."

"Susan, who is 'him'?"

"Just someone I knew."

"When?"

"Last year."

"And…?" She isn't making this very easy. I am running out of patience.

"And I don't want to talk about it."

"Oh. Well, what do you expect me to do when I hear you crying out loud in your sleep?"

"I don't know, Rachel. Honey, I'm sorry for waking you up. I really am."

"Just tell me what you were dreaming about." I thought I'd try one more time. The 'honey' thing is a bit irresistible.

"I don't think it's a dream exactly. I think what I dream really happened. Does that make sense?"

"Sure. Of course." I am finally getting somewhere.

"Rachel, I am so embarrassed. You don't understand."

"How can I understand if you don't tell me what's going on?"

"I know, I know."

"What makes you cry in your dream? Just tell me what is making you cry."

"*He* is making me cry, Rachel. That man. That horrible man!" She sets her empty glass on her bedside table and buries her face in her hands.

2

EXPOSED

"Alex."

"What?"

"Alex."

"What are you talking about?" I am sitting at the kitchen table in the bright, morning sunlight tearing at my pumpernickel bagel I left in the microwave too long. I can't throw it away. The guilt would be too much. No, I just sit here grinding away at it causing my teeth and jaws to ache.

"I mean Alex, Rachel. The man in my dream?" Her inflection is sassier than it should be for the tears that were spilled only hours ago.

"Oh." Now she wants to talk. Even though I don't know what it feels like to be hung over, I figure I probably am. I barely slept at all after our little midnight chat. It irritates me to see her looking so chipper with her soft corn muffin and coffee. "Michael's Alex?"

"Of course Michael's Alex. How many Alexes do you think I know?"

"Whatever." All I know is I am not running as I should be at this very moment. I can barely lift my eyelids, much less my legs.

"It's fine if you don't want to talk about it. I don't need to talk about it..." Her voice trails off as she goes to primp in the bathroom. She is put off by my mood. Good. Now she knows how I feel. I pop the last hard piece of brown bagel in my mouth and chew furiously while I finger through the morning newspaper. This is Michael's scene, the coffee and the paper. I very rarely sit down with breakfast when he is home.

Susan comes prancing back into the kitchen moments later with her black bag and jacket. I could ask her to sit down, to tell me about it. Tell me all about it, I could say. Like a mother, like a big sister. But I don't. I pretend to digest the tiny black and white print before me.

"I'm outta here."

"Bye." I try to sound as neutral as possible, as if I forgot all about her little attitude, and mine.

"See ya." She fishes around for some last words of consolation.

"See ya."

When the door closes, I put the paper down and begin feeling very alone and very sorry for myself. I just don't have enough for me and for someone else. Sometimes I don't even have enough for me. Enough of what, I am not sure. I think about calling Louise at the agency to tell her I am really sick or have bad cramps or something. It is amazing how much we get away with, being models. No one wants us to see clients if we are bloated, puffy, or generally irritable in any way. I am all of the above, but not because it is that time of the month. I feel mentally fat from missing my run and completely exhausted from missing too much sleep.

"Good morning, Models Incorporated." Nasal, East Coast, smoky throat voice.

"Louise? It's Rachel."

"Rachel, darling, I'm glad you called. Your composites are here. I need you to make the rounds with them. Go back to all the magazines: *Seventeen, Self, Sassy, YM.* They love you there. It'll give you a good excuse to have them see you again."

"How do they look?" I try to sound as unexcited as possible.

"They're gorgeous, of course. Hold on, I've got another call."

I stand there and look at my hands, noticing a grease stain from the bike, messy cuticles, the bump from writing on the left side of my right middle finger.

"Rachel?"

"Yeah. Um. Louise, I'm not feeling very well today."

"What is it?"

"I don't know. My head is pounding. I didn't sleep well last night."

"Well, I suppose we can wait the weekend. Monday morning, though. Unless you get a booking. Oh, by the way, *Mademoiselle* confirmed for the 14th. What's this, your third booking with them now?"

"Yeah, I guess." Poor me. How can I remember with such a headache?

"Rachel, I gotta go. The other line is ringing. Take care of yourself."

Not more than a minute passes when the phone rings, scaring me.

"Rachel, Louise again, sweetheart. I'm sorry to bother you, but that was Michael. He's found someone in Paris. They're still with Alex, but he wants me to tell you he'll be home in a week or so."

"What's her name?"

"I don't know. She's a blond. Anyway, just thought I'd let you know. Get some sleep now, okay?"

"Okay."

I don't know why as I stand there in my pajama tee shirt and shorts and uncombed hair that I feel jealous about Michael finding another girl to bring home. It is just another reason to feel sorry for myself, to bask in my excused depression. Sometimes I don't know what I am doing or where I am going. What I do know is how I feel is all too familiar. With each breath my heart sinks a little deeper into past confusion.

* * *

"Rachel? Did you dust this shelf?" The young girl nods her head as she sits upright in the top bunk bed. Her mother slowly sweeps her right index finger across the small blue shelf that houses her Raggedy Ann and Andy. The finger is then thrust into the child's face. It is full of a brownish, gray fuzz.

"Don't you lie to me! Get down here this instant!" The child is pulled off the bed by her arm. On the way down, her head hits the metal frame and she winces. The little boy in the bottom bunk lies frozen and scared, holding a stuffed monkey with long arms and a goofy grin.

In the bathroom, her mother holds up two of her father's belts. "Which one do you want?" The crying starts then, quietly. "You want something to cry about? I'll give you something to cry about! Pull down your pants!" At this the girl tugs at her baby doll pajama bottoms and is quickly pulled over her mother's knees as she sits on the edge of the tub. The belt is folded in half, and with the rounded part she beats her daughter too many times until her daughter is screaming from the pain. When she stands up, her mother's hand clamps itself around the girl's mouth, stifling the noise. She claws at her mother's hand, trying to pry the fingers loose from around her nose so she can breathe, but it is no use. She isn't strong enough.

* * *

In the bathroom, I find myself sitting on the edge of the tub taking off my shorts and tee shirt, still feeling terribly sleepy. It is times like these I hate to be alone. I want Susan to come back so we can talk again about her dreams. I should have been kinder to her, I think. I should have helped her.

Naked and numb from my thoughts, I sit there and wonder if I will ever be able to find what I am looking for. Modeling is only an excuse for me to be gone from the hideous life that had been led thus far. I want so much, and I can feel it is now within my grasp. But I am scared more than anything. There is nothing to go back to.

I can only go forward, running away from the past. As I let the warm water run down my face, I cringe at the word, the thought, the concept of family. I have no family. I don't even look like them.

Every few seconds I turn the plastic knob to the left to provide more heat to the water. I want warmth, comfort, cleansing. I want the shower to take it all away, every last memory and nightmare and cause for my stomach to turn over in panic.

Dad would get angry over some seemingly insignificant household detail and fly into a rage. Tables and desks were overturned. Precious statues and knickknacks were smashed to the hard floor in glee and psychotic triumph. I would take my brothers then, and we would go to the furthest corner of their room and sit and wait. Punches were thrown, voices were raised, and by the time his truck wheels squealed out of the driveway her eye would already be turning a dark purple.

I dry off my body, limb by limb, secure a fluffy white towel in a pile on top of my head, and wipe the mirror clear so I can see my face. A sleepy darkness surrounds my eyes. I pop a small, white zit on my chin and apply Susan's green facial mask until I look like a creature from outer space.

In Michael's room I find the remote, curl up under his sheets, and begin flipping through game shows and talk shows and reruns until an episode of "Little House on the Prairie" appears on the screen. Laura Ingles in pigtails with a handsome, wavy-haired father calling her half-pint and taking her fishing. One would never know how much this show provided for young girls like me growing up in old houses in the suburbs with overweight, angry mothers and childish, violent, obtrusive fathers who never once called their daughter by name, much less by a pet name.

I remember those Monday nights well. The ones in which I wolfed down my hotdogs and macaroni and cheese so that I could plop myself down on our scratchy, red couch to be taken away into a world so peaceful, simple, and good where families worked together and struggled to find a bit of pleasure at the end of the day.

I became Laura Ingles each Monday night, although most of the time I identified more with Mary, the elder sister who had to be more responsible. I didn't care which one I was as long as I had parents like that.

* * *

Susan comes with me to meet Dylan and his friends in the park even though we aren't really talking. She will not miss an opportunity to socialize, to be in the midst of things, because even though she is a near failure in the modeling industry, she delights in her success with the opposite sex. As far as I am concerned, most of it has to do with breast size. Since she is obviously gifted in this area, is it not expected of her to be a thing of desire for those who enjoy the sight of bulging mounds of flesh sticking out of the upper torso and distracting the attention of ones who are denied such soft and peculiar shapes? It's her job; otherwise what are they there for? A person must make use of what they are given, and for Susan I don't think this will include nursing a baby any time soon.

We walk the entire way there. Susan isn't the type to get on a bike, even if she had one. I am quiet with my own thoughts and picnic things growing warm in my backpack. I am beginning to doubt my initial love lusts towards a young man I barely know, and therefore walk dutifully instead of expectantly toward Central Park in the afternoon sun. I am doing this because I said I would. Susan is giddy enough for the both of us. She has prepared herself in a proper park package of short, floral, cotton shorts and a tight, lacy, white and basically see-through top that isn't even long enough to cover her belly button. "No imagination required" could be stamped across her forehead. She prances along beside me, smiling periodically at her audience of male and female onlookers. People just don't dress this way in New York, even if they are from the south. She is nearly embarrassing.

I trudge along in my modest jean shorts and clean, white tee shirt that reveal nothing, as I have nothing to reveal next to Daisy Mae.

The park is crowded, as it always is on Sundays when the sun is shining. I feel a twinge of panic run up the insides of my body. What if he isn't here?

I forget Susan and quicken my pace to find him. No one will make a fool of me. The picture of me and my little red basket hanging from my arm waiting in line for deli ham seems ridiculous. I don't even eat ham.

"Rachel, over here!" There he is. Just like before, with long, dark curls and his guitar. I walk over slowly and stand in front of them, blocking their sun. I am surprised to see them all again.

"Hi!" Short and quick and spunky from behind me.

"Dylan, this is Susan."

"It's all very nice to meet y'all."

Do I detect a curtsey, a slight dip to reveal the goods? So soon? Sit down!

"Rachel, come here." He is so slow and easy in his speech. It is like watching taffy turn, beautiful and interesting. Art almost. I take off my backpack, sit down next to him, and join the group to view the show.

"This sun sure is hot in the middle of the park like this. My, my. Who has somethin' to drink?"

I guess I wouldn't want to sit on the grass in those shorts either. We all stare up at this girl I brought as John pours her a cup of wine from the cooler. I find it fascinating, detecting the shape of her breasts in the different shadows the sun is making. I wonder if the guys can see the little pink bow holding it all together under there.

"We were all just going to play a little sack. Anyone up for it?"

"I'll just hang here, if that's okay."

"John, here. You guys play. Rachel and I are going to sit this one out." Why is he being so nice? What is he going to expect in return?

And so we watch Susan's butt cheeks wiggle as she bounces toward the small circle where the hackeysack is already being served to John. It touches his chest, knee, and the outer side of his tennis shoe before he passes it to Susan. Her naked, pale leg lifts itself in response, but the sack settles itself quickly in the grass before being picked up again and tossed to another one of the guys.

So I sit there next to him and am silent because enough is going on around us to distract our attention from each other.

"Would you like some wine?"

"Oh, I almost forgot." And I begin unloading the food from my backpack. "Sure."

"She puts on quite a show." He sees right through her.

"It's better than television." We sit and sip red wine from blue, plastic cups while my bodily lusts grow anxious and my brain grows pleasingly numb in the lovely sunshine.

When the rest of the group joins us again, Susan finds a spot of blanket near John and we all innocently toast to our great country. I keep my eye on my new boyfriend trying to figure out who he is. After a while, the two of us decide to take a walk while the rest of them watch our stuff. Halfway around Sheep Meadow, he reaches for my hand. I let him take it.

"What do you want, Rachel?"

"What do you mean?"

"What do you want out of life? What do you want for yourself?" His eyes look into mine and I feel as if I must have known him for a very long time.

The wine swims slowly around my head in search of an answer. Several make themselves available. I discard each in turn and say, "I want to know who I am." It sounds a bit odd, I suppose, but it is the truth.

"Tell you what. I'll find out with you." His tone is so mature and easy, as if he knows a secret I may never know. It's confidence, I decide. It's one thing New Yorkers seem full of, and I quietly hope that by just living here some of it will wear off on me.

"And how will you do that?" My personal insecurity overrides my desire to please in this instant. Maybe it is saying out loud what I want that begins the journey toward the answers. We are face to face with chaos and commotion all around us, and yet I don't hear any of it. He squeezes my hands in his and pulls me closer. I look directly into is deep brown dancing eyes. He considers himself clever, I guess.

"Time." He is smiling at me, completely engaged in this initial, philosophical chat he seems to be directing.

"Time." I consider it out loud with him, following along.

"All good things in all good time." Again with the smiling. And then I realize so suddenly that my spirit shifts; I am not alone. Until this moment under the green trees and gray buildings I'd felt absolutely by myself. No agent or girlfriend or guy had ever had this effect on me. I shudder in expectation, in fear. If this is how it feels to experience love, then I don't ever want to be without it again. And I am not saying that I am in love, only that I am feeling love for the very first time.

"You cold?" His hands are on my shoulders, supporting me as I stand as a witness to this. I am the silent observer, nodding in my acknowledgement of the intensity of the moment.

"Cold? No." I shake my head.

"You okay?" His smile is softer, but seemingly sincere.

"I never want to leave this moment." Maybe it is the wine, I think. Dare I speak so boldly so soon? But his answer is in his embrace, and because we stand at exactly the same height and our bodies match up so completely, I am no longer questioning. I am just being. Who I am supposed to be and who I have always been fade away as I hold him, not sexually yet, but spiritually.

"You don't have to." He's enjoying this, I can tell. He knows he's done what he's set out to do—capture my attention, make me want him. Check, check.

"Will we stand here all night then?"

"If that's what you want." What a gentleman. How long will such talk last? But I catch myself at the threshold of cynicism and yearn instead for more of the good stuff. Make it last. Why not? The rise is the sweetest part and it must be savored, like the first bite of food after a long hunger.

"This I want." He knows what I am talking about. He has to feel it, too, right? The connection is more than chemical; it seems like we've been here before. And so it only follows that he moves his right hand around my neck to cradle the back of my head. I give myself a mental nod of approval for doing a hot oil treatment just this morning. I can tell his hand is enjoying itself in a soft head of hair, a head that is slowly losing itself. His lips are perfect on mine, and I kiss him equally as he kisses me there under the sun God and my God and all of New York. And then he kisses me some more, and I find my hands around his waist as if we are lovers, as if we have done this a million times before.

When I open my eyes, I feel foolish. It is the wine. Two cups of wine on an empty stomach around his hypnotic voice and luscious head of dark, curly hair. If this is what I do in public, what will he expect of me in private? I pull away and with the back of my hand wipe my mouth, but gracefully, to signal conscious resistance of some sort. Is it too late? Apparently he finds this amusing because he just takes my hand back in his and gently returns me to our place in the park. It is not necessarily what he says, but the lack of it that intrigues me so.

On the blanket, sitting Indian style, with his recent conquest by his side, he brings his guitar into his lap and begins strumming a familiar Beatles' tune. "Strawberry Fields Forever." I drink some more wine, don't ask why, and attempt to sing along whenever I remember the words. I find myself relaxed enough to sprawl out sideways, with one hand under my head and the other secure around my blue cup. We mingle in a semi-circle of sorts, and for a moment, I am very comfortable, as if these are my people. I am careful to connect what I feel with Dylan to my singular soul, lest I get caught up thinking he is the only one who can make me feel so incredibly alive.

"He was shot not ten blocks from here, you know?" John speaks out loud to us, yet his thoughts have taken him far away. We briefly follow the direction of his gaze.

"Oh my. Who?" Susan is all eyes and ears.

"John Lennon."

She doesn't respond.

"John Lennon. The Beatles?"

"Oh." She finishes off her wine and gives the empty plastic cup to John, who fills it again and asks her quietly if she wants to take a walk. Dylan and I smile at each other as they get up from the blanket. We grin at them as if to give them our permission. Let them frolic in the summer breeze. Tomorrow they will have adult problems to deal with. Problems like love and what to do about it.

* * *

I lift Michael's pea-green bike into the elevator and press number three. It is getting more and more like work, searching for jobs in the pollution and humidity of the streets. My legs ache from riding all day, but it is a good ache and I am proud of myself for all my physical exertion. The sweat drips down my face as the elevator stops on the second floor. A very striking blonde girl stumbles in with an enormous suitcase that distorts her slight frame as she lifts it.

"Ah, hello. You can help me perhaps?" She looks at me inquisitively with her beady, brown eyes and then back down at the little piece of paper she holds in her hand. She squints at it. I know who she is.

"Sure." I will make her say it. I am feeling mean. The last thing I need is another beautiful girl around. I'd been competing against them all day and am burned out from trying to be the perfect smile, the perfect legs, the perfect size. This girl is naturally scrawny, I can tell.

"Oh, dis is very good of you." So polite. It is aggravating. "Is Michael Siegle here in dis building, do you know?" Clueless, and at my mercy. I don't know why I find it so hard to be nice.

It is an effort when I reply, "Sure, follow me. I live there, too." We ride up to the next floor together, squeezed in by my bike and her suitcase. We casually check each other out with sideways glances. Now that she knows I am a model, too, she seems more interested in me. I attempt an act of nonchalance while beads of sweat drip into my eyes. I wipe them away with the sleeve of my shirt and pretend I am doing a commercial for bottled water.

"You out for a bike ride?"

Sure. In my little black skirt and big, heavy backpack I like to take quick trips around the city for fun. It's such a great time, especially in the blazing sun during rush hour traffic.

"It's how I get around."

"Oh, I see. You have no metro here?" Naiveté at its finest.

"Yes, we have an underground system of transportation." No, you don't have to be an idiot like me and drag along a bike wherever you go.

In the apartment, I secure the bike in its corner and try a little harder with her. "I'm sorry, I didn't catch your name. Mine's Rachel." There. Just like on television when women are trying to be polite, but feel catty underneath. It is the effort that counts. I hold out my hand and she sets down her suitcase.

"Yvonne. So sorry I did not say it before. Yvonne Balard. It is good to be in America. Dis is my first time." Great. A million congratulations are in order.

"We all sleep in here." I walk ahead of her and assume she will follow. I am not being paid for this, although upon Michael's long distance request I have made up the extra bed for her.

"Susan. I didn't know you were here." But there she is, with a plate of peanut butter and jelly sandwiches on her lap, right on top of her white bed sheets. Her embarrassment is instantly evident, but her Southern upbringing kicks in and overshadows her desire to be viewed as a tough and successful New York model. The plate of sandwiches is swiftly moved to the table beside the bed, and as it teeters there Susan makes Yvonne's acquaintance via the bottled water spokes-model. I care about appearances, for reasons unknown as of yet to myself. I don't want to let just anyone "in." I will do the choosing.

"Would you care for a sandwich?"

"No, but dank you so much for ze offer."

"But you must be just famished after your trip! You look absolutely fragile! Rachel, doesn't she look absolutely starved?" Do I want to play ogle the new, skinny girl?

"She looks fine." And I am out of there. Nothing worse than two females playing mind games of fake flattery and jovial jealousy. But Susan lives for the social life; live to be viewed, live to be heard. And she is off with her new victim chattering endlessly in her heavy, Southern accent as she takes Yvonne's things and arranges them around her new sleeping place. Yvonne takes to this like any young, displaced waif would take to new, foreign surroundings: with enthusiasm and gratitude.

* * *

"Mom, can Tanya stay for awhile?" She looks up at her mother's face and knows even before she asks the question the timing is wrong. She should have waited.

"Do you realize you forgot to throw your brothers' dirty clothes down the shoot this morning? I told you before you left for school that this had to be done, that today was wash day. But what do I find now after four loads of laundry? Dana's favorite jeans all rolled up on the floor and Billy's soccer uniform all muddy from last week's game! It was under his bed, just where I told you to look. And he needs it tonight, Rachel Ann! You're just going to have to take care of it. I have to lie down. Strip their beds and wash the sheets. That'll make a load. They haven't been washed in weeks."

The girl stands there next to her friend, views her mother through Tanya's eyes, and shivers. What a beast of a woman! So large, so mean, so demanding. She knows she is reaching when she pleads, "Can Tanya stay and help me?" Her voice is barely audible. She knows her fear sets her mother off, gives her permission almost to be mean. It is like giving a dog the reason to chase and bite if you ran away from it with fear. "We have to start dinner in fifteen

33

minutes for Billy to be on time for his game. And we barely have enough to feed ourselves, much less all of your friends. How are you going to finish the laundry, help with dinner, and have friends over all at the same time? Answer me that? You should know better that on a school night I need all the help I can get with the three of you. God forbid I have an evening to do something I would like to do!" Her large, trembling hands are set squarely on her tremendous hips. Her face pulls itself into angry, ugly lines. She doesn't even want to be here, so why would Tanya?

"Come on, I'll walk you out." She scoots past her mother quickly, lest her hand find itself smacking the girl's behind as some sort of end punctuation to all that has been said. She watches Tanya walk down the sidewalk toward her own house. She doesn't wish to go with her. She doesn't live in a fantastical world of wishes and dreams. She lives in a world of laundry and responsibility and trying to make ends meet. But she promises herself that day she will never allow herself to be embarrassed as she had been. After that day, she never again asks any of her friends to come to her house.

* * *

About a week after Yvonne moved in, Michael comes home. It is a relief to know he is coming back, even though it is fun to have the apartment to ourselves. Susan and Yvonne act more like children than anything, and it is becoming exhausting dealing with them by myself.

Michael is a charming cross between Arlo Guthrie and the lion from *The Wizard of Oz*. He has a child-like way of looking at the other person that is quite irresistible to me. Yes, I suppose I will say I am attracted to him, to the way he talks, to the stories he tells, and to his enthusiasm in the kitchen as he prepares his scrumptious chicken and spinach dinners. I am intrigued by the careless way his coat hangs and familiar with the tired look he has in his eyes, always two seconds away from closing them peacefully even if he's fully dressed. He is adorable like Arlo Guthrie in *Alice's Restaurant*, and goofy like the lion, always joking around to keep things light and humorous and interesting. One certainly must appreciate this type of person; the one who keeps the rest of us smiling and entertained and distracted from our daily cares. He has dark brown, shoulder-length curls that always hang too close to his eyes. He is stylish and disheveled at the same time, and he loves New York. He will be the man to stay in Manhattan if it is the main target of nuclear attack. His loyalty to his city is a bit disturbing considering the filth and crime and poverty that drip from every corner of it, but I let that pass. After all, I live here, too. Michael is Jewish, like all the rest, although he doesn't practice, much to the dismay of his parents. But he calls them on Jewish holidays and goes out with them for bagels and lox like a dutiful son. He only acts on ideas or people he firmly believes in, but he has a definite soft spot for girls, thus his initial job as a model scout.

He was a scout for various agencies in New York before opening one only a year ago. Now he is the president of his own agency and our only scout, which is why he is often out of town.

"Bonsoir, ladies!" His voice sounds heavy as the door bangs against the wall. I jump from the bed and rush into the living room to greet him, but Yvonne beats me to it. "Mademoiselle! Comment allez-vous?" His face brightens as he hears himself speak French.

"Tres bien, tres bien, merci!" Yvonne is beyond giddy at his entrance. She is gushing. It makes me sick.

"And Mademoiselle, how are you?" He looks right at me with his soft, black, puppy-dog eyes. His voice sounds much more meaningful; I am sure of it.

"Michael, you're home."

"I am. How's everything?" By this, he means my work. He glances around at the apartment and smiles with his eyes and looks back at me so I know he has taken notice of how nice everything looks.

"I got another booking with *Elle* today. I don't think it's a full page, though."

"This is wonderful, Rachel. Don't we all wish we could be

working for *Elle* on a regular basis?" He looks at Yvonne, then Susan, who has come out of hiding to show herself in a big, baggy, black tee shirt that drops almost to her knees.

"But of course, Mikey, let me help you vith deez, okay? Mikey?" Yvonne goes to him, picks up the smaller of two suitcases, and starts walking to his bedroom in her short, black mini-skirt, which barely covers her buttocks. Michael looks at me, shrugs his shoulders, and picks up the other one, following her. On the way, though, he puts his hand to my cheek.

"Thanks for getting her settled and everything. Pretty hot, huh?" He always says this about new girls, and he always wants my approval. I am sincere when I answer him.

"She's okay."

Later we all sit around a table together at La Cour St. Germain, the most incredible and delightful restaurant I have ever been in. The whole atmosphere is peachy and dreamy. One entire wall is covered in mirrors that reflect three circular tables supporting the most beautiful and delicious tempting treats. Whenever we come here, I always notice the same piano man working away happily at his version of a Scott Joplin piece, a Simon and Garfunkel tune, or an Elton John ballad. Sometimes, if our table isn't ready yet, I will glide on over by him, sit on his bench with him, and make requests, singing with him if I know the words. He told me once that I have a lovely voice.

But tonight everything is ready, and I just sit there, sipping at my water with a lemon, looking at Michael looking at Yvonne. He seems to have quite an interest in her.

La Cour St. Germain is the restaurant we eat at for free. Lovely, lip-smacking food for free. All we have to do on our part is to dress the part, of models. Of models in short, black skirts with flowing hair and quick, pretty smiles for anyone who looks our way. This is my interpretation anyway. Michael never really listed any requirements. But we got the idea quick enough when one of the previous models acted as if she was ready in her gray, off-the-shoulder "Flashdance" sweatshirt and jeans. Michael just stood and looked at her.

"Is that what you're wearing?" he inquired. It's all he had to say as he looked at the rest of us with an approving smile and light in his eyes. What guy wouldn't want four or five gorgeous girl-women with long legs accompanying his every move? That's what we are. He is our date. He is our agent, our father, our brother, our landlord. And for some, it is looking like "lover" isn't far from the list. He is our provider, as long as we remain perfect. The fat ones go home. The skinny ones, too. It's difficult to imagine, but Michael actually sent a girl home because she was too skinny. The ones who miss their boyfriends seem to fly back home even before the purchase of the required black mini.

After our initial and colorless wardrobe is acquired, Michael proceeds to give us a character or personality of sort. Most girls who leave home at seventeen or eighteen are pretty clueless, clueless enough to allow Michael to make them into whomever he sees them as. We then act our part accordingly, like a self-fulfilling prophecy. I don't mind the little charade. After all, it is me who has no identity, no knowledge of self, no knowledge even of where I come from. But Michael knows. I come from Wisconsin, and therefore I am a Wisconsin maiden who grew up with the cows and the fear of God. The fear of God part is right, but no one in New York can believe I grew up with running water and a mailbox attached to the house after Michael is finished with me. I am a clear-faced farm girl, innocent in all respects, which is basically true. Naiveté suits me, he says. I am not going to argue. I can be naïve. I am not to be looked at as meat, like Susan perhaps, but as a precious and untouched treasure Michael has control over. This too is all right with me. I trust him. Someone has to take control. No one has offered so far.

But Michael likes all of us to be friendly and flirtatious, especially at the restaurant. As far as I am concerned, I am earning my meals. A skirt and a smile are small prices to pay for delicious, tasty meals in a delicious and tasty atmosphere.

I pull a piece of French bread apart and happily deny myself butter as I see Susan dig into it with her knife. Michael sits back in his chair with a cloth napkin in his lap; a black tee shirt and off-white blazer offset the fact that he needs to catch up on his sleep.

"I saw your composites this afternoon."

"Yes…" I am playing confident, flirtatious model. I decide to draw myself out slowly with my lack of words. I won't be in anticipation. The mellow, peach surroundings of the smoky restaurant put me in a mood. My soup is warming me on the inside and settling my hunger.

"You need a better body shot."

He is right. I totally agree. I won't let this throw me in front of Yvonne. I don't care about Susan. I put the bread down.

"I'll have to work on that. I'll ask Louise to set me up for some tests." I blink my eyes innocently. My heart is in my throat.

"You see, girls, this is a professional." Michael always likes to make examples of us, either good or bad, and I know this. I know his secrets. It's why he likes me, I think. I smile at him, knowing I am playing my part. I have a bunch of other comments floating around in my head—silly, witty things I can come up with this very minute to impress the crowd, to overshadow Yvonne's newness, which seems to occupy Michael. But I refrain to remain effective, as effective as Clint Eastwood when he comes strolling down the dirt path of a small Western town in which all the curious ones begin to ask him obnoxious questions that lose their entire importance once Clint decides to ignore them and remain silent.

The waiter comes back with our main dishes and sets them all around the table. He is an attractive man in his late twenties, hair slicked back into a ponytail. He is also playing a part. At Yvonne's place, he sets down a thick cut of prime rib that oozes from all sides.

"Merci beaucoup."

"Pas de qua." In New York, everything that is French is fabulous—French food, the French language, French people. It is imperative that all models move to Paris at some point in their career to work on their books and become educated in the European fashion. I know Michael wants this for me, too. He wants me to learn French and move to Paris. Fortunately, though, I started working in New York right away and am still working. I don't have any great desire to move to Europe, especially now since Dylan. But I know Michael is always thinking of it.

"Rachel, honey. You wanna check out … with me?" She jerks her pretty head toward the desert tables while keeping her eyes on Michael. His are on Yvonne. She is safe. I feel like stretching.

I move slowly, languidly, behind Susan toward the mirrors and desert tables. A waiter offers her a sample taste of a chocolate cake she has her eye on. She is doing her best to look like a skinny, laughing thing, but instead is really concentrating on what is under that thin, chocolate icing. Will it be more chocolate? Or will it be something else entirely? I watch her as she holds her hand under the bite of cake. Her attention is already focused on some other choices, and he is there, ready to fulfill every one of them.

I am more interested in how I am being viewed by my audience. In the mirror, on the other side of the table, I see myself through the smoky air. I angle my head slightly to the side and watch my long, brown hair fall in front of my shoulder. I observe myself and at the same time make sure no one else is watching me. The food from dinner digests itself slowly, and as it does this I begin to feel warm and almost sexual, if one can feel this way from food. I can see my whole body in the mirror; the tight, black mini skirt, my long, toned legs that look good in heels. I look like a model, the way I am supposed to look. And it makes me feel exposed, but I like it.

3

APPETITES AND
SUPPRESSANTS

I begin to enjoy the feeling of being hungry, at least during the
work week. If I don't feel hungry fifteen minutes after I eat, I feel
I have eaten too much. It is a game I play, and hunger is the captain.
The hunger is a signal saying I am doing the right thing. If I am not
hungry, I will be fat. Still, I eat good foods at least twice a day and
continue to run. I am very conscious of my state of mind. I know
what I am doing and why. The reasons are not controlling me; they
are keeping me in line. I know I have to starve a little, because if I eat
what I want I can't be a model. I might just be a good-looking
average-weight girl. I am not prone to skinniness, and yet this is the
image I have to keep up. I have to be thin but always think I am fat. I
have to stand in front of the mirror with the rest of the girls and pinch
my midriff and say things like, "I have the biggest ass!" and "I'm
never eating again!" This is what I have to do to be part of the group.
If I feel myself exempt from the madness, I will surely end up fat.

I begin to realize this after my first six months or so in New
York. I've worked a lot and have become comfortable with denial. I
can deny myself food and feel better than if I would have eaten
whatever it is that seems so tempting at the moment. It gives me a

strange sense of power because I know keeping myself thin is what is keeping me away from home. If I prove to be a little neurotic, I will no longer belong in Wisconsin, back with the people who never leave, who just accept the mediocre, who grow fat on steak and ice cream. I need to feel like I am in charge. I will prove a different destiny for myself. I will conquer the odds. Well, this is what I think running through the park every morning and speeding through red lights each day on the bike, breathing in the dirt all around me as if it is my food. The fact is I still need balance, something to calm my insides, slow me down, and keep me realistic.

I find this with Dylan at a restaurant called Souen. Here he pulls me back to Earth, making me eat their heavy, dark, homemade bread, their steamed vegetables, their brown rice. I feel alive inside after eating a meal there. I feel nourished. The place is a dark, wooden hole in the wall, lit only by candles and the naked, glowing faces of the waitresses. They look wholesome in their cotton aprons, like Mary from *Little House on the Prairie*. Their eyes are bright and unassuming, and they let us sit there for as long as we desire, breathing in the strawberry incense that burns in the corner.

We hold hands across the table, and I rejoice in my balance, in the fact that I deny myself when I am not with him, but allow myself when I am. I let myself eat a little more than normal, then wallow in laziness around his apartment while he smokes a bowl or two and reads me the lyrics from songs he is writing.

Marijuana is not an easy subject for me to deal with. I mean, it's illegal, right? It's a drug and it must be bad if it's illegal. But Dylan, in his honey voice and soft caresses explains gently about his drug of choice, as he calls it. No one has ever died from it, he announces, but over 125,000 people die every year from alcohol abuse. He tells me that it's been around since, well, forever and that it was first acknowledged in 2700 B.C. remaining legal in America until the 1930s. He even says that George Washington and Thomas Jefferson were cannabis smokers. He tells me lots of things while he puffs on his pipe and slowly exhales as his eyes turn a watery red. I tell him to keep it away from me. He just laughs.

His father and he share an apartment on the Upper East Side. His father allows him to live there without paying rent because he is in school at NYU pretending to major in business. But Dylan confesses to me he is religiously opposed to the confines of a classroom for learning and he could better educate himself through his own choice of text and teacher. I am not sure who his choice of teacher is, and as far as I can see his only current "text" in hand is *The Hobbit*.

When he isn't skipping classes, his days and nights are spent writing music and lyrics and practicing with and without his band. They all agree that a female singer is a good idea, and so Dylan's latest project is to write up an ad for the paper that will attract the right kind of girl. I keep my jealousies to myself. I figure I won't freak out about it until I see her.

He seems pretty intent on making it in the music industry. I suppose we are two of a kind, lost in the competitive cluster of chaos called Manhattan. Each of us is struggling to make it in a field where it is nothing short of impossible to come out ahead. Modeling and music. Any kid's dream, I suppose. The dreamy part of what we found, however, is not out in the streets of the city, but inside his father's apartment, inside each other's arms. Since Dylan's dad is hardly ever home, the two of us can play house together, pretending to possess that which we do not.

"Come here."

"You come here." I stand at the kitchen counter and look at him lying on the couch with his arms outstretched. I am the mouse; he is the cat.

"How'd you get to be so cute?" He sure has a way about him. He is a magnet. I walk over near the couch, and he swoops his arms around my legs and pulls me down. Captured. The first couple months I remained fully clothed, but lately even I want his hands on my skin. I have never been allowed such freedom in my life, to be with a boy so unsupervised. And now, since I never let him go very far, though further each time, our desires remain at a constant high.

At least mine are. Ocean waves of lust rush through my entire body, and all I want to do is kiss him and hold him. In a strange way, I want him inside me, and when I think of this I see all the love-making scenes flash through my mind from movies and on television; faces of delight and anguish, boobs and buttocks being caressed, moaning, pushing, pulling, sweating, sighing. I try to picture myself doing these things and find it difficult, but I like to fantasize about it anyway, about total animal nakedness and sexual fulfillment. I tell myself that if I could somehow achieve this, I might in turn symbolically free myself from my past, sort of make a break from it for good as I graduate into the life of an adult. Who am I kidding?

I know I have let it get intense with Dylan. And I know guys hate it when girls are a tease. He hints about going all the way every time I find myself in that same compromising situation; body on body, my shirt off, his pants unbuttoned, soft lighting, the smell of pot in the air, James Taylor singing *Something in the Way She Moves*. But there is something about the whole situation I just don't trust. Actually, there are numerous things. I want to scream, "What about venereal diseases, unwanted pregnancies, heartache, birth control, the loss of innocence, fornicating against the Lord's will? What about AIDS?" Surely the act of intercourse isn't worth it when one weighs all the pros and cons. So when the candles are lit and the music is low, with pillows all around me, and that whisper asks me in my ear, I shout back, "No," put my shirt on, and ride home innocently on my bike through the light rain and sounds of comforting traffic all around me.

The next day, he skips his afternoon classes and meets me at the Museum of Modern Art on West 53rd. I wait in the sculpture garden, as I have done before, and he comes up behind me, scaring me into forgiving him for any pressure he may have put on me the night before. He knows I have been thinking about ending it, for the sake of keeping my virginity. He thinks it's cute. I tell him I am serious. He says he knows I am.

It is during one of these early winter days where the leaves from autumn are blowing themselves into a cold and disturbing fury that we meet again at the museum. He says he wants to talk, and the whole day, swearing to myself for not bringing along gloves, I find my heart in my throat and feel tears welling up in my eyes at the thought that he is going to want to break up with me. It's the sex thing. I have been a tease for too long. Guys and girls are different. I have learned this from listening to stand-up comics. Comedians basically tell it how it is because how it is, is usually very funny. What makes people laugh the hardest is the truth, it seems. I even catch myself laughing here and there when I understand a sex joke. But on the way to the museum, I am not smiling about the fact that guys will do practically anything to have sex, that it is in their nature to do so, and that if they don't get it from one girl, they're bound to get it from another.

I stand in the sculpture garden with my back to the cold wind, pulling my thin jean jacket tightly around me, waiting for him to find me. A couple times I think I feel him touch my shoulder, but when I turn around no one is there. He walks straight at me, his black curls blowing up off his head, making him look like a clown.

"Hey, what's up?"

He wears a brown, leather jacket and light blue jeans; thick, brown socks; and Birkenstocks.

"Nothing. You're supposed to be at school, huh?"

"Yeah. Whatever. I haven't learned one damned thing since the semester started." He notices I am shivering and pulls me to him.

"Maybe that's because you never go."

"Listen, Rachel. If I thought business school was so important, I'd be there, okay?" He gives me a little peck on my cool cheek. I pull away.

"I don't get it. You don't care that your father is wasting thousands of dollars on you for no good reason?" I hear my voice speaking the irritation that's been in my throat all day.

"Hey, what do you care? He's not *your* father. It's not *your* money. What's gotten into you today?"

I hate that phrase. As if I had some sort of fleas or ticks or a virus or something that could change my mood and make me irritable.

"I don't know." I am tired and cold from being outside all day and don't feel like fighting anymore. My energy is used up.

"You wanna go inside?"

I nod like a little girl. I think my lower lip even falls into a pout. He leads me in and up to the second floor where he usually discovers everything first and then tells me about it, as he is the native New Yorker who grew up with all this amazing art around him. I am just the ignorant farm girl, after all.

"That's nice." I point. I like the impressionists, the way their brush strokes sit on the canvas without really being a part of it. The paintings aren't as perfect as in the earlier eras. For some reason, they give me hope.

We walk into the adjoining exhibit silently, each pretending to be preoccupied with the framed decorations that hang majestically and demand attention. I know what is on my mind.

"So?" My way of getting to the subject. I can no longer deal with the churning in my stomach.

"Rachel." He says this as if he has been holding his breath. Now I can't bring myself to answer him. I don't want to acknowledge the serious tone of his voice. I stand quietly, staring at Monet's water lilies. The deep and subtle greens and blues that now surrounded me take me in. By my faith I step onto the pink and white lilies and do not fall.

"Rache?"

"What?" I turn around and slip into the water.

"You know I love you." He does? Here it comes. Drown me slowly.

"Dylan, if you want to break up with me, just say so already." I am shaking from the inside, and the hunger I'd felt all day so intensely vanishes instantly. I look at him, trying to win him back with my eyes, trying to be cute and irresistible, like a kitten.

"Come here." It works. I raise my eyebrows slowly and fall into my ultra skinny, nobody loves me mode. "You sure do jump to conclusions, don't you? Jesus. I don't want to break up, it's just that…"

"It's just that you want sex, and you're not willing to wait any longer, right?"

"Settle. Christ." He looks around then, as if to say "sex" is not a word he is comfortable with me shouting in a public museum with so many respected and revered pieces of art listening.

"Listen, I just thought we should talk about it, that's all. I mean, doesn't it feel as if we should, to you?"

To me? Who is he kidding? Like he cares what I feel.

"Why? Is that how you feel?" I am as equally loud to show him he doesn't phase me. I become very self-righteous when sex is on the table.

"I feel that I want to make love to you."

Right. Good. Put it in womanly terms. Maybe that'll melt my heart of ice. Thing is, I have no idea what I want or how I feel. It is all too confusing, and I just want things to stay as they are.

"Well, I don't know anything about making love." I sit down on the wooden bench and stare at Van Gogh's sunflowers. Their brilliance disturbs me. He follows my lead and seats himself at the other end of the bench, turning his body toward me in his most convincing pose.

"We can learn together."

Good one, Dylan. Like I believe you've never done it before. I know he's had plenty of girlfriends. When he's drinking with John, things will slip out, but he's always been decent enough to stop himself after noticing how uncomfortable it makes me feel.

"You mean you can show me how."

"If that's what you want." Guys are so pathetic when it comes to sex talks. They know the ball is in our court, and yet they continue to serve ball after ball thinking we'll hit one back eventually.

"Eventually."

"What is that supposed to mean?" He stands up, blocking my view of the flowers.

Am I pushing too far? Will I lose him with this tough, virtuous girl act? Is it an act? I want to cry to the Lord, asking him why he condemns fornication the way he does. Isn't it a natural thing? Isn't it something we are just supposed to do to stay with the flow of nature? There is a part of me that wants to go with him, lie down with him, and get it over with so it will no longer be an issue. But a larger part of me wants to stay a virgin until I am married, as I've been taught in church. Besides, what is the big deal? I have seen my roommate sneak out of our room in college so she could meet her boyfriend and have sex. All that followed were days of heartache when her knight in shining armor eventually found some other princess to ravish. And the stress she went through over getting her period! I never saw anything more ridiculous than all the talk about whether or not someone was pregnant, how many days they were late, if they'd get an abortion or not. All to be prevented by just saying no.

"I can't have sex with you yet."

"Yet?"

He is waiting on my every word. I kind of like this. If I give into him and have sex, maybe I won't be so special anymore. On the other hand, I don't want to risk losing him, not now after finally finding somebody I feel important around. He is basically the best thing that has ever happened to me. But how much will I have to pay for this assurance?

"Will you leave me if we have sex?"

"What gives you that idea?" His hands push evenly into his front pockets as he stands there and stares down at me.

"If you get what you want, then you can move on." I have seen my share of movies on this subject matter. Teenage heartbreak when the girl gives in too soon. No loyalty to the slut.

"Rachel, it's not like that." He sits back down. "I'm really into you. I don't know what's come over you today."

An evil force has come over me, ill winds, a winter fever.

"Nothing has gotten into me or come over me." I am quietly thinking that it might be PMS.

"Listen, can we change the subject for a minute?"

Yes! Had I won?

"Sure." So nonchalant.

"You have to tell me what you think about this. It's totally up to you because I'm not sure if you'll have the time, but the guys and I were thinking about asking you to sing with us for a while. What do you think? I mean, you've got a really good voice and…"

"No one answered your ad?"

"That's not the point."

"Sure it is."

"What do you mean?"

"I'm thrilled that you asked me, Dylan, I really am." I am actually giddy inside. I can't believe he thinks this much about me, to ask me to join his band.

"Well, why don't you think about it, okay?" He stands up again.

"Of course." Of course I'll sing in his band. Is he crazy?

"Coming over tonight?" He begins to look anxious about leaving. He looks at his wrist, but there is no watch there.

"What time?"

"I don't know, seven? Why don't you take the subway, or the bus?"

"I'll ride the bike."

"You sure?"

"Sure I'm sure."

"I could come and pick you up, but…"

"Don't worry about it." I stand up to see the sunflowers and his eyes. "I like to ride at night. The air is almost refreshing." I put my arms around him, feeling hungry.

"I love you, Rachel."

"I love you, too." I did. In fact, I don't think I really did until right there and then on the second floor of the museum with the beauty of master painters shining down on us.

"I gotta go to practice."

"I know you do."

"See you later then?"

"Definitely." His kiss is soft and moist and I want him.

* * *

At home I fix myself a couple perfectly warmed in the microwave bagels and dip them in plain yogurt and try to visualize making love. I decide I will need two things: lingerie and birth control. I know all about the different kinds from college classes and college classmates. Condoms protect against AIDS and babies but are supposed to be a drag during sex. There are sponges, but I'd heard of a girl who couldn't get hers back out after having sex and she had to go to the hospital for help. There is the pill, but that doesn't protect against disease either, and most of the girls I'd known who'd taken it had gained weight. That is a definite no.

After finishing both bagels, I wait to make sure I am still a little hungry, then go inspect my underwear situation. The thought had never really occurred to me to make myself attractive in my underwear. Underwear is something you cover up with jeans and a shirt. It is embarrassing, but I still have in my possession several pairs of big lady cotton briefs Mom had given me for Christmas. They are actually quite comfortable. I bury them underneath my belts and bandanas and think about Yvonne's assortment in the dresser next to mine. I am tempted to try some of her stuff on, but refrain. Apparently her father owns a small boutique in the south of France that carries all sorts of lingerie and garter belts and pretty, lacy things. So not only am I incredibly jealous of her adorable French accent, but I want her underwear, too. She has the sexiest, satin sets—always matching with little flowered patterns.

I am just saying my last good-byes to my nymphet years, visualizing what I will need to purchase for the inevitable day, when I hear a loud thump coming from the bathroom. I immediately run to the door and put my ear up against it.

"Who's in there? Susan?" I think I remember Michael telling me he was taking Yvonne to dinner, alone.

"Agh!" It is the combination of a moan, a cry, and an angry shout of discontent. I try the door, but it is locked.

"You okay? Susan, are you in there?"

"Yes!" And then she begins crying out loud. She wants me to hear her.

"You want me to leave you alone?" I know she doesn't.

"I don't know!" I hear a loud sniffle and then the turning of the lock. I push the door gently open. She is sitting on the toilet seat in her underwear and bra.

"What are you doing?" I am sincerely curious.

"What does it look like? I'm trying to throw up all the goddamned food I just ate."

"Jeez." I close the door behind me. This is a behind the closed door kind of moment.

"I know. And the weirdest thing of all is that I can't do it." She stands up and splashes her face with water, then sits back down on the toilet with a white hand towel hiding her face. "I'm so damned sick of it." She takes the towel away from her face and looks right at me.

"Are you bulimic?" All the television movies rush into my brain about girls gorging on junk food and then throwing up, irritating their esophagi and rotting their teeth just to be thin.

"Well, if I was don't ya think I could throw up if I wanted to?" I guess she is right. "Don't you be tellin' anybody about this now."

"No way. Don't worry about it." Her elbows rest on her thighs as she leans forward to put her head in her hands. Her stomach protrudes over the elastic on her panties and her bra strap makes a noticeable dent in the fat underneath her arms. I stand against the wall not knowing what else to say.

"Guess I'll be fixin' to go home soon, huh?" She looks up at me as her pale eyes fill with teardrops.

4

CLAUDIA

Ever since Yvonne moved in, the bedroom remains in complete disarray. I had easily taken care of Susan's messy habits when there were only the two of us, but now the two of them have bonded together like unemployed housewives who watch the soaps and talk shows and chat all day about how dreadful their lives have become. Neither of them work very much, and since Michael left for Switzerland, Susan stays on with us, trying every new fad diet—Slimfast shake, diet pill, and every food labeled "diet" in the stores. She never seems to be able to focus on one plan for too long. She expects to see results overnight, I guess.

I invite her to come running with me in the mornings, and she did go once, complaining the whole way of her knees and her back. I think her breasts got in the way. I can't imagine having to deal with the bouncing. One good sweat was enough for Susan. Yvonne supports her complaints, and they are off to the bedroom reading about some new diet where you cut your carbohydrates down to almost nothing, but are allowed to eat as much protein and fat as desired. Sure. That'll work.

I begin to feel closed in, like I don't belong in the apartment because everything always needs cleaning and I can't keep up with them. I hesitate every day to confront them. I don't want to make myself the one that doesn't fit in more than I already am. Yvonne is too European for me to get on her case. I don't want to offend or upset her. She takes everything very seriously and is always apologizing for leaving food out on the counters or not doing the dishes or mispronouncing some English word. She seems sincere, but it doesn't matter. Neither of them get it. I am going crazy in all of their mess, and I am the only one working. It doesn't seem fair. But of course life isn't fair, or so I've heard from every adult who ever heard some kid complaining about what's fair or not. And yet they teach sharing and taking turns as if it's somehow possible anyway.

I stare up at the ceiling from Michael's bed trying to figure out why I am so preoccupied with cleanliness, why messes disturb me so much, and why I can't seem to do anything until everything is clean.

Clean is what made my mother happy. It was what she demanded, and cleaning was the only way I seemed able to win her approval on a regular basis. Who needs a psychologist?

I remember being introduced to the toilet at the age of six or so. She took me by the hand and pointed to the sink, tub, toilet, and around the edges of the outside of the toilet where my father and brothers always missed. It was a terrible day, the day I met the outside of the toilet where the yellow gunk grew week after week. The inside wasn't that great either. And I didn't get one of those toilet scrubbers with the handle so that I didn't have to touch the water with my hand. For all the fixtures in the bathroom, I depended on only two things, a container of Ajax and one of my father's rust colored rags from the gas station. The rags had dark blue printing on them, and I used one every Saturday morning with what mom called "elbow grease." She informed me that this could be used in the kitchen as well. I found that I needed it most washing the dirty rings in the tub. As a small girl, I would climb into the tub so I could get the best angle and work to my highest point of efficiency. The last step was to wash the floor, from behind the toilet to the door. I rinsed my rag often, but not in the sink, because I didn't want to get it dirty again. I rinsed it in the tub, the hot water burning my hands every time because the water got so hot so quick. When I finished, I rinsed my cloth one last time, folded it twice, and hung it over the pipes underneath the sink where it would wait until the following Saturday.

* * *

Billy rode his bright colored, plastic Bigwheel up and down the block with his friend from across the street. The little girl could see his obscured shape through the waved, glass-block windows in the bathroom. It was summer, and the children had just been gifted with a yellow swing-set, which now sat in the tiny backyard. The girl's favorite moments were spent singing on the swings in the yard.

As soon as she finished with the floor, she quickly rinsed the rag in the tub, folded it, and hung it on the pipes underneath the sink. She had almost made it to the swings when she saw her mother standing at the back door in her red flowered house shift and dirty tennis shoes motioning to her daughter with her finger to come. The girl was pushed into the bathroom by the back of her head and made to peer into the area around the drain in the tub. Leftover grime and hair stuck against the white of the tub as evidence of her carelessness. She rinsed the tub to perfection that Saturday, but she didn't get to swing on the swing-set.

* * *

It took me awhile to get everything right, but all the practice made me good at what I did. And what I did was clean. I cleaned to make my mother happy, and I cleaned to give myself something to do when I was nervous.

My favorite time to clean was when my mother went on her errands to the bank, the post office, rummage sales, and the grocery store. If she was going to be gone for more than an hour or so, I would scan the house and think of a plan so I could get everything finished before she returned. While my brothers sat on the floor watching cartoons and playing with their matchbox cars and Legos, I would get out a rag and the Pledge and dust the laminated end tables and the old stereo, the chipped lamp bases, and any other wood or fake wood surface I could find. I made my mother's bed and picked up all the dirty clothes in the bedrooms, throwing them down the shoot. I got the whole house in order, leaving the kitchen for last. I did all the dishes, washed the stove top, cleaned the bird cage and the fish bowl, wiped all the counters, dried all the dishes, put them away, threw out any old food from the refrigerator, emptied the crumbs from the toaster, then made it shine with glass cleaner. When I felt I was almost finished, I would run around the house fluffing the couch pillows, straightening throw rugs, wiping fingerprints off the doorways and doorknobs, and blowing the dust off pictures and vases and things I had missed the first time. The last thing I did was vacuum. I made my brothers sit on the couch with their feet off the ground and their toys in their laps, and then I would vacuum with all my might, smiling every time I heard dirt fly up into the vacuum bag. When the vacuum was back in the closet and Mom still hadn't arrived back home, well, this was my moment of happiness. I had achieved great and wonderful things, and it would be impossible for her not to notice. I had spent my time wisely and had done it without any help.

I roll over on my side, pull my knees to my chest, and realize I am still that person, no matter how far away I think I can go. I am now only who I had been, that nervous, frightened girl who was only ever out to please, who always felt alone. Sometimes I hate her for coming along. What I need is more time to lose the girl I am so I can be ready and new when I find my birth mother, my real mother. Then everything will be different.

That night, I decide to sleep in Michael's room. I set his radio alarm clock for 6:30 so I can catch the 8:00 train to Connecticut. I have a booking there for a couple days in the snow. And I have made some other plans as well, plans that might help me find my biological parents. It scares me, though, to think of my mother finding out that I am doing this.

I turn my pillow to the cool side for the last time and beg for sleep to come. I lie there restless, knowing I need a good night's sleep; but the knowing only takes me from it.

* * *

She recognizes her grade school playground easily. The day is heavy, with a gray and dreary mist falling from the darkening clouds above. She can barely see the three small children who play kickball on one of the baseball diamonds in the distance. Their laughter makes the girl shudder in the fake fur coat she wears that is two sizes too small. She hates the coat. It is dark blue and has large, brown buttons on it she refuses to use. The air blows its cool breeze at her and hits her where her coat is left hanging open. She doesn't feel it. Instead, she trudges on, pushing her hands deep into the worn and nubby pockets. Her thin wrists stick out of the coat, exposing them to the winter air as well. She feels the coldness there, and pushes her hands deeper into the pockets, finding in the right one the familiar hole.

The thought occurs to her that it must be Saturday, and she wonders why she is on the playground without her teacher and her class. She trudges on through the fog toward the children who she can now see clearly. But they do not see her. Their screams of delight and rosy cheeks scare the girl in the blue coat. Except for the children, the playground and all the surrounding streets are oddly vacant. As she walks, she feels alone, as if she is the only person on Earth, as if she has no home to go to because no one can see her. These thoughts make her feel very old as she stands away from the children now at the other end of the playground. Her journey has been worthless. Where will she go now? There is no one who will come looking for her, no one who will take her hand and lead her home. The mist becomes heavier, matting the fur on the coat, weighing her down, down into the ground.

Suddenly, from the speakers above, which normally sound the bell to come in, comes a familiar and eerie sounding song that brings her back immediately to the place under the table where all she can see are their legs and the legs of the table, for she was just a toddler. Their voices scream above the song, the same song that now plays on the playground. She knows then, standing in the deepening fog, hearing that terrible music, that she will never have the chance to live the way she sees other people living. It is something definite inside her soul that tells her this. And she believes it. She will never be small enough again to forget the terror she now knows.

* * *

The bright red numbers on the clock read 6:32 when I finally pry my eyes open, not believing that I have to get up already. It feels as if I have just fallen asleep, as if I hadn't even dreamt. But then I catch the end of the song that immediately sends shivers up my spine, and I remember.

The booking is in Hartford at the home of the makeup artist who is to be on the set. All I know is that her name is Claudia and she is expecting me. I am going to stay at her house to make things easier since there isn't a hotel for miles. On the train, I leave the city and enter the country and the snow, and I feel my mind clearing itself from the dream that had haunted me all morning.

I take a taxi from the station to her house and am dropped off at exactly five minutes to nine. Since I have a moment to spare, I just stand there looking at her home, at all the windows that reveal a multitude of plants, both dropping down from above and also sitting, reaching their leaves toward the warmth and light of the glass. The house is a dark wood with white shutters that blend nicely with the virgin coat of snow on the roof. There is no sound besides the birds chirping in the large pine trees that stand on either side. The walk looks as if it has been recently swept, for there are pine needles and pieces of pinecones lying in the snow on either side as I walk toward the large, wooden door that opens before I can knock.

"Are you Rachel?"

"Yes, Louise sent me."

"Of course, come on in. I saw you standing out there and figured it must be you."

"You have a beautiful home."

"Why thank you, that's sweet. Can I get you something to drink? Some tea or something?" Her voice drips like honey, and I am reminded of those phone sex girls who come on television late at night to tell you that you're not alone. At least not if you have a credit card. I follow her into the kitchen where I set my backpack down.

"Tea?"

"Sure. I think I'll have a cup myself."

My mind rushes back to the only time I had ever been given tea. I was sick to my stomach and sitting in the kitchen waiting for the water to boil, catching just a sliver of Sesame Street through the dining room doorway. My brothers were in the living room fighting over who got to sit in the recliner. When my mom told me to drink the dark, steamy liquid that sat in front of me, I did. I can still remember the horrible taste of it. Not two seconds passed before I went dashing for the bathroom where my mother stood over me telling me not to miss, to get it all in the toilet bowl.

"I have peppermint, Red Zinger, orange, Sleepytime. But we don't want that now, do we?" She looks over at me and winks as if I were a child. I look into the cupboard where she is rummaging. It isn't very organized.

"So?"

"Oh. Um. To tell you the truth I've never really had any of those types of teas." I sound like an idiot.

"Well, then, this will be a treat. Herbal teas are very calming to the digestive system. They're tasty and caffeine free." She smiles as she sets her black teapot on a back burner of the stove. Her positive attitude seems unique after living in New York for so many months.

"Peppermint for the both of us?"

"Sure." I don't sound very enthusiastic.

"Don't worry. If you don't like it you don't have to drink it."

In her white overalls and long, brown braid she seems so totally content with herself. I wonder how a person gets that way.

"Here, let's take your bag into the back bedroom."

I follow her as she swings my backpack over her right shoulder. The room is small and adorable, with colorful afghans thrown over the bed and embroidered sayings on the wall. I recognize one as the Serenity Prayer.

"This is so nice of you, really."

"Oh, it's no problem. I'm happy to have you as my guest."

"Thank you."

"Oh, the water. Let me get it. If you'd like, we can get started. Everything's in the dining room." She points to the right as she scurries into the kitchen.

In the dining room everything is set up, all her makeup brushes and hair brushes, combs, and Q-tips. There are sponges and tissues all neatly arranged on a clean, white towel that protects her table from her huge makeup case, which houses all shades of foundation and cover sticks, blushes and shadows and creams and pencils and lipsticks and nail polishes and anything else one might need to become perfectly and completely beautiful.

"Go ahead and sit right there, if you will."

I sit down on a wooden stool that is covered with a black, padded seat cover.

"Your tea."

"Thank you." The smell of it is like gum or mouthwash. I set it on the table next to the towel.

"Let it cool awhile."

"Okay."

She takes her largest brush and begins working through my tangles.

"I'm sorry. I tried to get them all out this morning."

"No problem. That's what I'm here for, you see." She continues brushing, slowly and methodically, and all around us are pretty angles of morning sunlight streaming in, nourishing the plants and giving us a pleasant atmosphere. On the buffet next to us I notice a framed 5 X 7 of a young girl with dark brown braids and big, brown eyes.

"That's Emma." I look up at the same eyes. "My daughter."

"She's very cute. I like her name."

"Thank you. She's named after her great-grandmother, the woman who painted all of those." She pulls her large, almond eyes up to the wall in back of her. Mine follow to see three equally spaced paintings, two of scenery and one of a dark-skinned woman whose deep, sad eyes gaze beyond the wall and beyond the house into a distance that is invisible while her black hair blows away from her face in ripples, like a flag.

"Is that her?" Claudia steps around so she can face the picture herself.

"Yes. A self-portrait, I guess. It's pretty close to the way she looked, oh, many, many years ago." Claudia pulls my hair into a lose ponytail and dots moisturizer underneath my eyes. "Grandma Emeline painted that soon after she was moved onto the reservation with her sister." The soft tip of her finger dabs the lotion carefully until it becomes invisible.

"She's Native American?" I decide to use this instead of "Indian." I remember my professor explaining that Indians come from India, and the term "Native American" was more accurate, more politically correct I guess. Yes. It was the people native to this great country of ours who became America's first victims as we pulled their land out from under them, made them sick, and tricked them with our treaties. Now, after their culture had been cast out, their homes destroyed, and their religion mocked, at least they got the title of being the first to have cultivated the land of the white man's America.

"Grandma Em is a half breed Apache, on her mother's side. I believe her father came from somewhere in Europe, though." Claudia is trying to find the right foundation to match my skin. She holds up the cool glass to my skin, shakes her head slightly, and tries another.

I gaze up at the woman in the picture again as Claudia seems to find the right jar of foundation. I sip at my tea now, following her lead. It is pleasant enough and feels good going down.

Suddenly the door flies open and we both turn abruptly, looking.

"Well hello! Good morning, girls! What a fabulous day for the shoot, don't you think?"

"Good morning, Antoine. Don't you knock anymore?" We both watch him as he storms in the house towards us. He cautiously peers into my face.

"Rachel, is it you?" His hand is on my chin, turning my face from side to side and scowling.

"Of course it's her."

"Why Rachel, you beautiful thing you! Why you just blossom out in this country air! You look absolutely natural! Claudia, do put some makeup on this girl."

"That *was* next on the agenda, sir." She gives him a coy grin.

"Fabulous. Then we can get started at once. Has the, you know, arrived yet?" His bright, blue eyes dart around, looking into all the rooms as his long, messy hair flies this way and that.

"Not yet."

"Who will it be? Were you informed?"

"Roversi, I think; if they can get him."

"Of course you were told. I'm never told about these things." He mumbles this as he starts sifting through the garments and accessories that have been sent for the shoot. I glance over at Antoine as Claudia dusts my face with powder. I hold in a sneeze. Antoine is the most gorgeous guy I have ever seen. He's absolutely stunning. His face is sculpted to perfection, and his cheeks glow with a natural rose color from right underneath his eyes to down below the cheekbone where the color fades into the perfect tone of his skin. He is tall and thin and wears big, black combat boots; faded jeans with holes in both knees; and a big, black, cape-like shirt that flows along with his hair, which looks as if it's never been combed. But it is his eyes that really do it for me. They are blue like the sky— light blue, clear, and bright. I have only seen eyes like that a few times, and every time they do the same thing to me.

When he opens his mouth, he is so clearly gay it is ridiculous to even think of him as being interested in the opposite sex—not that *I* am really interested. He is like so many other makeup artists and stylists I have worked with. They just have that air about them that is undeniable, as if they want it to be known because for some reason it makes them more creative or interesting.

"What an absolute contradiction of fashion! Claudia, are you seeing these things? My God, they're early eighties! What do they expect from me?"

"The country girl look. Middle America." Claudia leans toward me with the eyeliner. I know her perfume, but can't place it.

"I wasn't looking for an answer to that, sweet-cheeks. I don't want to hear about Middle America. Is our little country girl supposed to be embarrassed to walk outside?"

"Don't tell me you haven't had worse."

"Remember the cover shoot for YM? God, that ugly, yellow rain coat with that hideous yellow flower! I definitely wasn't up for that one."

"Did they pick it? The cover?"

"No. They chose a lovely beach shot from the Bahamas or something. I knew the coat wasn't going to work. Of course I couldn't say anything with that bitchy editor there that day. You remember?"

"Yes, I remember. She was a real peach, wasn't she?"

"She was not fabulous. That's all I have to say. Are you seeing these colors, Claudia? Turquoise? What do I do with turquoise?"

He holds out a sweater for Claudia to see. It has some sparkling, plastic, jeweled things on the front of it. I don't like it either.

"Work with me, Antoine."

"I'm trying, I swear."

The booking went well after Antoine sorted and arranged and borrowed half of Claudia's wardrobe. For two days we shot activities one can do in the snow that can keep a person fit as well. They had apparently chosen me for the shoot because I am a runner and am supposedly more athletic than the average cigarette smoking, chocolate bar eating, anorexic type model who gets most of the work.

It was like being a kid all over again, or for the first time. I went sledding and carried the sled up the hill, huffing and puffing the whole way, but not showing it. We drove to a frozen pond, and I did my best with a couple turns as Claudia's cream colored scarf blew in the cool wind. I put on snow skis and made motion of movement. I built a snowman, looking energetic as I did so, rolling the growing snowball until it stood almost half my size. And as I took part in all these good-for-your-health winter activities, my pink lipstick never smudged, and my blush stayed blushed to perfection. My mascara never ran down my face, and any unwanted bead of perspiration was quickly blotted off with Claudia's handy compact. My hat always matched my mittens, and all my gear was shiny and new. I was a goddess of the snow, showing to all the subscribers of the magazine that if they would just get off their couch and venture out into their winter wonderland, they too could look fit and glamorous and perfect.

And the whole time all I could think of was my mom out at dusk, chopping at the driveway with the ice pick and no gloves because her hands had gotten too warm. She would be out there in one of her thin house shifts, leaving her legs exposed to the below freezing temperatures. I can see her shoveling the heavy snow in her mauve earmuffs and red, furry, polyester coat from Fingerhut, which she left hanging open at the front. Her short socks were buried somewhere deep in my father's old, black snowmobile boots. She would chop at the frozen ice chunks until all the ice was loose, and then she'd take our biggest shovel and scoop it all up onto the lawn. When she was through, we had the cleanest driveway on the block.

I would catch glimpses of her outside under the moonlight through the living room window. I remember the guilt I felt for not being out there. But she had sent us in when it started getting dark, telling us to do the dinner dishes and make our lunches for the next day. She liked her time outside by herself, shoveling away, working up a sweat, and at the end taking off her coat even though the temperature stayed around ten degrees or below on those winter nights in Wisconsin. She chopped and shoveled for a long time, until it was time to go to bed. But when she was through, she stormed into the house just as big as she had always been, telling us through reddened cheeks to turn off the television and get to bed.

After we finish shooting on the second day, I say my good-byes to Claudia and Emma and the photographer and hop into Antoine's car, excited because I am going to start looking for my real mother. All the way to the train station, Antoine keeps asking me in various volumes if I am sure I don't want to come to Albany with him for the weekend, that he is meeting friends there, that he is sure they would all just adore me. He is sorry he can't take me all the way back to the city because of this. Am I sure I don't want to come along? Yes, I am sure. I have plans. But I don't mention the Department of Children and Youth Services that I am stopping at in Meriden on the way home. I don't want to get my hopes up with someone like Antoine. It would have been entirely too exhausting.

I take a taxi there from the train station, and after a twenty minute wait in a silent, gray room that is scattered with old, ripped up issues of *Field and Stream* and *Redbook*, I am introduced to Frank, an adoption specialist, who would like it if I could please take a seat. I do.

"So, Miss Murphy, how can I be of assistance to you today?" He is an older man, fifties or sixties, with a sweep of pure white hair that grows on one side and ends up on the other, barely covering the big, empty area in the middle. He has sun-drenched skin that appears to be very tough and leathery. On his desk is a painted, wooden carving of a man with a golf club. Underneath it says, "World's Greatest Golfer." I want to tell this man to find my real parents, to free me from the bondage of my past and give me a new life. I want to shout out loud and cry at the same time. He is waiting for an answer while he shuffles through some papers on his desk.

"I'd like to find my natural parents. Or at least my mother, if possible." There. I have said it out loud to someone with authority. I am making progress; I have taken the first step. What would my mother think if she knew? A chill runs down my spine and my shoulders jerk involuntarily.

"Are you cold?"

"No. Thank you. I'm fine." Let's get on with it.

"Well. Why don't you start by telling me what you know of your adoption and we'll go from there."

He slouches back in his black, vinyl chair; blinks his aging, gray eyes; puts his hand to his chin; and waits. What do I know? My mother was young when she had me. I had been in several foster homes that I don't remember.

"I think I was born around here."

"In Meriden?" He sits up and puts his elbows on his desk.

"No, I mean the East Coast. Maybe Connecticut. Maybe New York."

"Well these are very populous places, Miss Murphy. Are you sure you can't be more specific?"

I am going to break down and cry in front of this man who can't even call me by my first name. God forbids he gets too personal or anything. There is a lump in my throat. I can't speak.

"Might you know the name you were born with? That would be a great help." He takes a pencil from his pencil holder and puts the point of it to his yellow legal pad.

"No. I think my mother might know some of these things, my adopted mother, I mean. But I could never ask her. It would kill her."

"Well, that's going to make it quite difficult for me to help you. We don't have much to go on, here. We have no names, no specific place. Do you know approximately when it was the Murphys adopted you?

"In December. 1972." I am so proud of myself for knowing something. Frank scribbles this on his yellow pad. Every Christmas Mom would say I was the best gift she'd ever received, and every Christmas I would get a special ornament with the year etched on it, signifying how many I'd spent with the wrong family where I was treated more as a servant girl than as a special girl.

"Well, unless you can think of something else, all I can really do is enter your current name with the information you've given me today. You'll be in the system then, at least."

"The system?"

"The computer. That means that if your biological mother or father try looking for you under the name you have now with their information that's missing from your file, we'll be able to cross examine your birth information with your adoption information and come up with a match." He is casually rocking back and forth in his chair as if he'd said this a million times to a million people.

"So I'll never be able to find them unless they're trying to find me?" The lump is back.

"I'm afraid that's correct, unless you can come up with some more information. Now, if I can just get some identification from you that you are over eighteen, and verification of your name and address."

I begin shuffling though my backpack for the information I'd been told to bring. I will be in the system. I will have to settle for the system. My head feels heavy. This is it. It is over. I swallow the lump as two large tears drop down into my bag.

I walk out of the building in a fog and stand waiting on the sidewalk for what, I do not know. The day is cloudy, gray, and a little warmer than it has been. I stand on the street and watch the cars and trucks whiz by at great speeds. Any one of them could be my mother or my father and they would never know it and neither would I.

Back on the train, I try desperately to remember life before Wisconsin as I sit securely in my seat and watch the trees and telephone poles go speeding by. If I focus on each tree or pole, take just one from the distance and keep my eyes on it, I feel as if I am going slower and can see more detail than if I try to see them all at the same time. I tilt my head back, resting it on the seat, and try to slowly focus on my past as a baby and a toddler, but all I can see are table legs and people's legs—and then I hear that terrible song again and open my eyes with a start. That is my first memory. I don't know anything before it.

5

THE FIRST CATHARSIS

As I enter Grand Central Station, I realize what I have been missing, the hustle that distracts and takes away the attention. The thoughts that had brought tears to my eyes are now forgotten as I turn the corner and look up at the wall to find my subway connection. Within inches of my body people are scurrying by, dashing here and there to find where they need to go to try to save time so they can be with who they want, so they can find something that will allow them to continue the race that prevents them from worrying about their problems. I am no exception, and I am happy about it. I am back with myself, looking out for myself, moving to get ahead. I feel the commotion all around me and liken it to a carefully planned circus. Every performer has his part to play, and it has to be played to near perfection to win the applause and recognition of those watching. I can do this. It comes from my days of efficient cleaning. I could do a lot in a short period of time, and I could do it well.

In the elevator on the way up to the apartment, I think about Dylan and the inevitable. Maybe if I have sex with him I could forget about looking for what is obviously unattainable. I need something serious to cement me into my new life.

A small smile comes over my face as I push open the unlocked door, but disappears as soon as I enter. I can see them from the living room as I stand frozen in place, my backpack falling slowly off my shoulder. The bedroom door is wide open, exposing her in her flowered, satin set, her blonde hair, his dark curls. What is he doing with blonde hair? They are sitting on her bed together, side by side, as if telling each other secrets. I see him put his feet to the floor and start buttoning his shirt. I even think I hear him say my name before I run into Michael's room, locking the door behind me. I can't handle what I see, not in front of them. I don't want to. It is over.

I go to the darkest place in the room, in the corner behind an overstuffed chair, and sink into the floor, waiting for the tears to come. Their voices on the other side of the door don't matter to me. I am back instantaneously with all of my other nightmares, and these bring the dread of life into my chest as I curl into a fetal position and try to disappear. My crying is silent, and their knocking becomes annoying after awhile. I am alone again, the way I've always been, the way I'll always be as long as I don't fade away.

The disappointment I feel with people overwhelms me as I remain motionless. The sun sets and the gloomy room grows dark. I don't get up.

I can't help the questioning as it begins again in my mind. Why go on living when all is a constant disappointment? All anyone does in life is run around in circles, repeating day after day every mundane activity that only takes them forward to more of the same. Death is the only real excitement to look forward to. It is the ultimate freedom, the ultimate end to all the chaos, to all the people who can never be trusted, to all the people who only hurt me.

I cry until the tears no longer come, until my shallow breath is the only movement I make, and then I try to quiet even that. If I quit breathing I will quit hurting. If I have no eyes I won't have to cry. I will lie here until I become invisible, until I need no food to feed my hunger or blanket to warm me.

How could I have been so ignorant to think he would wait for me? Who am I? Some kind of prize? I am nothing to wait for. I have nothing to give.

I fall asleep behind the chair, and when I awake I can see nothing but the slight glimmer of the streetlight and the bright, red, digital numbers on the clock. It is almost 1:00 in the morning. I want to freeze time there for days. Don't ever let the sun come up, I pray. I slide under the cool covers with my clothes on.

The next morning does come, though. I know it before I open my eyes, and I curse the sun and the motion of the Earth around it and the movement of the moon around the Earth. I swear against all forward progression, all the sounds of the cars and the people walking, looking, working, for what? What the hell are they all doing?

I want to know why the blissful dark of the night goes so quickly with all its dreams of unreality, which can be halted with the blink of a waking eye while the day drags on to torture the soul with the very real and very bright problems that never seem to cease. I lie there motionless, staring at the ceiling pattern, which begins moving after awhile. I stay focused on this until I get dizzy, until my head begins to pound incessantly. The hunger in my belly pushes me from the bed. Major head rush. I open Michael's closet door to look in the mirror. I need some physical validation that I am still alive, that I am who I think I am. I am.

My eyes are red and puffy, and I have a white zit on the side of my nose. I squeezed it with my dirty hands until all the yellow stuff comes out. Now my eyes and nose match. I decide I look terrible and fall backwards onto the bed again to stare up at the ceiling some more. Maybe there is an answer there somewhere. That fucking bitch, is all I can think. They are nice, strong words that make me feel better. That blonde, fucking bitch who is somewhere outside the door. I feel physically and emotionally imprisoned. What are my choices now? I am light-headed from lack of food and realize suddenly that I haven't eaten anything since the strawberries and bran muffin at Claudia's for breakfast. That feels like years ago.

The lack of fuel in my body gives me the power that I need to cope. As long as I feel this empty, I am signifying my lack of interest in life. I will only take part because suicide is a messy alternative, and I can't stand messes.

I walk across the room and put my nose to the window, feeling an abrupt warmth. I am surprised. It seems unseasonable for the sun to be so strong. It has been months since I've felt the sun on my face. Deciding that today is a definite non-running day, I quietly unlock the door and slide into the bathroom to take a shower. It is Saturday, the lovely do-nothing day, and I am going to do just that. In the bedroom, while Yvonne is in the kitchen, I slip on my jean shorts, a thick tee shirt, my cream-colored Irish knit sweater, warm socks, and my hiking boots. I am ready to brave any element as long as I don't have to be cooped up in the apartment with the slut. I move quickly, without making a sound, packing everything I think I will need for the day, for my life, and then I ride to the park on the bike and find my spot, all without even saying a word.

I feel comfortably removed from reality as I sit in the Meadow with hunger pangs gnawing at my insides. Maybe I can just fade away right there under the sun. I don't need food. I am not doing anything but watching. I lay my head down on my backpack and pull a small part of the blanket over my chilled legs while directing my face towards the sun.

Within my view, I recognize a Hispanic man standing underneath a skinny tree. I have seen him many times hanging around the park with his huge, black boombox that echoes a loud mix of rock and reggae. He always does his business under the same tree, talking with his fellow park people, taking from them small wads of cash, giving them small baggies they immediately stuff into their front pockets. He has very black hair and a mustache to match. Once in a while, a woman in a hot pink skirt will come around with a boy child and they will all dance little steps under the tree.

Watching him helps me forget about myself and my stomach. It occurs to me that I haven't spoken to a soul since Frank. I am mute and hungry and fading. Only the sun keeps me breathing. My hair is now just about dry from my shower. It keeps flying in my face and distracting me from the nonexistence I am attempting to achieve. So I sit up slowly with my face to the breeze to comb and pull my hair into several long braids. I do this slowly and methodically, finding in my possession five hair bands to fasten them at the ends. When I am finished, I take a brown bandana from a pocket in my backpack and tie it around my head, securing all my braids in place so they will no longer disturb me. This is all very exhausting, so I lay my head back down on my backpack, pull the blanket back over my legs, and close my eyes to the sun.

Hours pass while I sleep on my blanket in the park. I am in and out of consciousness, staying aware of the people around me, and keeping a hand on my bike even though I have the wheels locked in place. I know where I am, but where I need to go for comfort is more important and too strong to stay fully awake.

I find myself in a protective cloud, looking down at my body objectively. I am so small, so alone in my big, cream sweater and sun-touched face. I console myself in my sleep, telling myself that there will be something better soon, something new that will break me out of the frozen existence I am dwelling in. At the same time I know what I am doing, know that I am really sleeping, but I can do and think other things while my body rests. I go back to Frank, but he just shakes his head and lowers his gray eyes. I go back to Claudia, and she picks up Emma from school and we all dance to the reggae music together, our braids flying behind us as we smile and keep the beat with our bodies. I think they are glad to see me.

I fly around the city in search of Dylan. I want to see what he is doing without being seen and I know I can do that now. I fly from the West Side to the East in seconds and find the apartment vacant. I am tempted to leave the city altogether, to fly far away where no one knows me. I don't want to be known. And so I run. I run into buildings and out of them again in my hiking boots. I run across busy streets, narrowly escaping getting hit. I run and run until I no longer know where I am. All I want to do is to get away. The whole time I know it is only my spirit moving while my body rests, and because of this I can move swiftly and without much difficulty. I have no body weighing me down.

"Rachel?" A shake of my body to make my spirit enter again.

"What?" Groggy, but aware, I grab for the bike.

"What are you doing sleeping here?" I look up and see his face looking down at me. How dare he? I put my head back down and feel my left arm start to tingle, as the circulation has been cut off. Other than that I feel strangely alive and well, recharged with a drunken awareness.

"What is it that you need?" My intention is not to be rude; I simply feel I have no use for someone like him anymore.

"Rachel, if I could talk to you?" Pleading.

"What you've shown me outweighs any words you might want to share with me."

"Rachel, what you saw yesterday was nothing. I came here to tell you that." He sits down inches from my blanket and continues to squirm.

"How did you find me?"

"I took a guess."

"Basically, Dylan, I think you're an asshole." The word comes out, just like that.

My first, real, audible swear word. I am proud. I sit up and stretch my arms above my head, yawning out loud. I squint into the sun, ignoring him completely.

"So you think I'm an asshole, huh? I see. I'm an asshole because when I came to the door yesterday your little French roommate, all decked out in her underwear, took me by the hand into the bedroom and told me to sit down, that you'd be home soon."

"Do you always do as you are told?" I am not impressed.

"Whatever. I didn't do anything with her."

"So why then, in the late days of winter, did you find the need to unbutton your shirt?"

"It was her idea. See, she—"

"Don't speak." I just want him to go away. I don't want to replay the image of them in my head one more time. I can't stand it. "Please, just go away. I was doing fine here without you."

"Yeah, sleeping in Central Park is a real bright idea." He looks around at the few other people who decided to brave the chilly winds. "You're lucky you didn't get mugged or raped or something. I don't know how you think you can just take a nap in the middle of the city like this. This isn't Wisconsin, you know."

"Really? I wasn't aware. Good try at changing the subject."

"Rachel, I never meant to hurt you…"

"Right. That's why you decided to get cozy with a naked stranger in my bedroom? Was this your way of welcoming me home?"

"She wasn't naked."

"Close enough."

"She came to the door like that."

"I don't care. You could have sat on the couch."

"You're right. I'm wrong."

"Of course you're wrong. How would you like it if you came home and I was sitting on your bed with John and he only had his underwear on?" I want to burst into tears. I want to make him hurt the way he'd made me hurt. I don't know what I want.

"I'd feel like shit. You know I would."

"Well, then? What? I'm supposed to forgive you the very next day?"

"No. You don't have to forgive me." He inches closer, probably feeling as if he is making some sort of progress. "I understand you're really upset. You have a right to be. I made a mistake. I don't know, she pulled me right in by the hand, said I could wait with her in your room. It was weird. The whole thing was weird."

"The *whole* thing? How long were you there?"

"I don't know. Twenty minutes maybe. I wanted to be there when you got home. I was going to take you to dinner. I've missed you, Rachel."

My stomach rumbles.

"Twenty minutes, huh?"

"She's one odd chick, Rachel."

"So that's supposed to make it all right? What did you do? Did you kiss her or something?"

"No, I didn't kiss her."

"So what? She kissed you?"

"I don't want to talk about this anymore." He leans back on his elbows into the cool Earth and looks away from me.

"She kissed you! That fucking whore!" Now I'm going to hell for sure. "And what, you let her? You enjoyed this? What?" I wanted to rock his world the way he'd rocked mine.

"I'm sorry, Rachel. I don't know what to say. I'm just sorry."

It just isn't good enough. The hurt is too fresh. I turn my face from him.

A couple seconds of silence pass, and then he gets up quietly and begins to walk across the park. I want to scream after him. I want to run after him. I want him back. But my selfish pride takes control, and I lay my head back down on my backpack and cover my legs again with the blanket. It is lethargy that keeps me from getting up. I am in an emotional coma induced by my distinct denial of life. I will just lie here forever, I think.

But then the sun passes behind a cloud and emptiness engulfs me. Tears begin to fall without effort. Feeling sorry for myself is easy. I count the moments, figuring if he is out of the park yet, wondering where he is going. I've been abandoned by everyone I know, and it is making me feel depleted and drained of emotion. I am as drained as my stomach. Pretty soon I'd just be a pile of bones. I begin to drift again into semi-consciousness.

"You gonna lie here all night, too?" He is back.

"I guess." I blot the tears with my sleeve.

"Did you really think I was going to leave you here?"

I sit up and pull my bandana back down over my forehead.

"I love your braids." He sits down across from me and reaches for my hands. I give him one.

"In your honor the moon rises,
the birds all sing your name.
Blue eyes deepest and clearest,
delicately beautiful brown braids."

Who can argue with poetry?

"That's precious."

"You're the one who's precious, Rachel. You're too precious to be treated the way I treated you yesterday. It'll never happen again. Forgive me, okay?"

"I don't have the energy." I don't. I'd never figure how someone could have fasted forty days and forty nights. I'd be dead in three or four for sure.

"What, are you hungry?"

"Past hungry."

"How about the dinner I owe you?"

Is this it then? I am going to forgive the kissing, the exposed chest, the going behind my back just like that? I am just supposed to roll with this, with the way men seem to be?

"Souen."

"No problem. Let's get you out of here." As if he is kinder or more fair to me than the grass and dirt of the Earth. I stand up, feeling a little shaky. Sooner or later I know I'll have to live again. I guess it's time.

"Thanks for coming back."

He stops picking up my things and pulls me up to a standing position. His black curls blow in front of his face, but his eyes stare straight into mine. We kiss underneath the dropping sun, and all that needs to be said is said with silent lips penetrating. Our lives and thoughts cease for these moments, and we let them. For that is love, the ability to put aside time and space to enjoy, to unite, to blend spiritually.

When we are finished blending, he picks up my bike. I give him the key, and he unlocks the wheels. I stuff my blanket into my backpack and swing it over my right shoulder, take his hand in mine, and walk out of the park.

It is twenty blocks to the restaurant, and we walk most of it without talking. Maybe we both want to give it a rest. I forgive him without telling him this on our way there. Life is too short and too lonely not to proceed onward with the best possible attitude available. If I am not going to die, then I am going to live. And if I live I want love next to me, even if it hurts sometimes.

"I don't think I've ever been this hungry."

"Haven't you eaten today?"

"Not since yesterday's breakfast."

"Rachel!"

"What?"

"I thought you only starve yourself during the week."

"And when I've been let down."

"I thought we were finished with that."

"We are."

"Here we are." He takes the bike and locks it to a nearby pole, placing the palm of his hand on my lower back, and gently guides me into the restaurant. I breathe in deeply. We find a table quickly and sit down, facing each other over the heavy wood.

I take their bread the moment it is laid at my fingertips. I pull it apart and set it in my mouth, remembering food. I eat squash and carrots and fish and brown rice until I have been fully revived. It humbles me to eat. I am still part of the earth, still cemented in a physical life. We sit at the restaurant with a flickering candle between us while I let my food sink in. I order peppermint tea. Dylan drinks iced tea and we soak in the ambiance of the moment, talking to each other with our eyes. He says to me that he is happy we are still together, that he is sorry, that he wants me. Mine tell him that I am comfortable here with him, that I am grateful to be fed.

The cry, the fasting, the sun, and the food have done me a good turn. In one day I have become more of who I want to be. I am so much more aware and at the same time so comfortably unaware.

Sitting there in the restaurant at sundown with him I realize is one of those moments I need to capture, to take a mental picture of. I do.

"Rachel?" I move my eyes back to meet his. I don't want it to end, this lovely feeling of fullness, physical and emotional fullness. I have fallen back in love with life. "I've paid the check. We can go if you'd like." His respectful caution with me makes me rise from my seat and follow him without a struggle.

"Okay." I grab my backpack and my keys and follow him half in a trance past the messy bulletin board that advertises yoga classes and group meditations, mountain bikes for sale, and roommates wanted. We walk through the dark, wooden doorway into a different world of cement and tall buildings, a million people and a million cars, greed and speed, rich and poor, exhaust fumes and perfumes, hot pretzels and cold drinks, energy and chaos and confusion. I don't want to be alone.

"Wanna come over? It's only across the park now."

"Your Dad home?"

"He's out of town for the weekend, in New Jersey for some business."

"Well, I'm not going home to her." We are just standing there with the bike between us. "And I don't know where Susan is. I don't think she ever came home last night."

"She went back to Georgia."

"She did? How do you know? Wait, I forgot, you have the 'in' with her best pal, right?"

"Whatever."

"Why'd she go back so quick?"

"I don't know. I didn't find that out. I don't really want to talk about it, if that's okay with you. I just want to make you happy again."

This is the first time anyone has ever said this to me. I am sold, right off the rack. Take me home.

Walking through the park with him at dusk I feel older or more experienced in some way. My own personal, individual life has been validated emotionally. I am standing on my own, but my legs are about frozen.

"I'm freezing." He walks the bike and holds the backpack for me. I feel silly for complaining.

"What possessed you to wear shorts? It is winter, you know. I've heard they have winter in Wisconsin. Are you familiar with it?" He is trying to be funny, testing the bounds. If I smile he is pretty much off the hook for good. I have quite enjoyed making him squirm. I give in and grin at him.

"Very funny." And then right there in the middle of the block on our way to the apartment he snaps the kickstand into place, sets my backpack on the ground, and rubs my cold legs with his warm hands, making me feel ridiculous and special. When he stands, I realize again how perfectly we are matched. Standing, we are nose to nose, hip to hip. All he has to do is move in close and there he is. Weird things turn me on like matching heights and the way he takes my arm in his as we stroll home towards warmth.

At his father's apartment, he has me sit on the couch with a blanket over my legs while he puts some water on for hot chocolate. He opens a Miller Lite for himself, sits next to me on the black, leather couch, and from underneath it produces his little black tray that holds his film container of pot, a red lighter, and the queen of spades. After cleaning the seeds from the buds, he takes the card and separates a bowl for himself. He pulls it this way and that, cutting it like Al Pacino in *Scarface* with his cocaine. When he has what he wants, he scoops up the greenish-brown granules and empties them into his shiny, brass pipe.

Lately I'd been taking mouthfuls of marijuana air from his mouth after he takes a hit and as he kisses me. Nothing ever happened even though I swallowed the air like he told me to. It seems harmless enough, and he likes it so much when I do it.

"Rachel." I turn and open my mouth to his, sucking in his hit and ending it with a lip smacking kiss. "Hold it." I hold my hit and hold my breath trying to make him proud. I figure if I never take a hit on my own it doesn't really count. Of course this is how the Devil gets one to sin, little by little, rationalization by rationalization. I like the smell of marijuana. It is just as pleasing to me as the incense burned at Souen. I breathe it in deeply, making myself forget myself.

"So, what do you want to do?" This is from the kitchen now where the steam rises from the cup and hot chocolate is delivered to me by a stony faced gentleman. I want to smoke. I want to take the pipe and smoke the way I've seen him do so many times. I've survived the last two days, and I've grown much older in the process. I am mature enough now. I want to put the finishing touches on the newness I am experiencing. My catharsis is nearly complete.

"Will you fill a bowl for me?" I sip at the hot liquid and pull away quickly, nearly spilling chocolate on my sweater. I am warm now. I pull the blanket off my legs to appear more serious.

"Ah, hello? Did I hear correctly? Does my pristine little princess want to get stoned?" He is sitting with his father's selection of compact discs, thumbing through them and scowling.

"I'm not that pristine." Molly Ringwold, *The Breakfast Club*.

"You sure?" He looks up at me from the floor.

"I'm sure."

"Cool. I'd always knew you'd come around."

"What is that supposed to mean?" I act offended, but I'm not.

"You're a funny girl, Rachel. Come on." He pulls me into his room and shuts the door. I am joining the secret club. "Pick out some music. Now you know there's a possibility that this is not going to affect you right away. It may take a couple times."

"Whatever. That's fine." Simon and Garfunkel, Cat Stevens, Donovan, Jim Croce, Bob Dylan. This is my mother's music.

"Here's one." He tosses me a new CD, still completely wrapped in plastic. *Led Zeppelin II*. There is so much music to learn. Dylan knows every song and songwriter, every word, every lyric, every drummer and date. I am fascinated and overwhelmed by it all.

"Cool." We are both sitting on the wooden floor in his bedroom in between the stereo and his bed.

"Put it on."

"Okay." I take the new CD in my hands and fumble with it until my bowl is ready.

"Give that to me. Christ. What, are they wrapping these things so they don't pick up a disease or a virus or something in the mail?" He pushes forward onto his knees so he can reach into the drawer next to his bed. In this position he is just inches from my body, and I can feel his energy. He snatches his Swiss army knife from the drawer and slashes the plastic CD wrapper down the center carefully, so as not to mark the case. "Here. You take this." He places in my hands the brass pipe. It is heavy and filled to the brim with weed.

"Gotta light?" This is the first time I say this. But for the life of me I can't hold the lighter and the pipe and suck in hard as I've been instructed, so Dylan moves into my lap almost, closer than he needs to be, and lights the thing for me. Inhaling deeply, I choke on the smoke immediately just as "Whole Lotta Love" begins reverberating through his intimate room. This is not my mother's music.

"I'll get you some water." He dashes out through the door and leaves me hacking to the weird and wild sounds of Robert Plant and Jimmy Page. I cough and cough until I think I might bring up a lung through my throat.

"Thanks." Water down, cool, as the guitars jam and the drums bang loud enough so I have a difficult time hearing him. "What?"

"I said, you want another hit?"

"Yeah." I nod to him. I figure, as long as I have started it. My mother always said, Finish what you start.

"Way down inside, woman, you need it." Dylan sings to me as he strums his air guitar and laughs beautifully at me as I continue to choke on the smoke. My eyes tear up involuntarily, and I am having a difficult time opening them after three or four hits. Something has definitely taken effect.

Dylan's head rests in my lap during "What Is And What Should Never Be." After figuring out the child safety device on the lighter, I am able to handle the process myself. My fingers run through his curls as the room turns hazy. Lazy is how I begin to feel. Numb, lazy, lovely, dreamy, and extremely interested in every instrument and every beat of the music. I follow the drum for several measures, then the guitar for a while, then the bass. I am inside of the music. I am in the middle of their stage, their set, and can focus easily on whatever seems the most appealing and engaging at the moment.

And the two of us lounge in his room for the entire album as we easily caress each other's faces and arms and stomachs without saying a word. It isn't necessary anymore to speak. With the lighter, I provide the flame to a vanilla candle that sits on his bedside table and the aroma of this is sweet enough to fill the hunger I am feeling.

My lips find his as I drift into a position on the floor alongside him. I close my eyes and kiss a kiss I will never forget for as long as I live. For the touch of his mouth to mine invokes every blazing sunset, every amazing rainbow, every lust and every desire I've ever experienced. It is an ultimate sensation. This kiss crescendos along with the pulsating rhythm of the drums towards a heaven I never want to leave.

6

TO FORGIVE OR FORGET

Several weeks later, I find myself sitting in church, feeling not that pristine, but grateful I haven't yet succumbed to all the Devil's temptations. I escaped Dylan's grasp that night on the floor only because I'd said I wasn't ready, which is true. But it is also a way to put off the whole mess of sex. The lingerie has been purchased. A girl ought to have something nice like that even if she isn't having sex, I figure.

I put the off-white teddy on in front of Michael's mirror when no one is home. The whole thing is lace. It looks good, I have to admit. It would look better with a tan, but it is seductive enough. It will do the job. I fold it delicately and place it in my underwear and socks drawer, right one top in case the boyfriend stealer gets nosy.

I've firmly decided I am not going through any great hormonal changes, weight gain, acne breakouts, or mood swings just to have sex. Plus, I don't feel I should have to pay for it. Dylan said he'll wear a condom, which I said is a good idea in case he had a disease or something, which he said he didn't, of course. What do I care if sex isn't as enjoyable? I already have a good time without going all the way. Still, the whole planning of such an occasion is a major turnoff, and I've kind of grown weary of it. And so I sit in church, still a virgin, contemplating why I've even partially agreed to such an

85

adult adventure. I know it is because I don't want to lose him.

Sitting quietly in my pew with less than Sabbath thoughts running through my brain, I notice the small boy next to me crushing Cheerios into the bench. He is on the floor, leaning his head down on the pew, crushing quietly and looking up at me with large, hazel eyes every once in awhile. When he catches me looking at him, I quickly bring my attention back up to the speaker at the podium.

I relax humbly next to this innocent youngster as an illegal drug user who is seriously contemplating full-fledged fornication. I drop my head in shame and stare at my folded hands in my lap. I am a sinner. I know this so clearly as I sit there in my Sunday best, watching the congregation all around me taking the sacrament. I am not worthy enough to partake. I bow my head further and pray silently for strength. Please, Lord, forgive me for falling away from your teachings, for sinning the way I have. Please keep me chaste and pure so I can remain worthy in your sight. I pray, but I do so half-heartedly, wanting to believe in my words, and at the same time knowing I don't want to live up to them. I am struggling. It is time to sing. I pluck the hymnal from the little wooden holder in front of me. All around me the congregation bellows. I join in with enthusiasm.

"I tremble to know that for me he was crucified, that for me a sinner, he suffered, he bled and died." I sing this loud and with conviction, but I know I sing more to hear myself sing than to praise and worship Jesus. But somehow singing the song makes me feel holy again, and I am pleased when I drop the hymnal back in its place.

I glance down at the little boy next to me whose mother is patiently cleaning up the Cheerio mess. She must have been so involved, not to have seen him doing that earlier. I envy her devotion. She pulls out a Christian coloring book and crayons, and her son begins working on a picture of Jesus rising into the air, his palms showing as witnesses of what he had undergone. He is evidence of life after death. The child takes the white crayon and begins coloring his robe, working hard to make it show on the cream colored paper.

It is nearly spring, and there is crucifixion and resurrection in the air. I try focusing on this, on why Jesus let himself get killed for us. He was put to death in his thirties for all the people who ever lived, for all the people who were living, and for all the people who had yet to live so we could all repent, be forgiven, and have a second chance. I figure this isn't such a bad tradeoff considering he would have eternal life, guaranteed, and that he'd live with God. I quickly decide I would have done the same thing.

"Though your sins be as scarlet, they shall be as white as snow; though they be red like crimson, they shall be as wool. If ye be willing and obedient, ye shall eat the good of the land: But if ye refuse and rebel, ye shall be devoured with the sword: for the mouth of the Lord hath spoken it." His voice thunders down upon me. I look up at the podium, too scared to meet the eyes of the speaker, lest they be focused on mine. I am a rebel. I will be devoured by the sword. I will never eat the fruit of the land. I shake involuntarily, feeling suddenly cold, sitting there alone hearing the words run through my body.

The following speaker isn't nearly as frightening as he speaks about forgiveness, how we can be forgiven, how we should forgive again and again, for it isn't our place to judge or hold anyone in condemnation. He is speaking to me. I have been treating Yvonne terribly, ignoring her completely, holding her in condemnation. The speaker tells me to forgive her, and when I do a weight will be lifted from my shoulders.

By the time church is over, I feel a glow all through my body as I shake hands and say hello to some people I know. Everyone smiles at me, telling me how good it is to see me here each week. The speaker on forgiveness steps down and takes my hand, and I tell him how much I appreciate his sermon. The glow radiates through all of us. We are all at once immune to life's deficiencies. We are warriors who will conquer all, for we know the way, the truth, and the light. We can overcome adversity and not blame, for we know all are lessons teaching us, helping us grow, to become more Christ-like.

Everything has a purpose, and there is eternal life for which we will all work for and be worthy of in the end. There is a plan, and we know it, know why we were here and where we are going. It is all very simple.

Yvonne isn't at home when I arrive, which gives me time to change. Away from church I never feel comfortable in church clothes. I know some people who can come home, loosen their tie or put on an apron and go about their business as usual, as if they are just as comfortable as ever in their suits and nylons. I need to get my clothes off as quickly as possible after church so I can feel like myself again.

I sit on Michael's bed in my jeans and tee shirt, feeling quite blessed. I am still warm in my face from church. My soul has been cleansed. I have been renewed, and as soon as Yvonne comes home I am going to be a good Christian and forgive her. I lie back on the bed and wait in silence, measuring how much room I have between my jeans and my flesh. I feel unusually thin, which puts a smile of vanity on my face.

When I hear the door open, I get the feeling in my stomach the same as when I am nearing the top of a long drop on a roller coaster, the same as when my mother used to call my name and I knew it wasn't for dinner. It is like the black hole has moved right into my abdomen and is especially hungry for all the fear I have ever felt. Confrontation of any kind startles me. I possess an imperative need to flee from even the slightest conflict.

Knowing not at all what I will say, I move toward her closed door, ready to forgive, ready to ask for forgiveness. I knock lightly only twice.

"Come in." She raises her voice at the end, as if she is asking a question, as if she isn't sure.

"Yvonne?" I say, with the same inflection as I inch the door open and peek in. Her body jerks slightly.

"But Rachel, come in. This is your room also."

"Yeah, I know." I sound stupid. I will never be able to pull this off. I look at her, seeing them together, flesh showing everywhere. I imagine her unbuttoning his shirt, trying to kiss him. I think I am going to lose it, so I just say what I have come in here to say. "I'm sorry about the past few weeks. I know there's been a lot of tension in the air. I just want to say that what happened is no big deal. It's forgotten." I lie so smoothly with such determined nonchalance. Inside I am shaking.

"Oh, but Rachel, it is me who should apologize, the vay I acted vas terrible. It vasn't his fault, anything. I don't know vhy I did it." She shakes her head from side to side, pulls her knees up to her chest, and covers her face with her hands. I feel relieved, hearing her say that it wasn't his fault. Anyone else could have easily made out as if he had been the culprit. It is usually the guy who is to blame anyway, right? I want to walk out then. I have done what I came in there for, but I can see that she has started to cry. I shift my weight from one leg to the other, feeling uneasy and foreign.

"Are you okay?" Please say yes so I can get out of here.

"I am so sorry. Ever since I left Papa…" At this her crying gets louder. I am supposed to hate her. What am I doing standing here listening to this chick who has come onto my boyfriend? I look out the window at the beautiful, sunny day that is wasting away as I stand amidst the mess and garbage of the dreary bedroom. Both her and Susan's beds are full of dirty clothes and magazines and paper plates and crumbs. The sheets are on the floor and the pillows are mashed in between the beds and the wall. My bed sits neatly in the corner with cleans sheets and hospital corners. I haven't slept there in awhile.

"Do you miss home?" I know I am just prolonging this. I am starving and am supposed to meet Dylan in an hour. I don't have much time for all of this. I know how girls can talk forever about nothing. I have listened many times to Susan when she is on the phone with her girlfriends in Savannah. The topics run from their weight to their hair, and on to talk shows, boyfriends, birth control, periods, what they hate about their parents, what they love to eat, and back to diets and cellulite and weight. It could have gone on forever, this endless chitchat, except Michael decided to put a long distance block on the phone.

"But of course I miss Papa. Mama passed away, you know, vhen I vas young." No, but thanks for sharing. "He is all I have. But I think he's not so happy vith me now, if he would know vhat I've done."

"About Dylan? Yvonne, it's no big deal. I already…"

"Ha! No. You think I'm talking about that? No. This is nothing."

Well, it may have been nothing to you.

"Then what are you talking about?"

"It vas in Paris, vhen I moved vith Alex. Rachel, you must promise me, please, don't say anything to Michael, please." Her eyebrows rise, and she squeezes her knees tight as she glances up at me.

"Say what?"

"No, but I can't tell you. I'm sorry. It is not your problem. It's just that I think about it all the time, vhat I did. And I can't say anything to anyvon. I promised. On my Mama's grave."

On her mother's grave? What is this? I can see myself getting pulled in by this, just like with Susan, listening to her bleak sob stories she could never fully get a grip on.

"Who did you promise?"

"But Alex, of course." I caught her. She pulls her knees in tighter. This girl is desperate if she is going to confide in me.

"Yvonne, what did Alex do to you?" I thought I'd cut right to the chase and stomp all over her mother's grave.

"How do you know?"

"Let's just say I've heard things about him."

"From who?"

"Other roommates."

"About Alex?"

"Yeah."

"I can't believe it. Are they still vorking?"

"You mean as models?"

"Yes."

"Some of them are. Some of them have gone home." I am really getting carried away with this.

"Susan?"

"Well, I really can't say."

"Vell, you know about him then?"

"I know some of it. He's not a very nice guy, is he?" I glance at my watch.

"But no. He's a terrible man. Vhat he did, he should be jail."

Jail? I sit down next to her, right on top of some clothes.

"Yvonne, I think you need to talk about whatever is bothering you. You need to get it out in the open so it doesn't end up eating you on the inside. It's not healthy to keep things inside, you know." It was all I could remember from the last Oprah on child abuse. The abused, now adults, had come on the show to let it all out, share their personal, intimate problems with the entire television watching nation.

"I know you are right. Alex is such an asshole…"

Even swear words sound adorable when spoken with a French accent.

"Yvonne, tell me. What did he do?" I am curious now, consumed in her saga, engulfed in her experiences with this man.

"Papa's store vasn't doing very good vhen I vent to Paris. He couldn't send me money so I could get my own place. Then I meet Alex, and he tells me it's okay, he vill take care of me. I vanted so much to be a model, you know? I didn't vant to go home to Papa a failure. So I moved in vith Alex. There vere some other girls there already, and it seemed okay." She was quiet then.

"Go on."

"Vell, Alex said to me that I vill model in Paris vith him, that I vill make money to send to my papa, you know? It seemed okay."

"So you moved in with Alex and…"

"Yes, it vas okay at first. He vas nice to me. Very nice, you know?"

No, I don't know, actually. I don't know this man. I look over at

Yvonne, who now has tears forming in her eyes again. Her chin has dropped to her chest and her body seems frozen in place when suddenly her hands move to pull her shirt up over her chest. "He made me get these! Look at them. They're hideous!" I scoot over on the bed a few inches to get a proper view. They look a little high and stiff. And then, just as fast, she pulls her shirt back down and begins crying out loud. "He told me they vould fall into place, but they didn't! Did you see?"

"Yes. Did you have them done?" I am still surprised from her outburst. What am I supposed to say?

"But of course! Do you think they look normal?"

That I don't want to answer.

"He made you get them?"

"Oh, but you don't understand."

"Yvonne, I'm trying. I really am. Michael has wanted me to get them, too, but I've been working without them okay." I wish I hadn't said that.

"Rachel, you're a beautiful girl. I see now I didn't have to do this. But it's too late." She pulls her hands down over her breasts, trying to push them into place I suppose. I hadn't noticed they were fake as she'd always kept them so carefully adorned. It is terrible, but all of this is helping me to hate her less.

"Yvonne, you have to look on the bright side." How cliché. "They don't look that bad. They look really nice in your pretty bras, totally normal." I really need some experience with this girl talk. I am stumbling all over myself, trying to care, feeling as if I probably don't, and then feeling guilty for that.

"It's not just this," she says through her dwindling, pathetic tears.

I offer her a box of Kleenex I notice underneath Susan's bed.

"Rachel, you can't tell anyvone. I'm serious."

"I understand." Do I? Or am I just curious for the gossip, hungry for a little drama that once heard is mine to do with as I like? I know I am making a pact with her, that I will not be able to tell anyone. Otherwise where is trust, loyalty, confidentiality?

"Then you keep your promise?"

"Yes, I promise." Now tell me what he did.

"Vell, it started out that he vould have these veekly inspections. He'd come into our rooms and check us over." She pauses, listening to what this sounds like.

"That's not that abnormal. I mean Louise did that when I came here."

"But vhere you naked?"

"Completely naked? Well, no. I had my underwear on."

"Vell, not us. No, he vouldn't have that, and of course I didn't know better vhen I first came there. I figure this I must do to model. He said this to me anyway."

"Every week though?"

"But of course, he said it was necessary to make sure we stayed healthy and thin. Fit, you know? No fat bumps."

"Cellulite."

"Yes, that. So every veek he vould measure us and veigh us. But this is not so bad, you know? I mean I vas raised to be naked, vent to the beach many times vith no top on. So I don't think anything about it until a couple veeks later vhen he starts touching me, telling me I need to have a boob job." At this she takes both of her hands and directs them towards her chest as Vannah White might have towards a brand new car.

"He touched you there?"

"Oh, but of course, alvays. That is not even the start of it all. Rachel, he had sex vith me many times."

"You let him?"

"It's not like that. I know you don't understand." She curls her legs back up to her chest and drops her head. I reach out and touch her on her shoulder, trying to act compassionate.

"Yvonne, I'm trying. Did you feel you had to do that?"

"Yes, vell, not all the time, I mean it vas just part of... oh, you don't understand. I feel so foolish now. Rachel, he is not like other men, not like anyvone I've ever met. Sometimes he vas so good to us, but then he's a monster, you know? Do you know that he paid for everything? He made us these shakes every day vith expensive Chinese herbs. Anytime ve needed a doctor he take care of it. He bought us clothes and music tapes. He treated me so good sometimes, like a princess, you know?"

"Yes, but he also raped you."

"Don't say that."

"Don't say that he raped a minor? What about sexual harassment on the job?" I had seen enough of those one hour news programs like *Dateline* or *Primetime* or *48 Hours* to know about these things. "Yvonne, I don't know what the law is like in France, but I'm sure he's broken it."

"You said you vouldn't tell! You said you promised!" She screams this and raises herself up, which causes us both to bounce lightly up and down on the bed a couple times.

"I know. I won't say anything unless you want me to."

"Vhy vould I want you to?" She seems angry now. She pulls her pillow up from behind the bed, sets it freshly against the wall, crosses her arms in front of her, and looks me straight in the eyes for the first time. "Rachel, this isn't your problem. It is mine, and I am here now vith Michael. Thank you for listening, but I don't vant to say anything more."

I rise from the bed, from the strange and ugly world I had been brought into, and walk away from her, mumbling some parting words as I leave. The grayness of the room has crept into my spirit, removing all the glow from church, all the happiness that I usually feel on the Sabbath.

I had done what I set out to do, but instead of having the weight lifted, more had been added to it.

7

TURNING POINT

On the bus to the East Side, with a pumpernickel bagel in my hand, I think about breast implants. I can't get the image out of my head of her raising her shirt for me to see her silicone chest. If Michael had been home, I know I would have been tempted to take him aside immediately and unload it all onto his lap. But maybe he knows more than he ever lets on. Alex is *his* friend, after all.

A chill runs through my body as I remember her words, but then the bus turns a corner and the sun comes streaming in the window. The warmth penetrates through the glass and lands on my face, erasing the unbelievable. I can't imagine how all of it could be taking place if Yvonne hadn't wanted it to. She is a big girl, just a year younger than I am. She can take care of herself.

I chew my last bit of bagel as I step off the bus, holding my breath as it moves away slowly, leaving a thick, poisonous trail of gray fumes behind.

Turning onto the side street where Dylan lives, I take notice of the budding bushes and blossoming flowers and other signs that spring is pushing to be noticed, that it is fighting for its rights amidst the hard cement and thick air. Spring signals a hope that nature is still giving, still willing to put up with man's overwhelming power and control, inventions, disasters, destruction, desires, selfishness.

Walking alone, with Dylan's apartment in sight, I understand the bush and flower, feeling consumed as well by the darkness of mankind, picturing Yvonne curled up in the corner of her bed, holding breasts that are not her own, lost in America, apparently terrified of Alex, not wanting to go home, not working in New York. But talking with her had freed me. I am no longer bound to her by my lack of forgiveness. I can not help her now. She will have to find her way on her own.

My desire to see Dylan has been heightened by the gloom I had been taken into by Yvonne. Next to him I am strong. There is someone else in my corner, on my side. I need to see his smile, and I need him to balance out my perfectly ordered life of exercise, work, church, sleep, and be good. He is my vice, my temptation, my lust, my experience, my life. Alone I do not truly live. I watch. I contemplate. I obey. But I do not live.

I push the small, round button that is found neatly under his apartment number. He is on the first floor, and instead of buzzing me in, he comes toward me through the small window in the door. His hair is a fabulous mess.

"Babe! You, my love, are late!" He seems crazier than normal, wild and excited and goofy. His eyes are punishing for a moment, to scorn my lack of punctuality.

"I'm sorry. I've been talking with Yvonne. She had some things she needed to get off her chest." If he only knew. I want desperately to relay the entire conversation to him, right then and there in the hallway. I especially want to tell him her boobs are fake. Any small-chested chick likes these things to be widely known. But I keep my mouth shut, feeling saintly. Besides, I just don't feel like mixing that life with this one any more than I have to.

"So, did you guys finally make up?"

"Excuse me, but who started the whole thing?"

"You know what I mean. It's been bothering you for weeks that you guys weren't talking." He pushes open the large, wooden door. John is slouching into the black, leather couch with a blue marble pipe in his hand, holding a hit.

"Hey! Good to see you, Rache." He blows out the smoke and sits up a little, unfolding a young Jerry Garcia on his tee shirt. "Wanna hit?"

"No thanks. I mean, I just came from church, you know?"

Dylan and John look at each other and grin.

"How was it? What'd you learn today, my little church girl?" Dylan falls into his father's rocking recliner and pats his knee for me to come and sit. I shake my head.

"The wrath of God, sin, rebellion, forgiveness, the basics." I am getting the feeling that something is up with these guys. They have a secret between them. I am in the dark, playing the game until I am let in on it. "So what's up with you two?"

"We have a surprise." All four eyes radiate a pinkish-red as they close halfway into a devilish smile. John strolls to the refrigerator and pops open a Mountain Dew. "Get me one, too. Rachel?"

"No thanks. I'll just get some water." I walk into the kitchen where John holds two sodas. Dylan can see us, as there is a large opening between the two rooms.

"Should we tell her?" Dylan is at the stereo now, changing the CD.

"Tell me what?" An uneasiness creeps down my body with the flow of cool water. Surprises make me nervous.

"I don't know. It's your call. She's your girlfriend." The Grateful Dead's version of "Good Lovin'" dances straight into the room in perfect volume.

"Rachel, I want you to know that whatever you do is up to you. But John and I thought we'd at least ask." Dylan leans on the counter from the living room, John and I from the kitchen. Dylan reaches into his front pocket and pulls out a baggie of what I think at first must be marijuana. "They're mushrooms."

"Mushrooms?"

He lays the baggie on the counter between us. There are dry bits of what look like mushroom heads and off-white pieces of stems mixed with hints of blue and purple.

"Remember when I told you about Ken Kesey, The Merry Pranksters, and the Acid Tests?"

"Yeah." One night as we had walked from my apartment to the park to find some privacy as his dad was in town, he'd shared with me the history of the Grateful Dead. And the way he'd explained it made me feel as if he was explaining the history of his family rather than that of a rock and roll band. Jerry Garcia was supposedly this mystical, magical father of the Dead Heads, of whom both Dylan and John pledge their allegiance. To partake in drugs at these concerts or shows is apparently part of the ceremony to Dylan. It seems like a lame excuse to get high. I know he's tripped on acid before.

"Jeez, Rachel, don't look so scared."

I am staring at the mushrooms on the counter.

"Mushrooms are sort of like acid, but they're easier on your body, and then you eliminate them just like food. They're totally natural."

"They're a lot healthier for you." John joins in on the sales pitch.

"Shrooms are just better all the way around, don't you think?" Dylan looks at John, acting as if we are deciding on whether to have Chinese food or pizza.

"Totally. I think I'm finished with acid, actually." Here they are in their early twenties already finished with acid. I try to picture all the times they've had together, all the memories they've stored already, all the life experiences, good and bad. I don't have these.

"Mushrooms are much harder to get, but it's worth it. It's a better trip."

They're going on a trip now? John gulps down the last swallow of Mountain Dew and motions towards the clock on the wall.

"Anyway, Rachel, we were thinking that you might want to join us. We're gonna take the Subaru to John's and have a fire on the beach later." The ball is in my court. Do I hit it back to them or out of the park?

"And eat mushrooms?" It is a motherly tone that I take, and it bothers even me. I am attempting to ruin any fun before it begins because I feel left out and emotionally unable to join in.

"It's what we bought them for. They're not going to do us any good getting old in my pocket here." He taps his jeans and has a "Let's go" kind of look on his face. "You think you can get the day off tomorrow?" He is moving so fast. What happened to my peaceful Sabbath day of feeling I can conquer all?

"I suppose you've already decided to skip school?" Mother's back. No sign of guilt on their end, however.

"This is better than any day at school. Come on and live a little."

This strikes a hard chord with me.

"I don't understand. You eat these?" Sold. But I need some more information if I am going to take a day off and make up a lie and everything. I am scared, but I want to do this. Besides, there is no going back now. How can I ever go back to purity when all I know of purity is that it is the absence of truly living? What have I accomplished anyway by shunning that which is not taught in church? There has to be more than abstinence and prayer and scripture. It is God and church I seek only because it stands in opposition of what I'd known at home. It is a safety net for me to abide by strict and religious guidelines out of fear of becoming like my family. I want to have a better life than my mother. I want to be stronger and happier.

I stand there bent over with my elbows on the counter as these ideas rush through my mind. Can it be that there exist more roads than two?

"Rachel? Are you listening to me?" Dylan peers into my face until our noses are almost touching.

"What?"

"Did you hear what I said?"

"About what?"

"About eating these?" He seems annoyed all of a sudden.

"So you eat them. How do they taste?"

"Like shit. That's why we drown them in applesauce or something. Just like we said."

"Okay. Applesauce. That sounds good."

"Rachel, are you okay?" Dylan puts his arm around my shoulder, and I stand straight up.

"I'm fine. Thanks." Growing up is like reading a good mystery. Each chapter unfolds more and more clues making the reader change his mind as to the outcome.

"Hey, there's a jar of applesauce in here. You want me to grab this?" John's head pops out of the refrigerator with the jar and another soda.

"Sure. So Rachel, you okay with this? You want to come with us?"

"Yeah. I think so." I need to start making memories for myself. I need to be young while I am still young even if I don't feel young, and my craving for this seems insatiable at the moment, as I suddenly remember a phrase from a novel in English class. Carpe Diem. Also the theme of *Dead Poet's Society* with Robin Williams. Seize the moment or forever hold your peace.

"I've got a phone call to make." Dylan turns down the stereo with the remote and I call the agency leaving a message that I have some personal business to take care of on Monday and that I'd call in by 8:00 Tuesday morning for my go-see list.

"Pretty slick, Rache."

What am I doing? Fear slides through my chest as I view Dylan and his accomplice.

"Well, we'd better get going if we want to be tripping by sundown." John finishes his second soda, crunches the can on the counter, and deposits it into the recycling bin next to the garbage can. He rubs his hands together and glances around the apartment with clear anticipation. "Bring anything you guys might need for over night."

"Here, Rache. You wanna bring these?" Dylan comes out of his room with an extra white tee shirt and a clean pair of Levi's I keep in his bottom drawer just in case, just like a modern day lover or something. I nod to him without speaking. I'll go through this with

100

them, but I can't seem or sound excited and optimistic like the two of them so obviously are. It isn't in my nature. I will follow this adventure, not lead it. I haven't the strength nor the knowledge to be a part of the forward motion. If this is my fate in life, so be it. I'll jump in when everything seems a little safer.

Dylan has a bright orange 1986 Subaru he hardly ever drives. It sits on the street collecting parking tickets while his father threatens to sell it, saying that Dylan is too irresponsible to have his own car and that he doesn't need it anyway. But it is nice for a change to sit in the front seat of a normal car and just drive, drive right out of the city. There is no stopping every couple blocks, no hanging onto the bars above me for my life while all around me stand strange, creepy, smelly people I don't want to meet eyes with. There is no worry that if I daydream a little I will miss my stop. There is no watching the numbers click forward every couple seconds, catching a glimpse of my driver in the rear view mirror while he catches glimpses of me. Taxis make me nervous, and I never know how much I am supposed to tip. The amount I have to pay just for the ride always seems enormous.

"Isn't this great?" He looks over at me, his black curls flying all around his face. We have three windows open and he has to yell for me to hear him above the noisy engine and the wind. I know he doesn't expect an answer. He is expressing happiness for the both of us. I allow him this. Dylan has the kind of face that glows naturally. He doesn't need church. His cheeks are forever a rosy pink, and the color slides down his face lighting up his eyes and making a beautiful contrast with his hair. He really is lovely, and thin. He is thinner than John by far. John, at the tender age of twenty-one, has already managed a small belly. He is rounder. Dylan is more sculpted. I fall somewhere in between.

"You'll love my parents."

"What?" I turn to face John, who was in the back seat.

"My parents. I think you'll really like them. Don't you think, Dyl?"

We slow to make a turn and Dylan answers.

"His parents are pretty cool. Didn't they used to smoke?" He twists his neck toward John.

"They were total hippies. Went to Woodstock and everything." He is yelling again so I can hear him.

"Do they do that now?" I turn my head slightly, holding my hair in place while yelling into the back seat.

"Ha! My parents? I doubt it. If they do, I don't know about it."

"They're total yuppies now," Dylan explains to me, while he laughs at John. "But they're cool because they dig the band. They totally support us on that. They even know about you singing with us."

I think about how the last couple practices have gone. No matter how hard I try to make Dylan happy, he always has more suggestions when it comes to how well I project myself, my rhythm, everything. It is exhausting with him in that tiny practice room on 14th Street. I mean, what do I know about being a singer in a band? But Dylan says I have to start somewhere. We all do. And he does try to have patience with me. I can tell. Still, I am not sure if I can ever live up to his expectations.

"Wow." I turn my head toward the front again to see the Atlantic Ocean, the spacious, cool water that separates us from where we came from, from a place still so foreign to me, so far away. It still bewilders me what lay on the other side, and what pushed our ancestors to come here. It seems now all anyone wants to do is hop on a plane to London or Paris. So chic. So cool. Back and forth in search.

"Like a different world out here, huh?" He looks at me and winks and smiles. He wants me to be happy so he can relax and be happy himself. I know he is waiting for the sign or signal that says everything is all right with me, go ahead with your friend and have your trip and I'll come along too so that we can all stay together. So far in the car I'd committed to no specific feeling. I feel neutral. In motion, but still on the fence. In church I'd learned never to be a fence sitter. Choose a side, choose the right, as if there were only two choices: white or black, good or bad, right or wrong. I feel nearly ready to jump off the fence as we pull into the driveway.

"It's beautiful." He knew the way as if he'd been driving to his own house. For most of the ride I'd been pretty quiet. I look over at him to see if he'd heard me.

"You're beautiful, Rache. Come on."

Flattery gets one everywhere. We all get out of the car and slam our doors one right after the other—slam, slam, slam. I put my hands above my head and stretch up to the sky, breathing in the air and allowing myself to feel a little intimidated by the sight of John's house. It is white and large and decorated with very green and perfectly trimmed bushes all along the outside. The grass has been recently cut, and the smell reminds me of summers in Wisconsin. Birds chirp, and I realize I am no longer in the city. I've been brought back to this different world where Claudia and Emma and other people who have established normal lives and homes in beautiful settings live. The air smells so good and everything seems so peaceful. I turn around to get it all in. How will I ever find this for myself? It seems an impossibility.

"Well, this is it. Come on, let's meet the 'rents." John takes me by the arm as Dylan follows close behind. I look back at him wearily. We tromp through the freshly cut grass to the back door where white, wicker patio furniture sits neatly. A large chestnut tree stands over the furniture, shadowing it. The patio is raised and made of a light wood that has been sanded to smooth perfection and polished so that it shines beautifully beneath my tattered, black cowboy boots.

I feet rebellious, entering a home like this on a Sunday afternoon in my jeans and boots with a man on either side of me knowing that shortly I will be consuming illegal, psychedelic drugs. I glance around nervously in search of the devouring sword. It has been only five short hours since I shuddered in my pew, consumed with guilt.

"Dylan, how good to see you again. Come on in. This must be Rachel!" John's mother is dressed in a casual, beige, silk outfit that flows dramatically with every movement of her waving hands.

"Mom, this is Rachel; Rachel, Mom."

I shake her creamy, soft hand and say that I am pleased to meet her.

"Dylan, you're a lucky boy, aren't you?" Her voice sings out high and low and then high again, all in one breath, while her arms move about her like butterfly wings. "Why don't you kids come into the den and have some of Bertha's homemade banana bread? She made up a whole big batch of it yesterday, and your dad and I will never be able to finish it ourselves."

With her flowing silk, she leads us into the den where we eat Bertha's banana bread and drink milk like children. Bertha, Dylan whispers to me between chewy mouthfuls, is the maid. I feel honored for some reason to be eating bread that has been baked by a maid. It is my first time.

"So what do you all have planned for the evening? Will you be staying?"

I look over at John.

"If it's okay, Mom. Rachel hardly ever gets out of the city. I thought we'd maybe make a fire later."

"Well that sounds lovely, really. Of course your father and I would love to join you, but we've just made plans with the Robertsons in the city. They've invited us to stay the night. They even booked a couple rooms at the Plaza. Of course Jane just begged me to bring all my things and stay so we can shop and do lunch tomorrow, but Dad's not sure. Either way I hope you will all make yourselves quite comfortable. John, you know where the extra blankets are, don't you?"

"Top shelf, hall closet, next to the blue bathroom?"

"Exactly. Isn't he just a peach?" At this she bends down to kiss him lightly on the forehead before she flies quietly out of the room, mumbling something about how she has to get ready and wake up John's father from his nap.

"Your mom is great." I mention this in a half whisper. I am stunned by her grace and charm. The small lines in her face appear as if they've been placed there only to show that she is in fact a wife and mother and deserves the respect these titles bare. Otherwise, her eyes sparkle and all her movements seem light and easy. I decide that I want to look like this when I am forty.

"Yeah. She's pretty cool. She has her moods like anyone, but she keeps them to herself mostly. Dad's the one I always have to watch out for. But, hey, wouldn't that be great if they decided to stay in the city?" He whispers, too, while Dylan and I lean our heads in together, listening and nodding. I finish my glass of milk, startled that it tastes so good. I gave up milk when I moved to New York. It is fattening and expensive.

"What if they don't?" I am worried about his dad.

"It won't matter, except that we'll all have to be quiet later. Mom's a light sleeper."

"They don't care if I stay overnight?"

"No, why should they care?"

I look over at Dylan.

"They don't care about that. Hell. They were probably doing it with all sorts of people at our age."

Doing it?

"People change."

"Rachel, don't worry about it. If anybody gets upset it's on my shoulders, okay?"

"Yeah. Okay. Sorry." John looks different to me in his big, fancy house. He doesn't match it like his mother does. His brown hair falls over his ears and his collar. His tee shirt is faded and his jeans are frayed at the bottom. He sits with one soccer shoe on top of the insole of the other and rocks them both back and forth as he speaks.

"So it's your call. When do you want to eat these? Oh, shit. We forgot the applesauce." Dylan stands up, shaking his curls back and forth. His hands push deep into his front pockets and his shoulders curve forward.

"Don't worry about the applesauce. Except I bet your father's going to wonder why it's sitting out on the counter."

"Yeah. I haven't eaten applesauce since I was a kid."

"Well, I can look and see what we have, or we can stuff them into some more of that banana bread."

"As long as we've got plenty of beer to wash them down, it doesn't matter to me." Dylan looks at me. I shrug as if to say this is fine. More banana bread and some mushrooms with beer. "Hey, you still have that case of St. Pauli Girl in the cabin down below?"

"Yep."

"The cabin?"

"Quite a few summers ago, John and I built, or tried to build, a little cabin in the woods. It's about a hundred yards down past the house and off the beach." He points in the general direction, as if I can see it.

"Yeah, but Dad had to rescue us at the end, remember?"

"Hey, at least it's still standing."

John wraps up a couple more pieces of banana bread, grabs two old blankets from his room, and the three of us journey out into the Sunday afternoon sunshine towards the alleged cottage in the woods. I stay silent, soaking in my new surroundings like the clean air, the lapping sounds of the ocean, and the tall, thin trees that soon envelope me. John is the leader of the pack now instead of Dylan. This is his territory, his woods, his cabin, his banana bread. He leads us quickly down a dirt path and in no time I notice a small, wooden structure to the right.

"God, I can't believe it's still here. Do you remember that night we were so wasted we fell asleep in here and your dad had to come and wake us up the next morning for that baseball game?"

"Didn't we lose that one by like ten runs or something?"

"It was a sad display. I think that's when I traded my mitt in for a guitar. Damn, I forgot that, too. I would've liked to have had that tonight."

"We still have that old boom box in here I think."

We all duck into the cabin, and John begins pulling up a couple floor planks, taking out bottles of beer and offering them to us. I look at Dylan.

"St. Pauli Girl, Rache. Have one. You'll need it for the shrooms." He grabs a lighter from his pocket, pops the top off with it, and hands the beer to me.

I am sitting on a small bench that had been built against the wall. Dylan comes over and sits down next to me while John sticks his entire head in his little storage place, pulling out a very dented and dusty boom box.

"Still works." He turns the dial past several stations, then stops. "A little Doobie Brothers?"

"Fine with me. You wanna divide these things up now?"

"I think it's cool. No one is gonna come around here." At this Dylan pulls out his baggie, moves to the dusty, wooden floor, and starts dividing the mushrooms into three piles on top of the plastic bag.

"John, help make these even." Dylan sits Indian style on the floor of the cabin in deep concentration as he divvies up the dry heads and stems.

"I don't need as much as you guys." I am having serious doubts. Worry slides into my stomach as I sit there, shivering, listening to the wind rattle the one plastic-covered window in the cabin behind me.

"No," says Dylan without looking up. "We all have to be on the same trip."

Even so, I feel separate from them. Do I want to stay that way? I picture myself running out the little cabin door, through the woods, down the beach where I would drop to my knees and pray to the Lord for strength. "Keep me from the Devil's world!" I would scream. I look into Dylan's face as he peers up at mine. And then I glance at John. These are my friends. Maybe they are my only friends in the whole world.

"Ready? Here. Just fold the shrooms into the bread. You'll probably never even taste them. They don't taste like anything, really. Have your beer ready, though." And Dylan hands me my piece of bread, the sacrament I had been denied in church because I wasn't worthy enough. It is the bread of a new life. I put the mushroom sandwich to my lips and jump off the fence into the yard next door.

"God, these things taste like shit." Dylan's cheeks fade to a light pink as his nose twists and his eyes roll. The beer and the banana bread are a poor combination, but I chomp along dutifully until all my bread is gone, hardly tasting what is inside. Then I take my beer and gulp a couple gulps until I feel my mouth and teeth are as clean as I can get them.

"Time for a bowl."

"Definitely."

"You bring your pipe?"

"Yep. There's still a couple hits in there I think. Rache?"

"No, that's okay. You go ahead." I just cannot believe we are going to do all these things at once. I am starting to get confused.

"I just have to get this taste out of my mouth." Dylan lights John's blue, marble pipe and takes a hit, holding it while Fleetwood Mac sing, "You can go your own way." I am still sitting on the bench, frozen in place, terrified now of what is going to happen and feeling too stupid to ask.

"Well, there's no going back now." Dylan smiles and stands up from his spot on the floor, dusting off his jeans. He turns around slowly, keeping his head bent slightly. "Jesus, either I got bigger or this cabin got a whole lot smaller."

"It's the cabin." They laugh together, and I wonder if this *trip* has already started. I'd been feeling happily normal until Dylan mentioned that there was no going back, no chance to change my mind, no pretending I didn't know better. My stomach squeezes together as I think about what I have just done.

"Rachel, you okay?"

It is John. Thank you for asking. Does this mean you care, I mean really care? Because I need to know.

"I don't know."

"Babe, there's nothing to worry about, I promise. Shrooms are easy. We're both here for you, right John?"

"Of course. Everything's going to be cool. Don't get all freaked out about anything. Just go with it."

"Yeah. You want to relax so you can have a good trip. I think Rachel needs to smoke a little. John, fill one, okay?" Dylan tosses him his other baggie and puts his arm around me. Now I feel patronized. The better part of me *is* okay. I want to stand up and be strong, go forward with my new decision and conquer my fear. I just don't know how.

When the bowl is filled, I take a couple hits to calm *them* and within seconds that tingling sensation comes back again, and I feel the fogged focus that makes me smile for no apparent reason. I am past it now, past the point of turning back. It is where I'd wanted to go all along, somewhere far away where her voice cannot reach me, where it is a little dangerous and completely new.

8

THE TRIP

The three of us step out of the darkening, dusty cabin and into the remaining daylight, blinking our glassy eyes. We are stoned. With beers in our hands, we begin looking for firewood at John's request.

"Get enough kindling, enough of the little stuff, so we can get it burning easily."

I bend down, and with my left hand begin gathering the twigs at my feet.

"We're gonna need a lot of wood." Dylan calls this from behind several trees. I can't see him, but John is nearer to me, and I see him nod.

"Definitely." And then he lets out a yawn that is quiet at the start and grows much louder at the end.

"The yawns already?" Dylan walks up to us with his arms full of branches and small logs. "How long has it been?"

"I don't know. Half an hour at least. Maybe more. You feelin' anything?" John is tugging at a good-sized log that is buried beneath brown pine needles and mud and weeds. I take a long sip at my warming beer and wonder what they are talking about.

"In my knees." Dylan's face has resumed its normal rosiness. He begins leading the way as John finally frees the log from its habitat.

"Me too. A little." What are they talking about, and why don't

111

my knees feel different? Panic strikes. What if I *don't* trip with them? Maybe it won't work for me since I've never done it before. I stand there with a few twigs in my hand feeling frozen in place. I am startled as John comes up behind me.

"Rachel, here. Will you take these and find a spot on the beach?" He takes my few twigs and adds them to his own growing pile.

"Sure. No problem. Okay." I take the blankets and turn numbly toward the sun, finishing my beer on the way. The sun, oh the beautiful sun! While in the woods I had almost forgotten it was there, fading with the day. Tragic and wasted is time not spent in the sun when it shines so warmly down upon us. I search for the perfect spot with my blankets and empty beer bottle, listening to the sound of their laughter back between the trees.

I want to find the perfect spot, close enough to the water and not in sight of the house. I figure they won't want to be too near the large picture windows in the living room. Does John fear the wrath of his parents? It doesn't seem like it. Neither Dylan nor John had ever expressed any concern over disappointing their parents. It is what made them so free, so detached and able to laugh like children. When John speaks of his father being the one to watch out for, it is out of respect that he is the owner of the house, the husband, the bread winner. He is the one deserving the respect of his son. I obey out of fear or guilt, to prevent guilt from seeping into me to make me feel less than I am, and always less than my mother. I can only feel worthwhile if she allows it.

I spread out each blanket, feeling incredibly drained. I remove my jeans jacket and lie down on top of both blankets to prevent either of them from blowing away while I close my eyes to the sun and search my mind for good thoughts. Freedom blows in from the ocean, into my nose, and I breathe deeper than I had known was possible. In with the ocean, out with the sun, concentration, deeper and deeper until I can no longer feel myself lying on the blankets with the beer bottle still in my hand.

"Hey!" And just like that I sit up with very little effort to the sound of his voice, quite conscious of them and their piles of firewood even though seconds before I'd been miles away. "Jeez, I'd thought you'd fallen asleep on us." He was grinning and carrying so many logs and twigs and branches I can barely see his chin.

"No. I'm awake." I stand up instantly to prove him wrong. I feel very energetic, alive, aware; so completely and entirely alive and aware as I've never been before. I want desperately to smile.

"Check this out." John drags behind him an enormous tree trunk, dead, and perfect for burning. "I'll be right back. I'm gonna get my dad's saw from the shed. You guys dig a hole. Whew, these things are comin' on strong. You guys need anything?"

"Beer!" My boyfriend yells this out and drops the wood simultaneously as it hits me. I feel it in my legs and in my stomach, a strange and free feeling that doesn't belong. I look at Dylan, who seems incredibly beautiful. He appears more exquisite and magical in a way as I witness the sun touch his cheek and watch the wind blow at his curls as if to cajole them into playing. Everything suggests that I take a more intimate look at what I see in front of me, and it all moves slower because it all counts that much more. All of it, Dylan and his face, the feel of my own body motions, the weather and the wind, all are more important because I possess the energy to appreciate them. I am seeing through different eyes and breathing in a different body, which are slightly removed from my own inner thoughts. Breathing becomes terribly fascinating.

"Hey, you over there, how you doin'?"

I turn again to face the splendid person he is. How can I explain this?

"Well…" I want to tell him how good it feels, but for some reason the thought embarrasses me a little. Perhaps the inner sensations are too intimate to define.

"Well, are you okay?"

"Yes. Absolutely." I sound so positive. This feels foreign and delightful simultaneously.

"You trippin' yet?"

"I think so."

"You'll know if you are."

"I am."

"Cool. Come here, Babe."

Babe. I am someone's Babe. I drift over to Dylan as my boots sink into the sand. We embrace in silence. I don't need to speak with all the energy communicating from deep within me. He places his cheek against mine and runs his fingers along the backside of my head and underneath my hair, massaging my skull and bringing forth every exotic sensation I've never known. "I gotta dig a hole."

I sit down on the blankets again with no effort. Every movement feels terrific, every bone and muscle, all the blood moving, all the oxygen sliding into my lungs. I am alive. I turn toward the ocean. It is so glorious, so blue, so inviting. I want in. I observe Dylan digging a few feet away. He catches me and winks. John saunters toward us with a saw in his hand. Everything that happens seems to be happening perfectly and for a very great reason. I feel completely in sync with the world, with every atom flowing around me, with the solid rays of the sunshine and the alluring sound of the ocean waves. Every word I hear uttered is meant to be said and to be heard. Everything is very important.

"John, how cold do you think it is?" My head motions toward the water while my hands remain clasped around my knees.

"Cold. Very cold. Why? You thinking about going in?" John raises his eyebrows high and shakes his head back and forth quickly, like a cat.

"I am."

"Did you hear her, Dyl? Your girlfriend's crazy." John has the saw in place and is already working on the tree trunk.

"Rachel, the water is freezing. I won't let you go." It is interesting that he thinks he has that kind of control over me. The greatest thing is that the issue of control has vanished. Nothing seems to be in charge except the energy within my body.

"I really think I have to do this." I am already taking off my boots, one by one, with absolutely no consciousness of the strength required. Magic takes them off, and when they are off I can't remember how they came off. My mind is speeding with different thoughts. Am I being too silly, too carefree? What if I try the water and it's so cold I just come running back? What should I wear in the water? Will Dylan think badly of me if I just go in my underwear?

"You're gonna get sick." He has dug a perfect hole, and they are building a log cabin with twigs in the sand on their knees. I wish for a camera.

"I'll be fine."

"You are one goofy chick, Rachel." John shakes his head as I remove my socks and unbutton my jeans.

"Just don't look."

"Yeah, John, no peeking." Dylan laughs, and I figure it'll be okay. I peel off my jeans one leg at a time and give in to the pull of the ocean. It beckons me and I run to it, like a magnet to metal, wondering if they are looking at my backside as I do so. I hope my butt looks smaller than it feels, if they happen to take a glimpse my way. I refuse to turn around. I am determined to go forward. The water brushes up onto my toes as I stand at the edge of this vast and colorful picture begging me to enter. I do, pretending it isn't cold. I step into this body of water for the first time in my life and keep going until the coldness creeps to the bottom of my shirt. I shake involuntarily and feel goose bumps running up and down my limbs. But the new energy drives me further and keeps me company as I sink deeper into ice. A small fire blazes back on the beach as I turn to make sure they are observing my courage. It is all they are doing. With the descending sun in my face and the water freezing my body in place, I whisper a small Thank you to God and whoever else is listening, and dunk my head back into the water, baptizing myself.

Am I an evil child? Is pleasure what I seek, and if so will this require a great deal of repentance? Can I ever return to the innocence I've now tarnished? How come innocence never made me feel this full of joy? How come I waited so long to feel so good? Up out of the water, I pull my hands over my hair and clear head as a song runs through it. "If loving you is wrong, then I don't want to be right." It makes sense to me for the first time as I pull my chilled flesh back onto the beach, destined to leave my heaviest of thoughts back in the Atlantic to mingle with the fallen *Titanic*. Some great and seemingly important things were never meant to survive.

Quite suddenly I realize how cold I am. I pull my tee shirt from my skin and wring it out onto the sand as I look at Dylan for some sort of signal.

"You look like a wet rat."

Thanks. I was picturing more of a *Sports Illustrated* glossy page spread with wet tee shirts and sunset scenes.

"So, how's the water, goofy one?" He looks behind him and then back at me. "John's getting you some towels and stuff. Shit, I didn't think you'd do it."

"I did it."

"I see that. Come here. Turn around." He pulls my wet tee shirt off over my head as I face the water, shivering. Then he takes off his long sleeved, gray shirt with just three buttons and puts it in front of me, still sheltering me from anyone behind us. I pull it over my head and smell Dylan, feeling much warmer.

"Better?"

"Better."

"You should take these off before you put your jeans back on." He slides his fingers underneath the wet elastic and up over my pelvic bone until I think I might scream. I turn around and melt into his soft embrace.

"I'm tripping my brains out." My body is fully charged now, my senses escalating to new and wild heights. I am fresh and clean and vivid.

"You all right? I mean everything's okay?"

"Yeah. I like this." It is one of the hardest things I ever had to say.

"I thought you might."

116

"You thought right."

"Here's John." I stay where I am as Dylan turns halfway around to grab two towels.

"I'm gonna say goodbye to my parents. I'll be right back." And he is gone again.

"John's cool." I am impressed by his respect for my wet nakedness.

"He's my best friend."

"I see that. You're lucky, you know?" Dylan is helping me dry off. He towel dries each leg while I fluff my hair with the other towel so it won't soak Dylan's shirt.

"Here's your jeans." I pull them on over my underwear.

"You're gonna catch a cold."

"You want me to moon everyone?"

"Who's to see?"

"You and whoever else is lurking in the woods or looking through big picture windows." I stand barefoot in the sand and smile a huge smile.

"They can't see you."

"No?"

"No. God you're beautiful. Have I ever told you how amazing you look with your hair all wet like that? You're fucking gorgeous."

"Fucking gorgeous?"

"Watch your mouth."

"Watch yours."

"I love you, Rachel." His fingers work themselves up over and around my ears, making me tingle even more.

"I love you more." I did. Right then and there I loved him more than anything, more than the world, more than the sun.

"They're gone." Dylan turns around and we face our friend. "Sounds like they'll probably stay the night. Dad sounds like he is up for it. Mom packed for it. So, we've got the place to ourselves. How are you guys feeling? Like I'm feeling, I hope?"

"We're right with you, Johnny Boy." Dylan looks at me as if to say we need to make John feel comfortable, that it is time to include him and be three instead of two. They'd done it for me many times. "Cool, you brought some tunes."

"Thought this one would give us a better sound." John holds a gigantic boom box. "Fuck. Dealing with the 'rents and tripping just don't mix."

"Don't know how you do it." Dylan playfully pushes John on the left shoulder. He topples backward slightly, sets the boom box down, and goes back for revenge. And here they are, two puppies in the sand. As soon as Dylan is on top, holding down John's hands, John's feet kick until Dylan is on the bottom. There is a burning energy in all of us, and this is what guys do with theirs. I just watch them, shaking my head with a smile, trying to find the same station John had found in the cabin.

"Hey, turn that up!"

Here it is, some classic rock station.

"Who is it?" I still am not able to identify every singer, but I am familiar with the song. I have to wait for my answer while they chase each other around and then land in a heap back on the blankets in front of me.

"Guess. D.B." I am given the initials, now I have to come up with an answer. The music is strange, but it speaks to my soul. D.B. I don't know.

"I don't know."

"Come on. David…"

"David Bowie?"

"You got it." I got it. I have it. "Space Oddity." Now that is a cool name for a song. Dylan and John seem to have exhausted themselves and are walking and talking with each other on the other side of the fire. I am alone and loving it. I don't need anyone because the power within me is more company, better company than I've ever had. I rise from my pose on the blankets and drift into the music, inviting my physical body and my spirit to dance together. Each note instantly choreographs the rhythm I need to communicate, and it is done. There is no thought or planning to the dance. My toes melt into the cooling sand and my arms stretch toward heaven, conducting the air and the water and the sun to join me. I lift my body and drift closer to the ocean as the music pulsates through my blood, feeding it. I dance the dance of energy, the dance of fire, of sun, of music. I dance the dance of woman, of the woman I am and of the one I will become. Dylan's shirt rises to expose my flesh as my arms swirl in circular motions, and the coolness of it is a balance to the warmth of the hottest star in view. My eyes see through my closed lids as I work the wet sand beneath my feet, my jeans allowing every bend and movement my body desires to make.

When the song ends, I bend at the waist to touch me toes, to punctuate the memory, and then I step lightly back to my spot on the blankets, still in my own space, but re-entering reality slowly.

"Your girlfriend is hot."

Do they think I can't hear them? I pretend not to.

"Find your own."

They stroll back toward the fire and Dylan sits down next to me. If a genie would have appeared at that moment to grant me three wishes, I would have given them to someone else. Each and every sense and human desire was being fed instantaneously and simultaneously so that there was no wanting, only being. We just were. And we knew it. We knew there was no need to speak, and when we did so it sprung only from a wanting to cement ourselves in the now, to remind ourselves of who and where we were. It seemed dangerous to silently drift for too long.

"The sun."

"It's melting." And so it does, right into the earth.

"Can you see the moon?" John points to the nearly invisible circle it is and to the sliver of it we can see clearly. "It'll be dark soon."

"We have the fire," Dylan comments calmly.

"More wood?"

"Yeah. A couple more logs."

"Okay." More are placed onto the thinning blaze and we watch them catch fire. "Rachel, C.S."

"C.S.?"

"The song."

"Oh. Cat Stevens. My mom has this album. 'Peace Train,' right?"

"Very good. Kudos to you."

I cross my legs in front of me and lean my face toward the fire, feeling its warmth.

"Careful."

"I am."

John has a stick and is messing around in the fire with it and staring up in the sky at the same time. I lean back into Dylan's arms digging the mushrooms in my body.

"Must be kind of a drag to be seen only when something else bright enough shines on you." Dylan and I glance at each other and then at John.

"You're not getting sappy on us now, are you?"

"I don't know. I've just been thinking about stuff lately. Like what life is all about. What's it all for? What are we here for?" John looks straight at the fire as he speaks. Dylan looks at me. I offer no immediate support. I am trying to think of an answer that doesn't come straight from the Bible.

"We're here for this." Dylan pushes for group optimism.

"You mean this moment, this trip?" John gazes into the flames.

"Sure, of course. All life is is moments. Some are just better than others."

"Most of them are pretty shitty, though." John seems unconvinced.

"So you celebrate the great ones and put up with the mediocre ones." I am impressed with my boyfriend. I could live with someone like this.

"And then what? All there is to look forward to is death, and no one seems to have much of a clue as to what happens then. I mean there's no proof. So we live through a great many mediocre moments, grow old, and die, with no guarantee."

I feel myself growing cold inside and hug Dylan closer. The warmness I'd created dancing is vanishing. I want to tell John about Jesus and that he died so that we might live, but suddenly I don't even know what that means exactly. The prophets and apostles who wrote those words were only men who lived a long time ago. What if the deal has changed since then—expired? What if they were only writing out of inspiration and hope or hearsay? Sitting there on the blanket in the sand, I suddenly feel as if I don't belong, not there or anywhere. I want to run, run away, far away from all the confusion. I need to go somewhere else. I stand up. Rising, I feel my energy source surge through my body. It grows from my pelvis, through my insides, strengthening them, through my heart and lungs, and up through my throat, out and back into my eyes. It is a cool energy that is keeping me awake and alive, and I realize suddenly that the clock has stopped, the one that tells us when it's time to eat and when it's time to sleep.

I walk a few steps from the fire toward my socks and boots. My gut wrenches with intensity. I feel amazingly thin and not at all hungry. Just the thought of food seems silly. I am living on something else that feeds my spirit and soul, not my physical body. Instead, this frame or temple for my spirit follows my soul instead of the other way around. At last, I am not being controlled by my physical hunger. I can concentrate on other things, like how awake I am. My eyes have never seemed so wide open before.

I walk back to the fire and sit down, feeling as if I had accomplished some great and important mission. I feel as if I belong again.

"But how do you know death is just a transition into another life? Do you have any proof?" John is looking up now at his friend, engaged.

"Who would create such wonders, such spirits, only to have them destroyed? You sit there, John, thinking, feeling, questioning. You are very much alive. That cannot end. No matter how old your body gets, that spark inside you will never die. It's too powerful."

Dylan reaches to his left without disturbing his sitting position, grabs two medium sized logs, and places them on the fire, causing John and me to move back a couple inches.

"I don't know. Of course it all sounds real nice and everything. But still, it's how you perceive the situation. Not everybody feels the way you do, Dyl. Sometimes I get this eerie, freaky feeling like I'm just gonna disappear."

Without a thought, I get up and go over to him, to John. I put my arm around his shoulder and say nothing.

"Hey, Rache." He places his arm around my waist and gives his attention back to the fire.

"Where the hell is the beer around here?" Dylan rises to a standing position and motions to John.

"There's over a case in the cabin. You know where. You need me to come with?"

"No, I got it." And then he pauses for just a second and I wonder if I ought to go with him. But then he is gone. We watch him as he stops for a second to light the pipe, then continues on his way.

"He's a good man." John seems in awe of his friend.

"I know it."

"It's really cool you came with us, Rachel."

"Thanks." I lean back on my elbows and look up at the darkening sky.

"Dylan sure is lucky to have you."

I glance over at John.

"I'm the lucky one. I don't know what I'd do without him."

"I know how you feel."

"Oh my gosh. Wow."

"What?"

"It's everywhere."

"What?" John backs up as I look from the fire to the pile of wood to John's face.

"It's in your hair. It's everywhere. Can't you see it?"

"Rachel."

"It's purple. It's geometrical. A pattern of purple everywhere." Everywhere I look I see purple designs in front of my eyes, and the pattern blends with each object, fitting to it and decorating each surface.

"Rachel, you're hallucinating."

"You mean you don't see it?"

"Well, I don't see it now. I haven't seen any colors since the last shows at the Garden. But that was with acid. You're peaking, Rachel."

"Euphoria." It was all I could think to describe it. And then the Doors come on the radio. I ask John to turn it up. I get up. I can't resist the alluring voice and seductive guitar. Jim is a spy in the house of love. Deepest secret fear. I move slowly and away from John, back into my space to meditate with the music. I have to take the moment and do this, or it'd be gone. My body drapes around each chord, and I breathe in the beautiful ocean air and become lost in the darkness. Each time I swallow, I swallow energy, and every time I breathe, I breathe life. My pattern shows brightly on the back screen of my eyelids, and the entertainment is pure and bright. I flow far away from the flames of the fire and nearer to the water until I can feel it. But there is someone there. I open my eyes as the song fades away.

"I didn't mean to scare you, Rache. I just want to tell you that I love the way you dance."

"Thanks, John. You didn't scare me." I face him and the pattern that is splattered all over his face. It amuses me so. The cool darkness all around us seems to separate us from everything, and the small fire that burns is only a reminder of what we've done and where we'd return. John touches the side of my face lightly and then pulls me toward him, hugging me without permission. But I hug him in return. Hugging is innocent, right?

"Hey, can I get in on this, too?" Surprised by the abruptness and closeness of his voice, we both turn to face Dylan, stepping away from each other and toward him.

"Dylan."

"John Boy."

"I didn't mean anything by this. I was just giving Rachel a hug. That's all."

"No big deal. I leave and you guys have your arms around each other. I come back and you're hugging over here in the dark."

"Dylan. Sweetheart. It's nothing. John is just being nice is all. I got a little freaked out by all these…colors." I am seeing them now, rivers of moving rainbows flowing swiftly in the sand. I bend down to get a closer look.

"She's definitely peaking."

"Here. Take these." They are quiet above me, making amends. John takes the beers and walks back to the fire. Dylan bends down next to me.

"You don't see them?" I can't take my eyes off the colors. They are so brilliant and so lovely in the dark.

"I don't see them, Babe. Rachel, promise me nothing was going on here." He is serious. I look into his face and through the colored pattern.

"I love you, Dylan. I think John's just a little lonely. He needs a girlfriend."

"Come here." He pulls my body into his so my back is nestled into his chest. His arms enclose mine, and we sit together there while I watch the colors and try to stay earthbound. "We're peaking. It's the zenith of the trip," he says.

"It's amazing, Dylan."

"I love you, Rachel." There isn't much need to say more. We sit together like that looking out over the water for several minutes or an hour while the stars fit into the pattern in my brain. I play connect the dots with the stars and try explaining it all to him.

"I had no idea when I woke up this morning that I'd be here like this with you tonight. So much can happen in just one day, huh?" I turn my face to meet his.

"You've got to make the moments in life count, Rache. You've got to have some fun."

"It's true." And then I can tell Dylan is feeling restless to get back to John, who we find drinking the last swallow of a beer and stirring up the fire with his stick.

"Hey, I didn't mean anything, you know." He is still pouting.

"Next time you need a hug, I'm right here, big guy." And they are at it again, wrestling in the sand and making me worry about their proximity to the fire.

"Watch out, you guys!" I stand there with my hands on my hips watching them, and loving them both.

"Christ, I need a beer." Dylan lands beside me, sweating. He opens beers for both of us, and then for John, who has placed three more logs on the fire. I pull the edges of the blankets back into place and dust off the top layer of sand at least. The beer feels good going down. I desire it. It falls down my throat easily, and I want more. Drinking alcohol has never been very familiar to me, but now I seem right at home with it.

"You tired, Rache?"

"Never been so awake in my life." But I settle down on the blanket with my head in Dylan's lap anyway, to gaze up at the stars and see what all there is to see. He begins smoothing out my hair, petting me like a kitten. And the two of them start talking again as two guys will, about their band and sports and other good time memories. Their voices are backstage. I melt under Dylan's touch into a very deep realm. I go back into my head, back to a time of forgetfulness. I lift from myself, still feeling a hand on me. I become androgynous, neither man nor woman, but both. I am simply a stream of energy, a very tight stream that runs all the way up to the stars. It is pure perfection and enlightenment. Perfection? Is there such a thing? Isn't the state of being perfect the ultimate impossibility?

I am one again with where I've come from. Have I come from God? It is my ego I left behind. There is no thought of the me, the identity of face and form. I am free from that now up where I belong. I am with the stars.

My stream of energy glides down from them then and instead swirls around in a circle. Behind my eyelids, I see a movie of swirling shapes as one would see through a kaleidoscope. It is a livelier force that shows me these pictures. Life is a cycle, a cycle of moments. Around and around and around. I see bizarre eyes and faces and animal shapes, all in a circle 'round and 'round. All the colors are brilliant, and I watch the whole moving movie trying to figure out how it is that I am seeing these things while my eyes are sealed tight. My body stays still for a long time. My hands are clasped upon my belly and the right side of my face is warm from the fire. I know I have been away from myself, and I am ready to return. My feet stir in the sand beyond the blanket. His hand is still combing back the hair from my forehead. I need to move.

"Hey, Rache." I sit up.

"Hey." I feel drowsy and light-headed.

"You okay?"

"Fine." I grab my beer from its spot in the sand and drink down several gulps to clear my mind from the colors that are slowly relaxing. They dim and depart gradually as I notice a flicker here and there of my purple pattern. I understand now that I have consumed a drug.

The rest of the night comes and goes as we watch the moon move around in our sky, first high, then settling to the side. We drink all the beers John has, one after another, as our only desired nourishment. I get buzzed, but the mushrooms are stronger still, holding on in my body, keeping all of us awake until the whole earth around us begins to lighten again. We notice it in the water and in the sky. We can see further now as the never sleeping sun shows its first rays of light upon our side of the world.

The light without a prior night of sleep seems creepy to me. Confusion sets in with my newly discovered lethargy and I want the dark back. I am thin and physically weakened as my mind remains annoyingly alert. Without a word, all three of us stand up and begin picking up beer bottles and blankets. It is quite understood that the trip is over. I try to pull my hand through my tangled hair. It is full of sand. There is sand in my underwear and between my toes, and I think of a phrase my mother used to use when she wanted to describe the utter physical dissatisfaction she noticed with someone. She'd say, You look like death warmed over.

All of a sudden, all bodily necessities, which had been ignored through the night, come rushing up to greet me all at once, begging for my attention like a little puppy dog. Clean me, feed me, find me shelter.

"Put those in this."

"Okay." John holds out a bag for the bottles.

"Mom's got a place to recycle these in the garage. I'll be right back." He leaves while Dylan and I fold up the sandy blankets. The morning mist of greens and blues and grayish fog fit our silent mood. I avoid his eyes, not wanting him to see me as death warmed over. The light of day reveals everything. Thank the Lord for the nighttime. Forget the day. Neil Diamond.

"Let's go, you guys."

We walk behind John with the boom box and blankets, coming to terms with reality once again—bright daytime reality of requirements and routine. The mushrooms are exiting my system slowly. I can feel them winding down, pulling me back to the earth and to my life, and it is not a bad feeling at all.

In the house, John brings us white, fluffy towels and tells us to take his room, that he is going to sleep downstairs. The carpet is soft beneath my feet. I feel like a guest in a hotel, his house is so perfectly neat and organized. I have much respect for all the time and energy it takes to make such nice surroundings, even if a maid is involved.

I gratefully accept my towel from John and feel like a rescued savage. My clothes smell of fire, and I can tell I've already walked sand into the house as I stand there holding my boots and socks.

"The shower is down the hall to the right. I'll get your stuff from the car." Dylan looks at me to make sure I've heard him. In his hair I see a flicker of the purple pattern. I nod and walk down the hall.

In the bathroom, I pull off my sandy jeans and fold Dylan's shirt on top of them. I feel scrawny and renewed. In the full length mirror on the back of the door, I scare myself by how different I look. It is experience that has changed me. It is the colors I'd seen that made my face look different and my whole image less important. My body is empty, but my mind has been fed so completely I don't think I'll ever be able to go back to the person I was. I don't want to. My hair is a matted mess, and I smile at this. It is lovely not to have to be concerned with the physical aspects of oneself for a change. Life is so much more than sex appeal.

I step into the cleanest, whitest, and shiniest shower I'd ever been in. Sand scatters itself across the bottom of the tub as I adjust the water to the perfect temperature, just below hot. Down with the water and out with the sand. I lather up with their expensive shampoos and soaps and enjoy every moment as I lose myself in the present. Through the small window in the bathroom I can tell the day will be a cloudy one. Already there is a noticeable grey cover in the sky, draping low over the water and between the trees.

The blue, furry rug feels soft beneath my washed feet as I towel dry my hair and find some lotion in the cabinet for my skin. It is Monday morning, and I am ready for bed.

9

THE SEX

"Did you get a shower?"

"Yeah. Down the other way there's another bathroom. They've got four total."

"Wow." I am wrapped in towels. One stands on my head as a heavy crown, the other barely makes it around. "You sure it's okay we sleep in here? I feel bad kicking John out of his room."

"He offered. It's actually the darkest in here. And we don't have to worry about making a mess. It's already a mess." Dylan seems cocky lying there under the sheets as I clear off a chair to sit down, ladylike, so as not to expose the goods. I have no idea what I am supposed to wear now. I think of my lingerie folded neatly back at the apartment in the city. Even if I had it, I wouldn't want to wear it now. It would seem so completely and sexually forward. I can't very well put my jeans on, which I notice have been placed on top of one of the stereo speakers. I grab my clean shirt from there, drop the towel from my head, and slide the shirt on, keeping the other towel wrapped around my waist.

"Come to bed, Rache."

Sure. Right. Like I'm some wife or something. I reach over the bed to twist John's black blinds to their tightest, closed position. He catches me and pulls me down next to him. I should have seen this coming. Or maybe I knew this was coming.

"Take this thing off." Unwrapped, just like a package. He tosses the wet towel onto the floor and pulls me close. My mind races with thoughts I know are lame but can't help anyway. Why do I love him so much more when he has his pants on? I can't keep my mind off wanting him when he is fully clothed and playing his guitar. Now he seems so vulnerable. All his attention is on me. I can make or break his expectant mood. And this is stressful enough without thinking about the fact that I still have not completed the sexual act and am therefore by definition and in the eyes of my judging God, a virgin.

Off the bed and crouching next to the stereo in the dimness of the bedroom is my naked man. Can he sense my, what will I call it, my sexual apathy? It isn't that I don't like having an orgasm.

Dark Side of the Moon or *Wake of the Flood*? His behind looks so white in the dark. He appears as a little boy to me. I've never seen him so completely stripped like this before.

"You choose." Having an orgasm is one of the most physically fascinating and delicious events. I remember the first time I had one. Eighth grade History class. Mr. Hanna looked like an owl behind his glasses. He could talk for a good long time without ever expecting a response from us. I was sitting in the middle row about three desks back. In that class were two of the most gorgeous guys in our grade. Not that their attractiveness had anything to do with my bodily motions. I'm sure my skin tight Jordache jeans were to blame, to thank. I didn't have to move very much at all, and I had no idea what was going on at first. A little movement to the side, a little back. It was a game. How long could I make this wild sensation last? It made the class go fast. I wouldn't have another orgasm until Dylan, until he placed his body on top of mine to kiss me on the floor in his living room just two weeks after we first met. Each of us fully clothed. No matter. We both came like crazy.

I settled back into the pillows as Dylan sprang back into bed. Pink Floyd made soft noise from across the room.

"Tired?" He seems so chipper, so eager, too eager.

"I guess. I should be, huh?" But the thought of sleep would not come. What am I doing lying bottom naked with him?

"I have something…just in case."

How convenient. So prepared. I wonder if he had been a boy scout. Was I going to have sex with a guy when I didn't even know if he'd been a boy scout or not? I try to nod from my place in the pillow so he knows I have heard him. And then he begins stroking my hollow stomach with his fingertips. This feels good. Too good. Do I know what I am doing? My body wants to give up, I can tell. It has been worked hard and wants to quit.

"Dylan, were you ever a boy scout?"

He lifts his fingers from my flesh to look into my face as if I am a loony tune.

"Cub scout. Then I got kicked out."

"Why?"

"I don't know, messing around. I didn't go to all the meetings. Why? Were you a girl scout?"

"Yep. I even sold two hundred and fifty boxes of cookies one year."

"Wow. Good girl." Too good for him, or am I just pushing the purity thing? How long can I hold out? He is back with his fingertips, rewarding me for being a successful girl scout. I try to relax my brain into the moment, but fragments of the trip keep butting in, keeping my mind moving in odd directions and away from sex. His hands are underneath my shirt as the screams of Pink Floyd get a little louder. I turn toward the speakers. I've only heard this album a couple times at his house.

"The Great Gig in the Sky." The chick sounds like she is having an orgasm herself.

"Oh." His music knowledge turns me on just a little. I mean, it is something. My breasts flatten as I lie on my back, even more if I raise my arms above my head. I bring my hands down to my sides and turn toward him, to see him, to determine how far I am going to let this whole thing go. The first time ought to be memorable, I muse. It should be with someone one feels strongly for. I look into his large pupils, into his face of wanting. The male sex can seem so desperate at times. The first time should be a positive experience, one in which the sex works. The first time ought to be on my wedding night.

His right hand is working my thighs now, up and down first the outer, then the inner and upper portions. My body is weakening. Pure exhaustion is taking hold. I can't last much longer. The thought that I am doing this in someone else's bed is now in the background of my mind. I haven't really a choice. I have no choice.

His breath and lips are on my neck, under my hair, over my ear. Impulse and nothing else drives my left hand around his body, feeling his young skin. I kiss his chest and finger the almost nonexistent hair there. Our bodies mold to one another easily. Everything is working in silent and slowing motion as the mushrooms dance their last number through my brain. I kiss his familiar lips and tug lightly on his curls as I've done so many times before.

The music chants its distant rhythms into the room, and my eyes close to see a bright image or two. Sex is natural, like the sun and the flowers and the motion of the air. I am just a girl with just a boy doing what makes the world swing 'round and 'round. I can feel him hard between my thighs and know there is no turning back. I keep my eyes closed while he fumbles with a package. He wants in. I am ready. Don't fight nature. Don't fight.

"I love you, Rachel. I do."

Right on cue. Come here. His body is on top of mine and in mine sooner than I think. It takes just a second or two for him to enter completely, and it hurts only a moment. In. He lifts my shirt so our chests can meet as he works. I close my eyes to concentrate. I want this to be good for him, too. I apply light pressure at the bottom of his back to signal that I want him inside me. The motion he is making, however, does very little for me. I concentrate on him instead, keeping my arms around him, trying to kiss him if he gets close enough.

Sex. This is sex. This is the nasty, terrible, evil, wonderful act. I am doing it. It isn't such a big deal. He comes sooner than usual and pulls out and lands next to me on the bed. I put my arms above my head again and close my eyes, feeling strangely liberated and a bit used. He snaps off the condom. I can hear it, but I keep my eyes closed.

"I'm sorry."

For what? I knew for what.

"Dylan, I love you." I had to, I am having sex with him!

"I love you, too, Rache."

All this love and sex is wearing me out.

"Come here." He pulls me to him again, to his warmth and into his afterglow. There are tiny beads of perspiration across his forehead. Words are not to be spoken. They will jinx the moment, and he isn't finished. His mouth finds its way to my stomach and down to my thighs. I closed my eyes again and go back into my head into memories of orgasm. This is absolutely the last shred of strength I have remaining. Yesterday and the day before are years past to me now.

I put my hand on top of his to relay agreement of place and position. I can't help but move my hips under his touch. Defenseless and susceptible, my body and brain zoom into involuntary motion. The Goddess of sex takes control now, to show me the way, to bless me with this freedom to come, to charge me with yet another drug. A thousand ocean waves of euphoria, a shudder. I keep my hand on top of his. I've never done this before, but I want it again. The energy within isn't ready to give up. Not even now after he is probably exhausted, not after an entire night awake, not yet. And I come again and break the silence with my cries.

10

THE MORNING AFTER

The day is gorgeous and warm and windy, windy enough to lift up my white, cotton dress and expose my tanned legs. I am on a beach near the ocean; the sand feels cool and smooth beneath my bare feet. It is early morning, and I know the day is special. It is for this purpose that I have curled my hair. I have the sides up and fastened loosely in a brown, leather clip. Twisted tendrils fall near my face until the ocean breezes blow them carefully away. I know, though, that I am missing something—an important element in all of this is gravely lacking. Is it that I am naked beneath my dress? Where is the lingerie I have purchased for this special day? A girl shouldn't be naked on her wedding day, I think. That is it. I am getting married.

The three of them walk toward me. I can only see the shape of them at first because the rising sun is behind them. I wonder if they can see through my dress.

Where is my mother? Why isn't she with me? Shouldn't a mother be at her daughter's wedding? I feel sick inside. I haven't invited her. I can't find her. That is it. I don't know how to get in touch with her, and now she's missing the most important day of my life. Regret pours upon me like the sun. I will never be able to make this up to her. It is all too fast. How can they come toward me like this? Don't they know this is all moving too quickly? Why can't I shout for them to stop?

The priest stands before us now. His weathered hand opens the holy book with the purple, silk bookmark that is frayed at the end. He glances up and peers into my eyes. Does he know that I am not a virgin? God, he can tell. Doesn't he know that I did it just once? Just once. That's it. I'm not as bad as you think I am.

"Miss Rachel, do you take Dylan as your husband this day, to have and to hold, in sickness, in health, in poverty, in wealth?"

"Yes sir."

"And Miss Rachel, do you take John as your husband this day as well, to have and to hold, in sickness, in health, in poverty, in wealth?"

I look to my left at John and to my right at Dylan. They are both smiling their glazed and gorgeous smiles. They wear full, black tuxedos, each of them.

"Yes."

"I now pronounce you husbands and wife. You two may kiss your bride."

Just as the priest closes his bible, I put my hand up to my mouth. All of my teeth are loose. I can't let them see my mouth. I turn away as Dylan tries to kiss me. Several teeth are in the palm of my hand now, and more are falling out. I hide from them as they shake hands with the priest. The priest shakes his head at me. He knows! It is the punishment of God.

* * *

I pry my eyes open and lie silently next to Dylan, listening to his steady and relaxed breathing. It is 11:34 on John's digital clock in the corner. The big, red numbers shout reality to me as I try to remember all the details of my dream. I grit my teeth quietly, testing their permanence. My insides are still in a state of panic. I wonder when John's parents will be home. Even though my eyes are heavier than I've ever known them to be, I rise from the bed and slip on my jeans.

"Hey…" His arms reach out to me as he lets out a short and controlled yawn. He is testing the water. I zip up my pants and give him a face of uncertainty. Who can know for sure if deeds done are deeds done right? Only the future will tell us that.

"Hi."

Hi, it's been a long time. Donovan. It is a long time since we've been just him and me, normal and normal, without drug or desire or destiny unknown.

"You getting up?"

"I guess. I don't know when his parents are coming back."

"They won't be back till later, I'm sure. Come here."

I feel silly standing in the darkened room amidst John's clothes and CD's and posters of Jimi Hendrix and Bob Marley as if I have some important business to take care of or something. I relent and walk toward the bed, knowing that I have, in fact, entered into a new dimension of this relationship. It is an adult avenue of agreed upon, mutual, sexual enjoyment, all the way, no going back. The hunter has captured his prey. Smiles. He is all smiles, as if we are supposed to be celebrating a happy day, an occasion to remember. I suppose. Why do I feel so glum?

We kiss some, but the gnawing hunger in my belly pushes him playfully back. I certainly am not ready to take another go at the sex thing. Guys are unbelievable. I sit down in John's desk chair and swivel to face the bed as I contemplate opening the blinds to face the day.

"I need a toothbrush or something." Anything to distract his attention away from our cozy situation he is begging me to enter once again. He is flashing me now, showing me he is hard. Jesus. He appears almost pitiful with his thing in the air smiling over at me.

"Come here." Always calling me as if I am his puppy dog or something.

"Why?"

"I want to show you something."

"I can see it from here."

"Yeah, but you don't know what it feels like from there."

I've never touched it before. I've never touched anyone's before. He is stroking his, up and down in the dim light of the room. What does he think he is doing? Is this supposed to get me going? What if it was, and I am abnormal? I can see it now. A cold fish, they'll call me. That's why her husband cheats on her; she's a cold fish. She doesn't even like oral sex. Really? Yeah. All he wants is an occasional blow job, and she won't go for it. He says she pulls her nose up as if it disgusts her or something. Jeez. I know. It's not like he's even asking her to swallow.

Shit. I head toward the bed. Is this the ritual of becoming a woman? Because I don't remember any other, unless I count the day blood seeped into my panties while I was playing cards with my brother on the dining room floor. My reaction was neutral. I told my mom, she got the pads, I stuck one onto clean underwear, cursed the female sex, and resumed my card game. The leakage of blood certainly hadn't turned me into any kind of woman. Not at fourteen. At nineteen, I stare at my first live penis in curious and confounded reluctance. It isn't even all the same color.

"You want to touch it?"

I have propped up a pillow and am sitting against the headboard with my legs outstretched and ankles crossed as I try to seem interested in his most prized possession. I feel like grabbing the ruler from John's desk and measuring it. Six inches is supposed to be average, as far as I've heard. I cock my head to the side. Is that at least six inches? I never was very good at eyeballing measurements.

"Do you want me to touch it?" I know he does. He just nods like a small child who's been asked if he'd like a freshly baked chocolate chip cookie. Boy, I have him right where I want him. I reach out with my right hand and slide it down from the soft head to the wrinkly body. It is pretty smooth. He seems to like this so much that I think I'd break his heart in half if I stop. Up and down, slowly, as if I am just exploring. His hands clasp around mine, then, and he pushes for me to speed up the process. I give in and let him move my hand as he wishes. I am actually getting a kick out of this. Now there is no going back. He is into it full speed and then his hand is gone and mine is still moving, up and down, up and down, as fast as I think I can go. My arm almost gives out before warm juices spurt out from the top and onto his chest and my hand.

"Huh." Pretty wild.

"Grab me that towel, will you?" I look to where he had thrown it hours before. It is still a little damp. I give it to him and he cleans himself up. I squint to see if any of it has gotten on the pillows or the sheets. That would be gross for John to find. I can't see any. I move back to the swivel chair and watch Dylan dress. There is a knock on the door.

"You guys up?" Up and down and up and down.

"Hey John. Mornin'." Dylan opens the door like a cowboy in his jeans and bare chest, wobbling a little from side to side to make sure the package is well adjusted and neatly tucked out of sight of the mighty zipper.

"Just barely."

"It's noon already, huh?" Dylan glances back at the red numbers on the clock, grins at me, then turns to face John. "Thanks for the room, Johnny Boy. That was real kind of you. We'd like to change your sheets at no cost if you don't mind."

Jesus, did he want to advertise our most personal experience to date?

"Don't worry about it. Bertha will be here around 2:00 or so. I'll leave her a note. She'll take care of it."

"You sure? It's the least we can do." He looks at me again with that face. He is the man.

"Come on, you guys. I'm gonna fix my specialty, Mexican breakfast tacos with eggs, cheese, peppers, and onions. A little hot sauce, and we'll all be back in business." He is already leading us both down the hall and into a glorious, sparkling kitchen of stainless steel pans hanging from above and smooth tile to be stepped on below. I don't want to touch any part of it. There is nothing more satisfying than to gaze at perfect cleanliness such as this.

Dylan and I sit on wooden stools and place our elbows on the counter to watch the show. I tuck my nappy hair behind my ears and carve the crust out of the corners of my eyes.

"The shrooms were excellent, don't you think?" Dylan's energy comes not from food.

John opens an amazingly stuffed to the brim refrigerator and plucks out a half gallon of Tropicana orange juice, not from concentrate, a cardboard carton of organic eggs, a block of cheddar cheese, a red onion, small green peppers, and several scallions.

"Powerful, yet friendly. Not too bad," answers John, as he opens the carton of eggs and counts the ones remaining. "You guys want some juice?"

We both nod, already tasting it.

"Rachel?" Dylan turns to me now and puts his hand on my thigh.

"What?"

"You like the shrooms?"

"I did. You know I did." He looks at me as if he expected a little more. I am still entranced by my partnership in male masturbation. I walk around the counter to wash my hands with hot water and soap. "You need some help, John?"

"Sure, Rache. You can crack these in… use this." He grabs a white, ceramic mixing bowl from the cupboard to his right and sets it down in front of me. "Scramble 'em up with this. I'll chop up the onions and we'll be eating in…twenty minutes tops." He glances at the digital clock on the microwave and retrieves a knife from its wooden holder to begin chopping.

"Well, while you two cook up a storm, I'm gonna check out the water." He grabs his glass of orange juice, gives me a warm and parting smile, and saunters out. I half want to follow him. I'd rather stare at the ocean than scramble eggs, but it would be rude to leave John. I whisk the eggs against the sides of the bowl and instinctively duck my head down when John reaches for the large frying pan that hangs from a hook right above my head.

* * *

It is the pan that frightens her each time she washes it, which is oft times twice a day. In it her mother fries the eggs, cooks the pancakes, and grills the cheese sandwiches. Every meal he demands something be cooked. He wants hamburgers or hash browns, and his meals are always served to him on the brown, metal snack tables in front of the red, scratchy couch where he sits and stares from when he gets home until he leaves again.

"Rachel! Bring me the ketchup!" Ketchup on the eggs and the home fries that her mother fries in the frying pan.

"Rachel? What are you doing sitting there when the dishes need to be done?" *Three's Company* is on while her father eats his fries with his fingers, licking them each time and staring straight ahead at the screen across the room. She's brought him the ketchup and has gotten caught up in trying to figure out why Jack is always acting like a homosexual with Mr. Roper when she hears her mother's voice and jumps. She knows she isn't supposed to be watching that show. It is off limits to her and her brothers. She walks diligently back into the kitchen, tensing up slightly as she passes her mom in the doorway. She will make it up to her. She will do the dishes and dry them right away and put them all in the cabinets without being reminded further. She will make it better right away so she won't get yelled at for watching that show.

The dish strainer is already full when she gets to the pan. It is time for the S.O.S. pad. The one in the sink is all rusty, though. It is definitely time for a new one, she thinks. The new ones are always so nice to use, so full of soap. She always uses S.O.S. on the frying pan because her mother is particular about it. Rachel bends down and leans her forearms on the sink as she uses the new pad against the stuck-on potatoes. At nine years old, she is surprised to find that her back is hurting her as she stands at the sink and scrubs the metal of the blackened pan until silver begins shining through.

"Does this look clean to you?"

The girl looks at the pan and then at her mother's face. "Well?" She knows the answer is no. She has missed some potatoes, which had spilled over onto the outside of the pan, and she curses herself silently for not double-checking it after she'd rinsed it. "Damn you. Can't you do anything right?" She knows her mother's rage is not completely caused by the dirty pan. She glances at her mother, at her large legs and angry face. She looks at the curlers in her hair and at the light aqua scarf that holds them tightly against her head. She notices the colorful house shift her mother has sewn herself, and at the rickrack around the scoop-neck collar. And then before the girl knows it she is on the kitchen floor, lying on the outdated linoleum which has been there since they moved in, which her mother curses each time she washes it. The pan comes quickly, too quickly to duck. But even if she could have found the moment to tuck her head to the side, she probably wouldn't have. It would have been another punishable act against authority. Best to take the punishment that is meant. She lets it happen to her, and then stays on the floor as she watches her mother's large tennis shoes walk out of the room. The girl puts her hand to her head and cries as silently as possible.

* * *

"Rache? Rachel?"

"What?"

"Those are the most scrambled eggs I've ever seen. Excellent job."

"Oh." He takes the bowl from me and pours them into the heated frying pan as they sizzle and begin to separate almost immediately.

"Here. Drink your juice."

"Thanks." I gulp down the pure, orange liquid and ask John if he doesn't mind if I take a walk outside. "No problem. Go ahead. Enjoy." I walk out of the kitchen and out of the past.

11

RIDING THE WHEEL

The endless, rambling, and wistfully playful notes of the Grateful Dead serenade our stomachs as we slowly digest John's tasty breakfast tacos. I have eaten two and am stuffed.

"*Live/Dead*," answers John, as he fingers the cover.

"I don't have that one yet. Give it here."

John tosses it to Dylan as Dylan passes me the pipe. I inhale my third hit, certain now that I am destined for hell, and "might as well enjoy the ride." We sit on the floor of John's room in a circle, still shoeless and working on facing the day. John wants to be gone before Bertha arrives. He says she becomes quietly annoyed with visitors. I want to leave right away, but the boys want to smoke. So be it.

"Jerry's not gonna hang on much longer, you know. We ought to get tickets for the shows in the fall as soon as possible."

"They're coming to the Garden?"

"I imagine. Last year they did eight shows, remember?"

"It's a bummer we only got into three. Maybe Rachel will wanna come this year?" John takes the pipe from me and re-lights the bowl. He sucks in hard. "It's cashed." He blows out heavily and looks toward me for a response.

"Sure." It is all they listen to, for the most part. My mind blurs into a dazed fascination of its own with the music.

Our ride back to the city is a quiet one. It allows me to think and ponder and reflect. In such a short time so much has changed it makes my head spin more than it already was. I look over at Dylan in the driver's seat and for the first time really feel a part of him. We are bonded now. I hope he feels the same. I stare straight ahead and get lost in my brain.

Being stoned means you never have to think about any one thing for very long. The one thing will be thought about deeply and in a way never thought about before, but then it's over and it feels as if one has gained some new and indescribable insight that has probably never been considered before. And then just as it occurs that this epiphany ought to be quickly jotted down on paper in detail so that it can be passed on to others to aid in better self understanding and enlightenment, it is gone. Gone like the wind.

The springtime breezes blow through the Subaru. Ten breaths. I count each one of them and hold them as long as I can. I want to savor the savory country air while I still can. I want to remember this moment and use it when I find myself stuck behind the large, grotesque city buses that are so slow to get moving and so quick to pollute all of the air surrounding them. I feel so violated when, struggling for air so I can pedal fast enough to go with the flow of the traffic, the bus will pull in front of me and cover me with thick, black exhaust. I will have to hold my breath then, and at the same time pedal faster so I can get in front of it before it stops again. It wouldn't be so bad if there were only a few of these monsters to contend with, but they're everywhere. They're in every biker's way and in every driver's way, lugging their heavy load back and forth as if they are the most important things on the streets.

I smile coyly in my seat. I'll have yesterday for the rest of my life. I'll have the cool waters and the smooth, pleasant air in my memory forever. The fire and the colors and the stars. I'll have it all at my disposal now; good times to access in moments of doubt and pain. They are mine.

"How you doin'?" His bloodshot eyes glance over at me and break me from my thoughts.

"Good. Real good." Marijuana always gives me that feeling. Invincible euphoria and peace. The food felt great in my stomach now. "Thanks for breakfast, John." I turn to him and smile. He sure is a good, little camper. "It was excellent."

"You're totally welcome. Glad you enjoyed it."

I turn back around and melt back into my mind. I am so grateful for the little things, like the warm breakfast and the way we bounce in our seats every time the car goes over a bump in the road. Pot makes me stop and enjoy the little things.

"Hey. I'm thinking about checking out the art museum this afternoon. You guys up for it?" John leans into the front with his upper body, turning his head toward Dylan and then to me. I nod to Dylan. Anything to make it all last even longer.

"Sure."

"I still have some free passes from my parents. I know how you guys dig the museum thing." He sits back and we notice the buildings coming into view, looming in front of us like Gotham City, large and foreboding, daring us to enter. Our cleared, country minds begin to calculate and consider all the necessary steps that will get us from here into the museum. Parking may be a problem.

"Here, before we get there." John passes up the pipe, cupping his hand over the bowl so I won't have to re-light it. I am still good and buzzed, but I take a hit to be polite and pass it to Dylan, who takes a hit with one hand and keeps driving with the other. I pass it back to John for him and shake my head when it is my turn again.

"I'm good, Dylan?" He is in a zone. Suddenly many cars are surrounding us as we near the Lincoln Tunnel. Things are back to serious now, especially because we are baked. All three of us gaze straight forward, tensing up if a car gets too near us, slowing down when the car in front of us brakes.

"I'm a much better driver when I'm stoned." He winks over at me, keeping both hands on the wheel.

"Why, cuz you're paranoid?" John places his forearms on each of our seats.

"Maybe." His facial muscles drop again to serious as we slowly become engulfed by the tall shadows of the skyscrapers around us. Cement above and below and to the sides of us. We are rats in a cage, in a maze, running to and fro, playing the game to receive our food pellets and our comfort pellets. If we turn here and wait here and drive down that one way street and wait again, then prance at the right time we'll find it. The ultimate, evasive, invisible parking spot. One where there are no tow away zones, no fire hydrants, no parking signs, no handicap signs, no stop signs, no cars, no trucks, no moving vans, no police cars, no taxis waiting.

We drive down Fifth Avenue, turn right onto 53rd, right again at Avenue of the Americas, and onto West 54th three times before Dylan notices a van moving out of a seemingly acceptable place to park only two blocks from the museum.

"There. You think?"

"Looks good." It is John from the back. Our speech has sped up along with the traffic and the stress. We are determined to park this car and walk safely into the museum. All of our bodies bend forward as our eyes search the spot and surrounding area.

"He thinks he's gonna get it." I point to a large, silver car with tinted windows.

"Not gonna happen, Mister." Dylan turns into the space and the car beeps at us, giving us the finger through the horn. You can just tell, the way he honks at us. Oh well.

"I can't believe it. You did it, Dyl." John taps him on the shoulder playfully and laughs.

"Shit. Talk about stress." Dylan rolls up his window and we follow, locking and closing our doors simultaneously. He walks around the car to take my arm, and the three of us walk safely on the sidewalk toward the museum. I am so happy to be walking I almost forget how tired I am. Our bodies are running on little more than breakfast tacos, and the pot doesn't help. After awhile it just makes me want to yawn.

John divvies out our passes from his wallet and we get in without having to pay eight bucks a piece.

We walk around for a few minutes until I come upon some of the most beautiful paintings I have ever seen. I stop in my tracks and gaze up at them.

"Look," I say to no one in particular, as I peer into the chubby faces of the cherubs; they hang motionless in between the clouds to keep watch over the fair-skinned women who are draped, naked and without caution, over red velvet couches. Their thighs are layered in flesh. I stand there amazed at the indiscretion. Their breasts are proportionally smaller than their hips and buttocks and each of their boobs are of an obvious different size than its pair. Still, they expose themselves without concern. It is fantastic, like a revelation to me. Big, fat, uneven, cellulite-ridden women who are comfortable in their own nakedness, in their own unexercised flesh. Amazing. Dylan draws me on. I follow.

Up a couple floors the three of us come upon a black and white photography exhibit that seems to reflect the bleakest arena of our humanity. For this particular showing, the more depressing the subject matter the better, and the more it has been enlarged. The unframed portraits whisper of poverty and despair. Each pair of eyes cry of suffering and grief. An old man in a dilapidated hat looks at his passerby with worn eyes and deeply creased skin. A burning cigarette finds itself between the arthritic joints of his first and middle fingers, the smoke frozen in the air forever as the man neither smiles nor frowns. His tattered coat hangs unevenly on his shrinking, rounded shoulders. With his eyes he speaks, *It all ain't worth diddly when it comes right down to it. Look at me. Look at what happens when you get old, old and withered like me. Might as well have a smoke.* Might as well. At least that's what he says to me. I want to reach out and touch his face, feel the smooth, matte finish of the print, but there are signs all around saying, *Please do not touch.*

There are photographs of children as they stand in rags with stringy hair on a dirt road, boot strings untied. Welts or infected bug bites decorate their little legs. Skinny urchins with young skin and old eyes that pop out of their sockets when they see something of interest. They are probably standing in awe of the photographer with his dark, denim jacket and expensive camera, which he holds out in front of his face to capture their spirits. They probably said, "Hey Mister, got any change to spare?"

We walk around in a daze, taking it all in—food for the soul. Museums are like libraries, quiet and serene. It is a good place to come down after a trip, Dylan says, as we make our way to another room.

An hour or so later we are ready to leave. Dylan wants to go back to the guitar store. John says he doesn't mind. We know what he wants to see.

"You ought to just buy it." We wearily walk a good many blocks to the music store where Dylan has his eye on some expensive, red electric guitar.

"Right." He fingers the fret and plucks lightly at the strings.

"What?"

"What do you mean, what?"

"You know what I mean." John sounds hostile.

"If I saved up for a year maybe. Shit. I don't even have a job. I mean, jeez. If we could get ourselves a gig someday, maybe." Dylan takes the guitar off the rack and places it against his body. The store clerk eyes us, then looks back at the customer who is buying sheet music.

"Well…"

"Well, what? We're not ready. Not even close."

"Maybe this is what you need."

"What are you saying, that I'm the one who needs something?"

I rarely witness Dylan on the defensive.

"I don't know. All we fucking do is practice, practice, for almost a year now. When are we gonna actually *do* something?"

Dylan looks over at me then. I keep my eyes on the floor. I am not sure if I can keep up with his pace, with his dream of some day making a record. I don't even know where I'll be living in the next year or two. I just can't commit. I need to make money like anybody else, and modeling takes precedence over music at the moment. Does he understand that? I move around the store, shuffling through songbooks and keeping my distance from them. This isn't my argument.

"*I'm* the one writing all the songs. *I'm* the one trying to pull this all together. A quarter of the time I don't even see *you* at practice." Dylan is almost raising his voice, but he knows he's hit a sore spot. John has become unreliable when it comes to the band. I know he doesn't want to scare him any further away.

"Well, I don't know why you just don't get your dad to buy you that thing." John shrugs his shoulders and shoves his hands into his pockets.

"You know damn well I want nothing to do with his money." Dylan places his scarlet treasure back in its place, checking the price tag one more time.

"That's why you live in his apartment and let him pay for NYU?" John has a point. I wait for the response to this one with a listening ear.

"I don't see your ass moving out."

Good come back. I am really the only mature one in the bunch. You grow up real fast when at eighteen your parents can't afford you anymore.

"Whatever." John shrugs his shoulders again. "Bet the Dead never decided when they were ready. They just played and people dug it."

"We're not the Dead."

"Yeah, like I think we really are. Jesus Christ, Dylan, you just don't get it. We're always waiting for you, waiting for your songs, waiting for your changes, waiting for you to tell us when to breathe. Some of us are getting bored with it, that's all. I don't know. Maybe I don't even want to hang out in New York much longer. It stinks here."

"Really. Where do you think you're going to go?"

I step in closer.

"I don't know. California." John stares sheepishly at the floor.

"Oh, you're going to California now. Thanks for telling me."

"Whatever."

"Listen to yourself, John. You're acting like a spoiled kid. You and I both know this shit takes time."

"Maybe I feel I'm wasting my time."

"Well, if that's really the case, no one's stopping you." Dylan walks out of the music store to punctuate his statement. John and I follow.

We are all realizing something. It stirs our souls. The choices we make now will affect the rest of our lives. Where we live and what we do is starting to mean something serious. I feel it. New York isn't anywhere I want to live for long either. And God knows modeling isn't necessarily my first career choice. I watch Dylan push the glass doors in front of him in earnest. We are attracted to him because he seems to want something specific and he works for it.

Out in the cool, afternoon air each one of us stands looking in a different direction trying to figure out how to get back to the car.

12

WHEEL TURNING

"It's this way." Dylan looks irritated as we step toward him and begin walking back to the car. I close my eyes for two seconds, then three as I walk. Fatigue doesn't even come close to describing my energy level. I am wiped out. I trip over a crack in the sidewalk and my nerves pulse through my body, waking me up.

"You okay?" He looks back at me. I am steps behind. His stride is too long for me at the moment. John is behind me.

"Fine."

"Sure?" He lets me catch up. All I can think of is bed.

"Yeah." Then I give him a look and a nod, signaling John's evident distress. His saunter has slowed to a stroll, and he is at least a half a block behind. Dylan raises his eyebrows in mock defeat.

"He's going to California."

"Maybe you should talk to him anyway."

"Why should I?" He pauses to think about this. "Wait here, okay?" He kisses me on the lips and I kiss him back. It is a soft kiss, not too wet and not too dry. My body gravitates towards him. There is evident lust in my bones.

"Go." And I stand in a sliver of sun that falls in between two tall buildings as he retraces his steps back to his friend in an attempt to make amends. I pull my jacket around me and try to keep my eyes open as I watch them. A song my mother used to play on Saturday mornings while we cleaned suddenly pops into my head. The worn album cover appealed to me; blue jeans and bare feet sitting by the window with a cat. My mother sang the songs with as much energy as Carol King while she folded the laundry, swaying her hips and head back and forth to the beat. "I feel the earth move under my feet, I feel the sky come tumblin' down…" I can feel the earth moving like a big wheel turning. Things are happening, choices are being made, choices will be made. Life is beginning to roll, to rock and roll straight into the future. I stand there sleepily wondering if I am ready for it.

"Boo!"

"Ah! You scared me!" I about jump out of my own skin. "Jesus, Dylan. Hey John." I can tell by their relaxed faces that things are basically back to normal.

"So. Let's go, huh?"

"I almost fell asleep standing up."

"We gotta get you home." Home. Is that the place with Michael's models and Michael's furniture? I need to get my own place, I think. Yeah right, I answer myself.

"What are you guys gonna do?"

"I don't know. I guess John's gonna stay the night. You'll be at practice tomorrow, right?" The sky comes tumblin' down. I'll have to deal with Louise in the morning, get my appointments, make it to practice by four. Time to make everybody else happy again. Mini vacation is over.

"Yeah, I'll be there. John?"

"I'll be there." We walk into the dropping temperatures, into the wind as our hair flies in crazy circles around our heads. I pull mine down and hold it to the side with one hand. Time to pull a brush through this mop.

"The trip was good. Thanks, you guys." Over the hood of the car I give them both a friendly nod as we all get in. They are my pals and together we survived psychedelics. All of life will be richer to me because of the altered state I've experienced. There are dimensions to be discovered I am now realizing. This isn't just a two-way highway anymore. There is more to life than black or white, good or bad, right or wrong. There is a tapestry of beautiful and amazing colors.

"Any time." John seems pleased. Dylan pulls out of the coveted spot as another car swoops in.

"What time is it?" I haven't had a watch on my wrist since Friday.

"Nearly seven."

"Man."

"I know. It's been a long day, a long night and day, a long day's night."

"You're gettin' goofy, Dyl." I look over at him.

"I know."

The familiar night doorman stands at his post as I exit the orange Subaru to say goodbye.

"I'll see you guys tomorrow." Dylan hugs me close, cheek to cheek, chest to chest, hip to hip. "I love you."

"Love you, too."

"Call me later, okay?"

Does he know what he's done to me? Has he any idea at all?

"I will." John moves into the passenger's seat and they wave as Dylan does an illegal U-turn to face east. I watch as he turns right at the park. The doorman opens the door, beckoning me to face my new reality. I nod politely, enter the double glass doors, and head for the elevator.

Inside the apartment I hear the television from Michael's room, then talking.

"Michael."

"Rachel." He smiles from his relaxed position on the bed, shoes off, pants on, shirt unbuttoned four buttons, arm encircling the silicone waif. That is so mean. I can't help it. "Where've you been, baby? Louise said you left a message at the agency, but that was it."

"Staten Island, with friends."

"You look beat." He crosses his eyebrows and wrinkles his

forehead, but smiles with his deep, dark eyes. "Come here." He pats the broad, open area on the opposite side of Yvonne. It looks inviting. They aren't even taking up half of the king size bed.

"What are you guys watching?" I step nearer, glancing quickly at Yvonne. She is snuggled underneath the covers, her head nestled near his hairy chest.

"Only the greatest movie ever made." His left hand holds the remote reassuringly.

"And...?" I turn to face the screen remembering something he'd said months before about his favorite movie. A young Al Pacino and Diane Keaton sit at a round table together. "*The Godfather*?"

"You know it. Come, have a sit."

I want food. I want a shower. I want to wait for Dylan's call in the other room, but I grant his request anyway.

"I haven't seen you in a while." I drop my backpack and take off my jacket.

"Miss me?" Is Yvonne even alive on the other side of the bed?

"Of course." It is true. I always miss him when he is gone. He fluffs the pillow, continuing his invitation. I remove my boots and slouch into the pillow on the bed, closing my eyes for a second.

"Tired?"

"Very."

"You should get some rest." Always looking after my physical welfare.

"I know."

"How's work?"

"I don't know. Fine." I know I have a shoot with *Self* magazine on Thursday, but it is only for a half day.

"You do those test shots we talked about?"

"Yeah. Christian and I shot a couple rolls on the fourteenth floor. Black and white." Christian is one of the agency photographers from Paris. He is a little man who doesn't say much. Sometimes he helps Louise answer phones.

"How does it look up there?"

"Empty." The agency is moving upstairs in the next couple weeks, up four floors. Until then we have both spaces at our disposal.

"It'll be a good move. More room."

"Yeah." And then we pause in our conversation to watch the Godfather himself, Marlon Brando.

"He's the man."

"Yeah." It is all I can muster. My heavy head falls to the side and I doze, while vengeful shots ring through the room.

When the phone rings I jump up. "I got it."

"Pretty confident you've turned out to be."

"Hello?"

It isn't Dylan.

"It's for you." I hand the receiver to Michael.

"Who is it?" He smiles.

"Alex." I gather my things and shut the door behind me.

13

MOVING FORWARD

At exactly 6:30 my eyes pop open. I am the kind of person who doesn't need an alarm. All I have to do is think about the time I want to wake up before I go to sleep and it happens. It makes me believe in a man's spiritual and individual entity. And woman's. It's as if my spirit is saying, Okay body, time to get up.

I glance around the room at the two empty beds and a mess I'd wanted to pick up the night before but didn't have the energy for. It isn't my mess, of course, but I have to look at it. I move groggily over and pick up some paper plates and torn magazines, stuffing them into the tiny bedroom waste basket, which is already full. I make a mental note to empty it. I make another mental note to grab a giant trash bag and bring it into the room instead. I can't believe I am playing maid to this girl.

I walk into the adjoining bathroom, which is the size of a closet, and sit down to pee. I can reach the sink from where I sit. I pull up my jeans, trying to figure out how strange I am for wearing them to bed. I know it is some kind of sign. Insecurity. Something left over from the nights of trepidation I'd experienced as a child. Maybe I thought I was going to go somewhere when I heard their voices rising higher and higher, waking me up from my first sound sleep of the night. I wonder if they knew I could hear them, if they cared about waking us up at night. And then I'd hear the chasing around the house, the thud, the angry cries. In my room, in the dark, without waking up my brothers, I'd step quietly over their Tonka trucks and Tinker Toys, over to my dresser. While I cringed inside at my mother's defeated screams I would take off my pajamas and put on new underwear and my favorite jeans. In the pale moonlight I could see my young reflection in the mirror above my dresser. A clean tee shirt, a brush through my hair. I'd be ready if I had to go, if I could go. All I'd need…. I looked around the room and found the sleeping faces of my brothers. I couldn't leave without them. But I'd be ready just in case.

I look in the mirror above the sink. I had left. I'd left all of them.

Alex. I remember now. My dream had been about Alex. How? I don't even know what he looks like. But it had been him. He had chased me all the way through my last dream of the night.

I pull back my mess of hair into a loose ponytail, splash some water on my face, dab a little Vaseline on my lips, and make my bed. 6:45. I have fifteen minutes to dress and confront Michael with what I had been putting off for too long. It has been weeks, but I'd known about it even longer, since Susan. The guilt of not dealing with this is weighing me down. And now it is affecting my dreams.

In my cut-off sweats and old Grateful Dead tee shirt of Dylan's, I make my way into the kitchen, past the sleeping Yvonne, with my socks, shoes, and walkman in my hands. Michael is up every weekday morning at 6:00 am no matter when he goes to bed. There is something a little comforting with such regularity. I'd been waiting for the inevitable end of his little affair with the French lingerie queen, but my anticipation has been in vain. I suppose my irritation with Yvonne stems partly from a vague jealousy. I feel Michael deserves more for himself. I suppose I consider myself more. I have a little crush on him, and I know it. I will never do anything about it, but that doesn't prevent the knowing.

"Morning." I say it quietly as I sit down and gently drop my shoes and socks to the kitchen floor. I set my walkman on the table and bend down to put my socks on in the most model-like fashion I can muster in the early morning light. The short, stiff hairs that protrude from my shins and calves ruin this experience for me, however. He hasn't even looked up yet from his ritual corn muffin, steaming coffee, and morning paper. I wonder if he knows this is a turn-on, the way he ignores people, the way he pretends to be engrossed in the tiny black and white print that communicates only what was, never what can be. I am much more interested in the latter.

"Morning, Rachel." Ah. He does know I am here. Neither of us are morning people, but we pretend to be because it is one of those keys to success. Early to bed and early to rise makes a person healthy, wealthy, and wise? Well, we can all hope. Each of us is determined, I suppose, to become very good at what we do—become someone strong, independent of others, a leader. I know I have it in me to make something out of myself, and he agrees. Where we conflict is what this is. He insists I am meant to be a great model, a super model perhaps, as long as I follow his advice and buy some boobs. He says he'll front me the money for this. I tell him that is very sweet, but quite unnecessary as I will never pay someone to rip open layers of my skin in order to shove man-made materials into my womanly flesh. Never. The idea sounds absolutely preposterous. He says he is just doing his job. I say I know he is. And it is moments like this when we have the most respect for one another.

I stand up. Both shoes are on. I stretch my leg muscles, touching the tips of my three longest fingers to the kitchen floor. Bingo. He looks up.

"Michael? You mind if I talk to you for a minute?" Spoken in a half whisper with a peer into the bedroom to check on sleeping beauty. This arouses his interest. I knew it would.

"Of course. What's up?" I sit back down.

"Well, it's about Alex. I know you guys are friends and everything." I am stalling, fidgeting with my walkman. I have no idea what I am trying to say. Yes I do.

"Rachel. Pumpkin. Spit it out already." He turns a page in his newspaper, keeping an eye on my confidence problem.

"You ever hear of Alex, well... have you ever known Alex to treat the models badly, you know, in a sexual way?" I am falling all over myself.

"You're talking about our Alex, in Paris." He calmly sips at his coffee.

"Yes."

"And you want to know if he's ever done what?" He squints his eyes as he sips, holding the cup too daintily for a man. Why is he doing this to me? Didn't he hear the first time? Out with it.

"I have reason to believe he's been raping some of the models who stay with him."

"And who, my precious, has he raped now?" He is saying, *Let me get this straight. You are going to accuse my friend, a fellow modeling agent, a man I've sent dozens and dozens of girls to? And you have the balls to bring up the "R" word?* That's what he is saying to me with his eyes, which never leave my own.

"It's not really my business to say." I had promised.

"All right." So calm. "Let's just say for argument's sake that Yvonne in there goes home to the south of France and tells her daddy that I raped her. Would she be telling the truth?"

"Of course not." My Michael, the man I live with? Never.

"No, of course not. I'm not a rapist, and neither is Alex. However, our similar occupation as agents makes us ideal targets for this sort of thing, you see." Oh, yes. It's all so crystal clear now. "You know it's not always the guy who makes the first move, Rachel, I don't care what kind of age difference we're talking about." I knew it'd been Yvonne who came on to him. This was obvious to everyone. Could it be, then, that they did the same with Alex?

"I know." His nose is back into his paper, and that was that. I knew it wouldn't be easy to talk to him about this, and it wasn't. And no progress had been made. I stand up again and put my headphones on.

"A man doesn't stay in the same business for thirty years without learning a thing or two. Give Alex a little credit, Rachel. He's very much looking forward to meeting you. I've told him fabulous things about you. Don't let me down, now." I am standing at the front door and can only see his back. This isn't an invitation for more conversation. It is getting the last word in. It is reminding me of what lies ahead. Paris. And there is no turning back. I have to go, to move forward in my career.

I close the door and bolt down three flights of stairs as fast as I can, to warm up my leg muscles, to prove that I am strong and can take anything. Only wimps use the elevator when it is time to exercise. I press "play" on my walkman and am taken into the loud sounds of "Brown Sugar" by The Rolling Stones. Mick Jagger's screaming voice pounds through my head and pulsates through my body, bringing me down the stairs and through the glass doors and out into the free world. I walk to the park then and stretch in the early morning sun. It is Michael's cassette. He lent it to me, expressing his deep devotion to the Stones. I do trust him, and I want to believe him.

I run around Sheep Meadow without knowing I am running. It is easy to do when many thoughts skip and prance through my brain without even enough time to acknowledge each and every one, much less solve all the problems and questions which arise as I think about them. Dylan, the band, Paris, Michael, Yvonne, Susan, Alex, modeling, singing in the band, Dylan. Each connects to the other, and I know there is no possible way I'll be able to handle it all. At least not now. Maybe in time. Maybe. For now, though, I make a decision to forget about looking for my real mom and dad. I check it off my mental list of what needs to be done. It is a stupid wish. I can see that now. I mean, they gave me up. They'd made the choice about me long ago, or at least my mother did. Besides, how in God's name would I ever find either of them anyway? I'd seen enough *Unsolved Mystery* episodes to know that most of the cases stay unsolved. Solved are the precious few who are videotaped as updated and aired in an effort to pull on our heartstrings even though the people are all old and overweight and can barely get their grateful arms around one another.

I have no need for my adopted family. I have no need for a biological one either. "You Gotta Move" pulls me around another two laps as I begin to perspire from every pore in my arms and legs and face. I can taste the salty sweat on my upper lip as I blink away the drops that fall from my forehead. I will just keep running. As long as I run forward, the past will stay behind me.

14

STANDING STILL

"You okay?"

"Why do you always ask me that?"

"I don't know. The way your face looks, I guess. I wanna make sure you're okay."

"I'm fine."

"Just asking."

"You don't need to ask."

"Whatever." I rise from our sexual, summer slumber party on the floor in the living room to take our glasses to the sink and to bring him another soda. Maybe it is the heat, or maybe it is the fact that I am leaving in two weeks. We are at each other's throats. But only after the sex. Before the sex it's as if we've never been together before, two innocent kids playing music and watching television. The seduction is brand new each and every time. His voice is kind and cautious. Mine is uninterested and curious at the same time— uninterested in his advances, curious about who's singing this certain song, as if I am playing final Jeopardy. He slithers up next to me, whispers the answer in my ear, and kisses the inside of my arm. My body tingles up and down and I move away. Come get me. If you love me, you'll chase me, even as a snake upon the floor. His tongue in my ear. My leg over his, and then there's no going back. Clothes are off and the deed is done. Conquered. No need for further niceties. It's like walking to the store to get a loaf of bread. Once the bread is bought, why walk to the store again? Not until more bread is needed, certainly. Well, it's not as cut and dried as all that, I suppose, but sometimes and most recently it seems that way.

"Grab me that bag of chips, will you?" Smoke, sex, eat, sleep. The cycle of life. It is snack time.

"Sour cream and onion?"

"Yeah." I look at the fat content. 17%. Settling back into the pillows and blankets I listen to him chomp away as I glance at the side of his tanned and rosy face. I am going to miss that face. My heart gives a leap. With his free hand, he flips from one movie to the next, from HBO to Cinemax to Showtime until we'd gotten a small taste of everything that is being offered at the moment. We've seen them all, or have decided at some point they aren't worth viewing. It seems that with the advent of video rentals, movies have simply become a line of production like anything else. Quantity is overshadowing quality. Movies are being made at a quicker rate than ever, and it is painstakingly evident with the many movie channels offered that show them over and over again until we know them all by heart. It is an embarrassing element of our current generation. We scan the video store shelves whispering to ourselves, Seen it, seen it, until we come upon some new release that seems inviting because of the title and all the many thumbs up and rows of stars. We take it home, press fast forward through all the previews, hit play, and wonder where the hell the movie is going until the end when we look at our fellow couch potato confused as we hit rewind to be kind. Back and forth to the video store or surfing the channels in search, in search for the ultimate viewing experience. We are hunters once again, motionless hunters in search for the something that brings us sustenance and purpose and answer. Is it to be found on the screen?

"What d'ya wanna watch?" His greasy fingers hold the bag up to me.

"No thanks."

"Wanna take a walk?"

I am in a stoned mode, not wanting to move, but I visualize us outside and the picture seems more inviting than the one we are in.

"Sure." I stand up and stand still while he puts the chips back in the cupboard and washes his hands.

"Got your shoes?"

"They're at the door." We both have Birkenstocks now, dark brown with two broad straps over the top and one around the ankle. They'd cost me $85.00, but they are the most comfortable shoes I've ever owned. I slide my feet into these earthy shoes and open the door, allowing him to follow and lock up on his own.

The streets are surrounded in a welcome and humid darkness. The day had been one of intense heat that baked into every living and non-living thing in the city. It scorched the skin and fried the sidewalks and burned the trees and grass.

"Hey, hold this. I forgot something." He hands me his cold can of Fresca and dashes back in the house. I take a tiny sip. Zing.

"Thanks." He retrieves the soda from me and we proceed to walk down the street as an old married couple might, hand in hand, keeping with the rhythm of life as we stroll together. Walks are made to enjoy the present moment, the present partner, but my brain darts back a year ago when we first met and then forward into the future of foreign tomorrows. It's amazingly difficult to be still with my thoughts.

"The band is finally sounding good. Too bad it won't be able to stay that way. Guess I'll have to look for another female voice." Jab. Into my heart. Doesn't he realize this is all hard enough?

"I'll be back." Weak response. Very weak. We both know the duration of time we will spend apart is an unknown factor in the equation of this relation. We turn the corner at the end of the block and are temporarily distracted by the onset of whizzing traffic.

"Want a sip?"

"No. Thanks." Paris seems so far away, and although an intriguing-sounding city for sure, I have no real keen desire to go there. I will have to start all over again, with nothing and no one. I had finally come to some sense of comfort in New York. "Dyl?"

"Yeah?"

"I won't be gone long. Really." I so want to believe this, to feel as if I have control over time and destination. I know no model really does, at least not in my situation. You go where your agents guide you, where there is work, where you can be "new." I am no longer "new" in New York. I need to leave and come back again to be new. I am afraid to ask Michael how long this might be. I can handle a month. Maybe two.

"Thing is, we can't wait on you, Rache. The band is ready now to…"

"Wait on me? I'm not asking you to wait on me." I stop in my steps and stare at the back of him until he turns around. The tension is thick in the air. I am having trouble breathing. Pot always makes me a little stuffy.

"Don't get pissed. I've just got to make some decisions. We need to go ahead with this thing before I start losing everybody." I know he is referring to John as much as to me.

"You're not losing me." In a sense, he is.

"Yes I am."

"How do you figure?"

"Rachel, you're a model, not a musician." Deep cut.

"What do you know?" I start to walk ahead again, leaving him behind. Thing is, I don't feel that talented in either arena. I can do each well enough, I suppose, but I don't see either as a lifelong career. The practicality of each eludes me.

We round another corner as he catches up to me. I turn to him under a streetlight and watch as he pinches a sizeable roach from his front shirt pocket and turns his back to the wind to light it.

I could have stood on higher ground and preached against his obvious need to patch up every awkward circumstance with some artificial method of relaxation, but I can't find the energy. I take a hit when offered to me and we pass it back and forth as we make our way down the dark street in search of answers neither of us can word the questions to.

I take another hit in silence and wonder quietly, as a numbing sensation fills my lungs and travels down to my sandals, what it is users of drugs are looking for by consistently getting high all the time. Is it purely escape from current circumstance, a momentary diversion from daily duties? Is it more than this? Can it be more than this? Can it be these people are seeking, are seekers just as any straight person is, searching for beauty and for truth and for that which is good and enjoyable? For certain. I glance at Dylan and he at me, the two of us knowing that for this moment silence is key.

Problem is, do drugs ever bring the ultimate high, the ultimate answer, the ultimate truth or beauty, or is the experience of the drug user a simplistic façade of these things so that the user will never, in actuality, be able to perceive the ultimate awareness of anything, as it will always be in a shadow or cloud of smoke? If the drug experience suffices, is there ever a reason to search further? Is there anything further? I want to ask Dylan these questions, but I am too stoned to formulate the words in my mouth. It is dry like cotton. Cotton mouth. I don't want to say I have cotton mouth, though. It makes me sound too much like a pot smoker.

"Want a sip?" He offers me his Fresca with red, watery eyes and a smile I know I am going to have a difficult time living without.

"Sure." Standing still and stoned on a side street on the East Side of Manhattan I drink down the last of a warming soda and swear to myself that nothing has ever tasted so good in all my life.

15

FALLING

We are going together even though I am not in the mood for it. My eyes are still puffy from the night before. The Visine has taken the red out, but the pain remains.

"Carl Platt."

"Dis is his name or ze studio?"

"Both."

"Vhere?"

"East Twentieth, please." I lean back into my seat. I can't believe Michael has me taking a taxi. I know it is because Yvonne is going, too. This annoys me even more. I am babysitting. Even getting paid to baby-sit. He'd handed me a twenty for the ride with that look in his eyes. I knew it wouldn't cost that much. He never makes me return the change. It is his way of helping me along a little without being obvious about it. Still, I am not in the mood for her sniveling French accent. Ever since she started her "thing" with Michael, she had been acting the princess. Her accent becomes heavier around him, and she appears lighter, if this is possible. I am not feeling interested in any of it.

"Yes, it's a test. Didn't Michael mention that?" She sits to my right and I stare straight ahead as I talk, as if the driver won't be able to get there unless I am watching.

169

"Vell, I don't know, Rachel. He say something last night." I feel hollow inside. I have nothing to give, especially to her, not to mention the camera. "Ze test. Ah, photo for no money, right?"

"Yes, Yvonne. You pose. You get pictures. Carl gets pictures. No exchange of money. Everybody's happy."

"Iz zhere something wrong, Rachel?" Her delightful, little wispy voice irritates me like the scraping of fingernails on what? Freddy Krueger in his striped sweater and scarred and laughing face come to mind. I glance her way. There are a million ways to answer her stupid, superficial, airy, insignificant question. All I know is that while I am being shipped off to France, she gets to stay in New York and snuggle in the sheets with her lover-boy while playing model for as long as she wants.

"Everything is fine." The night before had been a scene from a tragic romance novel. Whoever said that parting was such sweet sorrow only got half of it right.

"Iz my hair good, you sink?"

Shut up!

"It's fine."

"You sure now? Iz okay for dis?"

"Well, they'll probably have a stylist there to help hide the bleached out parts." I take advantage of the fact that foreigners rarely seem to sense sarcasm.

"Bleached out parts?"

"And your ends are splitting." This is fun. She pulls her bits of blonde straw in front of her face and scowls a waif-like frown.

"My ends?"

Why am I getting myself into this? Can't she read body language like everyone else in the universe?

"Well, you could use a trim." I fold my arms in front of me and gaze out at the traffic and the numbers clicking, showing us our fare.

"Maybe zhey cut it zhere?" So hopeful. So vulnerable. So pathetic.

"Maybe." It is what I said when he asked if I'd be back for the shows, for the Dead. How could I know or plan or be in charge of my own life? We were in his room in each other's arms in emotional limbo. The pain in my chest cut deeply with every soft kiss and tears fell silently from the outside corners of my eyes as he hovered over me with his gorgeous, black curls, which fell amusingly around his face. This is all I want. Who needs a career with this type of comfort and security? To freeze the moment forever, to hold him like that and feel his young body cover mine. It is all I want, and I am leaving him.

Then later, the phone call from John. They were making plans for the band.

"That was John."

"I know." I blow softly at a candle that is dripping wax onto his bedside table. It stays lit. I blow at it again.

"We need someone to take your place."

"I know." I stare at the candle, slowly losing the warmth.

"If you could just tell me how long you'll be gone…"

"I already told you I don't know." Irritation and my mother's angry tone creeps up through my vocal cords and resonates sincere displeasure with my entire situation. If I don't go to Paris, I don't stay in modeling. If I don't stay in modeling, I don't pay the rent. If I don't pay the rent, I don't….

"Rachel."

"What?"

"I love you." I look at his bare chest and bare feet as he sits on the golden, hardwood floor of his bedroom. His jeans fit him loosely and are faded with time. The right knee is nearly worn through. I stare at his toes.

"I love you, too." But what?

"I don't know how long I'm going to be able to live without you." So sincere, or is this secretly about sex?

"What do you mean?" Toes to eyes in a flash.

"I mean, well, do you expect me to wait for you, you know…"

No, I don't. Tell me.

"What are you saying?" He moves closer, and I cross my arms

over my chest. He quickly blows out the candle and slides one leg on each side of me as he pulls my reluctant bones close.

"I want you, Rache. I want you every day." That's nice. Kisses. My arms wrap around him and my lips fall to his skin, his chest, his neck, his shoulders. Lust is a beautiful thing.

"You can't have me every day." Reality. It is so wicked.

"I know."

We go back and forth for hours like this until his father comes home. Then we take it outside into the streets of noise and rage and we make our own noise.

"So, what are you saying, that you can't last, that you're going to have to screw other girls while I'm away? Is that it?" Shouting the word "screw" like that makes me feel so evil. I stand with my hands buried in my front jeans pockets, my upper body leans toward him, enticing him to take me on, to go a round or two with me. The street light has him in the spotlight. I can see him. I am the interrogator.

"Rachel." With his head back and forth slowly as if I have gone over the line.

"Well, tell me now because I don't need the surprise later. If this is what it's all about with you, then I don't want it." I don't. I actually mean this. Maybe this is what I need to get myself out of New York. Maybe I've been a fool all along, just like every other naïve girl who gives in to sex thinking it's love only to find out it is just sex.

"I'm just trying to be realistic about this."

Realistic? The lump in my throat grows two sizes, and I have to force the tears from an unknown source or I think I am going to burst open at the seams with emotion.

"Fuck realistic. I thought we were in love." That word sure does come in handy when needed. Get back under the light. I'm not through with you yet.

"We are, Rachel. We are."

Try harder, you bastard. This I decide to keep inside my head because his embrace has broken me, and we stand together in the dark as I sob and wipe my nose on the sleeve of his tee-shirt. Take that, and yet I need him to hold me. Who else is going to do it?

"41 East Twentieth. To your right." The driver points. I look at the fare. $13.75. I give him the twenty and shut the door. Sometimes squabbling about cash seems so petty. I lead Yvonne up the stairs and we walk in without talking. Maybe she's finally catching on. In the elevator I press "B" for basement and we fall to the bottom of the building in continued silence. It is Michael's idea that I do one last test before my European excursion. He wants to see something a little more dramatic from me—off-the-wall, black and white, slut-like, leggy, an attempt at cleavage, that sort of thing. I am not in the mood and yet here I am.

"Rachel, Yvonne, I assume?" He is a short fellow with round, wire-rim glasses and a balding head. "Carl Platt." And he holds out his hand. Yvonne beats me to it, which makes me feel even more like a snob.

"You two are gorgeous. Come on in."

"Thank you." I really am polite. It's just that I'm sad today.

"Rachel, I hear you're off to Paris in a couple days?" This as he leads us into his studio, his bald head bobbing back and forth to see where he is going and to make sure we stay with him. Don't remind me, please.

"Yes. Thursday, I guess."

"That must be exciting." This guy is a geek.

"Yes." It is the shallowest "yes" I have ever uttered, and I hope he heard me just enough to satisfy a conversationalist's desire for a response. I am not up for much more of this "let's get to know one another chit chat to ease the tension before the shoot" crap.

"Well, I should be able to get the proofs to the agency by Tuesday." The effort on his part to remain congenial is impressive for New York. I'm sure if I play the bitch much longer he will lose his energy for me.

"Thank you. That is really decent of you." There.

His basement studio looks like a million others I have been in. Cold, gray, cement walls, hard floors, high ceilings, an assorted supply of backdrops, both cloth and paper, a small vanity to the side with bright lights all around the mirrors, a stylist named Tracy who has done one too many things to her hair, and a little kitchenette around the corner with coffee available at all hours. Too bad I don't drink it; I could have used some. Oh, and the music. Always the music in one form or another. Without music there aren't any pictures.

"Tracy, will you get Yvonne ready first?" This is a compliment to me. He wants to get her out of the way. Maybe I can get along with this guy.

Carl and Tracy fuss over her hair for a second or two while I pluck through his portfolio. It is the polite thing to do, after all. I point here and there at this and that, commenting on what I think is interesting to feed his ego just a little. No harm done. Might as well make this as pleasant as possible. I enjoy sitting around and waiting my turn. I don't have to be the silent body and face just yet. I can be a personality for a spell. I close his black book and begin fingering through the numerous CD's, which are scattered on and around several orange milk crates that hold a gigantic boom box.

"Would you like to hear something?" He walks back from where Tracy is twisting Yvonne's hair into tight little fans that stick out all over her head. She looks ridiculous. I smile.

"Whenever this is over." It is some non-ending jazz piece that was going nowhere and affecting me in no specific way.

"No. Go ahead." He hits stop as he bends down over me and then eject, as if I can't figure this out for myself. I am on the floor with no place to go and am forced into sniffing his cologne. He smells too fancy for a New York photographer. "Play whatever you like."

"Thanks." Now a photo shoot isn't the type of place for the Grateful Dead or Cat Stevens, and I am almost pleased when I don't find any of Dylan's music right off or I'd be tempted to play it, thus inviting conversation that will get too personal. Music is becoming more to me than it ever was in the past. I am forming a relationship with it and with the artists, if only from afar. I am interested in their lives and their pasts and what the words and stories really mean. Music is nearly a religious experience for Dylan, and I am catching his fever. My heart sinks, and I have to press the pause button in my thoughts to bypass allowing a new lump in my throat to graduate into tears.

No, for photo shoots the music needs to be either mindless and meandering, like his jazz, or empowering and energetic, which is why, unbeknownst to Dylan, I have taken a certain keen liking to a little, purple man-child called Prince. This music from a Minnesota-born, guitar-jamming, hip-thrusting, ego-driven, androgynous creature is enticingly sexual, nearly forbidding, and completely shunned by Dylan. Men have a difficult time understanding someone like Prince, I suppose. Of course male photographers are a species of their own. They have to be. I press play and immediately start bopping from side to side to "Sign of the Times," to his voice, the wicked beat, to the music that is not Dylan's. Independence. I can do this. I've fallen hard for Dylan, but my search is not over for who I am going to be. I have to be more than just his sidekick girlfriend and number one fan of the band.

Carl walks toward me as Yvonne receives final touches on the set. He holds out a black leather jacket and some large, silver jewelry, a low-cut black top, and an old pair of ripped-up jeans that look like they just might fit. Bring it on. No words needed. Let the music speak. On with this thing. Come on, Tracy. Lights, camera.

Action prevents the thoughts from coming. If I can just keep active I can keep my heart hidden from connecting with the thoughts in my head. Let the forbidden music drench me in the new phase of my future.

"Keep her hair straight and slick, okay?" Carl calls over to Tracy as he puts the light meter to the side of Yvonne's face. Our French baby wears a short skirt and pink, cropped tee-shirt, which reveals her flat belly. Her breasts perk up as her shoulders pull back. She looks almost pleased with herself.

"Sure. Sit here, okay honey?"

"Okay." Make me up and don't bring me down. Remind me of nothing but the present moment, and I'll perform for the pictures.

And I do. And the shoot goes on for six rolls of film after Yvonne takes the subway home to meet Michael for a dinner date. I am sure the sun sets outside while we keep the music on and take the clothes on and off and attempt to make the girl next door into the girl the boyfriend of the girl next door will want to cheat on with. I go along with all of it, intrigued by my own detachment. My tears from the night before have built an invisible, immovable mask between myself and my reality, and it helps immensely in becoming the image I am expected to portray. I even pretend to have cleavage.

On the ride home, I sink my rounded back into the rounded, plastic seat and stare at the despair on the faces engaged in attempting not to be engaged in anyone else around them. Stone cold are the stares at the floor or the tiny print in front of their eyes. Better stone than clay, for clay is more easily destroyed, picked apart, manipulated. New York is full of cement and tough, selfish, smart people; people who aren't fooled by the soft touch of love or the forecast of sunshine. They know, the somber citizens of the city; they know that all there is, is me, when it comes down to it.

I watch them all as they board and exit the train. They keep moving out of the fear of ending up like the lonelier, other half of the city who spend their days and nights looking up at the rest, begging for money inside their cardboard boxes and behind their cardboard signs. The needy and the homeless seem to have given up the race to find something worthwhile after they found that there was nothing to find. Perhaps. Perhaps they are smarter than the materially gifted. When one has what one needs, the race becomes tougher, lonelier. The search and race continue, but the prize at the end keeps moving further and further away because there is no compensation called complete contentment in the outside world. There is only a wanting forever. Maybe the people in the street have this figured out and have given up on purpose, concentrating solely on acquiring just the basic of necessities for mere survival, laughing quietly at all the rest as they hurry by, dropping quarters and trying not to look.

I observe the women with hurried and worried expressions as their nylons rub together between their thighs. They glance at their pretty watches and wonder if there is enough time for the gym before the kids have to be picked up from daycare. There isn't. There is rarely any time for anything anymore. But the bums in the street can sit in the park in the sunshine or take a walk for hours if they feel like it.

I watch them as they study the lines and veins in their hands, as they contemplate their age and the stage they're at in life compared to the woman in the seat across the aisle. They fidget with their wedding rings or with a ring that replaces the one they want or no longer want. And they fear with every bone in their body that he's cheating on them with another and that he's been lying about it all along.

I notice all these women and the men who appear superior to those who lie beneath their feet. At least there's scum down low to give definition to those who rise above.

I notice them all, the whole cycle of rich and poor, of determined faces and desperate faces, of the chaos and confusion of a city that moves too fast, too late, and too competitively for anyone to find any inner peace anywhere. I see it all, but I don't see the crack in the sidewalk that catches the heel of my shoe and pulls me down to the hard cement in one agonizing and embarrassing New York second. I fall, and as I am falling, I wonder quickly where I really fit in. I am numb, mute, alone, and empty. Where dignity and purpose have been, there is instantly nothing and it scares me how quickly this comes. At least fifteen people pass me in the darkening, summer evening as I peer at my bleeding elbow with the help of passing headlights. Fifteen people walk swiftly by my place on the cold, hard cement, and not one looks down to see me.

Until now I have certainly considered myself a well-dressed, hurried person with a mission, as those above me were. But as I gather my backpack nearer to me and work my arm back and forth, testing its strength, I have to contemplate myself as the wanderer, quietly and quite desperately at times searching for food and shelter, looking up at all the rest, wondering where they are going and how long it will take them to get there and when they will finally decide it isn't worth it.

Join me on the cement. Take off your heels and ties and stop for a moment, won't you? Is it worth it? Will you tell me? Should I begin the race of the adult world in the world of adults and cash flow and competition and calendars? Should I use sun screen and eat green vegetables and go to the gynecologist? Is it worth it? Someone please come down here and tell me. Will I feel this alone all the time? Will there ever be an end to it and a beginning of happy? Can't you see I have fallen?

16

FLYING

"Put your tables in their upright positions. Secure any loose, carry-on baggage in the compartments above or under the seat in front of you. The pilot has turned on the 'no smoking' light. We will be taking off momentarily." I have been sitting on the plane momentarily for going on forty-five minutes. In my impatience, I have almost decided to get up and try running off the plane, back into the airport, and back into his arms—which are the only security I am aware of on the entire planet.

But then we start rolling slowly down the runway in the hot and muggy evening. Rolling now into my future. The next soil I will step on will be foreign. The language where I am destined is unknown to me. I could have shed tears sitting there in my three-seat row by myself. If I wanted to, I could have.

"And what would you like to drink?" She stares down at me, me with my baggage beneath my feet and my tray table down now. I am her customer, her patient, perhaps even her irritation. I have seconds to make up my mind and tell her what I want to drink. Why is it so difficult to tell someone what I want? I'd rather just grab the can of apple juice off the cart myself. Why should she go through the action of serving me? I am capable. I can get it myself.

"Here you are." A plastic see-through cup with six cubes of

airplane ice and a dribble of apple juice all on top of a square, white, airplane napkin. I don't want ice.

Several moments later my cup is empty, save the ice and the napkin I stuffed into it. I want it in the garbage now. I don't want to stare at it, at the napkin as it soaks up little apple juice particles and grows soggy with the melting ice. I sit there, the prisoner of the airplane. I have no say up here in the sky. It will take her forever now to make her way down the aisle and then come back with her small, white garbage bag to collect our waste.

I try figuring out how long it will be until I arrive in Paris, and what time it will be when I get there, but the thinking of it wears me out quickly and I give up, not caring when or where I arrive.

The plane is large, decorated in the orange-reds and deep blues of other airplanes with the same company name. I sit in row 27, seat C. I lift the small shade to look out the window once again. The clouds are heavy, and it is difficult to see the ground below. Just as well.

Dylan. The thought of his name makes my stomach tighten. I am afraid to leave him. I am insecure without the knowledge that I can go to him if I need to. Our good-byes had been the last time I felt worthwhile and a part of something. I am already fading like the knees of his jeans as he stands there and presses his body against mine so that something inside me stirs, something that will not be able to express itself. Instead I am becoming numb from the inside out as the drone of the plane becomes the backdrop for the droop in my smile. It is gone. A hard and familiar lump replaces it near the back of my throat, and I fight to keep it from breaking into rough, raindrop tears.

But by the time we are over the Atlantic, I have conquered the lump and quietly accept the fact that my fate lies now in France. Careless emotion isn't very appealing, and I need to begin my preparation. In Paris I will play my part, pretending to be a model. If I play it well, the results are likely to be as pleasant, perhaps, as they are for any character in the movies. Why not? Of course I have no idea what results I am after. I glance at the shadow of my reflection in the little window as I sit in row 27, seat C. It is a face yet void of any discernable expression, a face too young to be called old and too old to be called young. I am stuck in the middle of a life, between heaven and earth, numb in a plane flying from one agent I knew to another I am trying not to think about.

I open my new Margaret Atwood book on my lowered tray table and stare down at the words. They pull me in as I have meant them to, and I finish two chapters before looking up again. When I do, I catch the stare of a man. He is no boy, this creature catching unwarranted glimpses of me. Two rows up and two seats to the right of me he holds a magazine in his left, manly hand as his prop. He knows I have seen him and is now smirking under his slick, graying hair and dark blue denim jacket, which has been left unbuttoned at the cuff. The side of his face is beautiful, shaven, rugged, smart. Instantaneously, I am shocked at my own observation and thoughts and attraction. My watch reads two and a half hours since my departure from Dylan. I begin chapter three. Halfway through it, I get out my comb and compact. A little lip gloss is quite necessary at such an altitude. My reflection in the darkened plane invites me to be what the image advertises back at me and I am once again shocked. The static electricity in my hair brings me back to my God-fearing reality, and I wish now for the melted ice. I lick my fingers and bring down the rebellious strands, patting them back into place.

A casual glance upward and in his direction reveals the stranger's sincere interest in whatever article is laid upon the page in front of him. I put my foolish, girlish items back in my backpack and begin another ridiculous wait for the return of the woman and the cart.

"What would you like to drink?" Time to drink again. Time for my feeding. I am on the prisoner's clock. Now choices. It is now time to eat and drink. Now or never. Steaming foil is set down on my tray table. I place my bookmark in the middle of chapter three and set it on the seat next to me. More ice-laden apple juice, napkins, plastic silverware. A breaded chicken breast, side salad, mashed potatoes, green beans, low-fat dressing in a packet, a toilette in a packet, and a chocolate chip cookie in a see-through plastic package. I have milk with my dinner and the entire meal ends up tasteless to me as I wipe my mouth with the rough, little napkin and try to clear the chocolate chips from my bottom molars.

The plane's rhythmic droning works my meal into the place hunger had been and I accept the food because there is no other choice. No choice, no guilt. Still, a piece of original Trident gum helps the cookie taste vanish. I am tempted to peak at myself again in my mirror while I rustle around in my things to find the gum, but I resist as the manly man in denim seems to have lost interest in me. I'd glanced over his way several times during feeding time, but he appeared to be lost in his own, little airplane world.

All of a sudden I am exhausted. Maybe it is the air so high up or the food lying so low down. I barely finish chapter three before my eyelids drop like the little shade covering the window next to me. I secure the tiny, white pillow between my head and the roaring plane, and drift fast into an odd slumber.

* * *

The pilgrimage is a secret, sacred one. I have been chosen to go, to make the journey and see the snake. I am alone on my trip. As I near my destination, many others crowd my path. I am one of many, but I talk to no one. The building we enter has many rooms, and by some natural instinct I know where to go. I know that I have earned the right to be here, and am humbled by this knowledge. I can hear the snake talking in the front of the room, and I inch my way into the crowd. It speaks of truths that begin to scare some of the closer people away. I have a chance to move closer. I want desperately to be near the snake, to hear him speak, and to understand. It is a cobra, and I think this appropriate, as the cobra seems to be the most powerful and alluring of all the snakes. Finally, it is my turn to be in front, to meet the snake. I so desire to know the truth. Does the snake see how humble I am? Does he see that I am ready to hear him speak?

* * *

"The pilot has turned on the seatbelt sign. We are experiencing mild turbulence. Please remain seated and fasten your belts until the pilot removes the seatbelt sign." My body jerks me awake and the pillow falls to my lap. I fasten the buckle on the much discussed seatbelt and reach for my left arm. It feels as if I've been stung or something. And then I remember. The snake had bit me.

I have to pee. All I want to do is get up, stretch my limbs, pee, walk around, and shake the airplane air from my brain. But the light continues to shine through the seatbelt picture above me. I won't dare get up and break the rules on the airplane. Rules and turbulence and lights shining. I sit there dispirited. I had been bitten by the snake, by the one who was to have had the truth. What does this mean? It is a pity my dream book is tucked away somewhere in a suitcase. I'd picked it up at a second-hand bookstore when Dylan and I had been traipsing around Soho on a day cool enough for hot chocolate. I'd stood there in the store and looked up teeth, remembering my dream about getting married on the beach. It said that if your teeth were falling out, you were having difficulty understanding something, that it was too hard to swallow or something. I figured everything I'd done that night had been pretty difficult for me to swallow, both literally and figuratively. I bought the book for $4.00 and we wandered to a tiny cubicle of a restaurant to eat clam chowder and bread while we read through parts of the book together.

The lump so yearns to turn into tears, and the fact that I am being held in by the seatbelt gives me all so many reasons to let it go, let it flow, like a baby who never holds anything back. But as adults I guess we learn to control such emotion, such angst. And then all of a sudden we can't fall asleep at night and therapy sounds like an interesting idea. I just want to pee.

Finally, the little light goes off accompanied by a short ringing— ding, ding, ding. I unbuckle myself from my cell and stand up as at least ten others do. Luckily, I am close to the restrooms.

It feels so good to be standing, like the first time you eat after having had the flu. It is a familiar and needed thing to be doing. I open the little door and walk into the one square foot of space, turn around, and push the lever to the left so that it will read "occupied." But the lever never makes it all the way over. When I feel tension from the other side, I pull harder on the door to show whoever is out there that this is my cubicle for the next three minutes, but then I see the hand and the unbuttoned jeans jacket sleeve and I freeze. Stepping back an inch or so, I forget I have to pee. He doesn't move the lever to the left. He just stands firmly against the door in the dim light. I think about screaming. It would have been the thing to do in a situation like this. The girl screams, the man pulls a sharp knife from his pocket and slits her throat. She falls limply to the floor. He walks out casually, and the next passenger needing to use the bathroom finds the girl in a pool of blood. The man is shown back in his seat offhandedly reading a newspaper or something.

His hand slides around my neck and travels up the back of my head. His fingers massage this erotic area without messing up my hair. It feels so good, and I really have nowhere else to go. I am backed up against the toilet. His back is still planted against the door. He says nothing. Staring into my face, he takes his other hand and brings my body next to his. The way he is rubbing the back of my head is hypnotic, and I find myself letting him kiss me gently on the lips. The foreign thrill of anonymity heightens this perfect, sensual, exciting, intriguing moment, and I am not scared. In fact I realize this is something I like, that I might even choose—something that I would check the "yes" box on when filling out a sex questionnaire. And as soon as this thought is over, I begin creeping back to a reality of feeling utterly ridiculous, so I pull away and land hard on the toilet seat behind me, allowing the confusion to finally set into my face. He smiles just enough to bring out the creases around his eyes, and then he walks out. I move the lever to the left, put the toilet seat up, my pants down, and pee.

It's what I wanted, down deep in my psyche. And realizing this brings me no peace. It makes me consider how deeply disturbed I must be. The God-fearing church girl act is just that—an image portrayed out of an absence of experience, even personality. It kept me unscathed and pure until I figured out what it is I am and what it is I want.

Reflection check in the buzzing of the florescent light. My face seems odd and unfamiliar. I spot some gunk people call sleep in the corner of my eye and pull it out with the tip of my pinky finger. Suddenly I realize there must be a line of people waiting for this very cubicle so that they too can relieve themselves and find some personal, momentary space. And as I pull the lever to the right I wonder how many of them have ever kissed a stranger in an airplane restroom.

I walk down the aisle and see him on my right, sitting there in his masculine strength and Levis. I settle back into my row and seat, next to the window.

"Our feature presentation for this flight will be *Batman* starring Michael Keaton and Jack Nicholson. Headsets are $3.00 each. Please have your money ready. For the comfort of our viewing audience, we would like to ask that all window shades be lowered for the duration of the movie."

$3.00 to see a movie on an airplane. My ticket had cost nearly $800.00. Couldn't they find a way to include the movie? I mean, we'd had chicken and a chocolate chip cookie without any further money collecting. I want to see the movie, too. Not that *Batman* is any major enticement. I just want the complete distraction of it. Having watched a couple movies without ordering the headsets in the past, I know how annoying the whole hour and a half can be. And yet, when the stewardess with the black headphones wrapped in clear plastic nears my seat I remain still and frozen as I peer ahead, contemplating this ridiculous $3.00. And after she passes me and is making her way back up the plane, I am still considering how fine it would be to escape into a movie to take my mind off everything, including the bathroom rapist. By now I am considerably appalled by what he has done, by what I had allowed him to do. Considerably appalled.

I enjoy the phrase as it swims around in my brain, making me feel righteous once again. Yes, the headphones would have certainly helped me make this break between that and this, but then the movie starts. The dark blues and blacks of Gotham City fill the screen and I am not part of the hearing audience.

All the little shades are lowered. There is barely enough light to see the words in my book until my eyes adjust to the darkness.

"Here." It is the bathroom rapist offering me headphones wrapped in clear plastic. "If you want." Seat B is now suddenly and totally occupied. Headset plugged in and everything. He stares up at the screen as I stare at the side of his rugged, gorgeous face.

This is innocent enough. I did not provoke this. I haven't even looked at him until now. I quietly wonder who he is, where he lives, and if, God forbid, he is married. I wonder what he does when he isn't making moves on airplanes. I glance at his left hand. Nothing but manliness. Dylan has boy's hands. They are even soft. They are guitar playing hands. This guy has earth hands; strong, thick, wide hands. Are they warm hands? Mine are cold as I lift the headphones over my head to begin watching one of the most exciting films I've ever viewed. The characters appear on the screen in a fantastical way, with their faces and voices seeming ever so close and interesting. I can't take my eyes off the screen. Where else could I place them? Not on him, not any more. It would be intrusive at this point.

And his eyes never look my way either when his fingers touch lightly upon my thigh, caressing the softness of the jeans, and the rough inseam. As Michael Keaton's quirky eyebrows lift up and scowl down, I feel my entire soul begin to seriously tingle, and I am at once brought into a place of caring for little else than complete physical sensation. After all, what are we really human for, if not to experience the bodies we are born into?

His hand molds to my thigh, and I crouch lower in my seat. With fascinating dexterity, he unbuttons and unzips my 501's, bringing to the touch satin and lace. And although his face expresses not a thought, his hand speaks as it moves and warms me. A softer than firm belly. Small, tight breasts. Nipples and then under the satin. I crouch even lower and stare straight at the movie as his experienced fingers press into a spot I never even knew was there. The moment stands still and at the same time lasts forever as my thoughts tumble to the background of sexual rhythm and drive. It matters not who it is who is doing this; it is mine and I want it. And with the shriek of Nicholson's laughter, I clench the armrests and shake the most pleasurable shake a girl can ever wish for.

17

FRANCE

It is raining in Paris when I arrive. The freshness in the air stimulates my senses after the long, strange flight, and I stand outside the airport with my luggage and backpack waiting for a taxi, wondering where I am and not really caring in the least. So much and so many miles are behind me now. I turn around and what I see is nothing; empty space. I am nothing here yet. No one knows me. It feels like a splash of cool water on my face as I stand there in the grayness of the rain underneath the cloudy sky. I am pleased the day is dark. So many possibilities in the dark. I smile to myself, then look around to see if anyone is watching.

"Ou pourrais-je trouver un taxi?" Do I look French? I begin searching my backpack for the French dictionary Michael had given me as I run her foreign sentence back through my head.

"Taxi?"

"Oui, Mademoiselle." She is a woman aged by circumstance rather than by attitude. Two, small, round-faced children snuggle next to her to avoid the drops of rain. She stands there peering into my face, weighed down by her seemingly heavy bags.

"Here taxi." And I point to the right of where we stand as I walk there myself. The fact that I don't share her language appears to make no difference to her.

"Merci." And she moves next to me and waits.

I look at the mother and the children, realizing I am neither child nor adult myself. I am not French, but I don't necessarily feel American now that I have been placed on different soil. I know no connection to the country or state from which I come. There is no allegiance or devotion to New York or even Wisconsin. It is Wisconsin from which I have escaped, even though the bumper stickers there read, "Escape to Wisconsin." Escape the mother and fathers and endless winters. Escape the mediocre, the mundane, the middle class of the Midwest. I will be anywhere but there. And now I am here, as blank as a computer screen showing only the tiny, blinking line begging for the attention, craving the creation of the one who has fingers to type. What will be typed upon my blank, Parisian page?

A taxi pulls up just as the raindrops seem to get heavier. I step up to the door and open it for her. The driver stows her bags in the trunk, slams it down, and walks nonchalantly back to his door. Once her children are fastened into place, she smiles up at me with her eyes.

"Merci beaucoup," as if I had really done something for her. She waves as the wheels of the taxi throw water up onto the curb, and I find myself waving back at this woman who I know as well as Paris knows me.

In my own taxi several minutes later, I peer into my compact at the face that Alex will see in less time than it takes for me to quell my fears and suspicions of him. I apply lipstick and darker, black lines to the top of my lids. A brush through my rain-moistened hair finishes the image of near-perfection I am so destined to create for myself, for my self-confidence.

I shuffle through my bag to find my wallet with the francs Michael has given me from a past trip of his. He said he had them "left over." Three hundred francs just left over. I know why I am sitting in the taxi on the way to meet Alex. It is for Michael, to make Michael proud of me, and to show someone that I can do something, make something of myself. "Go the distance." My field of dreams is spreading wide over the Atlantic and to a man named Alex now, who will be pivotal in shaping my destiny, like it or not.

The many streets leading from the airport into the city become increasingly narrow as the whole of Paris begins to invoke a feeling of tightness. Tight, little cars with their odd license plates. Tight buildings, tight apartments, tight parking spaces. The streets curve this way and that as we bump over the cobbled roads and the meter clicks more ridiculously large numbers at me. Maybe three hundred francs isn't so much after all.

"Ze address again, Mademoiselle?"

I hand him the slip of paper with the directions to my destination. Butterflies flit and float all around inside my body, bumping into one another, and falling to the pit of my stomach momentarily before flying again. "Tout droit. Ah, straight ahead now. Zis is your first time to ze city?"

"Yes. My first time." First time meeting Alex. I must give a good first impression. Shake hands firmly. Speak only after he speaks to provide an illusion of mystery. Keep talking about oneself to a minimum. Information is ammunition. What else do I know? Why do I care to impress this creep, this criminal? I am ashamed of myself. You should be ashamed of yourself, she would say to me after I had done or said something wrong. Those words grate on my entire soul.

I hand over what seems to be too many bills to the driver and head in the direction of his forefinger, up the steps, next to the black iron railing and through a heavy, glass door. Plush red carpet covers the stairs as I nearly tiptoe up them. At the top I recognize myself in the gilded-edged mirrors that line the entire front hallway. Dare I ring the bell and begin this crusade?

It is opened by a small and faceless man who greets me with a nod as if he's seen me many times before. I stand alone at the edge of a sitting room for a brief second or two taking in the strange and richly luxurious surroundings, daring not to enter further. I quietly place my suitcase and backpack against the wall and secure my left hand in my front pocket.

"Bonjour, Mademoiselle. Comment allezvous?" This is it. I shake hands with the dream rapist.

"Bonjour." And a little smile to boot.

"Rachel, Rachel." Deep and throaty. "Let me see you. Turn around." And he directs me in a swirl motion with his crooked finger up in the air. I am reminded of my ballerina who twirled endlessly on one toe to the music in my childhood jewelry box. I would wind it up on the bottom and watch her go 'round and 'round until the music dwindled and then stopped. I turn around for him without showing the least evidence of embarrassment.

"Charming. Lovely. How long have I waited to meet you, dear! Michael has told me a good many things about you. He's quite fond of you, you know."

"I am fond of him as well." So if you even think of...

"But of course, darling. Please, do sit down and we'll get you something to drink. What do you desire? Your trip has surely made you thirsty, no?"

"Evian will be fine, if you have some." I know the answer to the drinking question in France. Michael has drilled this into me. Evian, Evian, Evian. The key to weight loss, prestige, purity, regularity. To be seen drinking anything else is simply unacceptable in his opinion, for models at least.

"But of course we have this for you, darling. And yet, a girl cannot survive on water alone. Isn't that right, Sam?" A darkish figure with pale, thin legs skirts across the hallway and slams a door loud enough to bring Alex's hand up to his chest as he winks back at me. "Samantha is a charmer, isn't she? A brand new guest to Paris as well. We'll have to introduce the two of you when she's in a better mood. Now then." He'd been pouring my water from a bottle into a glass in the kitchen around the corner as he speaks. And now, as he walks toward me with the glass, I dare for the first time to look up into his tanned and leathery face, noticing all too quickly the severe scar that runs from his forehead through his right eye and onto his cheek, making that eye appear as glass. I sip at my water, leaving lipstick on the rim.

"Your apartment is not so far from here. That way we can stay close, no?"

"Yes. I mean no. I mean yes." I take another sip of water and wonder if this girl named Sam will make another appearance. It is creepy just being in the presence of this man. I don't know how to explain it to myself as I pretend to be delighted at the news of my new living quarters. He doesn't seem to speak English like the taxi driver. He pronounces each consonant sounding more British than French to me. And sitting across from me in an oversized, red velvet chair, he takes on the appearance of near royalty as his gold chains glint in the afternoon shadows of the room. He sips noisily at his dark, steamy liquid as he lights cigarette after cigarette, never smoking the entire length of any of them. The whole apartment reeks of stale smoke, heavy cologne, and dust. If dust has a smell, I smell it in this room.

"Tonight we'll dine out to celebrate your first evening in the city. Maybe Sam will join us. Won't that be a treat?" He grabs at one of the chains around his thick, creased neck and glances toward the hallway where we had both last seen her. I try hard not to crease my eyebrows at the sight of this man's costume. It seems as outdated as the décor of the room. The gold chains around his neck are not alone. Rings and bracelets add the glitter to his already shiny, silk shirt, which hangs loosely on his shoulders, exposing what I figure he figures is a sexy, manly chest with gray and curling hairs wrapping themselves around the chains. And all this jewelry continues to hold my attention as his emphatic gestures dart here and there, leaving just the trail of smoke and disturbed dust.

I want out of this house.

His one good eye is considerably glazed over, as if age has produced a light film over it to hide the terrors of growing old—the wrinkles, the crinkles, the drooping, dropping bones. For although Alex certainly intends to give the impression of virility and vitality, his past gleams through every cell of his body, and it is neither good nor attractive. He is a fool, and yet I remain completely afraid of him.

"I imagine our dear Rachel will like to get settled then. We'll call you for dinner around 8:30 or 9:00. Make sure you're ready. Call Rachel a taxi, will you?" He speaks indirectly to the faceless man and is up and in another room in seconds assuming that on this first night away from anyone in the world, I will want to spend it with a grotesque, aging, bisexual, French hipster agent who holds my livelihood in the creased palm of his cigarette-stained hand.

I wipe the lipstick smudge off the rim of the glass and set it carefully on a ceramic coaster nearby. I stand up. Standing, I feel freer.

"Here." He approaches me abruptly and out of nowhere. "The latest fat girl who couldn't live without her boyfriend left these. And here are the directions to the agency. Early Monday morning, I'd like to see you there to get weighed and measured. The market here is quite particular, Rachel. No cottage cheese or a flabby bum allowed." He smiles coyly. I take the small booklet of maps and a metro guide from him and observe the butterflies waking up. My confidence has withered within me slowly, bringing the corners of my mouth down, down with dust and the smoke and the hidden scenes that create the wicked energy surrounding this place. Holding out my hand to his, I try to shake it firmly and say "Au revoir" with the spirit and enthusiasm such a French word requires.

18

ALONE

My apartment is on Rue de Saussure, a quaint-looking, quiet side street. I run the name of the street over in my head a couple of times as the tiny elevator squeaks, pulling my luggage and me up to the sixth floor and toward my new residence. And then alone, I step over the threshold into a place composed of foreign space and an old-fashioned black telephone that sounds no familiar dial tone when I pick up the heavy receiver.

The apartment smells of dead, dilapidated air, overworked from moving around and around in the same space. Standing there I wonder for a second or two why I am standing here. What has brought me here? What fate? Is it really where I am supposed to be?

The distraction of departure and travel, handling of baggage, the anticipation of Alex, and then Alex himself has all of a sudden drifted silently into this very moment where I am alone in a scantily furnished apartment thousands of miles away from people I don't really want to be with anyway. Well, except Dylan. But now that I am here I wonder painfully if he would even be the one, the destined knight in shining armor, the future father of my children. Suddenly I am not quite sure of anything at all except that I need to lie down. And when I do, on top of a lumpy, white comforter in the bedroom closest to where I had been standing, the tears of self-pity come furiously from my weary eyes, and I search my brain for more things to cry about. And they are there, ready to be cried out onto the musty pillow beneath my head. The only thing I think could add to the whole situation would be an audience, or at least the possibility of one; the hope that someone who cared might hear the tears falling and come to comfort. Knowing this is an impossibility makes the tears come quicker, and I bury my head in my hands and sob without a sound. It was the noises I made crying that bothered her the most.

After a minute or two I decide to make myself more comfortable during my unaccompanied weep-fest. I take off my shoes and arrange my body horizontally to let the tears run down the sides of my head, dampening my hair. I stare up at the unpainted ceiling, the angled planks of wood that seem to hold the room together, wondering what is going to keep me together here. And then I fall into a fitful slumber as the sun sinks down low and into the nearing night.

Waking from the nap, my whole soul feels eerie and out of place. Had it escaped my body while I slept? Did it travel to see what I cannot see lying here, drenched in self-pity? The room is dark now, just dark enough so that it is getting difficult to see. I snap on the little lamp, which sits on a small table next to the bed. I snap it on as if to say this darkness will not scare me! Once the light is on, I look around the room, realizing how cute things look with the golden wood everywhere and the large window revealing just the faintest, pink streaks of a setting sun. I am immediately upset with myself for crying like a child. After all, I am in Paris! I am by myself in Paris in an apartment with my whole life ahead of me. And I am a model. I had almost forgotten.

In the shower I turn the antique-looking handles up and down and up and down again until I figure out the right water temperature. The pressure is low, but I lift my face up to the dribbling warmth just the same, to wash away the nap and tears. And then down with my chin to my chest as the water pours onto my hair. And there they are, the small, rounded breasts, and the muscular thighs. I close my eyes into the water again and despise myself for despising my body.

Larger breasts or smaller thighs? Is it too much to ask?

On a little, wooden chair in my room I sit and brush and blow-dry my mane upside down, feeling the blood rush to my face. Then in the little mirror above the sink in the bathroom, I apply my makeup carefully. Each stroke of liner or shadow or blush I apply in anticipation of the approval of Alex. To be found favorable by such a man must be something, I decide silently. It is my job now to do this, to be this thing I really am not. But when I think of any alternative to my current situation, I know that I can act the role of whatever it is I am supposed to be. Anything to stay far away from where I'd come from. I'd do the job, letting time pass, letting a new me come to pass until—until what I did not know and knew I didn't have to know. As long as the old reality never catches up with the new illusion I now lived in, things will be okay.

I choose my snuggest blue jeans, my whitest tee shirt, my boots, and my only black blazer—the incredible black blazer that covers what one has too much of and too little of at the very same time, while giving off the air of attitude and professionalism. Michael bought it for me at a second-hand shop in Soho. It had cost less than $20.00. I had long since paid him back for it, but still think of him each time I put it on.

Waiting for my ride, I decide to scope out my new surroundings. I open cabinets and drawers, test shades, and look in closets. The second bedroom is larger, but it is down the hall all by itself. My bedroom is right next to the kitchen and bathroom. It is smaller, cozier, friendlier, and safer, as far as I am concerned. I need to feel safe.

Without losing the just-combed, fresh-from-the-shower look, I place my clothes in drawers and store a few other items in the closet, along with my luggage. And then I stand by the window and watch. I am still five minutes early. I think about reading, but I am not in the mood.

Alex, his assistant, and Samantha show up fifteen minutes late. Needless to say, these fifteen minutes waiting bring back my earlier feelings of despair as well as drain all real and artificial color from my cheeks. I step out into the drizzle of the night and into a car with three people, none of whom I am really looking forward to spending the evening with. It's surprising sometimes to see what I do simply because I haven't yet decided what I want to do.

Glancing sideways at Samantha, I can tell she isn't thrilled with her current situation any more than I am. But neither of us seem to have any affect on Alex's flamboyant flirtations with anyone and everyone who pass his way. He is the director of his own supper symphony, waving his tawny, creased, cigarette-stained hands through the air as the gold on his wrists clink together providing musical interludes to his non-stop chatter in fast French or easy English. Both languages roll off his tongue just as quickly as the red wine slides down the opposite way. He seems to know every other person in the restaurant, nodding, throwing fake kisses, introducing Samantha and I briefly as if we are simply his newest commodity. Squish goes cigarette after cigarette into the little glass ashtray.

I wait until his fifth or sixth glass of wine to really look at him, to notice the deep orange silk shirt that creases this way and that with every emphatic gesture. My eyes are drawn to the folds in his neck, and how the leathery skin hangs in tiny layers beneath the gold chains. His face falls low and his eyes seem foggy, glazed over by deceit and superficiality and too many cigarettes. He is a terrifying creature with that scar running through his eye.

"Girls! Another glass?" Grinning, he holds the wine above us, ready to spill it into our glasses. Samantha puts her hand over the rim of hers. I just look at my glass, which is nearly empty. How many glasses have I drunk so far? "Drink up, my beautiful child! You're a virgin in this city, and Paris welcomes you openly, yes?" Glancing toward Claude, the faceless assistant, Alex beseeches some company in his drunken quest to make his American guest feel welcome. Claude nods, barely looking at me, and we both know Alex is at the point where the alcohol is now the spokesperson of the soul of this man. And although a drug has no literal voice, it often speaks the truest truth from the deepest depth. Finishing my bowl of cous cous and vegetables, I sip at my wine and watch as

Alex whispers things to Claude that provoke no change whatsoever in the countenance of this quiet man.

"Samantha! You're such a little brat, aren't you? Why don't you have a drink to welcome Rachel to Paris?" Another nudge at Claude, as if this man has a persuasive bone in his body. "I don't even know why I take you out these days. All I see is you sulking as if you have it so bad." At this he lights another cigarette and motions for the waiter to clear the table. I sip more wine in an effort to take the attention off Samantha. It isn't helping.

"She's just a little bitch sometimes. You really never know when she's going to act up like this." He peers apologetically into my face, and I wish to bring forth the correct expression, but I am not sure what it is supposed to be. Samantha appears unaffected.

"Claude, pour her a glass. I want to see her drink and have some fun." Claude pours, Samantha ignores. I know I should be feeling uncomfortable by this, but the warmth of the wine has settled in my belly, making my legs feel like jelly, and this is what I am thinking of in the moment.

Samantha stares weakly at her full glass and lights a cigarette of her own as she slouches over the table looking dismal in her black tee-shirt and wispy hair. I squint at her trying to figure out what she looks like on film. Then without notice, her dark eyes dart up at me, as if daring me to speak my mind. I blink quickly a couple of times pretending there is something in my eye, and then I take another sip of wine. My head is spinning. Alex snaps for the check, stomping out a cigarette. Everyone is getting antsy. She would always ask me if there were ants in my pants if I began to fidget and look nervous, as if a child ought to be still until being told she could move again. I want out of here now. I almost stand up before Alex does, I am so anxious to exit the smoky, crowded restaurant. I push my chair up against the table as Alex pulls French cash from his fancy wallet. How much longer do I have to play this charade before I totally lose it? My brain swirls with a thousand emotions, the main one being complete detachment from the company I have kept on this initial night in Paris. I need to get away from them, and not just because I am completely buzzed. These people are not my people. I wish desperately for Dylan then, and my eyes well up for the good times with him that now seem even more fabulous from far away.

Walking to the car, I begin to consider my financial well being. I have enough money for rent and food at the moment. And there are several jobs I haven't been paid for in New York. Michael will send the money when it comes. But for the first time I feel really alone this way, on my own. Alex is not Michael, and I can never imagine living with him. Samantha is one of the most miserable girls I have ever met, and it doesn't look like Alex is doing much to help the situation. I try picturing what it is they have going on in his house, and then immediately decide not to dwell on such a thing at all. I have to look out for myself now, make money, and get back to New York.

When Claude returns me to my little apartment on Rue de Saussure, I am definitely dizzy from the wine. In my new bedroom I take off my boots and sink between the lumps in my quilt, letting my head spin a minute and attempting to enjoy it. Certainly this is the most drunk I'd ever been, I think quietly. I wish the phone worked. I want to call Dylan. And then I don't. What if he isn't there? What time is it there? Thinking of it puts a drain on my brain, and I begin searching for fresh air to clear my head. The window in my bedroom is large and when I pull up on the bottom of it I receive no response whatsoever. The thing is quite stuck. I take a short break to gather my strength, and then try again. But socks on a wooden floor give no leverage or support, and I nearly land backwards. I look around for something to break the painted seal. The heal of my boot looks like the closest, hardest item around, and so with it I hit the frame around the window several good times, drop the boot to the floor, and give it another try. Nothing. Not even a budge.

In my mind I put shoes on and take the elevator down six floors and stand out in the street. It seems silly. I sit back on the bed and stare at the window for a long time thinking. Then I go to the bathroom to pee. When I come back I sit and stare at the window again. Everything is so quiet, so still. Where is the noise of New York City?

Quite determined, I rise from the bed to tackle it once again. And like opening a jar of applesauce or a working a key in a lock, all of a sudden my persistent attempts make that window shoot up so quickly I lose my footing and fall backwards onto my behind.

Back on my feet, I draw myself to the cool breeze that is already floating in. And then I am in the window myself, my long legs scrunched up to my small chest creating a dinner bulge in my stomach. It sticks out and it takes me a second or two to realize this is not necessarily a good thing. But for good reason I don't care as the night air begins calling to me. Out of the window and up the fire escape I crawl in my jeans and socks. Up, up until I am on the black, slanted roof. And then I see it and stare in awe, in European reverence, at the Eiffel Tower in the distance. Here I am alone, but the interesting, enticing, romantic, fantastic thing about it is that I am in Paris. And the wine softens the roughness of the roof for me as I lie on my back and stare up at the stars.

19

A DAY IN THE LIFE

It takes me several weeks to settle on a comfortable course for running. The first several times I venture out, I find myself darting up and down busy streets in a chaotic fashion around my apartment. But on one of these frenzied and required bursts of energy, I spot an area of green which, as I get closer, transforms into the most beautiful and serene park place I have been to in a long time. It is clean and emerald green and trimmed and fresh, and it is my new, daily, outdoor gym. Unlike a good deal of the exercising public, I do not need expensive equipment, mirrored walls, various weights, sweaty mats, an egocentric aerobics instructor, or a yearly membership fee to feel worthy, eligible, or inspired to get my heart pumping for thirty to forty minutes a day. I just need a non-polluted path to follow and a pair of reliable running shoes.

It's a good thing to lock myself into a routine, and the daily, morning run helps launch each day this way. It's the consistent similarity that gives me purpose and security. It promotes familiarity, stability, and a sense of balance, all of which are necessary ingredients while living alone in this foreign city, or any city, for that matter.

And so in the morning I rise an hour after the sun and breathe in the morning breads and pastries that bake in the boulangerie below the apartments. The fragrant air feeds my morning hunger pangs as I quickly bend to touch my toes, stretching my calves. With my hands clasped behind me, I pull them up to stretch out my arms, to wake up my blood and body enough to pull me from sleepy slumber to invigorating exercise.

To the park I run, then, with thoughts of a lean, strong body in mind. I feel as powerful and as fast as the wind as it whips through the strands of my hair left hanging after the braid down my back has been secured. With my walkman in my right hand, I fly past the small, round-faced children on their way to school. I peer down at them and they up at me, our eyes making contact for a second or two. I wonder what they think of me.

And then one morning, as I round the corner back onto Rue de Saussure, I meet the eyes of a girl my age, standing, looking out of place. I pat at the sweat that has gathered at the top of my cheeks and above my lip and remove the headphones from my ears, trying not to get the wire tangled in my hair. I think about putting my hand out to shake hers, but it is pretty wet with sweat.

"Hi." Her eyes sparkle as she looks at me. She doesn't look like a model. "Do you live here?"

"Yeah." My eyebrows cross inquisitively. "Did Alex send you?"

"Alex. Yeah." Her eyebrows rise up underneath loose strands of wavy hair. "Now there's a character. What a creep." She bends down to set her suitcase on the step. "I'm sorry. I'm Eliza. I didn't mean anything by that. Or maybe I did." She laughs and moves her right hand toward me. I wipe mine on my shorts and shake hers. We both give a nice, friendly shake, not too hard and not too soft.

"Don't worry about it. I'm not a fan, if that's what you want to know." I am very interested in this girl, in having some kind of company. "Here, let me get that for you. I'm Rachel, by the way." I move in to pick up her suitcase for her. After all, I am the strong and powerful one.

"Thanks. You're on the sixth floor?"

"Yeah."

"I hope you don't mind having a roommate."

"I think it's exactly what I need. So where are you from?" I am standing in the elevator now, pressing number six. For some reason I am neither intimidated nor put off by this girl.

"California, for the most part. You?"

"Wisconsin. Where in California?" We both wince at the squeaking sound the elevator makes, then smile.

"Sacramento mainly. It's where my mom is now."

"Well, here we are. There's a pretty big bedroom down the hallway. It's all yours." I look back at her, leading her to her room. As she sets her things on the bed, I bend down to stretch out my legs.

"So you run, what, every day?" She opens her large suitcase on the bed and then just sits down next to it.

"Nearly. I can feel my ass growing the minute I miss." I had gone ahead and used the "a" word in the spirit of newfound friendship.

"You look great. I gain all my weight here." She points to her lower belly as she sits with her arms set squarely on each leg. This girl is not the feminine type. "So what's up with Alex? Hasn't he shopped in the last twenty years? What is going on with his clothes?"

I laugh and untangle myself from my walkman completely. Then I pull up the only chair in the room and sit with the back of it in front of me, straddling the seat and resting my arms on the back.

"I don't know. I guess he thinks he looks stylish or something." I hadn't thought of mocking him in this way before. But now it seems well past the time I should have.

"So this is the fashion for French modeling agents?"

"No. I think our Alex is one of a kind. What did he say to you?"

I can't believe how high I feel sitting there talking with this new girl. How much have I missed friendly conversation with someone who speaks English as her first language? In this back room I am back home. Where is that again?

"He said all sorts of creepy stuff, asking me questions about my boobs, if they were real. And I was like, *you* get real, you know? What the hell?"

"I know."

"I mean it's not like I've landed my dream job here or something."

"What? Modeling?"

"Yeah. Everyone seems to think I should be all grateful and everything to be a model, as if it carried some supreme importance."

"I know what you mean." My eyebrows furrow as I gaze at her, realizing I have been taking myself too seriously.

"I mean, no offense, but modeling hardly requires any special talent."

"True." She is on a roll.

"Alex is all wanting to measure my waist the second I arrive, and I'm like hold on a second, you know? Like my waist measurement is going to determine my future success in life. Get real." She begins unpacking her suitcase, still facing me.

"So you don't really want to be a model?" Quietly, I think, me neither.

"No." She holds up a handful of brushes held together by a rubber band. "I want to paint. I mean, that's why I really came here, I guess. But don't tell anyone. I just couldn't pass up the opportunity to fly to Paris for free."

"For free?" I get up from the chair, turn it around, and sit back down.

"It's what I won. From the contest. And the modeling agency there is apparently hooked up with Alex here. Don't get me wrong. It's cool that I'm here. And I'll try and everything, to make it worth it, you know? But I won't be staying long." She pulls a framed picture out from underneath some tee shirts. "This is Ty."

"Cute." I hold out my hand. She gives me the picture. He is cute.

"We got a phone here?"

"Yeah. I got it hooked up last week. I haven't used it much. Valerie calls with my schedule at night. Hold on." I run into my room to get a picture of Dylan, who is also cute. The only picture I have is of him with his guitar in his room. It is in my wallet. I pull it out and throw my wallet on the bed. "Here. This is Dylan."

"He's a doll."

"Yeah."

"Do you miss him?"

"Of course. But I guess I have to be here for a while. Do my thing. Get some stuff figured out." Why did I sound like an idiot to myself?

"I think Ty's the one."

"You mean…"

"Yeah. I think we'll get married some day."

"Wow."

"He's the reason I'm here, I guess. He dared me to enter this contest in Sacramento. It was the silliest thing I ever did. I don't even know how I won, you know?" She sits down on the bed, still holding the picture in her hands.

"It was a modeling contest?"

"Yeah."

She shakes her head back and forth, and I wonder what time it is getting to be. I have appointments, but I feel frozen in place in this small world of ours. I feel that if I sit there long enough, I will never have to put on my black skirt and head out to meet the day. I feel transfixed by this girl and her disrespectful spirit. I observe it entering mine.

"I mean, I'm a basketball player."

"You play basketball?"

"Well, not any more, really. Except with Ty for fun. I played center in high school. I averaged ten rebounds per game my senior year." She seems proud of this and I guess that ten rebounds must be a lot. "Even had a scholarship. But I'd rather paint, you know? I've kind of lost the basketball bug . . . Smell this dresser."

"What?"

"This dresser." She is putting her clothes in the drawers haphazardly as she talks. Now she is sniffing it. "What is that?"

"Smells like marijuana."

"Yeah, marijuana." Again, she seems lost in herself. I am proud of myself for identifying the smell for her. "You don't have any, do you?"

"No. Wish I did, though. I kinda got used to having it around back in New York."

"Shit, Ty and I haven't smoked since the Crosby, Stills, and Nash concert."

"You saw them?"

"Several times."

"You like that kind of music?"

"What kind? Classic rock? Sure. But I'm into a bunch of stuff."

I can tell we are the same age, but she sounds like she is at least thirty. I feel fourteen.

"Well, I should go. I have a bunch of places I need to be today."

"Really? Where?"

"Um. Madame Figaro, French *Cosmopolitan*, and a couple photographers."

"I have to go to the agency." She sounds empty.

"Valerie and Vincent are great. They'll totally take care of you there." Who am I trying to sell?

"The blonde?"

"Yeah. She's really sweet."

"She told me to drink Evian. Can they really tell me what to drink?"

"I don't know. They think it's a magical solution. Drink and eliminate all unnecessary fat."

"So she thinks I'm fat."

"I wouldn't worry about it, Eliza. Valerie is very cool."

"She's really pretty herself."

"She used to be a model."

"Not anymore?" Eliza is just about finished unpacking, and I can tell she wishes to detain my company longer.

"I guess she's too old now."

"Too old? What is she? Twenty-five?"

"I'm not sure. About that, probably." I really need to get a move on, as my mother used to say. But I don't want to be rude.

"Over the hill at twenty-five? Cindy Crawford is older than that, isn't she?"

"Cindy Crawford is a super model."

"I don't know what's so super about modeling. I haven't even done it yet, and I already feel completely self-conscious. I've never felt that way before." We are both standing in the hallway now, as I am trying to make my break from the conversation. Eliza looks lost. We both know she belongs here even less than I do.

"If it helps any, I think you're beautiful." I did. After studying her for the last half hour or so, I've decided that Eliza will probably look very good in print.

"Thanks. You're sweet." Was that a "you're sweet, but you don't matter"?

"Well, I really have to get a move on if I'm going to make French *Cosmopolitan* on time." Was I trying to impress her now with the modeling talk?

"I guess I should get ready myself." We give each other a last, friendly glance before we go off to our separate quarters to ponder whether or not we liked what we saw. I hope I made a good impression. The apartment already seems so much more desirable now that she is in it. I don't want to lose her.

After a shower, I sit on the lumpy quilt with my hair up in a white towel and stare down at my map in search of Rue de Mail, Rue Daguerre, and Rue Milton. Some of my appointments can be seen during the entire morning or afternoon, but others have specific times set to be seen. The trick is to make my daily rounds without wasting too many steps or time riding the metro back and forth. I look from my appointment book to my map to my metro schedule and try to come up with a successful plan for the day while listening to Eliza's music play from her room. This is what I have been missing. All I have for music is my walkman, which doesn't help much around the apartment. I get up and plod on the hard wood floors with my bare feet toward the bathroom.

"Who is that?" I yell pleasantly over the music.

"Nina Simone." She walks toward me so she doesn't have to raise her voice.

"Sounds like a guy."

"I know. Cool, huh? She sings the blue right of the blues." She stands behind me as I comb through my spray-on conditioner, which has settled into my hair, making it more manageable. I can see her in the mirror looking completely detached from my hurried, modeling mode. I envy her, trying to think of what to say after such a statement. I have no idea who Nina Simone is. Then I notice she has gone.

"Here." Back behind me. I turn around. "This is Nina."

"Huh, she's sort of different-looking, isn't she?" As soon as the words fall out of my mouth I would have paid to gather them all back in, as I glance at Eliza's face exuding nonchalance and non-judgment of both me and Miss Simone.

"She's got a voice that flows like a river water over mossy stones. Don't you think? I mean her beauty is there, all right. It just doesn't look like the glossy cover of a magazine." She steps away lightly, and I feel as shallow as the river water. Have I just ruined what could have been a very good thing? And now do I try to repair it or will that make it worse? What is the cool thing to do? And if I am trying to think of what might be cool, then for certain it can never be. I pull the loose strands of hair free from my head and hold them over the little wastebasket hoping they will fall in. Then I walk toward her room, not knowing what to say and hearing the great music that makes me feel so bad.

"I didn't mean anything." I stand in her doorway, now not worthy enough to enter without permission.

"It's cool. I guess this is my world now. Things are beautiful or they're not."

Shit.

"She has a great voice." Hello. This has been said already. I am sinking deeper.

"Don't worry about it, Rachel. It's just that I'm not used to judging everything by the exterior surface." She is so cool, and I am so not cool.

"Well anyway, I'm sorry."

"No big deal. I'm serious." She stands there in ripped bib overalls and basketball shoes. Tiny, silver earrings dangle from her ears as she turns around to sort through more of her things. I go back to the bathroom to dust my face with powder and gloss my lips to greet the world of beautiful or not.

Back in my room I check the time and forget Eliza as I grab a white tee shirt, my short, black flared skirt, black shoes, black backpack, black portfolio, and black appointment book. Neutrality equals a readiness for anything and a blending with everything. Make me. Create me. I have not yet created myself. I am pulling my white quilt up over my pillow and turning around to do one last check in the mirror when I see my new roommate leaning against the doorway. I back up for her to enter. The clock reads twenty minutes past the time I should have been out the door, but I sit back down on my bed. I need this friend.

She has one knee up with her tennis shoe on the chair in my room. "So how long have you been modeling?" I quickly calculate how I can skip the first appointment, call Valerie before I leave to tell her I am getting Eliza settled in, ask her to reschedule for me, and get to my next appointment on time as long as I spend only fifteen more minutes in the apartment. I run Eliza's question around in my mind before deciding on a response I know will instigate further probing.

"Not long. Perhaps too long. Long enough to know it's not something I will be doing much longer."

"Why is that? Because it's a ridiculous, superficial, artificial business that attempts to make women into objects for men to ogle at and for women to compare themselves to, never quite measuring up so that their self-esteem remains so low they end up on some anti-depressant buying cellulite creams that never work?" One knee down, the other up. Is this going to be a twenty-minute thing?

"Well." My eyebrows dart up, then pull their way toward the clock. People from California can be so overwhelming sometimes. "I suppose it's something like that. My own self-esteem...." I don't know how to finish the thought. I am supposed to be making my way out into the world of models dressed in black and white to be made into something artificial for men to ogle at. I don't have the space in my brain to seriously contemplate my self-esteem right now. I don't want to face the emptiness I feel about myself. And who is this girl anyway?

"Having a good opinion about yourself shouldn't be all that difficult when you look like you do."

"Well, that's a pretty superficial thing to say."

"Not if your self-esteem is based upon your exterior surface. Isn't that what you were thinking about?"

She has me. I am. Thighs and boobs and the zit on my chin. All stuff having to do with body shape and skin. Things I nearly have no control over.

"How can I not? I mean every day it's pack it up and head off to be inspected by foreign photographers or stylists or agents who will determine whether I'm going to be able to pay the rent this month or eat dinner tonight. Every bite of food I digest wondering if it will make me fat. Every minute under the sun I know my skin is aging, wrinkling away my youth and marketability. Every shower I take reminds me of my uneven proportions. Every time I look in the mirror I absolutely dread finding any kind of imperfection. We're not allowed to be human, Eliza. I'm not sure if this whole thing is for you."

She is obviously way too casual about her appearance. I need to get out of my room and face my reality.

"No, but is it for you?"

"I don't want to be rude, but why do you care so much?" Cringing in my head, I hope this won't piss her off.

"I don't know. I guess I just don't see the attraction. You seem like a beautiful girl who could be doing anything. I'm just curious as to why you chose this." She stands up and smoothes her overalls down over her thighs. She knows she is keeping me, but now she also knows she has stirred me up.

"I guess I just don't have anywhere else to be right now. I got into this thing and I'm going to see it through." Finish what you start, she used to say. And no game or puzzle was ever put away until it was completed. I stand up and grab my backpack. "Anyway, we can talk about all of this later if you'd like. I really have to go."

"Rachel?"

"Yeah?" I turn back from the door.

"You can do whatever you want, you know?"

"Sometimes I wish I knew what that was."

"You'll figure it out."

"You sound so sure."

"I am." Who is this girl coming into my house telling me what to do?

"I gotta go."

"See you tonight then?"

In the elevator I feel more troubled than ever, but at least the thoughts take me away from my lack of self-esteem. What do I want? Not this. Not this daily microscopic investigation into my body so much so that it gets to my soul. And back to the self-esteem. But here I am on my way to the metro to ask for it some more. Look at me and tell me if you want me.

* * *

The afternoon is bright and sunny as I feel all the muscles in my legs carry me from place to place. I want to tell the sun to turn itself down. A dimmer switch on the sun would have provided some relief, for I feel dim and confused and I want the weather to reflect it. My third appointment is French *Cosmopolitan*, a double intimidation in my opinion. In the elevator to the fourth floor I brush my hair upside down and pat powder on the zit as I check my strange reflection in my compact. I swipe at a small dot of gunk in the corner of my eye as the elevator door opens right into their office. I pull my portfolio from my backpack and pretend to be delighted.

"Bonjour, I'm Rachel. Valerie sent me to see you again."

"Ah, Rachel. Yes, yes of course. Do sit down. I'll grab Monique. She's just dying to see you. Monique!"

Past covers of French *Cosmopolitan* cover the walls in a consuming fashion so that as I wait for Monique I nearly think I'll kill myself unless I end up in one of their magazines. I pull my thighs from the leather swivel chair as Monique approaches.

"Rachel, Rachel. So, so cute. Let me see." I hand her my portfolio and remain standing.

"I did vant to see it again. I think you'd be so, so perfect for this shoot. Ah, dis one. Who took it? New York?" She points at the body shot where I had been pretending to have a rather shapely top half.

"Yes, New York."

"And how long have you been in Paris?" Said without pronouncing the "s."

"About a month now."

"I see, I see." Monique's orange lipstick nearly matches her severely short hair, which bops this way and that as she turns the pages in my book, shopping. She is very pale and wears gobs of accessories that jingle as she speaks.

"Rachel, vill you do us one small thing?" It is the guy who first greeted me. "Sure." Do I have some kind of option here?

"Vill you try dis on in dhere?" He points his long, stylish finger behind a black curtain toward the back of the room. I take the yellow bathing suit and what is left of my confidence, and walk like a model to the curtain, and then behind it. A bathing suit! A yellow bathing suit! What are they thinking? A hundred thoughts run through my mind as I dutifully begin to take part in my own torture session. I could simply tell them I won't fit it. I could pretend sickness and run. I could…. The bottoms fit well, but without a tan won't look well. I pull my tee shirt up over my head carefully so as not to get any makeup on it and look down at my 36 A's. Why am I continuing with this charade? What makes me play this ridiculous role in which I remain at the bottom for people to step on? I fasten the back of it and inhale deeply. In the full length mirror to my right I squint and inhale deeper. I can't pull this off, can I?

"Ah, Rachel. Yes. Come on out."

Come on down. I am on the wrong game show wishing desperately to change the channel. There is nothing to say. I have no voice in a bikini.

"Turn around please." It is Monique. You turn around first. And then the quiet talk, secret whispers in front of the model to remind her that she is less than human, and even more so if she doesn't fit the clothes.

"Thank you. We'll be in touch with the agency." The guy with the stylish finger points me back behind the curtain as if I am not fit to be seen in their office any longer. Get out of here, you hideous monster, I hear them say as I scuttle back to safety. I nearly detest my little black skirt as I pull it up over my hips. It is offering something no one wants. Pulling my clothes back on, I wonder what a prostitute feels like after the deeds are done. Used, humiliated, ashamed, confused? I experience the great need to walk out and pretend none of this had happened. Denial. Bring in superman and turn back time. I don't feel like having the memory of this.

They barely glance my way as I exit with my black catalog of myself. False advertising. I deserve the scorn.

For nearly a mile I walk in a daze in the haze of the sun as my shoulders droop further and further under the weight of my backpack. I check my watch, realizing that the agency will only be open for another forty-five minutes. I drag my breast-less body to the metro silently, deciding to retire from the ridicule. Surely I am meant for something more than this.

Valerie and Vincent sit at the circular desk in the dropping sun that glares at me through the window as I trudge into the agency. I sink into the black, leather couch with just the silent swoosh of the cushions under my weight.

"Rachel…" Valerie sounds as sweet as a sister might. I feel I have let her down. "*Cosmo*?"

"Oui. Zhey called."

"What did they say?"

"Ah, Rachel. But of course you know dis, no? But Madame Figaro books you for two days next veek. So dis is good news. Good money vith ze catalog, no?"

It is true. Catalog shoots paid five times as much as magazines did. So why do I feel like an utter failure in France?

"Really? They booked me for two days?" Good news or compliments must be heard a minimum of two times.

"Rachel. Don't worry about the *Cosmo* thing." It is Vincent, and he has gotten up from his appointment book to come and slouch next to me on the couch. Vincent is someone who doesn't look like he works in a modeling agency. He drives a motorcycle and is way too cute and way too straight to be so involved in the industry from this angle. I have just a little crush on him. He clasps his arms across his chest and peers at me sideways with a comical grin. "*Cosmo* is for slutty models, Rache. You're too clean for them."

If only this was true, and the fact that I have no breasts wasn't true, everything would be just fine, I think. I am not one to buy into false, flattering, consolatory excuses. He can tell it didn't take. "Anyway, there are a lot of other clients out there. Just try to keep your head straight." How did he know it was tilted?

* * *

At home it appears as though Eliza has been a busy little homemaker. There are art posters up in the living room and salads and wine on the counter in the kitchen. I drop my backpack inside the doorway of my room and call to her. She comes cruising in from her bedroom barefoot and paint-stained.

"Hey!" She is cheerful from ear to ear.

"Hey yourself."

"Do you like?" She waves her arm up at the posters.

"That one's Monet, right?"

"Good girl." All smiles.

I take my shoes off while we both stare at the brush of light oranges and blue-grays. There are silhouettes of boats in the distance and two darker, smaller boats in the foreground. An orange circle setting represents the sun. It is reflected in the water reflecting an easy end-of-the-day peace.

"So what have you been up to?"

"Nothing much. Painting a little. I bought some supplies at a cool little shop on the way home from the agency." She begins looking busy in the kitchen, and I begin feeling like the husband.

"So you did go."

"To the agency? Of course. Or, but of course, as they like to say here a hundred times a minute." She laughs out loud then as she pulls two wine glasses from the cabinet.

"Wine glasses?"

"I couldn't help myself. Merlot?"

"Please." We are playing. I will play along.

"A toast." She raises her glass in the air."

"To what?"

"To Paris! I love this adorable city, don't you?" She so wants me to join her in her youthful energy and spiritual discovery. I still have only one thing on my mind.

"I have no boobs." I just have to say it out loud.

"So? I weigh a hundred forty-five pounds. Let's get drunk."

"Okay."

20

HALLOWEEN

You want me to grab one for you, too?"

"I guess. Shit, I wish we had some more of the yellow ones. They seem to go down so much easier."

"I know. But we ate the last two yesterday. You don't feel like getting more, do you?"

"I feel like I'm going to faint."

"You and me both."

"Should we weigh ourselves before we go?" She seems so anxious.

"Let's wait until the morning. It's always better to weigh yourself in the morning. You can be like five pounds heavier at night."

"Good idea." On our way back to the laundromat, Eliza and I dodge the drops of rain that dot our path as we chew on yet more apples. For three days all we have been eating are apples. We have eaten red delicious, granny smith, yellow, green, sweet, sour, sliced, chopped, peeled, and shredded apples. It is a diet Eliza read about in a magazine. I agreed to do it with her. At the end of three days we were supposed to have lost up to eight pounds. I figured it couldn't really hurt. I am doing it to support her, I guess. I know all about fad diets and that they are a scam. I know that thin people can't lose eight pounds in three days, and yet the allure remains. You wish.

You hope. You dream that such a thing is possible, that after only momentary suffering and sacrifice your troubles will end and ahead is only the skinny, beautiful, perfect life of self-confidence and perfect acceptance by all. Well, Eliza and I are dreaming of this anyway. I know it can never hurt me to lose a few. In the modeling business ninety percent of the models can all stand to "lose a few." Words so easily said by the agents, photographers, stylists, and clients. I'd like to see them try it.

"Eliza?"

"Yeah?" She is back in her bib overalls. The past few weeks have taken a toll on her. She is paler, less inquisitive, less cheerful.

"What do you want to be when you grow up?" I am asking her the question because I want someone to ask me the same.

"I am grown up, Rachel." She is very serious.

"I know that. I mean...you know what I mean." She does.

"Well, I don't want to be a model. That's for sure."

"Me neither. Did you grab the quarters?" All of a sudden I remember that we have forgotten them. They are still sitting on the counter in neat piles ready for the dryer phase of our weekly laundry experience.

"Shit." She seems really pissed.

"I'm sorry."

"I can't fucking deal with this anymore." And she drops to a small spot of grass under a tree that is two steps away. I crouch down next to her and put my hands on her knees in an attempt to comfort.

"Eliza?" I am so quiet with this.

"I'm sorry. Christ! I need some food, Rachel. I can't do this anymore." Tears are coming out of her eyes fast. This triggers mine into action. "I feel like I'm fading away here, Rache. I mean, what the hell? I don't need this crap. God, I have everything I need back home."

I wish I could have said the same.

"Eliza, all I know is that this modeling world is not all it's cracked up to be. It's all about image and persuasion and enticement and seduction and making people feel less than they are. None of these things is important, really. Right?" I thought I'd ask a question to keep her involved and test whether or not she was listening to me ramble.

"If you mean that this place has made me feel less than I am, then I'd have to say that's pretty important, Rache." I give up crouching and just sit on the moist cement.

"Yes it is. You're right. But how do models make other people feel? What I mean is what we are doing isn't really helping anyone, you know? I know I feel like crap next to Rachel Hunter or Cindy Crawford. So if what we're doing isn't very important, in the scheme of things, then there's no reason to get all bent out of shape about it." Who am I talking to? Peering into the sad face of my friend under a tiny tree while raindrops fall seems like a strange thing to do while our laundry sits washed and not dried. I am beginning to feel bent out of shape myself. My brain isn't functioning normally, and Eliza remains in a dismal daze. I pull my hair back, twist it around, and set it behind me. I haven't had the energy to comb it out and put it in a braid.

"Modeling is like gambling, Eliza." I am trying again. "You put so much of yourself out there on the line, so much of your self-confidence and self-worth. If you win, you can win big. If you lose, you wish you would have never played. The trick is to know when to play and when to quit." I am starting to get cold.

"But I haven't played very long." She takes her white hand and ring-less fingers and pulls her tears off to the side of her face. I blot mine with the sleeve of my jeans jacket, then shiver out loud.

"What we need is food, Eliza." I know how the lack of it can grossly affect one's mood.

"But we need to weigh ourselves in the morning." She sounds so desperate about it. This is not the Eliza I know.

"I know." I knew better than anyone how terribly important it is to see certain numbers on the scale. It can mean so much to have lost just a few pounds. "Come on." I help her up and we walk back arm in arm to the apartment for our quarters.

* * *

That night we go to bed early and get up early. It is time to weigh ourselves. Eliza steps on the scale first. She is completely naked.

"Wait!"

"What?"

"Did you go to the bathroom?"

"No. Jeez, you scared me."

"Sorry. Go to the bathroom first."

"Okay." I walk out and stand by the door until she opens it again. We know how silly we are. In the back of our minds somewhere we realize we are being utterly ridiculous with our apples and our starvation and our ritual weigh in, but it's all a part of the bonding females do, and none of it can be helped.

"So... go ahead." It feels strange looking at her, but I do anyway. She has large breasts that hang down and wobble a little when she steps onto the scale. She has no fat on her that I can see. Her butt is smaller than mine and a bit flat, I suppose. I step beside her to peer at the numbers as the needle dangles then stops.

"One forty. You lost five pounds!" I am sincerely happy for her.

"Yeah." She seems a little distant. She grabs her blue robe off the sink and puts it back on. "You know what's weird?"

"What?"

"I don't even feel hungry."

"Me neither, really." I step on the scale then, with a towel wrapped around me. At the last minute I dropped the towel to the floor and squint down at the wavering needle, hoping that Eliza isn't checking me out as closely as I had her.

I remember watching the overweight watchers of their weight at Mom's meetings when my brothers and I were young. We would play in the inside or on the outside of the circle they all sat in. They were congenial women who laughed at Dana and Billy as the boys made goofy faces and rolled around on the carpet. During the meetings, each person would take a turn on the scale. The numbers were written on their chart in their file. Each time weight was lost the circle would clap. I wonder what they would have looked like naked on that scale.

"Three pounds, looks like. I lost three pounds. Oh, well. It's probably all water weight anyway." I know I'd probably gain it back in a day or so. My body fights a good fight. It likes food. Exercise is my only true weapon.

"It's so early."

"Yeah, it is." I secure the towel around my deprived body and sigh.

"I'm gonna go back to bed. Rachel, you were so cool for doing this with me. Thanks."

"You don't want to eat anything?"

"No." She is dragging herself down the hall.

"You sure?"

"Why ruin a good thing?" She closes her door and I put some clothes on and tromp expectantly into the kitchen. My mind is swimming with a million food options that do not include apples. I am almost giddy with anticipation, but don't want to put the kibosh on the three-pound deficit so quickly. I decide to break my apple fast with a bowl of oatmeal and a banana. It is Sunday, and although I have ceased my dedication to organized religion, the Sabbath is still a day in seven to ponder what it is all about and whether I can make any good sense of it or not. It is a day to consider my existence deeper than the exterior, material, superficial, mirrored image of what I am.

The oatmeal is a nod to deeper thought. I could never feel spiritual with a stomach full of eggs and bacon and butter. And the oatmeal tastes like heaven to me. Cardboard could have come in a close second after the endlessness of the apples. Every savory bite is smooth, dreamy, yummy, nourishing, and comfortable going down. I am cementing myself back to the earth, returning to my body. Perhaps my spirit had wanted out if I wasn't going to provide a warm and happy home.

I wash my bowl out in the sink quietly while heating up some water for peppermint tea. The right tea can top off a meal like the right hat completes an outfit. Tea carefully warms and relaxes all inside mechanisms that could have been mistreated by chunks of food not properly chewed or digested. Tea provides closure to the meal, and gives the mouth a refreshing sensation that allows one to feel satisfied and complete. Tea allows me to feel I am finished eating, even if I want more.

Setting my mug on the bedside table, I drop onto my bed with my latest Margaret Atwood book. And as the steam swirls up and out, I drift down and in to the words that ring so true inside my head. My only worry is that I am running out of them, these Margaret Atwood books. This makes me read each page slowly as I savor it, like the tea I sip and set back on the table.

The sun is getting brighter from the window ahead of me, but this only gives the room a warmer glow, so that even though I am not sitting in a pew in church, I can say that I am feeling the spirit or whatever it is that puts me into a mood so that just sitting and breathing is all I need.

So I sit and breathe and sip and read and try not to think of the Monday model I will have to be in twenty-four hours. Hours. Five hours difference from here to New York. And this is also what I am trying not to think of. It is nearly 9:00, which makes it 4:00 am in New York. My stomach does an oatmeal flip as I think about where he might be. Safe in his bed alone, is my positive mental image. Passed out at some stranger's party house next to who knows is my fear. I sip my peppermint tea and listen to the clock tick. I won't be able to call him for at least another five hours. I know the wait is going to ruin my momentary serenity. Something always does.

At least this week I have the ball in my court, as they say. It is my week to call, and Sunday is our day to talk. Last week it had been dark outside before the phone rang. The long distance relationship thing is seeming nearly surreal to me, as if all we have been through or done together is fading, splitting into tiny pieces of my creative imagination that could conjure up only what had been good, making the memories sweeter and more heartbreaking now that we are apart. I look at the words in my book, but my mind is busy seeking the truth I have with Dylan. Is it good or is it all I have to hang on to?

Either way, I am not finding any peace with him. He is now only a voice on the phone when he used to be my only vice, escape, pleasure, temptation, enjoyment. He is just a Sunday phone call now. Slowly, slowly I can see our relationship quivering in the great winds that separate us and blow over the mighty Atlantic with a cold and careless shrug. What do time and nature care of human experience, of human need and comfort? Not much. Time cares not at all. It doesn't consider that each day ticking away is another contributing to the weakening of ties. And time knows that unless you're Michael J. Fox or Superman, it cannot be brought back or bought for any price. Time does not play by our rules. We play by the rules of time with our clocks and watches and scheduled appointments. When we want time to speed up, it only laughs and slows down. And when we wish for time to stand still it hurries forward without even a backward glance.

I look at the clock again. Maybe I can call just to see if he is there? I could pretend I forgot about the time zones. I could tell him I miss him so much I couldn't wait. But would I want him calling me at 4:15 in the morning? What would I do if he did answer?

"Hey."

I looked up from my book.

"Hey, sleepy head. Hungry yet?"

"I don't know. I guess. What did you eat?"

"Oatmeal."

"Yuck." Eliza stands there with her blue robe hanging untied at her sides. Her hair is everywhere, and dark circles pop out from beneath her eyes. We have quickly gotten past the point of trying to impress each other with our appearance. The task is too exhausting.

"I know. But you wouldn't believe how great it tasted." The memory is going to be a fond one, and will assist in future meals consisting of oatmeal.

"Anything would probably taste good right now."

"It's true." She takes a seat then, and reveals a tight, white, ribbed tank top that makes her breasts look huge. With her fingers she plays with the edge of the silk, paisley boxers she wears.

"These are Ty's."

"Oh." I assume she is talking about the boxers.

"I miss him like crazy."

"I know." I miss Dylan like crazy, too, but probably for different reasons.

"What are we going to do Rachel?" It is a broad question, but I know exactly what she means.

"You wanna go back home?" I am hoping she'll say no. It is daring to even ask this, seeing as she is my only friend and I want to keep her in Paris.

"I don't know. If I did I'd feel like a failure."

"You're not. Jeez. You think you have to be a model to be successful?" I give myself silent kudos for not looking out for my own self-interest.

"I know this sounds lame, but I think Ty is really getting a kick out of me being here." She crosses one skinny leg over the other and continues. "I mean it's the only thing he talks about lately."

Ty calls his girlfriend no less than three times a week.

"I guess I feel like I'm doing it for him, you know? If I went back I wonder if..."

"Eliza..." It is a scolding tone.

"Well, shit."

"It's ridiculous to think that way. You guys are in love, right? And you had something way before this. He just wants you to feel good about your choice to be here." What the hell do I know?

"I'm not sure anymore."

We both understand that being models is an exciting concept for those we know. We also realize we are doing it partly for them, for the ones who look on and brag about it to their friends. We do it for our mothers. Even me.

"I just can't let them down, you know?"

"Yeah." Although I am staying away for more reasons than this.

"I've only been here what? A couple weeks? A month?" She pulls her legs up so that her knees give her a place to set her chin. "I'd be giving up way too early. I'd regret it the rest of my life."

"That's what they say." It is an excellent ploy used by the agents when they think they might lose a working model.

"I feel like I could eat everything in the apartment. That, or nothing at all."

"The apples were easy, huh?"

"Yeah." She comes over and lies on the bed next to me. I move over a little for her. She curls her body up tight and we both are quiet for some time. Sometimes words can get in the way of insight or truth or knowledge. The room glows brightly with the noonday sun, and I wish for the cool of the evening again so I can slip out of my window and witness the Parisian night lights from the roof. It is my favorite time of day, the night.

"You need to eat, Eliza. Let me make you something. What would you like?"

"Do they have Pizza Hut here?"

"I haven't seen one."

"A medium pan cheese, please." Her arms are over her head; her eyes close as she continues her fantasy order. "Don't forget the parmesan cheese and a large Sprite with extra ice." Now she is smiling.

"How about some low-fat pancakes with honey and orange juice?"

She opens her eyes at me.

"You're gonna make pancakes for me?" She inquires this in a high-pitched voice that makes her sound giddy. Now her legs go up and she begins doing criss-crosses with them. I just stand in the doorway watching. "Maybe if I just lie in bed all day I won't have to eat."

"Novel idea."

"I can just go out for appointments and jobs, if I get any. Then I can come home and get back in bed. Of course I'll allow myself water."

"Of course." I sit on the chair as she turns onto her side to do leg raises with pointed toes.

"You're really gonna make me pancakes?" Her doubts about my cooking desires are certainly to be expected. She has been the one to do any fixing of meals, if we eat together.

"Really I will, if you want them."

"I want them."

"That's all you had to say."

* * *

At exactly 2:00 pm I dial Dylan's number on our ancient, heavy black phone in the living room. Eliza is out gathering more food. She has been born again with the pancakes and realizes her starvation ideas have been utterly absurd.

I pull the circular dial piece around, saying each number in my head to make sure and get it right. The receiver feels like a three-pound weight in my hand, but it is thin. I hold it up to my head and under my hair. I pray to God he will answer. It is still pretty early there.

"What?" responds the groggiest, grumpiest voice I've ever heard.

"Um." Clearing my throat. Why hadn't I done that *before* I dialed? "Is Dylan there?" Please don't be mad I called.

"Who is this?" Yikes! Why do I feel so hollow inside? Every reprimand I have ever received comes rushing into my chest.

"It's Rachel. Calling from Paris." This always makes it sound important, and it seems to work because his tone of voice changes immediately.

"Rachel, yeah. Hold on a minute. Let me check." Clunk. Let me check? Doesn't he know if his son is in the house or not? What kind of a father is he?

"Rachel?" This is him, the voice I have waited a week to hear again.

"Hi." As if I called all this way to say nothing but.

"Hello." Can't he think of something else to say?

"Is it too early?"

"No. I mean we were sleeping in."

"Oh. You were still in bed?"

"Yeah. It's okay though." He gives a little waking-up-groan, and I can visualize his thin, naked chest rising and inflating with air.

"So, what did you do last night?" I cut into the groan a second or two before it seems completely finished. I am not paying to hear that!

"Not much." I have asked too early. I pushed it too fast.

"Where did you go?" I can't stop myself.

"I don't know. Here and there." God, I wish I had my own life so I didn't have to horn in on his!

"Did you go out with John?"

"Yeah. So what are *you* up to?"

"Nothing." I can play the game. Is he trying to evade my questions? No such chance! "Eliza and I just completed our three-day apple fast." Boy does that sound stupid.

"What do you mean? You ate apples for three days?"

"Yeah." At least I am getting his attention.

"What did you do that for?"

"To lose weight, obviously." I am trying to convince myself.

"Rachel, you don't need to lose any weight." Oh, thank you, thank you. Reality check. Long distance reality check.

"I lost three pounds." Why do I feel the need to grab him in this fashion?

"Rachel, don't be stupid, okay? Jesus. You know those dumb diets don't work." Is he calling me dumb? Why does he sound so irritated with me?

"Dylan, I need you to be honest with me, okay?" I don't feel like paying for senseless chit-chat that is getting me nowhere.

"What?"

"Just tell me the truth."

"About what?"

"Do you promise? Can you just promise to be truthful with me?"

"What?" Irritation all over the place.

"I am just wondering if you'd, you know, slept with anyone since I left?" I squeak it out not even really wanting an answer.

"Have *you*?" Is he evading the question or really wondering?

"That's not the question."

"Sure it is. It's just as valid as the one *you* asked."

"Fine then. No." I think about the incident on the airplane and it comforts me to know that just in case he lies I have something, too.

"Me neither."

"Really?"

"Really. Don't you believe me?" No. After all, *I* wasn't even telling the whole truth.

"Yeah, I guess." It doesn't matter what he says or if I believe him. I will never really know the truth from this far away if he doesn't want it to be known.

"Rachel, I still love you. I don't know why you have to always question me like this." *Still?* He *still* loves me, as if it is a chore or something, as if we've been married fifteen years and he deserves some kind of medal?

There is a silence then, and I wish to God I had a developed sixth sense to cut through all the crap and just read his mind. I give up and enter a new topic of discussion that could disappointment me almost as much.

"So, did you find someone new for the band?"

"Rache…"

"Well?"

"We did. Are you happy now? How long did you expect us to wait for you?"

"Longer than this." I am pouting.

"Anyway, John thought we should get someone more professional, you know?" His timidity feeds my confidence and continued curiosity.

"So, what's this professional's name?" I have never truly intended on making his band a serious career choice, but I am not going to give in so easily. I sound hurt on purpose. "Who is replacing me?" In how many areas?

"Her name is Annie."

"Annie?" As if I don't have good hearing. Did he say Annie in a personal or professional way?

"Yes, Annie." There. More professional than personal, I guess.

"Does this girl have a last name?"

"I don't know. Something with an 'M' I think."

"You don't know her last name?" What am I trying to get at here? It's probably good he doesn't know her last name. Then again, I don't even know the guy's first name on the plane.

"Rachel, I don't care about her last name."

"Oh. How old is she then?" Will I never relent?

"I don't know." Guys never know anything.

"Well take a guess." Don't be an idiot.

"Mid-twenties. I don't know." His irritation is mounting once again. I am running out of innocent sounding questions. In my brain I am a prosecutor. Are you attracted to her? Does she have a boyfriend? Has she been to your house and for what reason? Is she thin? What color hair does she have?

"So how does she sing?"

"She wails." Excellent word choice. It makes me feel like a squeaky, unprofessional mouse who nibbles all day on apples and nothing more. I can't wail. I can't even sing harmony all that well. Now I feel like an idiot for even practicing with them.

"We actually got a gig on Halloween. Annie knows the owner of this dive bar in Brooklyn. It's not much, but it's something." Finally, some excitement in his voice. And none of it has to do with me. My heart sinks to my toes.

"That's great. I'm really proud of you guys." How *did* I get that out?

"And John's got a place in the city now. I told you that, didn't I?"

"No. Where?" How long? What other information is he keeping from me? And how could he not keep track of what we have told one another?

"Lower East Side. He wants me to move in with him, split the rent, you know?"

"Are you going to?"

"Maybe. If we start getting some paying gigs it could work pretty well. Anyway, my dad's been on my case again about school." All of a sudden I realize I am talking to a boy, a kid, who has no idea for the future, no long-term plan that may or may not include me. I wonder then how I could have slept with him. Time and distance allow for greater and deeper reflection. "Rachel?"

"Yeah?" I sit in a daze, staring at the dust on the living room blinds, picturing myself trying to clean them, but not having enough of a desire to really do the job the way it ought to be done.

"I should probably go. My dad needs to use the phone." His dad just woke up. Who does he need to call so soon? And how dare *he* say when the conversation is going to end. I am the one calling long distance from Paris.

"Who does he have to call?" None of my business, but who cares at this point?

"My mom."

"Oh." If it is a lie it is a good one. And what can I do thousands of miles away? I can't entice him with my charm or touch him on the arm to plead for more time to work through all of this.

"I'll call you next Sunday, okay?"

"Yeah, okay." Said hesitantly.

"I love you."

"I love you, too." Dial tone. What can a man do with a woman's voice? Scratch that. What can a kid do with a long distance romance? Not much. Who am I to try to keep him on a leash that extends to connect two continents?

* * *

232

On Halloween night, Eliza and I are sitting in the living room on the thinly carpeted floor, drinking Merlot and staring at three flickering candles we have purchased together when we hear a knock on our door. No one except Alex has ever been in our apartment. We look at each other hoping it isn't him.

"I'll get it." Eliza springs up on her long, strong limbs, sets her glass on the counter, and peeks through the hole in the door. "It's Sam."

"Sam? Let her in." I stand up, a little wobbly from the wine, but fine.

"Hey. Do you guys mind? I can't fucking take it anymore over at the whorehouse."

"Come on in." Eliza and I look at each other in disbelief. Who is this bold intruder knocking on our door on the night of all nights? "Would you like a glass?"

"Definitely. Anything you got." And she is in and on the floor with her large bag of a purse thrown next to her. Sam is what the business calls petite. As far as I know, petite models don't work very much. It's such a specialized market.

"You okay?" Eliza settles near her and resumes drinking.

"I'm fine."

"It's cool that you came over. I mean, Eliza and I were just sitting here bored out of our minds." She doesn't respond to this. I approach her with her glass and she looks up and into my eyes for the first time. Hers are dark, mysterious. She has short, jet-black hair cropped close to her face. She wears heavy, black liner on her top lids and a good deal of mascara. Her lips are dark purple.

"You guys get high?" Again we look at each other without Sam looking at either one of us.

"Sure." I hadn't really thought about it for a while. But I guess I do. I had. Yes.

"Sure." Eliza follows my lead as we watch Sam unload several items from her purse. Out comes a black tray, a baggie, and a pipe with what looks like the head of a monster or some grotesque animal. She begins with the seed separation I have witnessed so many times. Then with her tiny fingers she breaks the stems away from the leaves and tears and rips until she has a nice little pile of pot ready for the monster pipe. And then out with the lighter.

Outside our window, the city is dark. It rained earlier and the living room window still has a wet look to it, droplets smattering near the bottom edge.

"Look at the moon. There, you can see it." Eliza and I tilt our heads to get a view. The three of us have formed a circle around the candles, which makes passing the pipe an easy endeavor. We pass and puff and cough and we light the leaves again, inhaling the smoke, the earth, the night, the magic, the hope, the air, the fire, the THC. I bring the bottle of wine to the floor and fill everyone's glasses a second or third time.

"I'm glad we decided on the big bottle." Eliza whispers this to me as if it might disturb Sam.

The air is becoming thick and smoky. I decide to open the window. In rushes the after-rain aroma and cool breezes. Sam shakes involuntarily in her tight, black tee-shirt. Torn and faded blue jeans wrap themselves around her little body; her feet are disguised by black combat boots with laces going far up under her jeans. I close the window and sit back down, this time against the wall with a pillow in my lap.

"Don't you guys ever go out?" Again, a mutual search into each other's faces.

Eliza offered, "I guess we would, if we knew where to go." She looks at me and shrugs her shoulders. I shrug right back.

"We'll have to go out some time."

"Sure." I am feeling good. Real good. Warm, high, low, happy, comfortably unaware. Moments like this are excellent. I look toward my room where I've left the small lamp on by my bed. It makes the room look cozy. I feel safe. I stare at the candles and try not to think about Dylan.

"We should really hit the pavement tonight, being Halloween

and all, but I don't feel like it. May I?" She holds up a cigarette in her dainty paw. Normally I can't stand the smell or knowing what it does to my lungs.

"If I can...?" I nod to the window and she nods up and down. I crack it slightly, and while Sam smokes hard on her cigarette, she tells us a story, casually flicking the ashes into her hand and rubbing them into her jeans.

"Last Halloween seems like a million Halloweens ago. I was living in Detroit with my brother. He brought me along to one of his college parties, said it was going to be a real bash, you know. The only thing was we had to dress up, and I didn't have a costume. So I went as a gypsy. It was easy enough. My hair was down to the crack in my ass then. Anyway, the party was already insane when we got there. People were smoking all sorts of shit. I was just drinking from the barrel and smokin' a little weed, nothing major. So pretty soon I can't find my brother anymore. The house was fucking packed. I mean wall to wall. It took me twenty minutes to find a bathroom. I thought I was going to pee in my pants by the time it was my turn. So I'm feelin' pretty good, but I still can't find my brother. I figure, oh well, he probably got lucky or something. He had just broken up with this girl he was really digging, and I felt sorry for him, you know?

"So after a couple hours I'm pretty buzzed, and I'm standing in line for another beer and there's this pirate standing next to me and he says he and I should get together, you know, because of our costumes. He was really cute, from what I could see. He was a big guy. I remember thinking he probably lifted weights, which normally turns me off. But I was getting lonely and figured I probably wouldn't see my brother again anyway. He tells me his name is Scott. Says he's majoring in business or something. So we start making out, but by this time I'm getting really tired and figure I should probably get back to the apartment. So I tell Scott that I need some air and I'm gonna go outside. He follows right along, just like a little dog."

By now all three of us are lying on our backs with our feet up against the wall. My glass of wine is teetering on my flattened chest.

Sam is working on another cigarette and the smoke is sailing politely toward the open window.

"It was a cool night, like tonight, and the fresh air felt good in my lungs. I just wanted to walk forever, you know, maybe wake up from my drunk so I could enjoy my buzz. So I tell Scott I'm gonna head home. I mean I don't really give a fuck about him. He's just one in a million of arrogant, horny, self-serving, alcoholic college boys. So he says that I can go fuck myself, and I tell him that I probably will, thanks for the suggestion. And he heads back to the party in a huff. Meanwhile, my head begins to clear a little and I'm enjoying the fact that it's Halloween as I kick through all the fallen leaves on the side of the road. But no sooner do I turn the corner when Scott is back with three of his buddies. They're all yelling and screaming and falling all over each other and I know I'm up shit's creek with a broken paddle, but I remain calm. The skeleton comes up on the right side of me and wants to know why I don't want to party some more, that he's got something that'll guarantee a good time. I tell him I'm sure he does, but I'm not interested. Then the priest and the football player run up ahead of me and turn around and begin walking backwards. I look around for a place of business or something, you know? A light or a house that I could run to because I've seen my share of HBO specials on the subject. But, and I'll always remember this, it was so dark where we were walking that I couldn't even see my hand in front of me when I went to light my smoke. They kept calling me 'little gypsy.' 'Hey, little gypsy, don't you want to play?' and so on until I wanted to scrape their eyeballs out with my fake fingernails. Somehow or other I'm entirely surrounded by these guys, and Scott starts demanding I finish what I started. I'm wondering where in God's world could my brother be, and I want to shout out loud for him, but I don't want them to see I've lost my nerve. So I keep quiet and light another smoke. The priest steals it from my mouth and tells me they have a better idea. Somehow I get knocked to the ground and my skirts gather all around me in a big pile of leaves. Scott pulls out this needle and the distant light of the moon suddenly shines on it, making it glitter

"'Now this is what Halloween is all about, huh?'

'Yeah. Hey, you sure you want to waste that shit on the slut?'

'You wanna have a good time, don't you?'

'Yeah, man.'

'Well, then.'

"And with a flick of the needle, he jabs the thing into my arm as the other three hold me down. By this time I'm screaming my lungs out, but the football player has a nice, tight grip over my mouth. And then my body goes ecstatically numb all over and I feel like I'm in heaven but I know I'm in hell. Sure, I've done drugs. But I've never shot up, you know. And all I can think of is AIDS. I'm gonna get AIDS. If not from the fucking needle, then from…

"'I'm first. You keep a lookout.' Scott says this to the skeleton as he unzips his black, pirate pants, and with his un-patched eye he looks right at me and has the balls to tell me to have a good time. Funny thing was, I didn't give a shit if the whole neighborhood fucked me, I was feeling so great. But I was still pissed off, inside. Somewhere deep down inside I wanted to fight so bad. I wanted to kick that asshole so bad, but he was on my legs. When he got up, I managed to do it, too. But that only cost me a punch in the face. Not even a slap, you know? He had to use a closed fist. That really pissed me off. Anyway, I must have passed out there in the street because when I woke up to the early light of November, Raggedy Ann and Andy were standing over me trying to talk to me.

"'There, sweetie. There's your purse.' Ann was trying to make my blouse go back together while Andy turned his back to us. I thought that was really nice of him, you know?"

21

CONFRONTATION

Time is easily spent fulfilling the requests of others, keeping scheduled appointments, working jobs that have been acquired, and maintaining self and surroundings so one is able to keep financial and other obligations. We work to maintain, and we maintain to work. It is a vicious cycle of the human existence, which none of us ever really wants to admit to. We want to think of ourselves as free as the birds, able to take off whenever we please. We would like to fancy ourselves not prudent, cautious, or guarded, but nonchalant and easygoing when it comes to our basic requirements. But being alive, and growing up is so much more complicated than we ever imagined. I wonder if Adam and Eve knew what they were getting themselves into. Washing, brushing, organizing, shopping, mopping, scrubbing, sleeping, filing, writing, paying, cleaning, calling, showering, finding, buying, thinking, drinking, eating, combing, clipping, cutting, driving, walking, fixing, listening, sewing, scraping, shoveling, digging, applying, and restoring, all due to the daily upkeep of the human body and home. And it's all done again and again, as if we had forgotten we had done it already. Just yesterday. Just last week. Time spent on maintenance and upkeep is time spent in a zone of forgetfulness.

We do not want to acknowledge the busy, repetitive state in

which we have found ourselves. And so we decide at some point that we will take a break, a vacation, a hiatus from the circle of scheduled, daily chores to contemplate and attempt to find meaning in it all. Some do this every evening, some do it every weekend, and some only find time this precious here and there when they think they can afford to. But everyone experiences this break in the wheel when the cycle slows down and we think we will finally be able to think.

But then, what is there to think about? A dangerous question asked on hiatus. All of a sudden we search for meaning, for identity, for something worthwhile to live for. Why? Because we finally have the time. It is interesting to see what people do with their free time. Do they find a hobby? Do they socialize? Do they search for more maintenance? I have seen people, like myself, who actually go searching for more things to "keep up." We notice the baseboards are dusty, and we dust them. We find that the keyboard to the computer is dirty, and so we get out the q-tips and alcohol. We alphabetize our compact discs, vacuum behind the couch, re-write our "to do lists," organize sock drawers, and unravel telephone cords. On the other hand, it seems that some people do nothing. Literally. They sit with the remote control and a cool drink and stare at their 36 or 57 channels and seem entertained by the same commercial for Tylenol over and over again. These people can watch the same movie six times and think nothing of it. It's a disturbing image the dawn of the moving picture has brought upon us.

I think the quality of a person is based on what they do when they have nothing to do. For the person who can create worthwhile activities and contemplations without being coached, is a person who is on the brink of discovering the meaning of life, or at least the meaning of their life. I am trying to become one of these people.

"Rachel?"

"What?"

"I'm gonna miss you when I go."

"I'm gonna miss you, too." Eliza is sitting on our only stool in the house sketching me. She is left-handed, and it looks funny to me to see her rounded wrist move up and down and sideways as she peers at me so seriously. I stare at the walls ahead of me, trying to stay still, amused at her patterings of paint that are finding themselves all over our apartment. They really warm up the place and make it ours. I am beginning to feel like Paris is my home. It is still strange thinking this, though.

"Can you bring your hand back?"

"Sorry." I had scratched the tip of my nose and forgotten to place my hand on the back of the chair where she wanted it. I am sitting backwards on it in nothing but the lacy piece of lingerie I had purchased for the initial encounter. My hair is down and draped in front of me. One leg is extended slightly, with a pointed toe. The other is propped up on a rung underneath. I face toward the extended leg and look melancholy. That is Eliza's word. She wants me to look sad, but more than that. Thoughtful. And then she finds the right word and seems satisfied as she looks up at me and then down again at her large sketchbook. I can do melancholy.

"You cold?" She glances over at the robe she's brought out for me.

"No, I'm okay." We are making good use of our time. It is almost a freedom not having a television. Its absence inspires creativity and greater human contact. There is no annoying sound distraction or competition for our attention blaring at us. No pretty, pale-faced women sounding serious about plastic versus cardboard applicators. No singing dogs or dancing cats or glamour girls shaking their shiny hair and looking seductively at the viewer to sell a certain brand of shampoo. Clutter. Commercials clutter the brain the same way dirty dishes can clutter a sink. Without all this clutter I have been accosted by during my nearly twenty years of life, I feel almost pure again.

"You're not painting me naked, are you?" I try to keep a serious face as I stare sideways.

"Would I do that?" She gives me an authentic grin, which makes her eyes light up.

"Probably."

"Do you want me to?"

"No." Natural, Christian impulse.

"This is actually looking pretty good."

"Is there any resemblance?"

She stops for a minute and extends her sketchbook away from her body. "A little." Again she smiles.

"When will you be back?"

"Tuesday, I think. It's a three-day shoot."

"This place is going to be empty without you."

"A little less melancholy, please." I like Eliza more than I have ever liked any girl, I suppose. She has a boyish quality and never attempts to compete with me as girls are accustomed to do. For her there is more to life than this, than being driven by personal beauty, recognition, self-preservation, and competition. I have to admit that she is probably a better person than I am when it comes to vanity. I am the kind of person who believes I have to be in constant competition with any girl, but will never let on as such. I can find a girl's finest features in a matter of minutes, and at the same time quickly detect her most inadequate flaw. If a girl has beautiful, unmarked skin, I will notice that the shape of her face precludes her from wearing her hair up. If a female person appears to be well-endowed, I notice the slope of her small, rounded shoulders as she turns sideways. If a girl has a shapely behind, I will notice the pucker of fat as she crosses her legs in shorts. And if a chick has nice, thin legs and pretty ankles, I will notice that her second toe is longer than the first, making her feet unattractive. It's all a curse that comes along with the modeling business, I suppose. The mini-competition I find myself in day after day automatically transfers to the rest of my life, and I am afraid it always will.

"Done."

"Really?"

"Yep. Take a look." I shake the frozen position from my bones, drape Eliza's blue robe over my shoulders, and walk across the room to stand in front of my first portrait.

"Wow." I am just impressed she has actually done it. I recognize my profile. That is me, all right. She has brushed soft colors over her sketch, giving the picture a quality that demands some attention. "This is nice." I touch the paper not knowing how to critique it. I am not really qualified. "I like it."

"You're not just saying that?" She keeps her gaze on her finished piece.

"No. It's good."

"We'll put it here." The paper is torn from her book and slapped up on the wall between the flowers and the fruit. "Bring me a couple thumbtacks, will you?"

* * *

The next day she is gone and the apartment feels emptier than the day I moved in. Eliza has gone to the south of France to do an advertisement for expensive jewelry. Dressed up and made up, Eliza has an elegant quality that has begun filling her portfolio. I am exactly the opposite. My pictures show energy and sunshine, bare faces and smiles. It reveals perhaps not what I am, but what I could become.

I wander up and down the hallway the first morning she is gone, wondering what to do without my friend. Saturdays we do laundry together, shop for our food, and clean up the place. Alone, I don't feel I have the energy for it, though.

Slowly, and out of habit, I begin wiping the counter and emptying the small trash cans into a large trash bag. In my tee shirt and underwear I've worn to bed, I crouch down in front of the refrigerator and throw out the soft end of a cucumber, two flexible carrots, expired cottage cheese, and three rotten apples. Neither of us has much of a taste for them anymore. I sweep the kitchen floor with our little broom and wash the top of the stove. I move around the house slowly, in my zone, doing what I have done a million times for my mom and for myself. I imagine the years ahead of me in which I will have to do this same thing and more. Perhaps some day for children, too. Where will all the energy come from?

I flip over a tape that is in Eliza's small boom box and moan along with Enya as I make my way into the bathroom with my can of cleanser, rubber gloves, and a rag.

Cleaning in my underwear gives me a strange sense of freedom. It seems almost taboo, I suppose, compared to the neatly dressed mothers in the laundry detergent commercials. They always appear so normal and well-coordinated in their preppie outfits and light lipstick smiles as they wipe their child's knee and nod to the viewer that the blood stains will come out of his favorite jeans. I wonder how many housewives clean in dress shorts, blouses that require ironing, and white, spotless tennis shoes? Not to mention full makeup and headband.

After the bathroom, I decide to pick up Eliza's room, a routine habit leftover from childhood. She is not the neatest roommate, but I'd take her over Susan and Yvonne any day. I fold her clothes and put them on top of her dresser. I pull her bed together and dust off her end table where she has a picture of Ty and herself somewhere on the coast. I sit down on the bed to look at the picture closer when I hear a noise at the door. Panic rushes up through my body and my heart begins to thump in my throat. I am not sure if I should run to the door in my underwear or hide or call someone.

"Hello? Anyone here? Hello?" His French voice bellows around the apartment. I feel awkward and embarrassed and confused and naked. I grab Eliza's robe from the chair, put it around me, and peek out the doorway.

"Alex?"

"Oh, sorry. I didn't know anyone was here, sweetheart." Hadn't he ever heard of a doorbell? "I just came to check on the sink."

"What's wrong with it?"

"I was told it wasn't working properly, dear. Don't mind me."

I do mind you! What are you doing here?

"The sink works fine, as far as I know." I slink toward my room, racking my brain, trying to figure out if Eliza or I had ever mentioned to him or anyone else that we were having trouble with our sink.

"Well, as long as I'm here…" In. Quickly, off with the robe and on with my jeans.

"Rachel, dear. You don't have to be embarrassed in front of me." His large hand casually pushes open my door. "My entire business deals with the female body. There's nothing I haven't seen, believe me." I zip up my jeans and cross my arms over my thin tee shirt. I have no idea what I am supposed to say or do.

"How's the sink?"

"I might need to get a plumber in here, perhaps." His darkly creased face and scarred eye try their best to look friendly. He is in jeans today himself, with a nylon jacket and boat shoes. It is one of the first times I've seen him look halfway normal. "The pipes are very old in these apartments, darling."

"Oh."

"So it looks like things are going well here with the two of you, no?"

"Yes. Eliza and I get along well."

"Very good." And he proceeds into the living room to view the sketches. "Is this one you?" The paper rattles underneath his fingers as he touches it.

"Yeah." How embarrassing.

"It's quite beautiful."

"Eliza's pretty talented." Why can't I just stand up to this man and be confident? Inside, my whole body shakes.

"Yes, yes she is. I want to thank you also for making her feel so at home here. I know it's because of you she's doing so well now. Michael told me you'd be a good influence with the other models." He places his hand on my shoulder as a proud father might.

"Thank you." His hand remains, weighing me down on that side. If there is anything I try to avoid in life besides getting pregnant, sick, fat, or being sent to hell, it is conflict. I don't want conflict. I don't deal well with it. I want life to be smooth without any bumpy loud anger, violence, abuse, or dissatisfaction. Everything I do I do to avoid the unpleasant.

"Rachel. I have to admit that I came here to talk with you as well. I hope you'll forgive me."

"Of course." *What is it? Get it over with and leave me to my cleaning.*

"Well, honey. Valerie has explained to me that you've lost several important bookings since you've been in Paris." His hand is back down and in his jeans pocket, but he remains just as close. I take a baby step backwards, hoping he won't notice. "You know why, don't you?"

"Yeah." I say it fast and soft, still clutching my arms across my chest. His breath is heavy and close. I can smell the cigarettes he'd smoked earlier.

"Well, sweetheart, part of my job is to look out for my business, you know. Someone like you should be working every day." I raise my eyebrows. "You don't think so?"

"I don't know."

"Sugar, all you need... Come here." He pulls my arms to my sides to expose my small breasts, which stick out of my shirt like anthills. And then his hands are on them, on top of the shirt as I stand there without moving or making a sound. All I can think is that he'll be finished soon and I can get through this without making a fool of myself. "Yes..." His right hand works its way over them, massaging them as his left holds on tightly to my arm. "You have a nice shape to them. It would be so easy, you know." And then without asking, he lifts up my shirt like a doctor and feels around again with both hands this time. I take the chance, step back, and snap my shirt down all in a split second.

"There now...." He moves a step back himself looking a little put out. "I wanted to get an idea. Rachel, you know you wouldn't have to pay for them yourself. I will take care of that and you can pay me back after you begin working like you should. Rachel, dear, you really have no idea. You could be big. I mean really big. Supermodel big. Don't you want that, sweetheart? I will help you out with everything. We have an excellent plastic surgeon here in Paris that has helped many of our models. You really have nothing to worry about."

By this time I was seething with anger at his ugly, sheepish, scarred face. How dare he do this to me! I want to scream out loud right there in front of him, only I have no desire to be comforted by a rapist. Instead I walk casually over to the refrigerator, grab a bottle of Evian, and take a cool sip. "I don't want a boob job." I set the bottle down on the counter because my hand is shaking.

"No, of course not. No one really wants to have one, dear. They want the results of one. What are you, a 34 A?"

"36." Do I really have to stand here and discuss this while the cleanser sits in the tub?

"All the more reason, Rachel darling. A girl like you with such a nice body and shape needs a little shape on top, wouldn't you agree?"

I hate him, I hate him, I hate him! In the back of my mind I know this conversation is going to stay with me the rest of my life, for the rest of my years I have to look at myself and see this inadequacy.

"Well, I'll let you alone with your thoughts now. You come and see me about this soon, all right? Michael would be so proud of you if you did this. You know that, don't you?"

I watch this old man give me a sly grin and walk out of my apartment as if I am the one in need of a makeover. The tragic thing about it is I believe him.

22

THE SECOND CATHARSIS

After the door is closed I go to it, securing the deadbolt as I should have done earlier. I want to bang my head against the door, but instead turn my back to it, slide to the floor, and sit there as the tears begin to drop. The familiar sensation of confused defeat and warm tears on my cheeks quickly pull me back again to all sadness, all unfairness, all depression I've ever experienced. Inside my body, inside my ribcage, probably very near to my heart, I ache deeper than I have in a long time and I break down and sideways, falling onto the wooden floor in the hallway. These are the times I suck myself into such deep self-pity that I begin to contemplate a self-decided end to it all, like in the movies where the young, pretty girls are found dead in a tub of red blood, sliced wrists hanging over the edge, hair floating all around as if unaware that the peace of life had been disturbed. Who would end up cleaning that tub? I wondered.

As romantic as this picture seems, it just isn't me. Suicide suggests a selfish thing, sweet only for the solitary moment, then stupider than all my silent tears combined.

So I inch my way onto the living room carpet like a soldier creeping low to keep from getting his head blown off. I grab a small, blue pillow and place it under my head so that my crying can be a comfortable thing. I freeze into my new pose and peer into the dreary-weathered day, finding solace in the lack of sunshine.

The tears from one eye drip over the bridge of my nose and join the tears from the other eye as they fall to the pillow, making a darker blue spot. The whole process tickles a little, but I don't care to use the energy it will take to bring my hand up to scratch. Every non-effort is praised by my inner soul who screams to be taken from this earthly state of repetition, worthlessness, and inevitable demise. My thoughts travel to a darker place and I question why I should even try if I am just going to grow old and die?

My energy has been sapped by the one man I swore I'd never let hurt me. I mean, Christ! I had been warned! And yet there I stood alone with him breathing on me like some pervert. I want to call my mom and cry to her. I want a mom I know I could cry to. And then I simply lie there as still as expired breath. I run out of the energy to make tears.

* * *

The three of them walk in the darkness of the night away from the bright lights of the carnival. Mom and Dad hold onto their small daughter's hands on either side of her. She is barely tall enough to reach them. The happy, crazy, noisy sounds of the carnival fill the midnight air. Colorful and distracting spots of light blink from the roller coaster and Ferris wheel nearby. Children walk along the designated paths of the fair with large, pink wads of cotton candy and big, stuffed animals. Red rings are tossed at small-topped bottles and wrinkled dollars are traded for white balls to be thrown at a target.

Suddenly, the little girl looks around and realizes she is alone. Her parents have continued walking ahead of her and don't seem to be looking back. She steps between crowds of people trying to get a glimpse of her mom and dad as they fade into the distance ahead. They are no longer holding hands, holding her hands. She is losing them quickly. She decides to fly. She wants to. She has to. She pushes off with her small legs into the dark, summer air. Up, up, up she flies. Soon she is so high that it frightens her. But she knows if she gets too scared, she will fall. So she finds her desire again and flies forward with her arms stretched in front of her. And then she spots them. Her mother wears a dark, navy windbreaker. She can see it. It won't be long now before they will hear her yelling to them. But when she tries to scream for them, nothing comes out. Either that or they can't hear her. Or maybe they don't want to hear her. Maybe they don't even want her. But where else can she go?

She flies forward as the lights from the carnival fade into the background behind her. Below her, their distant shapes begin to melt into the blackness of the night. She tries once more to scream to them, and this time something does come out. But it is too late. Neither one of them even looks up.

* * *

My neck is sore as I rise from the floor and try to remember what I have been doing here. My head is dizzy with depressing thoughts and dreams and I want to shake them from my hair. I pull my hands over my chest and vow once again never to get a boob job. Why did I even let that creep get to me? I feel hung-over, but this bleak emptiness and head throbbing is a good thing, a distraction from the plodding seconds that punctuate the clock. There is a space out of time where I have gone to escape, and the physical sensations are the souvenirs that I've been away.

And so I get up and make the best of the rest of my day, vacuuming up tiny particles of food and dirt with the dust buster I'd picked up at a second-hand store. It will only run for about a minute and a half at a time, but this is fine with me. It is more like a game than a chore this way. I arrange all of Eliza's art supplies neatly in the corner on a table in the living room, fluff the pillows, make my own bed, pull the laundry and garbage together, and decide to go running even though I haven't eaten all day. I stand for a second, after my work is done, gazing out the front window at the drizzle that has turned to sheets of rain. Hunger gnaws and grows in my belly, and I wonder how it is that I've ended up a flat-chested model in Paris in the rain with a running addiction when I'd grown up an adopted child in a poor, abusive Midwestern family. How does one thing lead to the next, and if I've gone this far, how much further can I go?

The rain makes a beautiful sound against the windows as I pull my laces tight and tie them. I will go out into the pouring rain and run, as I have done in the summers as a kid. She'd send us out to play in the puddles in the gutters and our hair and clothes would get glued to our skin. She'd stand at the back door in her big, colorful dress and laugh at us when we'd look concerned or start to shiver. "You won't melt!" she'd exclaim. And before long we were splashing around and opening our mouths to the sky, feeling special somehow, that we were allowed this type of spontaneous freedom. Rain wasn't an excuse to sit indoors and pout. It was an opportunity to go out and find a little danger or be a little different from the rest.

All grown up now, I dart into the drops and am soaked in seconds as I run my course, weaving here and there to avoid an umbrella or a telephone pole. Running pushes me ahead of myself and allows zero opportunity for looking back, especially in the rain. The path ahead looks a bit bleary, but it's all I have. And so I plunge through the pools of water and into the vacant park where the grass is greener than any green when the skies are clear. On a spot of earthy carpet I pause and hang my head down to my knees and stretch until water runs into my nose. I blow it out onto my shirt, turn around, gather strength, and speed with the wind that now blows at my back, racing home through the dwindling rain. Running I am anyone. I am not this girl or that model or her daughter or his sister. I am a runner flying into any possible future, strong in my strength as I carry myself. I need nothing but my two legs, two feet, two shoes. I don't even need the sunshine. Running I am a motion. I don't hold still long enough to be judged. I don't require approval or direction, for a runner goes wherever she goes. It is the running that is the goal, not the destination. And today, I don't even require food, until I stop steps from the apartment to stretch again and breathe in the wonderful and sensuous aroma of the baking breads and pastries from the boulangerie. Such punishment I seem to inflict on myself, and all in a day.

I squish my way into the elevator in my soaking shoes and begin to conjure up the perfect meal to break such an unintended fast. As I exit the shower and re-enter what I'd maintained as a pretty balanced life in such a foreign place, I wonder why it is that the extremes seem so much more fascinating than in-between the extremes. Starving and binging, sleeping and running, living like a puritan and tripping on psychedelics are easy. Anyone can jump from one spectrum to the other in search of meaning and excitement and distraction. It's the standing still and breathing in one place that makes one squirm.

After a bowl of brown rice with sliced avocado and a large glass of distilled water, I carefully take Eliza's paints and brushes and paper out of their neatness, disturbing the perfection of it I have created, and slowly pour a small pool of all available colors on a piece of thick cardboard. I look at a blank piece of paper and begin. Choosing a medium-sized brush, I dip the tip in red, then purple, then green, then yellow. When the brush is gushing with color, I press it into a spot on the paper and twist it around and around in a gentle, circular motion. Then I rinse and repeat, except with different colors this time. I slowly and methodically fill the piece of paper with these bright kaleidoscope patterns. After this, I take a larger brush and instinctively place a black dot in the middle of each of them. Detached lines falling from the bottom of each finish this session of therapy for me. I let the picture dry as I clean up my mess.

Hanging my flowers on the wall amidst all the other sketches and paintings makes me decidedly proud of myself.

23

BIRTHDAY PRESENT

The lumpy, white comforter covers me from toe to chin as I sleep until the dawn, until the earth tilts and turns just enough to allow the golden rays to pierce through the hemisphere and room I currently live in, sleep in, wake in. My dreams have been jumbled, as if the dream master had been impatient with the remote control, unsettled in his decisions as he flipped from the shopping network to the discovery channel to all the various HBO options with a hundred commercial fragments in between until finally settling on VH1 with the volume turned up. The Rolling Stones ring through my brain. What tune, I can't place. Either way the night dramas have ended. It is time to awake to reality once again.

I splash my face with cool water in the bathroom as it falls from the small, silver, ancient looking faucet heads, and I peer into the tiny mirror above the sink, letting my face drip. I am curious to see myself in this most naked fashion without any deep cleansers, astringents, creams or powders. I stare at the image that stares back at me while I lean against the porcelain sink and remember I have to pee.

I once heard that during an average life span of seventy some years, people spend nine of it sitting on the toilet. Nine years. What a waste of time—pun intended. In nine years I could do so many things. I'm not sure what I would do if I had an extra nine, but I could do something more useful than sit on the pot.

Back in the mirror and a little more awake now, I spot two whiteheads on my chin and zoom in on them with my index fingers. How many times had I read that I should never touch my face, never squeeze a zit? Many. But to me it is just the common sense thing to do. I mean, what am I going to do, let them sit there and turn yellow until they gush from my face? Or worse yet, let them fester and cause craters. Don't ever play with a pimple, the pamphlet said; you could push it deeper and cause scarring. I picked one of these up at the clinic in college while I was waiting to experience my first pap smear. Another apparently necessary grotesque part of keeping up the female body in all its complexities and modern maladies. Prevent cancer, prevent scarring, prevent wrinkles. Have this test done once a year, use this cream twice a day, take this pill in the morning. Don't go in the sun. Sun damage causes premature aging.

Scarring and aging seem to be the worst evils of the day, and I am well on my way towards both. Two fine lines have already given themselves a comfortable home underneath the outer part of my eyes. I smile at my reflection and they sink deeper. Brown spots or freckles land across the tops of my nose and cheeks and I remember the summers in the backyard when I'd run out with the baby oil after I'd finished hanging the laundry on the lines. I'd slather on a good deal of it and lie still for as long as I possibly could while my brothers played with the hose and the sprinkler. Thirty minutes on my back and thirty minutes on my stomach, and then onto my back again until I had been roasted a deep, dark brown all ready for dinner.

"Rachel! Come set the table for supper!" She'd call me in then, and I'd pull my face up to the sun one last time, check my tan line, gather my things, and say goodbye to my sun until tomorrow. I loved the sun and I loved being tan. Still do. There's nothing better than those warm rays piercing my skin and changing it to make my teeth look whiter, my eyes bluer, my body thinner, and my soul warm and glowing. What magic! Being tan means more confidence with less makeup. It means that clothes look better and jewelry sparkles more attractively against the skin. But now it's bad for you, and on the news they show beaches of stupid sun searchers as they discuss malignant melanoma and irregular skin formations and the ozone layer and sunscreen and being "sun smart." I don't want to have to be smart in the sun. That is the whole beauty of it. It is so simple, so magical, so warm, so delightful. You go out in the sun and play or swim or read and you come home a changed person, a happier person, a warmer person. Now the warmth means spots and the sun means cancer, which means chemotherapy and radiation and the spread of cancer and hair loss and medical bills and death.

The first white head comes out easily and smashes into the mirror. It startles me to see the power of the zit as it sails at lightening speed toward my reflection. Splat. The other one oozes a little, like a dud on the Fourth of July that spins around slowly and then sputters out. I know there is still some stuff in there that needs to come out, but decide it isn't ready yet, like a cake that hasn't risen. So I leave it alone, and get out my cleansing lotion and begin to cleanse in a circular motion with my fingertips for several minutes as I walk around the apartment and open the blinds. Eliza isn't awake yet, so I am quiet.

After I rinse and pat my face with a towel, I take a cotton square, douse it with toner and slather it all over my face. Then I rinse again because I don't like the feel of the toner. Dots of under eye moisturizer soak themselves into my fine lines and wrinkles promising to diminish them. With my hair pulled back into a loose ponytail, I lean hard on the sink and peer in deep at my image. Here I am now, all grown up, no longer a teenager. It is the day of my birth. I am twenty.

* * *

"Rachel, it's for you." She hands me the phone while licking her fingers. We are having croissants and jam for breakfast. She insists as it is my birthday. Lovely, buttery croissants that crumble sweetly in your mouth and in your hands. They are so good. Too good. It's dangerous eating such tasty food when it's so denied.

"Hello?"

"Rachel, honey, it's me."

"Hi." It is my blonde booker.

"Good news. You've been confirmed for two veeks in Arizona vis zat German catalog. Remember vhen you saw Volfgang Kischnik at ze agency a mons or so ago?"

"I think so." I literally scratch my head to remember.

"Vell, he loves you. He sinks you are perfect for ze shoot. Anyvay. 1600 Deutsch Marks a day. Dis is fabulous, no?" She is excited for me.

"Yes. Thank you." My mind begins racing. "Arizona?"

"Oui, Madamoiselle."

"Why so far away?"

"Ze sunshine, of course. You know zhey need zis lighting for zhe long catalog shoots. It's alvays sunny zhere, no?" Ah, yes. Sun. "So anyvay, you leave in sree days. Alex vants your hair trimmed before you go, Oui?"

"Okay."

"Same place you go before. Just remember ze tip. Ozervise it is free to you." As long as I had been a model, I had never paid to get my hair cut. "Rachel, I must go. Ze ozer phone is ringing. Chow!"

I stuff the rest of the croissant in my mouth with confidence and satisfaction. This is a good birthday present. Now I won't even feel bad if Dylan doesn't call. Yes I will.

"Are you going to Arizona?"

"Oui, Madamoiselle. Can you believe it? Two weeks. With a German catalog, I guess. Catalog work pays really well, doesn't it? What's 1600 Marks in dollars?" I begin figuring 1600 multiplied by two weeks in my head. My eyes look up to the left, as if I can see the numbers there.

"I don't know." She looks at me with the same look I had given her when I knew she was going to leave. Wonder, confusion, sadness, jealousy. A model's life is so unpredictable as it is. It is rare to find the comfort of home and family Eliza and I are attempting to create together. Perhaps this is what a marriage is like—building days upon days with another person until that is what is most preferred, until that is the most desired reality and none other could compete. "That's a long time to be gone. Two weeks." First she had seemed like the man going away leaving the woman, the wife behind to clean the bathroom. Now it is I who have to depart as Odysseus to seek adventure and gain truth and knowledge, along with the rent.

She walks around the counter and disposes of our paper plates. "You want this?" She shows me the last of my orange juice.

"No thanks. I wonder if I'll go through New York?" I slide off my stool and begin walking around in circles, thinking.

"You're thinking about Dylan, aren't you?" Still in her blue bathrobe with her hair secured in a scrunchie on top of her head, she carefully washes two knives, two glasses, and a few mugs from yesterday. I thoroughly enjoy this, being the recipient in the endless cycle of clean-up. Had anyone ever cleaned up after me? As far back as I can remember, I'd been the busy one with a rag in hand, scurrying to wipe up the entire world before it came crashing down on me like Oscar the Grouch in his garbage can. The fact that it could please him so, the mess, the dirt, the rotten, foul things, well, it was a near epiphany to me. If there is me and there is him, surely there is a balance in between.

"Of course I am. I wonder if there's any way I can see him in between flights or something. I really need to see him, you know? I just need to see him." I walk in a few more circles and then into the bathroom to brush my teeth. I use the white baking soda toothpaste. I like the taste. The blue pastes and the stripes seem too fancy and colorful just to spit down the drain.

"You still wanna go to lunch later?" Eliza yells this down the hall at me. I come out with my toothbrush and nod to her as white foam drips from the left corner of my mouth. I slurp it back in and step back into the bathroom. She has offered to buy me lunch at this quaint restaurant on Avenue de Friedland we always pass on our way home from the agency.

I walk into Eliza's room right after her with a small towel in my hand to dry my mouth.

"So when do you leave?" She takes out the scrunchie and shakes her black hair from side to side.

"Thursday, I guess. Valerie said three days." I sit down on her chair and cross my legs. I am already dressed and just need to comb my hair. It is always the very last step in my primping sessions.

"This Thursday?"

"Yeah."

"So soon…" Her voice drifts as she drops her robe and clothes herself in the usual blacks and whites we wear every day.

"I know." And I want to be with her, in her anticipated loneliness, remembering how it had felt for me, but my mind wanders directly to Dylan and how much I want to see him. Our phone calls have become shorter, and he has missed calling me once. Why this makes me desire him more is beyond my understanding. I know all about absence making the heart grow fonder and all, but I know it has to be deeper than that. It is the human condition to want that which it feels it cannot have. It is the competitive spirit within us, the will for more, for better. We are creatures in search of something. I know I am. I am in search of a true lover, a mother, myself.

"This too short?" She tries to turn her head around to see her own behind. She wears a black mini skirt and her question is not whether it is too short in general, but whether it is too short for a normal day together, as chicks instead of as models pedaling our faces and figures around the block.

"No. It's cute." It is. Her thighs are thin enough and just the fact that she is not a vain person allows her more leeway than normal, in my opinion. Had she truly wanted to turn on every guy on the street to get her kicks the skirt would have been too short. But Eliza is a practical girl, a deeper girl than that. All she wants to do is impress the two of us. She does. My partner in this little marriage makes me proud.

"You should try and see him. I would. I'm nearly out of my mind without Ty."

"But what if he found someone else and hasn't told me?" A painful aching rushes into my chest and sits there, spoiling my happy birthday mood. "What if he's totally into that singer now?"

"You mean Annie?"

"Yeah." How can a name like that bring a sick feeling of defeat into my gut? Wasn't Annie a red-haired orphan girl? Not anymore. Now she is the boyfriend stealer, the opposition, the competition. "What if he's slept with her?" When am I going to give myself a break with this? As if I have any control over the situation.

"Have you asked him?"

"How can I?"

"You're right." She is fumbling with a silver charm bracelet. I get up to help. "Even if he was, even if he did, it would be the rarest thing for him to confess it to you all these miles away."

"There." I even have trouble getting the thing on her wrist. But when it is finally fastened, she shakes her arm a little and we are both thrilled with the looks of it. I smile at her and can tell she is feeling good about herself. We both are. We are feeling strong, grown-up, young, free. "You don't think he'd tell the truth?" My naiveté is often written across my face. I can tell from other people's reactions to me.

"Rachel. If it's one thing you need to learn it's that men lie. And what they lie the most about is sex." All of a sudden, Eliza seems so much older than either of us.

"How do you know?" I sit back on the chair in nonverbal communication. I want to know a lot more about such a thing.

"I just know." Her back is to me as she goes through her top drawer looking for something.

"How?" Obviously I am prying. Obviously she has no desire to see this conversation further. Nonetheless it is my birthday, and I feel I deserve just a little extra opportunity to press the situation. It works. She closes her drawer and falls heavy onto the bed, her skirt rising up her thighs.

"I just do." She looks right at me with wise eyes—eyes I wanted, too.

"Ty?"

"Yes, Ty."

"He cheated on you?"

"Yeah. And I don't think the pain from it will ever really go away. That's what sucks the most, I think."

"With who?" Here I am, wanting all the gruesome details just like an audience member on the Jerry Springer show or something. Why is this type of thing so intriguing? I try to look like a very caring person, like I am there to console her if necessary.

"It doesn't matter really. He was drunk. Probably stoned, too."

"Oh." I can tell she isn't up for this. Still, where else am I going to get such an education?

"How long ago?" I think it a safe question.

"A year or so."

"Did you guys break up?"

"I wanted to. I tried to. Then he'd come over and we'd end up in bed like nothing had ever come between us." She is working on a hangnail, trying to pry it free. "Men are different, Rachel. Men are boys." What is that supposed to mean?

"Different how?"

"They act first and think later. They lie."

"Everyone lies."

"Men lie more." She is certainly sounding old. "They lie like children who don't want to get caught. A boy grows up to be a larger boy and a girl grows up to be the mother the boy used to lie to when he was smaller."

I think she is getting a kick out of this now, this shedding the light on the matter for me. I am not sure I want to hear any more of it. I think of Dylan on the bed with Yvonne. Twenty minutes, he'd said. He'd been there twenty minutes. All that needs to be done can certainly be done in twenty minutes. Shit, it could've been done twice in twenty minutes. And who is to say he even knew how much time he'd been with her? He never wore a watch. Remembering what Yvonne had been wearing begins to make me ill all over again.

"All men?" I still don't want to believe it. I want the sick doubt in my chest to leave. Should I have not believed him that day in the park when he said he didn't kiss her, that she'd only kissed him? What the hell did that mean anyway?

"All men." How could she know? She doesn't know all men. "Trust me."

"Okay." I want out. I want out before I am too deeply in. I can see all the pain ahead of me, all the doubt, all the…. But my thoughts stop there as Eliza pulls me off the chair and down the hall. We clomp in our boots on the hard wood floor, speaking to the air and our future that we are not going to go quietly forward into this life of lying men.

* * *

At lunch, Eliza surprises me with a cake and twenty candles. The waitress brings it and sets it down in front of me, and I am taken back to all the birthdays before, all the ones that have led to this one in an expensive French restaurant with a girlfriend from California sitting across from me and a boyfriend in New York waiting for me. He said he'd be there, at the airport at 7:25 pm waiting for my flight. I had until 9:00 am the next morning to spend with him. Valerie helped me arrange it this way. He had even sounded excited, I guess. It was difficult to interpret this perfectly over the phone, especially since all I wanted to do was re-drill him on the whole Yvonne situation. But what would it profit?

"My mom hasn't called." We are daintily stabbing at the tiny pieces of our chocolate cake. Lunch has consisted of too much French bread, creamy vegetable soup, and side salads. The atmosphere is dark for the sunny afternoon that it is. The restaurant is old. The wooden chairs and tables are mahogany and deeply marred from years of lunch and dinner seekers. Who has been at this table before me and how many will come after? I wonder too, where I'll be next year at this time. At this juncture it seems I could be anywhere in the world. This gives me pause for serene reflection, and I am nearly startled when Eliza swallows her bite of cake to answer me.

"The day's not over, Rachel." She looks at me in the dimly lit restaurant and tells me with her eyes to stop complaining while she is taking me out to lunch.

"I know."

"Don't worry about it. Enjoy yourself." I can tell she is into the moment, of the cake and afternoon Parisian crowds out the window just beyond our table. She is enjoying herself and wants company in the now, not in the yesterdays of regret or the tomorrows of trepidation. I watch her pretty face as it looks up and into mine. Eliza knows me and I know her. We have shared just about everything from our religious beliefs to our birth control methods to our philosophies on death. I have even told her about the guy on the airplane. It takes girls approximately three days tops to know every single thing there is to know about the other, if they're willing to honestly share, which we are. I know her father had slept with three women before her mother found out he was cheating on her. And I know that her mom had a breakdown because of it and had to go on medication to prevent her from killing herself. She knows about my adopted mother and my fears about becoming like her.

In a way I suppose girls are their mothers whether they like it or not. We know and are what we are because of what our mothers know and are. We grow up saying the same things they say, like, "Finish what you start," and "If you're not going to do it right then don't do it at all." Our moms teach us how to fend for ourselves at the playground when the kids are mean and call us names. "What you say is what you are." "Takes one to know one," is what she was famous for saying when my dad would call her nasty, unforgivable things I cannot even repeat. Right back at you, like a boomerang.

"You know what I wonder?" We are both finished with our cake and have pushed our china plates back a bit, laying the thick, cloth napkins back up onto the table. I am aching to stand and walk off the rich foods before they settle into my thighs forever.

"What?" She is looking for the waitress, for our check, but her brown eyes come right into mine as she speaks.

"I wonder if my real mom is thinking about me today."

"Of course she is, Rachel. Women don't forget about having a baby. Even if they give it away. She probably thinks about you more than you know."

"You think?"

"Absolutely." She uncrosses her legs and brings her elegant elbows squarely onto the ancient table.

"But I wonder if I'm like her at all. How much are we shaped by our biological makeup and how much are we formed by our environment?" I'd always hoped there was some gene within me that was so different from my adopted mother, something that would prevent me from falling into her footsteps.

"It's a little of both, I'm sure. And there's probably a lot more to it than that."

"Really?" Is my friend becoming weary of my questions? I can't help it. I am twenty, want some answers, and don't know where else to go for them.

"Sure. There's quite a lot of evidence to suggest that we've all lived before many times."

"Reincarnation."

"Yeah. My mom's totally into it. Once when she was hypnotized she regressed so far into the past that she ended up in a previous life."

"Wow."

"I know. I totally believe it."

"Really?"

"More people believe in reincarnation in the world than don't. Plus, I've read all the Shirley MacLaine books."

"Oh." I don't know about those books or much about

reincarnation. And it all makes me feel much younger than the candles on the cake. The waitress comes over with the check and Eliza slips the requested amount of francs and more into the black booklet left there for that purpose. "Thanks, Eliza."

"No problem. Quite a calorie fest we've had today, huh?"

"Yeah, and the day's not even over." So wicked we are for our bread and cake.

"Nope." We both stand up tall and slide our chairs back into place. We look around, noticing we are being watched by several male patrons, and smile.

"Thanks again for lunch." I really am grateful.

"Of course, silly. It's your birthday. But I expect a dinner out after you make all that cash in Arizona."

"For you, anything." It is Eliza who knows me in the now, in the moment and for the person I am today, and for this I love her.

With this we saunter out into the cool, Parisian sunlight in our model skirts and boots as one of the men at a table near the door speaks some beautiful French in our direction. It matters not what he says, for he speaks with his whole demeanor. And it makes us giggle loudly as we turn the corner with our arms wrapped around each other, stepping into the street to meet with our future.

24

HAPPINESS TO TASTE

Now I have heard about several creation theories during my young life, and as far as I am concerned none of them make too much sense in the believable scheme of things. In church I was taught about Adam and Eve in the Garden with the tree of knowledge of good and evil. They had been created in the image of God on the sixth day and he instructed them to be fruitful and multiply, which they apparently did. It's difficult for me to imagine a God, any God, who looks like us and creates a world in six days and is so pleased he or she decides to take the seventh day off. I mean, just like that? Bing, bang, boom world created, man and woman happy in the garden naked and not ashamed? I can understand the creation of a song or a piece of art. One uses tools like paper and paint, piano and guitar. But how does a god snap his fingers and create mankind? From the dust of the earth? Was it magic dust?

Now, it would have been sweet had Eve not fallen into temptation the way she did. But the wicked woman was curious. Can you blame her? God apparently did, and thus suffering of all kind was born. Pretty sneaky way of getting the bad stuff there in with the good, as far as I can see. There they were all naked and happy and enjoying the earth and then God has to put a big tree right there in the middle and say, don't touch this now. You may eat of all the other trees freely, but of the tree of the knowledge of good and evil, thou shalt not eat. And he told them if they ate, they would surely die. Now, if they did not know of good or evil or much of anything else, how in the world could they know about death or what it meant to die? This story is difficult for me to envision. It puts a good deal of the blame on the woman, for one. And it shows that the character of God is initially deceptive and manipulative. It is quite obvious he put the tree there on purpose so they would eat of it. Otherwise, why put it there at all? It's like putting a three-year-old at the table with a plate of warm, chocolate chip cookies and saying, now don't eat of them. If you eat of them, I will have to slap your hand. How long is the kid going to sit there before she reaches out and grabs one?

In my freshmen Biology class, I was introduced to a scientific approach of the creation of the universe that seems to have begun over 15 billion years ago in a fit of flames. Slowly, signs of soft-bodied creatures began creeping and crawling and inhabiting the land mass called earth. Darwin and his theories of evolution struck me as cruel and correct. Survival of the fittest is something I can understand, but did we really evolve from amphibians to reptiles to mammals to homo sapiens? Were my ancestors gorillas? Maybe. At least I could see a progression with the scientific approach. It wasn't so magical as the creation theory. And there was proof here and there of this chain of evolution. Proof is important. I used to think the scriptures were proof. Now I'm not so sure. It's not difficult to write a story, to give an opinion on hearsay. I am sure the prophets of old didn't see all of what they wrote first-hand. And even if they did, there's always the author's slant, the author's idea of how it happened, of what took place, of who said what and when.

It's actually quite a strange thing to ponder, the beginnings of it all. And to speculate concerning how it all began is to wonder how it's all going to end. For everything has a beginning and an end, right? But what about the in-between? And why is the in-between the way it is? Why does it seem that so much of it is heartache and hardship, and so little of it happiness? Could it simply be because

Eve succumbed to the temptation and ate of the tree of knowledge? The bite heard 'round the world, except no one was there to hear it. Why are we punished for Adam and Eve's transgression when we weren't even born, and when it was set up by God anyway?

No. There has to be a better explanation. I have heard many myths and legends, folklores and fables. One story is as wild as the next when it comes to who made us and why.

Perhaps there was a great and mighty chef, God's chef. And one day God was bored of just eating all day and watching the animals play, and he said to his chef, "Write up a recipe for Life, for the life of all mankind who I have yet to create. You are such a good chef and should do a fine job at this. Together we will make an existence greater than the animals, and smarter. We will form them in our own image so they are interesting to us. Then I will be happy and have something to do with my time." And so the chef thought great, now I have to write a recipe for Life and continue to cook God his breakfast, lunch, and dinner and feed myself. When does he think I have the time? But the chef was obedient, and he took out a heavenly quill pen and during his free time he sketched out a recipe for God. And he figured, since his life wasn't all that great, why should anyone else's be? And he wrote:

LIFE
1 8-ounce package of troubles
½ cup of satisfaction
2 pints of unidentified pain
4 teaspoons of success
6 tablespoons of comfort
3 pounds of confusion
1 ounce of peace and quiet
8 slices of worry
9 packets of fear

Combine all ingredients in a heavy sauce pan and bring to a slow boil. Allow mixture to thicken, stirring constantly until Life begins to form. Boil for five minutes, remove from heat, and allow to cool. You may or may not want to sprinkle on joy or happiness to taste, depending on your preference.

Creates 4 to 6, depending on the size

Of course the chef didn't know God would decide to multiply the recipe by several billion. Who knew that this was how he would be spending the rest of his god-given life? Most of the time he didn't even sprinkle on the seasonings at the end, out of spite of course.

I am in my room packing almost everything I own into my big, black suitcase I purchased with money I made modeling. Some of the jobs I'd done in New York were finally paying. It is amazing how long it takes to get paid as a model. Three to six months seems like the normal period of time elapsing between the click of the camera and the smooth feel of the check between my fingers.

"You okay?" Eliza pauses in my doorway as she is making her way down the hall.

"Yeah. No big deal." Earlier I shed a few tears of self-pity.

"Sure it is. She should have called."

"I know. I told you she wouldn't. She would never make a call to Europe during the week. It's too expensive. She'll probably call on the weekend."

"You think so?"

"Yeah, but it'll be too late."

"Why don't you call her?"

"I probably will. As soon as I'm done here." I fold my tee shirts and jeans and black skirts neatly and arrange them in my suitcase. My mother had not called me on my birthday. Then again, it isn't a very important day in her life. What had she known of me the day I was born? For all I knew the day of my birth caused her pain. I am slowly trying to see things from her point of view, yet all I want is to forever flee the force she has over me. It is the force of motherhood, of years together and of a child raised and trained to act and react in a certain fashion simply because of the elements surrounding her. So if I am so repelled by the whole situation, why then do tears fall when she doesn't call? She is my mom, the woman who had sewn my clothes and fed me. She was the person who had played the tooth fairy, the Easter bunny, and Santa Claus. And she was the person I needed to hear from on my birthday. Mark time with me, Mom, as we have done all my life. Acknowledge that I'm older and that you're proud of me. I need you to wish me a Happy Birthday to make my birthday real.

But my birthday had been two days ago, and there hadn't been a call from anyone in my family.

And so I pack my suitcase with a fierce determination to once again be a survivor alone. I will rely on myself only for happiness. I know I don't have what other people have, what Eliza has. A home. A place of refuge. Even a family I can depend on. And being adopted seems to make the situation even more pitiful, yet it gives me the strength to separate myself from my past. I can tell myself that even though it feels familiar, it isn't really mine. I don't belong in the cold winters in Wisconsin getting fat on cow meat and cow milk and hating myself. I can't breathe in the middle of America, suffocating between the energies of the east and west coast. I don't fit the Midwest stereotype of mediocrity. I want more. I want to experience more than the same, more of what I already know.

And so my comfort and satisfaction is found not in loving voices and supportive family members, but in mystery. Mystery allows almost any possibility, and I know I'll have to be satisfied with that.

Still, later that evening, I find myself dialing the 414 area code. The phone rings twice, and I hear the familiar voice of compassion and distress.

"Hello, Mom?"

"Who is this?"

"It's Rachel." As if she has any other female to call her mom.

"Rachel, it doesn't sound like you. Oh, you know I was just thinking of you. I know I didn't talk with you on your birthday, but you'll be getting something soon. The reprints I wanted to send you of the boys weren't ready until yesterday, and I wanted to have everything together. I made copies of their report cards for you also. Billy's not doing so well this year, but he made the Varsity soccer team."

She sounds very excited about this. "I just wish he could do better in school. I'm afraid he just doesn't care about it, you know? He needs you, I think. He needs your good example around the house."

"Tell him I'm happy for him, for making Varsity. Anyway, I just wanted to call to—"

"Rachel, you just can't imagine how it is here without you. I miss you so much. There's just no one to talk to anymore. And no one to keep me from eating all this junk food these guys make me buy. It's terrible. I must have gained twenty pounds since you left." And then there is a pause.

"Mom, I'm going to Arizona for a job."

"Arizona? I thought you were in Paris?" She sounds put off that I haven't offered the least bit of sympathy, that I haven't pulled her from her dreary self-esteem issues out into the light of new possibility and hope.

"I am."

"Well, Arizona's a long way from Paris." Really.

"Yes it is."

"When can you make it home?"

"I don't know." Home? "The catalog company I'm modeling for is paying for the flight. And I'm coming back to Paris afterwards."

"I really wish you'd come back home. The boys really miss you. Nothing's the same. I'm so lonely, you know? I need my friend back." She means me. I can't believe she is calling me her friend. "Next week is ten years since the divorce. Can you believe it? Ten years. I need a man. But who will want me, the way I look?"

And we talk that way for a while on my money with her barely listening to anything I have to say. She comes close to tears a couple times, her voice cracking, begging sympathy. I pretend not to notice. I have to keep it light or she will lose it on the phone and dredge up all sorts of further unpleasantness for me.

"That her?"

"Yeah."

"So how'd it go?" It is excellent having someone on my side, someone who knows my past. A confidant. It is all about knowing the past to understand the present. A friend is someone you take the time to tell about your past so that present conversations are easily comprehended. Eliza has become this person for me, perhaps the first one who I've really let in, inside, into the person I am deciding to be because of and in spite of who I've been.

"Okay, I guess. She doesn't sound very happy."

"It's a symptom of middle age. Unhappiness." Sometimes she sounds like her mother might sound.

"It's a symptom of being alive." She laughs at this and pours herself a glass of water. She wears a white, ribbed, knit shirt and baggy blue jeans. Her hair is pulled back in a short, messy ponytail. She isn't wearing a stitch of makeup. Her dark eyes are compassionate as we talk. And I realize how incredible it is to share life with someone who is honest and comfortable and similar to myself. Eliza encourages me to do whatever I want to do, without judgment. She listens to me, and without knowing it, is teaching me how to be a friend.

Suddenly there is a loud banging at the door and we both jump and look toward it. The tape in Eliza's boom box has just ended and the apartment has been completely silent.

"I'll get it." She walks toward the door.

"Look through the peephole first." I get up off the floor and walk up behind her.

"It's Sam."

"Let her in." As if Eliza needs my permission.

She unbolts the door and opens it as Sam staggers toward us. Her right eye is swollen and her lip is cut and bleeding.

"Oh my God! What happened?" Eliza helps her into the living room where Sam sprawls out like a shivering rag doll. Her purse falls from her shoulder and comes crashing down next to her. Her gray tee shirt shows drops of blood from her lip, and her jeans are torn at the seam of one leg. She is barefoot.

"Jesus, you must be freezing. I'll get a blanket." I dash around looking at the hall and my bedroom as if to find a closet full of guest blankets and towels. There isn't one. I grab the white comforter off my bed and jolt into the living room with it. Eliza already has ice on her eye. Sam isn't making much sense.

"Fucker... I'll..." Her one good eye keeps rolling back into her head and her body continually shakes involuntarily, maybe from the cold or maybe from the fight she still thinks she is having.

"Christ, what are we gonna do?" Eliza looks panicked. I am not sure how I am supposed to react. Is there a 911 in Paris?

"We have to talk to her. Keep her awake. I don't know, maybe we should call a hospital or something." I feel like an idiot.

"No hospital, no hosp..." Sam tries looking over at me. Her face is really messed up. Black mascara and black eyeliner are smeared down both cheeks. Her lipstick has traveled all over the outside of her mouth, despite the obvious outline of lip liner.

"We're gonna have to take her to the hospital. But I don't know where one is." I figure I would want someone to do the same for me, especially if my eye was rolling back like that.

"Alex will know. Let's call him." Eliza looks at me. Sam's arm rises up and strikes her on the side of her head.

"Ouch! Jesus!" Eliza drops the hand towel with ice.

"No fucking way... no Alex, do not call that... that... bastard." Sam stammers this out slowly and in a voice that is not her own before both her eyes shut and her body falls inevitably limp, as only a rag doll would.

Eliza props the small, blue pillow under her head and stands up. "Jesus, Rachel. What are we supposed to do with her?" She begins pacing two steps in one direction, then two steps in another. She pulls her ponytail holder out and refastens her hair with it three times while staring down at Sam. I bend down and begin wiping her delicate skin with the moistened towel, not really sure how to feel or what to do. All I know is that when there is a mess someone has to clean it up.

* * *

They are all sitting around the dining room table. It is winter, and the mom and daughter have prepared chicken noodle soup, sandwiches, and hot chocolate for an early dinner. The family has just moved into a new home that has wall to wall carpeting, and it seems special and unique to eat in the dining room on carpet like this. The young girl is proud to have such a nice picture in front of her. Her father sits at one end of the table, and her mother at the other. One of her brothers sits across from her, and she has placed her baby brother in his highchair with a clean bib before anyone else had come to the table.

The conversation begins quietly enough as the family slurps at their soup and blows a cool breath at their hot chocolate. But quite abruptly the voice of her father begins to rise in an eerie fashion. Her mother's takes on the familiar tone of a pleading child. The young girl puts down her spoon and sits motionless, listening to the words as they become nastier.

"You fucking bitch. I told you never, never . . . how many times have I told you—"

"You didn't say. I never heard..." Her mother inches back in her chair as her father rises from his, large and mighty, like a horrible monster from the sea. The girl watches, terrified and bewildered, as her father takes his end of the table in his two giant hands and lifts it off the floor. Soups and mugs slide down the slick, Formica surface. The boy and girl stand up and back away from the torrent of crashing foods and liquids. The mother grabs her baby boy and screams for him to stop as she presses the child's small, blonde head against her chest.

After the entire dinner has spilled onto the carpet, the father is still not satisfied. His anger rises again as he brings the table back into the air, breaking it in two. He glares gruesomely across the room at her mother, and the daughter knows what to do. She stumbles across a couple broken bowls to her mother, who releases the infant into her daughter's arms. The girl motions silently to her brother and the three of them find temporary refuge behind the archway in the living room. The young girl bounces her heavy, baby brother on her hip in an attempt to keep him quiet, but it is no use. And it seems that each terrible shriek from the child only ignites her father's rage, for he dashes after his wife as she tries to flee from him. But where is there to go?

He bashes her in the face with his fist again and again as she comes crashing down to the floor in all her heaviness. Her wails are louder than her child's. They scream out in complete and utter defeat, anguish, physical pain and horror at what her life has become.

The daughter stares at the disaster her father has made out of the picture that had looked so perfect only fifteen minutes earlier. His truck squeals out of the driveway as the children try to help their mother up. But she only screams at them to get away and clean up the mess.

25

CAGED BIRDS

I pull the solid plastic shade up to watch gray Paris grow smaller and think about Sam's deep purple eye and the one who did this to her. I know my time in Europe is ticking down to its final hour.

"What would you like to drink?"

"Apple juice. No ice please."

Alex is becoming more than just a pervert. He is a demon, an evil force to be reckoned with, or not. I have no desire to provoke the demon; nevertheless, there is something that draws me to him. He is his own master. He does what he wants and takes what he pleases, and this is intriguing, despite the damage he has done. I want to flee from the fatherly grasp he has on me before I am damage done. Not that he can. Not that he will.

Samantha told us, after she came to and much later in the evening, that she probably deserved it seeing as she had kneed him in the balls. She is apparently used to getting knocked around. She didn't go into much detail about why they'd been fighting. She was ashamed—in the sad, pale, beat down state she was in—to be seen as she was and thanked us for not taking her to the hospital or calling Alex. She was quiet for a long time while Eliza and I sat up with her to make sure she was going to be all right. I could tell she didn't enjoy us fussing over her. All she wanted to do was take long,

277

deep drags on her Marlboro cigarettes and blow the smoke out the open sliver between the window and the frame, which we let her do. It made the apartment colder, but who can argue with a black and blue face?

I feel slight exhilaration as the plane bumps up and down in the air. I want more, like on a roller coaster. I love the lifting off and landing. The sensations of fright and flight make me feel out of control and relaxed. When I have no power over my situation, this is when I am most at ease. I have no responsibility, no choices to make, no place I have to be but here, wherever that may be.

But these situations rarely arise—which is why they are often self-induced.

* * *

When the pilot lands the plane with a screech and a halt, the butterflies and many of their friends dance wildly in my belly in anticipation of seeing and being seen by Dylan. Yet I remain in my seat when the seatbelt light goes off along with its familiar "ding." I am not one to rush and bang into people while they are unloading their things from the overhead compartments. I'd rather wait and swim around in my feelings of anticipation, even with the butterflies. Let everyone get their baggage and their children and their newspapers and purses. I will wait and walk out last, or close to last. There's usually always some man who insists on allowing me to walk ahead of him. And so I do. Long live chivalry. Any way I can get it.

I try to picture Dylan as I walk down the fake, gray hallway with my fellow stragglers. I have worn my hair down. I have on my usual jeans and white tee shirt. My backpack is on my back, hanging off both shoulders equally. I am all in one piece, ready.

And then I see him standing in the distance by himself and it's as if I've seen him every day of my life and never. He's so familiar to me compared to the rest of the crowd of expectant faces and families. Who belongs to me? Who is waiting for me? Who holds the sign with my name on it? Him. Curls and smile and hands in his pockets. It seems like centuries.

"Hey, girl. Look at you." He bobs his head up and down while he checks me out. "I forgot how beautiful you are."

"Thanks." Just a bit on the sarcastic side. How could he forget? But alas, I find I'd forgotten just the same. My bags are at our feet, and we stand and embrace. I can feel his whole body as it fits into mine. He is the missing piece to my body puzzle.

"You have a suitcase or something we have to get?"

"Yeah. Just one."

"Well, it looks like it's that way." He points to the sign that says "Baggage Claim" and we make our way in that direction with him carrying my backpack and my duffle bag. I feel light, airy, sleepy and excited. I try not to think about tomorrow when I have to walk back to the ticket counter, check my bags, and board another plane.

He walks ahead of me a couple steps with his New York City energy, and I watch his round behind in his Levis. His "behind," as if I'm a mother ogling my newborn's backside. Look at his adorable little behind, the mother would comment to her friend or older child as she bathed her slippery infant. Ass would be more appropriate at my age, I suppose. He's got a great ass, girls will say when they see a construction worker in the street with tanned, bulging muscles and snug blue jeans. Or buttocks, as Forrest Gump would stammer out in his charming, inhibited southern way.

"I love your butt." I quicken my pace and place my hand on it. I can't resist.

"It's all yours, babe."

"Is it?" Now I've done it. Shit, I can't even wait to get out of the airport.

"What is that supposed to mean?"

We step on the escalator going down. He is ahead of me one step and shorter as he faces me with an irritated look. I peer into his brown eyes trying desperately to figure out if this is authentic irritation. It's tough with guys. They're such good liars.

"It means what it means." It means that right now, at the moment and tonight for sure, it's all mine. For one whole night that I truly need a good night's rest it's mine. And what am I acting so possessive for anyway? I'd been away from Dylan's embrace for only hours when I'd allowed the guy on the plane to have his quiet way with me. And if I had even this one little sex secret, then the rest of the world must have plenty more, including the cute butt that is standing in front of me.

"Watch out." He turns around just in time to hop over the metal strips at the bottom. I'd heard that a young, barefooted boy had gotten his toes sucked underneath those silver claws at the bottom of the escalator once. Ever since I'd tended to leap over that spot.

The slow declining stairs part of our journey is over. Now it is back to thrusting and darting our way through crowds of cranky people who, like us, all want to be somewhere else. It is difficult holding a conversation with him earnestly pursuing the baggage claim, as if that is going to distract me.

And then the race is over and we stand at the revolving machine as it introduces suitcase after box after bag through the heavy, black rubber flaps that willingly dangle and give way to each item, new or old, for all those waiting with eyes glued.

"Rache, be honest with me, will you?"

"Sure. Of course," I say, loving that he shortened my name like that, as if we've never been apart; I got ready to lie if needed. There's no way I'll tell him about the guy on the plane. Never. He'd never understand.

"Is that it?" I look closely at the suitcase zooming toward us.

"No, mine's newer." With my shoe, I slide my duffle bag closer to me. My backpack is securely on my back now, and my hair is stuck underneath it. I don't feel like freeing it, though. It will cause too much static electricity. I am trying to be as cute as possible with him so near and so new again.

"We'll talk in the car."

"Okay." And we both stand there motionless with the growing, noisy audience of people all around us. When someone's luggage moves near to us on the conveyer belt we graciously step aside, almost in congratulations. Well done. Your suitcase has arrived. Go ahead and claim it and get the hell out of here while we have to wait and stare.

Exiting the JFK is a headache, and I realize I am in America again. I had forgotten how large and loud Americans are. There is no reservation. All is decidedly poured out into the open like the insides of an unsettled stomach. Heavy, sausage-armed mothers nagging at their children to hurry up. Boisterous men in cowboy hats roaring with reddened cheeks, as if there is no one in the airport besides them and their herds of self-indulging children and cousins and uncles and mothers. It all shocks me into utter silence next to Dylan as we trudge our way through so many strangers. But these are my people. This is my country. Apparently.

* * *

Dylan stops the car on a deserted street under a bridge on our way to John's. The only light we have is provided by two yellow streetlights on either side of the car. It is growing colder outside, but I don't think either of us really notice.

"Rachel, I've been thinking." He brings his right knee up toward the back of the seat and turns to me while his left hand rests on the steering wheel. He is still the driver, the one in control. I am the passenger.

"About what?"

"About us. I missed you. A lot."

"Really?" Tell me more.

"Yeah. I've never missed anyone like this before." So what does this mean? That he saved himself for me? "But long distance relationships don't work." The rise and fall of the heart.

"I know." I know.

"I need to know how long I'm gonna have to wait, Rachel, because it's too hard to be away from you."

What exactly is too hard? I would have liked to sit there and believe all the emotional aches and pains he seems to be suffering, but television has taught me a thing or more about the male species. On Sally Jesse Raphael, or some such program, I'd heard that guys think about sex on an average of once every minute. That's over a thousand times a day. Since my departure, my boyfriend has apparently pondered the sex act nearly a hundred thirty thousand times. And there's only so much thought until subsequent action. Of course, there's always masturbation.

"So, have you seen other girls while I've been gone?" Might as well get right to it.

"Rachel." His eyebrows crunch together, causing the flesh on his forehead to bunch up.

"Well?" Had he been a spotless virgin during the interim, certainly he'd be announcing this proudly by now.

"Well what?" He isn't giving in. Why should he? I'll be gone again in the morning.

"What about Annie?"

"Annie who?" Dead giveaway. "You mean Annie from the band?" Nice save.

"Of course Annie from the band. Who else do I know named Annie?"

"Annie's got a boyfriend, Rachel."

"Does that matter?"

"With me, it does."

"Does that mean that if she didn't have a boyfriend you'd consider her?" Am I relentless or what? I can't stop myself.

"Consider her for what?" Again, not buying it.

"For sleeping with." Sleeping. How did the sex act ever get melted down to sleeping?

"Rachel, I don't know what you're trying to get at. What I was trying to say before is that if we're going to be together then we need to be together. I want to be with you. I want you to be with me." Words feed the female, sex feeds the male.

"I want to be with you, too. If you want to know the truth (like I did) I don't think I like it much in Paris anymore. I don't see myself there much longer."

I drop my eyelids as if I ought to be ashamed of this. I haven't gotten any approval from Alex or Michael about this, and they both have a say in any career move I might make. As long as I am a model. Thing is, I am growing weary of the whole business and of feeling so alone all the time. I want Dylan. Girlfriends count, but not in the largest scheme of things. Most chicks feel that it's the ultimate thing to be with a guy, to have a boyfriend to call your own. Girlfriends act as the sounding boards for the in-between times, be they good or bad. If there isn't any action with the opposite sex, what is there to talk about? Blame it on the fairy tales. Blame it on Kodak commercials. Blame it on patriarchal religions. Women are to seek a man, settle down, make a happy home, be a wife, become a mother, and stand by their man. Men are the goal, the prize, the illusion that all is complete somehow. Until it's not. Then it's back to your girlfriends for what is really real. And we find out again, with them, that what we want is that goal, that prize. The illusion is so much more interesting. The girlfriend will always be there, but the man is the challenge.

I look over at Dylan wondering if he is the one I want. How does one even know? As much as I want to appear the self-sufficient model and world traveler, I don't feel I can keep it up much longer. I need someone to share my days with, even my future. I need to have someone around to make my life worth all the energy it takes to live.

"So what don't you like about it?" I look up quickly from my thoughts to answer him. After all, who wouldn't like Paris? I can't tell him about Alex. I wouldn't know how.

"Well, for one, you're not there." At this, he takes my face in his cold hands and kisses me deeply. I close my eyes and hug his soft, sheepskin coat.

"I love you, Rache."

"I love you, too." My whole body loves him. I mean girls think about sex, too.

It is difficult making love in the front seat, but not impossible. Maneuvering around the steering wheel isn't very pleasant, but the feeling of him beneath me is worth it. I want to cry I have missed being with him so much. The only thing that bothers me is that he pulls a condom out of his wallet so easily and casually, as if he's done it a hundred times before. I wonder what this is supposed to mean. Is he assuming I was going to get down with him before we even got to John's? Does it mean he always has one there ready for any kind of action he might run into anywhere? These questions fly around in my brain in disgust and puzzlement, but not until I have experienced orgasm and pull my jeans back on.

"Jeez, look at the windows. They're all fogged up." He is happy with himself. His rosy cheeks beam under his careless curls, and I envy men their simplicity. Seek, find, conquer.

"So do you always carry one around in your wallet?" I am helping him wipe down the windshield on the inside. We are using the sleeves and cuffs of our jackets. He looks like he is fishing for a good answer. His response takes too long.

"I've always kept one there."

"I don't remember ever seeing one in your wallet before."

"If you want to know the truth, John gave it to me because you were coming. I wasn't at home, so I stuck it in my wallet."

I like this answer better.

He starts the engine and his orange Subaru carries us through the cool, dark night to the one who makes a couple a crowd. I think we are both in need of some outside distraction. On the way, we smoke a bowl out of his tarnished, brass pipe and make peace. I do, anyway. I don't have time for more conflict. I want to leave him wanting me.

I look out the window at the dark, crazy city fondly. It is the first time I've come back here and it feels oddly familiar and nearly comforting. I lean back in the seat and let the THC rush through my body as the smoke pulls me into a tingly, relaxed state of awareness.

Being high definitely has its perks. It unwinds the mind, but it doesn't turn it off. On the contrary, the brain seems to think wonderfully interesting and imaginative things on marijuana. One thought so quickly leads to another in a warm and jumbled fashion, and ideas seem new and uncharted—even visionary.

"I should probably warn you about John, Rachel."

"What?" Wake up.

"John. He's changed some."

"How?" Immediate new interest arises.

"I guess you'll see for yourself. We're here." His head cranks to look this way and that as we drive around the block twice without saying anything more before he finds a place to park. I let my high entertain my mind while he drives, cursing everyone in his way. Sometimes when the male species is behind the wheel it's best to just let them be. As soon as the gears are in park, he grins again and announces that John's place is the new band hangout.

"I'm not officially moved in yet, but we can sleep here tonight. John won't mind." Anyone stop to ask me? We walk with my bags under the bright lights of the city toward the apartment building. I've left my suitcase in the trunk. All I can think is how badly I want and need a shower.

We are beeped in and take the sterile, silver, fluorescent-lit elevator to the third floor while I keep my eyes to the floor. It is some of the worst lighting I've ever been under, and I am not up to the scrutiny of it after such a journey.

"I bet you're tired."

Why, yes. Sweet of you to think of this before we enter party-land. I am tired and wired and worried about the shoot in Arizona.

"Rachel! Hey!" John shoots up from the couch as soon as we walk through the doorway. I hug a much thinner version of our friend and give him a little peck on both cheeks, as they do in Europe.

"It's good to see you, John." It is. But it is the whole effect. Dylan, John, the Grateful Dead playing in the background, the posters on the walls, the metal tin of pot on the coffee table, John's drum set, a guitar propped up against the wall. As much as I want to complain of my weariness, I am also so pleased to be home.

"What can I get for you, darling?" His hair is longer, hanging down into his eyes. He keeps jerking his head to the side and tucking loose strands of it behind his ears. "Water?"

"Water will be great." There's an unspoken connection between the boyfriend's girlfriend and his best friend. Keep it cool, play nice, have fun. The relationships are too close, too interdependent. And so the ones on either side learn how to keep it light and even enjoy it. John, although visibly changed, has kept right in step with me. Dylan and I just watch him for a while as he darts and dashes around the house in a frenzied manner, picking up an empty Doritos bag and clearing a dirty sweatshirt and several magazines from the couch.

"You guys have a seat." He pats the cushions domestically.

"John?" I look at Dylan.

"Yeah, what is it? What can I get you?" He glances around, realizing what he's forgotten, then forges toward me with a glass of clear water. I am so thirsty I drink half of it before answering.

"Mind if I use your shower?" I wipe my mouth off with the back of my hand.

"Of course, Rache. Shit, you must be really tired, huh?"

Do I look it? Probably. Why I feel this is slightly sinful, I don't know.

"Hey, just let me get some of my stuff out of there first. I was actually gonna do that earlier. Hold on." With that he cruises in there and we hear him banging around and sliding the shower door back and forth.

"Is he okay?" I whisper, sitting still. It is easy to do when someone else is flying around. Balance.

"He's fine." The couch is a beige, tattered rummage sale piece with cigarette burns on the arms and sagging cushions that have very little life left. I feel as if I am sinking into it, but when I bring my butt forward my thighs rest on the hard edge, which eventually pushes me back into the softer part again. Dylan nudges me to look. I do. Into the small drawer in the middle of the coffee table to find white lines of cocaine spread out evenly on a small mirror with no safe edges. The fact that it is hidden away like that while the pot remains scattered across the aging face of Neil Young on the cover of a *Rolling Stone* magazine makes it seem all the more illicit. Dangerous, unreachable, inviting, exotic, enticing, wicked, curious. This is what John is on now. It makes sense to me, even though I've never touched the stuff. Hollywood movies had given me a decent drug education. Dylan is apparently thrilled with this party pad they've created.

"It's all ready."

I spring up from the dilapidated couch being careful not to bump the coffee table. Coke table.

"Cool. Thanks." I grab my duffle bag and look back at Dylan with a scolding look. Not much I can do being far across the sea and far across the country tomorrow. Still, in the present, I am who I am, and this girl is not pleased. Marijuana is a gentle drug, something to be inhaled deeply into the soul, something that is shared easily. It provides easy euphoria, heightened hunger, desirable sleep, more intense orgasm, awareness of hidden sounds in music, deeper ponderings, and an overall sense of sweet relaxation. It is a substance born a long time ago, shared between our founding fathers and the Native fathers before them. It is a medicine to me. Cocaine, on the other hand, is the chosen drug of the bad guys in the movies. Consumers of this drug are the money hungry mobsters, foreign thieves, unhappy, skinny, wealthy women, and the tramps their husbands are sleeping with. It is the drug not shared, but hoarded and sold for great amounts of money, which always entails someone getting shot for no good reason. It is the drug of the selfish. It is the drug that is never enough that pushes the body for more and more until the sun rises in the sky, bringing to light the greed of the night.

I step into the shower, which is remarkably clean, and turn the nozzle toward my face. I wash away the flight, the dirt, the sex, the cobwebs from my brain. I am happy to be with Dylan, but it is temporary. I have a gig of my own, and who knows what next? I can't let myself get too worked up about what I have no power over. And yet I know I will probably do just that.

Just thinking about Dylan putting his nose down to that mirror gives me severe angst and confusion, curiosity and jealousy. What do the drugs have that I can not supply? A mind on medication is a mind distracted from the face of reality. It is in fact the very purpose for it. But why? What is there to duck away from on such a daily basis?

I shower quicker than I had wanted do, dress over my semi-wet body, then squeak a clean circle on the mirror with the outer part of my fist so I can see my hair enough to make a part down the middle. I am not in the mood for makeup, and it is just about time for bed anyway. I am not sure who was going to join me in this decision though.

As I am gathering my dirty clothes together, I hear a strange voice. Well, maybe I'll just pat on a little powder. A quick sweep of lip balm. A gathering of long, stray hairs I'd lost in the sink from brushing too quickly while it was still wet. I close the shower door and hang my towel neatly on the rack, thinking I might use it in the morning.

"Rachel! How do you feel?" The little mirror is on the table, empty, reflecting their overly friendly greetings.

"Come here. Sit down." Dylan pats the sagging couch next to him. One of the other band members is slouched in a chair next to John. "Rachel, you remember…"

"Yes. Good to see you." I smile for the sake of it all, the one night opportunity, the smell of comradeship in the air.

"You, too." The bass player.

"So, feel better?" It is my cheery boyfriend, who is well into his high, desiring for the moment that all things be high right along with him. For some reason this makes me feel low.

"Yes. Thanks. I think I'll just sit on the floor." I bend down and sit Indian style on the green, shaggy carpet. I am happy the lights are low. I can pretend it is clean.

"What can we get you, Rachel? You hungry?"

"A little." There is a gnawing pain in the pit of my stomach, but it has been overlapped with dread. It is dreadful the way I feel I can never keep up with the company I keep. Haven't I done my time with these two? Aren't I "in" now? But now they've distanced themselves again, and I am only a visitor, an onlooker of their cozy, coke scene.

"You guys wanna order a pizza or something?" At least John is trying to be nice.

"Not hungry."

"Me neither."

"We'll order one for you anyway." And he is up looking through the phone book. "Balestreri's is the best one around here."

"Don't worry about it, John."

"But you need to eat. I don't have much…" He begins opening cupboard doors and closing them quickly. "Here. Clam chowder."

"That's fine. I can get it myself."

"No. That's cool. You're the guest. Let me do it."

"Thanks, John. You're sweet." I glance up at Dylan from my position on the floor to see him with his guitar in his lap, strumming slowly. It is what I had come all this way for, to see him like this. What a beautiful sight. It inspires me to pick up a half-smoked bowl and fill my lungs and brain in anticipation for dinner. Also, it pleases all the guys to see me partake. I draw in the wicked smoke and hold my hits long in my mouth before swallowing. And then, properly adjusted, I walk into the kitchen to help John.

"So, you want some bread or something?"

I stand with him as we stare at the contents of the refrigerator. Three bottles of Becks, half a loaf of white bread, Dijon mustard, some leftover Chinese, and a head of very wilted lettuce.

"Who does the shopping around here?" I grin, not needing an answer.

"The maid's been on vacation. Please forgive our hostile environment. You deserve so much more." He closes the refrigerator door and pulls me around to face him, backing me up against the coolness. I notice no one can see us from the living room. We can hear Dylan strumming. "He doesn't know what he has." His right hand is on my left shoulder, holding me in place while his left hand secures itself around my lower back. It is a delicious and confusing three seconds when we kiss. And then it is over.

"I don't think I need any bread. The soup will be fine." The kiss has knocked the hunger right out of my belly. Why are my cheeks flushed? We both continue to glance toward the living room. But as long as we hear Dylan playing, we know he is sitting. I could have kissed Dylan all night long, and my body would not have felt the charge it experienced up against the refrigerator. There is a reason people flirt. It fills the need to feel needed, wanted, desired. It is a rare thing to have just one person fill this role—especially one all coked up and entranced in his own music.

As I pour the soup from the pan into a wrecked, wooden bowl, I wonder about John's intentions. What had he seen Dylan do that made him tend to me so? Or is it simple jealousy manifested under the influence? Stoner thoughts turn into stoner hunger, and I sit down squarely upon the floor without the use of my hands and begin filling my belly with warmth, chewing and swallowing and not interested in the least in trying to catch the eye of either one of them. I eat faster than a lady ought to and rise quickly to wash my dish, lest I add to the chaos already found in the kitchen.

I am standing over the sink trying to rinse out bits of clam with the water running loudly when I feel him come up behind me and hug me with his whole body. I jump inside myself and turned around to meet the best friend of the boy I kissed minutes before.

"You okay?" His eyes are glazed, grinning, goofy.

"Yeah. I'm fine." Stock answer. Works every time. It's what everyone wants to hear. Am I? I put my arms around him in response, in recognition of my girlfriend status. He pushes into me against the sink, and I can feel the shape of his body beneath his clothes.

"Babe, I didn't know if you wanted to do any, you know?"

"Any what?" I am still wild inside from the flirtation.

"We still have a few lines if you'd like to try it."

Goddamn the pusher man. Nothing confuses me more than drugs on top of drugs. Isn't being stoned enough? "How often do you do this anyway?" I push him gently away and fold my arms across my chest.

"Not often." He is slightly amused with me. I can tell. "Not like John, Rache." It's no big deal.

"Maybe it is for me."

"Whatever."

"I mean I'm only here one night." I am loud enough so the guys in the living room can hear. I don't care.

"That's the occasion."

"The occasion?" Voice rising. "My visit denotes a reason to snort cocaine? I don't think so, Dylan." I sound lame to myself. The problem is that I don't truly know myself or what I want. Does anyone? Most think growing older assists in such quandaries, but I am not so sure. Older people might have more experience, but this just means that the questions become more complex and the answers less definite. I know there should be something blissful about being young, but I never can feel comfortable enough to allow that. And if I can't be joyful just for the sake of being so, how can anyone else?

Were drugs the door to manufactured bliss, the escape from a natural state of non-bliss, or just an opportunity to ponder the possible blissfulness of what lies in between? Whatever they are, they cloud my brain enough for me to feel that what I think on them seems insightful and therefore purposeful. So why can't I transfer this from marijuana to cocaine? No matter how I try, I cannot.

"How about just one line?" Relentless. Can he not hear my thoughts?

"Just one line?" I am out of my mind with this. And it is mainly because I don't know why I shouldn't just go over there, plop down on the couch, and sniff in the next drug on the menu. Smoke 'em eat 'em, breathe 'em in.

"I hear sex is amazing on coke."

"You what?" This comment pisses me off in more ways than one. Our sex is apparently not amazing; he thinks he is going to get lucky with me twice in one night, and the last thought that pops into my weary, worn-out brain is that he had (of course) already had amazing sex on cocaine.

"You hear? Do you take me for a fool? Are you saying that what we have isn't good enough; you have to sniff shit up your nose now? Is this what you do with all your conquests? Bring them over to the pad where John hands out lines and condoms and lets you use his bed?" I push him hard with two flat hands into his chest. He takes two wobbly steps back, seemingly stunned. I feel ready to take them all on, all the horny, coked-up guys in the world who can think only of satisfying their momentary desires with temporary pleasures.

"Jesus, Rachel." He looks to where John is sitting and shrugs his shoulders.

"What? I'm here for one night and this is what you decide to do? I can't fucking believe you." I turn to walk away, but there is really nowhere to go, seeing as I don't know where I am. No place is mine - no cubbyhole, no spot, no familiar bathroom to cry in. I want out. I want a hotel room. Why have I even bothered with him? Tears form in my throat, and I walk around the corner and into the hallway where John and the bass player can't see. He follows me. He better follow me.

"Rache, come here." The tears are warm and overwhelming. I back up against the wall and slide down until my knees sit under my chin. My hair brings curtains around on each side, and I bury the rest of my face in my hands. So many reasons to cry, so many rivers to cross. Will I ever find the right place to be, the right guy to be with, and the right me to cry about? On one hand, I feel as if I might cry forever. On the other, I wonder how I can think I have it so bad. I am a model with a rocker boyfriend. I live in Paris. I am on my way to a job in the sun, where I'll be getting paid very well for smiling. I am healthy and twenty and sexy enough for two guys to want me in one evening. My apparent boyfriend stands in front of me with fabulous curls and rosy cheeks, a beautiful body, and the desire to cheer me up. Count your blessings, name them one by one.

"You come here." Come into my cave and comfort me. Tell me lovely things and that everything is going to be good again. Tell me I'll be okay. And then tell me you'll love me forever and never want another.

Dylan crouches down beside me and kisses me on the top of my head, blessing me with courage to move forward. I peek my tear-stained eyes up at him. If I go lower, deeper, darker than he, he can then seem higher, better, and more secure than me. Sure, he is coked up and probably fucking any decent prospect that crosses his path, but I am psychologically lost, mentally confused, and insecure. So is it a match?

"Just tell me why you have to do coke now." Meaning why is this the new drug of choice—this one that costs a lot more and makes you so extra sexual.

"I like it." So simple for him I want to throw up. But the clam chowder is resting nicely in my belly.

"Well, I don't." I put my head back down. Kiss me again.

"How do you know?"

"Hey, you guys okay?" It is John. "Am I interrupting something?" He jerks his head and slides some hair behind his right ear.

"No. It's cool." What is so cool? And now I have to be charming and pretty for both of them. I am just so tired I don't even want to be seen.

"Thought you might want to jam on that new song."

"Yeah. We'll be right there, okay?"

It is the "we" I want to be a part of. Doesn't everyone? What a lovely word. We. We'll be right there. We will come when we are ready, when we've got our shit together. We come as one.

"Wanna hear it?" The question is, has he done his time with me? Have we kissed and made up enough to join in again? Has he paid his penance for being a coke-fiend? Probably not. Not really. But when the time is so limited, so must all of it be. Mini-meals, mini-make-up sessions, miniscule amounts of sleep. I am not awake enough to care enough to make him suffer any longer. Be in the moment and enjoy it before it's gone, before you're gone on an airplane across the country. Be a big girl, dry your tears, and act like an adult already. I stand up to my full height, my full sexuality, my full age, and tell Dylan I would love to hear them play. And I do.

His voice. Do anything to me. All I need is to hear you sing, to watch you play, to be your number one devoted fan. You are an artist, a beautiful, sensual artist who requires mind trips to set yourself free. Strum the strings and sing sweetly the song you seem to surrender to. I will sit here on the ugly carpet in awe, in my dirty jeans and jealous heart. I will watch you through my weariness. I will clasp my untalented hands across my shins and find you grinning beneath your curls. I will devote my ears to the sound you create before me, and in the words you sing, I will try to find you.

I know there is air to breathe
Yet I sit with caged birds that can't fly.
Crosses burning on the lawn
Crosses burning all night long.
Seasons have come and gone.

It is a strange disease
Sometimes you catch it
Sometimes you are cured
Sometimes you're not.
Once you leave home, you can never go back.
That's right, Jack
It's time to make new tracks.
Seasons have come and gone.

The house is burning from the inside
The flowers melt in the breeze.
There is no laughing, only decay
The only thing to do is leave.
Seasons have come and gone.

I see through him. I see him as the very young man that he is, searching and struggling just as I am. I witness him creating and debating within himself. Who am I to expect some kind of long distance control over a soul as sweet as this? We are so different and the same. We want what our parents want for us, but we also want the more each generation tries to prepare itself for. He is a boy. I am a girl. And this distinction will forever drive us 'round and 'round in search of the other.

My thoughts run around with the THC in my brain as we drift into a strange land of slumber. If I had the energy, I would have told him I understood. I would have released myself from him and him from me and allowed the distance to finally settle it. But I started dreaming before I could form the words in my head to words on my tongue.

26

A LITTLE INDIAN

I wait until the orange Subaru is illegally parked in front of the airport doors where gruff, black men in fitted polyester suits and company hats are handling baggage while their morning coffee cools in white Styrofoam cups with plastic tops to say it out loud. It has been with me in my restless sleep and all through the morning rituals we dragged ourselves through. Neither of us greeted the morning light very pleasantly. It seemed to remind us of the reality from which we so beautifully escaped the night prior. Even Dylan's cheeks have lost their glow.

He puffs on half a joint while I comb through my hair yet again. When there is so much to say, sometimes it's best to say nothing. There isn't enough time. There isn't enough devoted energy. And the obviousness that neither one of us is in each other's daily lives is as evident as the burn holes in the dilapidated couch and the pieces of artificially colored Doritos scattered in the outdated carpet, where I'd placed myself the night before. Everything just seems too true in the sunlight.

He splashes his face with water and changes his shirt from a dirty white Bob Marley one to a baby blue one that makes me want to cancel any plans and kiss him in the park all day long. His jeans, he grabs from the floor, stepping into them while the curls fall loose in front of his face. What is it that drives the female to the male? For as I am sitting there, I've forgotten to take a breath or two. And this isn't how I feel when I watch Val Kilmer or Richard Gere in the movies. They are beautiful. They are yummy even, given the roles they play, the costumes, the perfect lighting. No. Watching Dylan get dressed in front of me while I sit on the edge of his bed puts me in a speechless mode. He has no idea of his loveliness. If he did, he'd look in the mirror at some point before he heads out the door. Certainly he'd want to enjoy the beauty that waits for him there? But even while he pushes the toothbrush back and forth in his mouth he stares into the sink, spitting quickly, rinsing and waltzing into the kitchen like a prince for a cup of coffee. The future is with this young man. He lives in the center of the world at the beginning of his adult life ready with bodily strength, physical beauty, and musical talents. He can have whatever he wants. And why not?

"Let's just say we both have our own thing to do right now, okay?" The time is ticking on the little digital clock in his car. I have no more than 32 minutes to get from the car to the seat in the plane for takeoff.

"What are you saying?" He decides not to make it easy.

"There's no use in holding onto each other from so far away. It's not fair. For either of us."

He looks at me gently. Parting is so bittersweet already, without breaking up right along next to it.

"Rache…" I am getting out of the car with lumps in my throat and severe loneliness in my belly already.

"I love you, Dylan. I do." I do. But I also know there was no way to hold onto such a specimen, such a one I desire to control and cannot.

"Are you sure this is what you want?"

Are you sure you could hang onto our long distance relationship, stay true to me, call me regularly and be totally straight and sober when I arrive back into your life, even if it means waiting a couple more months? I can already hear him thinking to himself that this means he wants me even more and that it finally allows him to be who he is being anyway, without the distant pressure from a basically nonexistent girlfriend.

He jumps out of the car and runs around to my side, getting nasty stares from the people in the car behind us who have no intention of parking and loitering. "I love you too, Rache. So much." He takes my morning face in his warm hands and kisses me with soft lips. "You better go. You're gonna miss the plane." He could just have easily said thank you for giving yourself to me, for being my girlfriend, but you're right this ain't gonna work. Now go. That's how it feels anyway. Still, as I turn to look back with my suitcase weighing me down on one side, he is still standing there watching me even though people are starting to honk their horns.

* * *

My life's anchor has released itself and sunk into the swirl of heavy mud. I am without a dock, a port, a place to call home, my own. I feel terribly nauseous and out of control. My stomach is in square knots, not to be undone. I am giving into the feeling of dread again. And being on another airplane isn't helping matters. I feel too closed in now. I want to jump and scream and tear my hair out, but I have to remain in my seat with my belt securely fastened.

Now what am I going to do? The same stale exhaust fumes I'd left the day before come seeping into the plane, and I begin rehearsing shortened breath. Either way I'll get a headache, so I may as well cry, I think, as warm tears drop down my lightly powdered cheeks. I remain motionless in an aisle seat, fantasizing about making a run for it. Belt unclasped, darting down the rickety floor toward the shocked stewardess who'll have no control over me as I force my way out. Out of the world of responsibility in which I've found myself. Out of the ridiculous business of modeling. Out of this stupid plane and into his arms again, into his world where I at least felt wanted. Am I wanted? Where? In his bed, by his best friend, as the model I've come to be? Does a person go where they are wanted or do they go where they want to? When does it become one in the same?

The large African American man sitting next to me glances over once or twice, but I stare straight ahead, not wanting to get into it with a stranger. It might just make me feel better, and I am not up for that. Not yet.

The flight is crowded. We are slowly served a Salisbury steak with mashed potatoes and green beans. The anticipation of this disgusting little meal is nearly hideous. People all around put down their little trays and close their magazines for something I lapped up like a dog in grade school but can no longer touch as an adult. I jab at the mashed potatoes with my spoon-fork combo utensil and try to make sense out of the fact that I live in Paris, have just broken up with my boyfriend in New York, and am flying to Arizona where I know absolutely no one. High in the sky it all feels like a dream, and I want it to be. I want to wake up and have a life that makes more sense—like the ones in the movies where the young women go to important universities where their parents pay their tuition and housing. There they learn about themselves in a safe environment and go home for Thanksgiving. The life that I am in is an insecure one that matches every day in my memory. It makes me weary.

Dylan is gone. My first love and my first life. I unbuckle my belt and walk swiftly to the bathroom cubicle. Vacant. In. I rock back and forth on the toilet seat and blow my brains into the wad of tissues I've pulled from the container on the wall. And then I cry and before I decide to be done, I cry a little more, to make good use of all the tissues. I feel worthwhile if I try my best not to waste things. It is a start. It has to happen somewhere. And in the occupied bathroom, it does. It is in there under all the very bad lighting and claustrophobic possibilities that I grow up just a little bit, for when I break through the narrow door and onto the cat walk in front of me, I begin to feel a bit freer and a lot lighter. Not having eaten breakfast or lunch helps, but nonetheless, something deeper has also taken place. I realize I am on the road to find out.

Cat Stevens sings in my head to me as I continue through the magazine I'd left the day prior. The ads are amusing enough. And then I close my eyes in gratitude of the things I've been given. It is all about perception. I can look at it this way, or I can look at it that. I can be an abused child with no true parents, poor and broken, or I can be a chick who tackles the world with a passionate mind and sturdy soul. Why not choose the latter? And isn't it all about choice in the end? In the beginning it may not be. But towards the middle, it most certainly is. It is then that we must begin for ourselves our own desired reality, regardless of past mistakes inflicted upon us. Looking back is certainly a prerequisite, but remaining present and glancing forward is the subject itself.

Many most important possibilities mingle around my mind as I press myself west into the singular sun. There's no turning back now. There never was.

* * *

The Arizona air is a crisp, bright blue and the sun is warm and beaming. I am shown to a luxurious hotel room with heavy, dark curtains, cable television, two queen beds, and the most perfectly clean bathroom I've ever seen, complete with the toilet paper folded into a point for easy use. It is probably my most favorite aspect of the whole room, the triangular point given to the toilet paper. It is so lovely that someone has done this for me, although it does seem a bit excessive. After all, one tug and roll, and it is gone, flushed.

The young, pale-faced porter moves me in with my bags and suitcase. I give him five dollars and feel like a queen. A queen? A queen wouldn't be traveling alone and tipping porters. Perhaps I feel like a model feels, a model who's been summoned across the globe to wear catalog clothes and smile for a very large sum of money.

Either way, I am somewhere I've never been being treated extremely well, and all of this did distract me just a little from my earlier morning despair. I want to call someone and tell them how great I have it, to make it real, but I am not sure who. I can't call Paris from the hotel, and Eliza is the only one I can think of who might be happy for me. Maybe Michael.

Instructions and an envelope have been waiting for me at the desk. I am to report at 5:00 am to room 115, where the makeup artist will be waiting to do my hair and face. The envelope contains five hundred dollars that is to be used for my expenses. I am not sure if I've ever seen five hundred dollars all in row like that before. Nothing lifts the spirits like a nice wad of cash.

In my room, I pull the plastic rods outward to reveal a setting sun and the parking lot. I sit down at the small round table by the window and look at the money again trying to decide where to put it. It is the money for my meals, but I can't imagine wasting it on food that will only end up as waste. Five hundred dollars. Enough even for a cheap car, a fast getaway. I fancy myself taking off without doing the job. Disappearing like Thelma and Louise down the vast and boundless highway in my own car, free, running away from all of it. All alone on the sunny, dusty roads of the southwest. Who would care? Who would miss me? It is almost a freedom to decide no one would.

The room is too quiet and hotel windows never open. It seems so sterile with the rough bed covers and empty drawers all around me. I would like to breathe in different air, get a feeling for the weather and winter warmth.

I turn on the television for company, for proof that I am not alone in the world, for noise and distraction from my dangerous and destructive thoughts of disappearing into nothingness. I finger the money once more and put one hundred into my wallet and the rest I tuck into *Bodily Harm*, my latest Atwood novel. Then I bounce heavily onto the bed with the remote control and try to figure out what I am going to do with my gnawing hunger. I haven't eaten all day.

Kentucky Fried Chicken appears instantly and is plucked open as steam rises from the white breasts. Doughy biscuits, mashed potatoes, corn on the cob dripping with butter, coleslaw. Tempting, certainly, but this is something to be eaten with a group of people around a picnic table on a summer afternoon in the park, right? I flip the channel. Two all beef patties, special sauce, lettuce, cheese, pickles, onion on a sesame seed bun. The picture of it on the screen oozes with fatty juices as large fries and a coke are planted on either side. The American meal. Fat on a bun, fat and sugar on the side. Yum. Yuck. I had memorized the ingredients though, as a kid. It was required of a fourth-grader. Mom had even bought us the tee shirts with all the words. That made it easier. It helped us to impress our friends.

I roll off the bed and undress, still flipping though all the channels, trying to allow television to redeem itself. It has been a spell since I'd viewed American television and it brings me back. It had been such an important element in our house.

* * *

"Rachel! Come get your father's dinner!" The mother screams this from the kitchen around the corner. Rachel has her eyes glued to *Happy Days* and is reluctant to move with Fonzie in the room. He is so cool in that black, leather jacket with pretty girls hanging on his every "Aaay" and "Whoa."

"Rachel!"

The girl walks swiftly and dutifully to the kitchen and brings back a plate of spaghetti, which she sets on the veneer snack table in front of her father. His place in the house is on the red, scratchy couch. Lately he even sleeps there, that is until his wife tiptoes in and turns off the television without permission. Snapping it off snaps him awake, almost immediately. Then he'd roar angrily at her to turn it back on, which she would. No one wants to provoke a sleeping lion. But then he'd be up again, watching old black and white movies until dawn.

"You make a better door than a window." He is talking to her, but what does this mean? The little girl stands there perplexed as

Laverne and Shirley comes on. She likes to see them do their little step dance on the sidewalk, and she is enthralled for some reason at the lonely glove Shirley puts on a passing beer bottle in the brewery where they work.

"Move!" She jumps and backs away toward the front door, looking at her father, who is making an ugly face at his dinner. "I told you I can't stand this shit when you mix it all together like this! Are you hearing me?" He almost gets up from his spot, but then she appears in the doorway with a hand up to her face. She wears a printed, red housedress and blue tennis shoes from Woolworth's. The mother and daughter stand on opposite sides of him and are equally and terribly startled as they watch him throw his entire plate of spaghetti onto the white wall of the living room in rage and disgust. Some of the noodles stick, as well as the tomato sauce, but the meat and most of the noodles fall to the floor in a messy heap.

"Fat bitch! Get the fuck out of my sight!" The snack table is then overturned as he makes his way toward the back door. As he passes his wife, he makes a violent movement as if to backhand her in the face. But apparently watching her flinch and hearing her squeal is sufficient.

* * *

The water pressure in the shower is not so good, but it still feels sweet to wash away the flight. I need to feel new again. Fresh for dinner, whatever that is going to be. I decide I will probably just walk around near the hotel and find something suitable enough to get me through the night.

But before it gets too late in New York, I decide to take a chance and see if Michael is home. It has been a long time since we've talked. I sit on the bed and press mute on the remote, listening to the ringing and trying to figure out what time it is there.

"Hello?"

"Hi. Is Michael there?"

"Yeah. Just a sec." Phone down. I can't tell who it is. It doesn't sound like Yvonne. It could have been any girl from any town, USA. They all come and go so quickly through his apartment.

"Good evening." He sounds serious.

"Michael, I hope it's not too late."

"Rachel?" Oh, how lovely to be recognized.

"Yeah." I want to say something French because he loves that so much, but nothing comes out.

"Wow. Good to hear from you. Are you in the states?"

"Yeah. Arizona."

"Yes, I know. Alex told me. Congratulations."

"Thanks."

"Everything going well?"

"Yeah. Well, it hasn't really started yet. We start shooting tomorrow."

"I'm happy for you. I take it everything is going well in Paris?" He pronounces it with a silent "s."

"Well… that's kind of the reason I called." My voice shakes slightly, although I hadn't meant it to. I stare at the crazy, colorful images of a Mountain Dew commercial and try to think. "What do you think about me coming back to New York?"

"So soon?" He sounds far away. I miss him. "Rachel, things are looking up for you there. If you come back, you could be missing some excellent opportunities. I'd like to see some European tear sheets in that book of yours, sweetheart. Alex told me you haven't really gotten the editorial shots we were hoping for."

"Michael… about Alex." I should have rehearsed this before I dialed the phone. "I just don't trust him."

"What don't you trust?" He is sounding irritated. "His business sense? Because this is the only part of him that concerns you, Rachel." I know how Michael likes to have his evenings to relax and unwind without dealing with a lot of stress. He is trying to pacify me quickly, probably knowing very well the character of Alex. But pacifying only works with babies.

"I just don't like him." Treat me like a baby, and I'll act accordingly. And then before he has time to respond to my infantile whining, "He hit one of the other models."

"He did?" I can hear a deeper registering of our conversation.

"Yes. Her name is Samantha. She was all black and blue when I left." So there.

"Well, try not to trouble your pretty head about it. I'm sure there are two sides to the story." Which there are, of course. "I'll try and sort things out from my end, all right?"

"Michael, you can't mention to him that I told you this."

"Well, that's going to make it much harder now, isn't it?" He is forever the practical man. "You want to tell but you don't want to be the tattletale. I'll do what I can. You just focus on your shoot."

"I will." What else can I say?

"Rachel, I've got another call coming in. You take care of yourself now." I can tell he already has the receiver halfway to the phone. And then it dawns on me quite suddenly that everyone is just looking out for their own ass. If I gained twenty pounds, I'd be gone from this business in a flash. None of them would give a shit about me. If I broke out into a rash, if all my hair fell out, if I accidentally shaved off both of my eyebrows, there'd be no more five hundred dollars waiting for me in an envelope. It is an exterior business with exterior values, and no matter how good it could be today, tomorrow I'll just be older and less marketable. I need to get out while I am still the one to decide such a thing.

I snap the television off and toss the remote back onto the bed. I need to eat. I grab my backpack and key and wander out into the darkened streets of Tucson.

* * *

The hotel phone rings so loudly in my ear I can feel my insides clench tightly before I pick it up, whisper thank you, and drop the receiver back in place. What a startling way to awake! Not conducive at all to the dreaming state. The sound has scared my sweet nocturnal images into hiding and I rise from the crispy, white sheets in a daze. It is 4:15 am.

Rubbing the sleep from my eyes, I stroll listlessly into the bathroom to begin the morning ritual. Toilet, shower, face cleanser, razor, soap, shampoo, conditioner, detangler, towel, deodorant, body lotion, toner, under eye replenish gel, SPF 40 for the face, comb, blow dryer, brush. And then I have to get dressed to meet the makeup artist so he or she can do my face and hair! Make me presentable! Make me a model.

In the elevator going down, I shut my eyes, trying to get in just another wink or two of sleep. I yawn a large, silent yawn just as the door opens onto the first floor. The arrows to room 115 point to the right.

I walk down the navy blue carpeted hallway looking to one side and then the other until I come to the correct room. It seems almost insane to knock on a stranger's door at 5:00 am.

"Good morning. Are you my five o'clock?" She looks right at me, and I know immediately that I have seen her somewhere before.

"Claudia?" There she is, as she had been back in the snow in Connecticut, with her long, dark braid and bib overalls.

"Do I know you?" She shows me into the exact room I had slept in.

"Rachel, from that booking we did at your house. Remember?" I had remembered her.

"Rachel. That's right. Wow. What a coincidence. How have you been?" Her tone is warm and she looks extremely well rested in the predawn setting. "Would you like something to eat? We've got some bagels and juice here if you're hungry."

"It's too early for me to think about food." As it was, I am probably still working on digesting the tacos I'd chosen for dinner. The cheese tasted fake and the lettuce was wilted. Yesterday had not been a good food day.

"I agree, but I thought I'd have them send some stuff anyway, just in case. You're my first this morning. There are three more models coming." She shows me over to a chair that sits facing a mirrored cubicle, or makeshift vanity.

"Oh." And I realize I had been the dupe elected to wake up in the middle of the night to get my hair done.

"Tomorrow I won't see you until 6:30. You get to sleep in." She smiles a friendly smile, reading my thoughts. "We rotate every day. To be fair." She slowly begins combing through my hair. "It's good to see you again."

"It's good to see you, too." It is. I'm not just saying that. The woman who stands behind me is a beautiful woman in her late thirties, maybe early forties. I wonder if I'll look so good twenty years from now.

"So you haven't told me how you've been?"

"Okay, I guess." I never am any good with these types of questions. "I've been living in Paris for the past couple months."

"Wow. They booked you all the way from there?"

"Yeah. Actually, I was surprised to see you all the way here from Connecticut."

"I do this catalog every six months or so. Most of the time we're in Phoenix or Tucson. It gives me a chance to see my grandmother. I think I told you about her...?"

"You did." I distinctly remember the portraits on the wall she'd painted. Claudia gently touches my chin so that I will move my head back. This way she can make an even part.

* * *

"Hold still!" Her giant, trembling hands clutch the sides of her daughter's head, making her momentarily deaf. The daughter wiggles one last time, trying to sit as straight and tall as possible. The hands shake her head back and forth abruptly until they settle on a position. The girl tries to freeze in place. This is where her mother wants her. She will try not to move now. But her nose tickles.

"Stay still." Her mother's middle finger plants itself on the tip of her daughter's nose while the right hand works the comb from this vantage point up and across the top and deep into the scalp, making a line all the way down the young girl's neck. But it still isn't right, and so the mother pulls the comb again, from the forehead to the nape of the neck in an attempt to draw a straight line into the skull. Done.

"Here." The mother gives her daughter the plastic bag in which all her hair accessories are kept. In it is a jumbled mess of ribbons and barrettes, headbands and bobby pins. Each ponytail has to sit high on the head and in the exact same spot as its pair. To get them just right takes a good deal of brisk brushing and tight handling. Small, colored rubber bands hold them in place.

"Find the yellow ones, with the blue dots." The yellow ones with the blue dots, the yellow ones with the blue dots, the yellow ones with the blue dots. The little girl has only so much time before the other ponytail is fastened into place. When this is accomplished, her mother will want the ribbons immediately. At least one. She doesn't like to wait for them. If she has to wait, she would become extremely irritated and grab the bag away from her daughter. The girl knows she can do it. She can find them. There is one. She snatches it, holds it up, and looks at her mother in the mirror, who is still wrapping the rubber band around the second ponytail. Her face is reddening and coarse, and her own hair is graying at the roots as she scowls determinedly at her daughter.

Too early. She isn't sure if she should watch her mother so she can be ready with the one or begin searching for the next one. She decides to hold the bag up a bit so she can see both, but the mess of the wrinkled ribbons and hairy rubber bands block her view.

The ribbon is plucked from the girl's hand. Her mother brings it first underneath the ponytail, then ties it, makes a bow, and then ties the bow, tight. So tight the girl winces as she finds the matching ribbon and holds it up for her mother, who has been kept waiting.

* * *

Claudia is finished with the second braid. At the ends of each, she has taken a small portion of loose hair and carefully wrapped it around the hair band, disguising it.

"Braids?" I look up at her in the mirror.

"What can I say? They're back in fashion." She smiles at me softly.

I stare straight ahead. "They make me look like I'm six." I turn my head to the left and watch her bring her makeup case over.

"How old are you Rachel?"

"I just turned twenty. I feel so old."

"Twenty? But you look much younger. Claudia is closely applying a beige foundation to my entire face with a clean sponge. I can smell the foundation and her perfume. It is the same she had worn during the first shoot, and just as familiar.

"Well, that's what they say."

"Look up." Dots of white concealer under my eyes. "So when was your birthday, if you don't mind me asking."

"November seventh."

Claudia backs into the cubicle and bumps into the counter behind her. She looks at me closely as she holds onto the counter in back of her with both hands. The sponge has fallen to the floor. We both look at it as she reaches down to pick it up, then toss it into the wastebasket by my feet.

"I apologize for my clumsiness. It's just so early in the morning." I look back at her with my perfectly blended skin.

"No problem."

"November seventh?" She grabs a fresh sponge from the bag, clears her throat a little, and resumes her work.

"Yes. That's my birthday. I guess I'm a Scorpio, but I'm not sure what that means."

"Yes. Yes you are. And it means that you're probably pretty intense and have a good amount of energy." She smiles in the mirror at me then. "They say that Scorpios are the sexiest of the 12 Zodiac signs."

"Really?" I can't imagine that the stars could determine who would be sexy or not. Nevertheless I like hearing it. "What's your sign?"

"Pisces. Also a water sign."

"So what do they say Pisces are like?"

"Apparently we're always moving in the opposite directions, trying one way, then turning around and taking the very way we chose not to go. It makes life quite disturbing at times. We can also be very creative, but then lack the self-confidence to see something through. Maybe that's why I've ended up doing makeup. It's not the most challenging occupation, but it feels safe." It sounds strange to hear her reveal herself like this.

"Nothing wrong with feeling safe." I would have loved to be her, to live Claudia's life. She seems so at peace.

"You hungry yet?" She looks at her watch.

"Do they have any juice?"

"Yep. Let me get it for you. We still have ten minutes. The rest of your makeup won't take very long." I look at how she'd created me thus far, and in the mirror I see the little girl I'd been and the woman I am becoming.

* * *

The day is bright, just like the one before. A large recreational vehicle has been rented for our use. The hired driver has taken us out at sunrise and we've driven almost an hour before the photographer seems satisfied with the location. We are now out in the middle of nowhere, in the desert with nothing but cactus and giant black bugs flying into our faces and in front of the camera. The space feels too wide open and vulnerable compared to the safe craziness of the cities.

There are two other girl models and one guy, who is quite taken with himself and thus completely unattractive, to me at least. I watch him in front of the camera—his chiseled face, wavy dark hair trimmed to perfection, dark, penetrating eyes—and feel nothing. Back in the trailer, he sounded just like a girl, wincing over the sleeves of his shirt not falling long enough in his opinion. But he is all we have, long arms or nothing. And so the stylist tries convincing him he looks fine, tucking in his shirt for him and pulling on the sleeves a little just to satisfy. He insists on seeing himself full length before he traipses out into the desert dirt. For this we all need to back out of his way so he can get the best glimpse of himself in the mirror on the back of the door. He spends more time primping than all three of us girls put together, and it is certainly our greatest entertainment of the day. Well, that and dodging the big, black bugs.

The other girls are both younger than me and different. One has naturally curly red hair and is fair. The other is a dark blonde who has a body like the Commodores sing about in "Brick House." But both are pleasant enough as we all take turns changing in the cramped quarters and smiling our catalog smiles out in the sun. It is their turn to go out. I am in.

"Rachel, while I have you alone I thought I'd ask you something."

"Wha...t?" My mouth is open, then closed to blot. Claudia is changing my lipstick from the deep red that has gone with a striped tee shirt to a soft pink that is to complement the flowered dress hanging on the rack to my right. I am picturing the mood I will project with it on, with my hair, now out of the braids, cascading behind me, rippled from the bends that have been made in it. The shot is a single. The other models are doing group shots in matching polo shirts and dress shorts. Claudia has given the girls side ponytails.

"This Sunday, after we're done with the shoot, I was thinking maybe you'd like to join me."

"Join you?" My eyebrows rise up in question as I stand up to put on the dress, then turn around so she can zip me up.

"To go see my grandmother."

I turn back around.

"On the reservation?" This idea appeals to me. Yes. Definitely yes. I can't believe she wants to take me with her.

"It's a couple hours drive west from here. It will take the entire day. I like to visit with her as long as I can." Her voice drifts and her eyes drop down to the small table where her makeup case sits. She picks up the compact she's been using on me. "Up."

"I'd love to go with you." I look up as she pats powder under my eyes. And then I look into hers. We are exactly the same height. She powders my nose, chin, and cheeks.

"I hoped you would. I little more blush, I think." She picks up the large blush brush and taps it lightly into a soft rose powder. Then she sweeps the color over my cheekbones and stands back to inspect her creation. "With your hair down like this you almost look a little Indian yourself."

"I do?"

"You do."

27

PILGRIMAGE

On the holiest of days, I sleep in until eight o'clock and wake feeling pleasantly refreshed. My hotel room has become my own. I've gotten used to feeling clamped in by the tightly made bed, looking out the window at the parking lot, and having my room and bathroom kept tidy by some faceless woman in a gray dress with a rounded white collar. No maid has to knock on my door to see if it is okay to make up the room. I am always already gone. And when I return, the slightest mess I may have made between dinner and dawn is anonymously whisked back into perfection in my absence.

I watch the maids in the hallway in the morning on my way out, pushing their carts full of fresh and dirty towels around from room to room and wonder how they do it. Do they just make it through each day to see the moment when it was time to quit, time to drop the dress and climb into sweats for an evening of television and eating on the couch? Do they make their own bed before they go to work? Do they make a triangle in the toilet paper for themselves?

I am decidedly against any future occupation of this kind. Never could I walk the streets with mail, delivering from house to house, box to box, letters and packages that will never stop coming. I could never wear the uniform. I could never wear a uniform. I could never endure such repetition. Yet so many do. And they are grateful for the opportunity to do so.

I so appreciate each fold and tuck and dumping of my trash. Having fresh towels every day is such a treat. All of a sudden, I feel the routine of life easing up for me as the mundane chores are being handled by someone else. It is a lovely thing.

I stretch my limbs away from my body until I feel every major muscle group, pull the clean covers off my rested body, and stand erect when the phone rings. I know who it is.

"Morning, Rachel. Did I wake you?"

"No." This is a "no" with a smile attached.

"Good. Is ten o'clock still okay for you?"

"Yes," I say, glancing at the numbers on the clock. "I think I'll go on a quick run first, and I'll meet you for breakfast then." I am already sliding off the boxer shorts I wore to bed and pulling on my running ones. The phone is sliding off my shoulder, and I have to stand on one leg to secure it back under my ear before proceeding with the shorts.

"That'll give me some time for my meditation. This week has been so crazy I haven't had a moment to stop."

"I know." I can tell we are both pleased the day is Sunday. We all have an extra day in Tucson, if we want it. We had finished our part of the catalog shots and the photographer was satisfied things had gone as quickly as they did. It helped to be able to count on the non-stop sun.

This is the day to renew and reward the self. It is finally a do-as-you-please day, and every bone in my body is grateful for what is now done and what can be. As hard as one can work, the balanced counterpart awaits. The important thing is to seize the moment, take it and be in it, breathing deeply until you are called upon again to run for someone else. This morning I am running for myself, and not because I am trying to be thin or burn last night's calories. I am running in the sun because it feels good.

The warmth pours down upon my lightly tanned cheeks and I recall the week that has passed. Claudia has become a friend. It is with her that I work and eat and talk. She listens with her eyes as we sit over bowls of split pea soup and salads at a nearby health food restaurant. She encourages me to express how I feel about breaking up with Dylan—offering me her napkin when my tears fall, noticing mine has food on it.

As we drove around Tucson one evening after dinner in her black, convertible rental jeep, she told me she'd been a runway model back in the seventies when looking ethnic stopped being unacceptable and started being cool. She showed me an old picture from her wallet with bent corners and fading colors of when she'd first met Emma's father. Her lips were a frosted pink, and her hair was down long, reminding me of Cher in those days.

"Are those fake eyelashes?" I held her wallet up to a streetlight. We were back in the hotel parking lot, but had decided to sit outside in the evening breeze with the top down as our conversation continued past the point of the parked car.

"Believe it or not." She smiled as her thoughts remained back in time.

"So that's Emma's father?" I pointed to the man in large dark glasses and striped pants.

"Long before I had Emma, of course." She took her wallet back and pressed it shut. "He still comes around to see Em, but it's been over between us for a while." She sighed a knowing, contemplative sigh.

"Do you still love him?" I wasn't sure if I was overstepping my boundary, but it seemed as if her thoughts were still on him.

"David? I'll probably always love him. But living with someone you love is a lot more complicated than just loving them." I sat there in my ignorance and knew there wasn't anything I could say to make it seem better, as she'd been doing for me. Then maybe understanding my silent inadequacy, she continued. "He was there for me when my life was turned upside down. It's a story that I'm sure I'll tell you some day, but not today." She dropped her wallet back into her bag and began snapping up her plastic window. We better get to bed. You're first tomorrow, aren't you?"

"Yeah." I snapped my side together and we pulled the top into place.

The two of us walked into the hotel lobby doors and before the elevator stopped on her floor, she turned and gave me a hug. I hugged my friend back to communicate what need not be said aloud.

"Sleep well."

"I will."

And I had. There is something so reassuring about Claudia. She is at peace with herself and can therefore radiate peace to others, making them feel calm with themselves. This is how I felt, anyway, and it was completely different from how anyone had ever made me feel about myself before.

Over a breakfast of oatmeal, bananas, and peppermint tea, Claudia sits at a table by the window in her fitted, faded jeans, black tee shirt, and cowboy boots and tells me of her grandmother's failing eyesight and incredible insight.

"Visiting Grandma Emeline is…" Claudia sips at her cooling tea and looks at me gently with her almond eyes and olive skin. "It's almost like a pilgrimage to me."

"I really appreciate you asking me along." I'd been a couple minutes late to breakfast and was feeling as if I might be holding up her trip. I swallow down the oatmeal, glad that I didn't really need to chew it.

"She'd want to meet you. I know if I told her about you and you weren't there with me she'd be disappointed."

"She would?" The peppermint tea is refreshing. My whole body tingles with good energy, from the run and the company and the food and the money I'd made. I wish I could take the moment—this one between an accomplished end and an anticipated beginning— and freeze it, capture the present for future tears I know will come. Instead, and in my post-teenage wisdom, I realize that moments like these define the others and vice versa, and for this ebb and flow of all things I should be grateful and accepting.

Still, I wonder where the photographer is now, now that I need *him*. Shoot a roll of us here at the breakfast table before our journey with our tea. The light is just right, and our hair is combed and braided. Shoot the important stuff. Shoot me *now*.

But five minutes later, after paying for our breakfast, I prop my soft-soled leather boots up on the black dashboard and lean back, watching the road and Claudia's profile underneath her sunglasses as she drives with the strength and carelessness only a woman possesses. She turns the dials on the radio, adjusts her rear view mirror, and changes lanes all at the same time and with no sense of reservation.

As we turn onto the freeway with the wind blowing through our hair and the southwestern sun shining down upon us, I think, *Here we are, just as I'd imagined.* It is a Thelma and Louise getaway into whatever is waiting for us on the other side.

Maybe I am on the other side of me, now. Maybe just enough time has passed living on my own that I've begun a new reality. In searching for it for so long, I'd barely recognized it until I am made to sit and stare at nothing and everything in front of me. The colors are amazing—rich, bold, and large. The red rocks, baby blue sky, and the small clouds stand still to me, requiring only my quiet attention, inviting a new me to look over at the old.

"You cold?" She has to nearly scream this at me as the wind whips at our ears, giving the trip a droning, meditative feeling.

Cold? I am not anything but perfect. Everything is completely tentative, just the way I like it. This isn't where I live, it isn't my car, I don't know where we are going or who will be there. I have no one I am responsible for and no one who is responsible for me. I am free. I am quite nearly in a state of bliss.

But it is in such a state that only the very enlightened, or the newly dead, are to remain. The rest of us need the continual ups and downs all in an hour or a day to keep us from our fear of too much happiness. Actually, it's not the happiness we fear, but what comes after it. As soon as we soar so high we inevitably fall just as low, 'round and 'round as the wheel turns, sometimes so quickly, and sometimes so slowly we forget that the downs have ups and the ups downs. The sweetest thing is to experience the ups after having the downs for so long. This is how I am feeling. I am remembering the high after a long row of lows.

The trick, I think, is to somehow keep it all balanced just enough so that each day's mix of highs and lows can be no more unsettling than the breath we first take in and then release. This way, there might possibly be a very slow and steady evolution of rising highs with fewer lows because of a foundation that is created a little at a time, like interest accruing on money sitting in the bank. At first, it may just be pennies, but add it up over a lifetime and there's a sum to be recognized. This is what growing older is about. It isn't about losing youth or freedom, it is about gaining a sturdy foundation of balance and wisdom simply by being in the moment and gradually releasing from the ups and downs of daily life.

This is what I see when I look over at Claudia. I don't see the wrinkles around her eyes or the raised veins in her hands. I don't see the graying roots of her hair and feel superior that I am as yet wrinkle free. I see her peace and feel deeply my uneasiness with myself. I watch her be comfortable in her older skin while my skin remains my only marketable commodity. How odd our culture is for the emphasis it puts on surface beauty when the only truth is that none of it will ever last. Every perfect baby face will some day gravitate into one with the lines and spots and scars of life. Every supple petal on every flower will eventually dry up and fall off, back to the earth from which it was born. And every model will look in the mirror at some point and realize there's a bit more to life than looking perfect for the camera.

The surface of the smooth, black road seems to go on forever as we push through the rough and looming red rocks on either side of us. I pull the collar of my jeans jacket up around me and bring my feet up on the seat, securing my arms around my legs.

"Rachel, is it too windy for you?" She yells this and turns her face to me twice briefly, while wild wisps of hair dart and fly all around her face.

"I'm okay!" I say, loud enough so she can hear. And then I turn to face the front again, breathing in the chilly winds and loving it. This is an adventure, and during adventures certain elements and periods of discomfort must be overcome for the greater experience, for the overall satisfaction of having endured the event. What satisfies me is not luxury and being spoiled and having plenty. What satisfies me is unique sacrifice, surviving danger and breathing and eating the earth as much as possible. Of course I am making this up as I go along, because what do I know except what has already passed? I need to feel alive to be happy. And to me, Claudia seems alive.

I catch her looking over at me and grinning as the sun shines down upon her, making her spirit glow. I know what I do best. I am a sponge around people I admire. And for now, I am soaking up all that Claudia is. It seems a very natural thing to do.

We've just passed Red Rock on interstate 10 and are making our way to a place called Picacho. The small reservation is in Maricopa. I peer into the distance searching for signs that we are getting closer. I have to pee. From the tea.

"Why would anyone live on a reservation?" I'd asked Claudia several days ago. Why would her grandmother choose to live on a place her people had been pushed onto? I had an image of the Native American people from the books I'd read by them and by films shown in school. Geronimo spent his life as a warrior, fighting against and escaping from those who would confine him. It is said to have taken 5,000 troops over a year to finally apprehend him. In an attempt to conquer land, the American settlers had to force out the Indians, pushing them further west and into designated areas, which if found attractive became land to conquer once again. The Native people ended up in the poorest areas, separated from their families and their tribes.

This was the history of America that made me sick. It made me weep for people I'd never known and now could never help. This country was completely "conquered" long before the pilgrims arrived. It was being farmed and esteemed and it was most certainly occupied. This land was home to thousands of tribes of people who were involved in the natural seasons of the earth. They were a culture I would have loved to know. Teach me the quiet ways. Tell me about the animals and their spirits. Help me to revere the elderly, to find them rich with wisdoms, not just irritating and slow the way my culture shows. Remind me of the four corners of the earth and of the symbols in my dreams. Guide me to live in harmony with Mother Earth as she provides easily for all of us. And let us use that which we kill, and use all of it.

I know the life of the Indians was far from perfect, but it was most certainly more perfect than the way we rush around in a selfish attempt to acquire that something more that will bring us that something that seems forever lacking. The white man exists to conquer and consume. The red man existed to be and let be. Who won? And did the white man get what he was looking for? Were they finally satisfied with all the land and the buffalo, the oil and the gold, the death and the sickness, and the killing of an entire culture?

And why would an old woman live on a dusty piece of land that had been roped off years ago by the enemy?

Claudia said it was her home and no matter how many times she invited her to move east with her, Grandma Emeline resisted. Perhaps she did so with the same spirit her ancestors had when resisting the inevitable change that was to come upon them so abruptly and so fiercely.

"What are you thinking?"

How does she know I am thinking? She looks over at me and grins a knowing grin. She is quite aware I won't be able to scream my thoughts back at her with the noise of the jeep and the wind, but I answer her anyway.

"I love it here!"

"Me, too!" She smiles again and looks back at the road as our bodies bounce in our seats.

Arizona seems to be forever climbing toward heaven as the sun pours down glorious, golden warmth to turn the soil brilliant colors, blessing the earth abundantly. We are a million miles away from anywhere I've been before. The gray cement and polluted noise of New York, the small, foreign feeling of Paris, the normalness of Wisconsin all seem to dissolve out in miles of desert beauty. We push our way in search of what so many before had been looking for. What is beyond all of this? Where does such vastness lead? For some it becomes the mountains of Utah and Colorado. For others, only the coast of California will satisfy the hunger for adventure. Quietly I wish we could have taken it that far, that the two of us would just continue west until we found the best Jim Morrison was so fond of.

What would I be leaving behind but a fading career and a mother who I try not to think about? She is there, though, in front of her sewing machine, then folding laundry at the dining room table with a solid look of defeat on her face. She'd leave the dishes in the sink for someone else so she could finish her sewing, her foot pressing the peddle, making that familiar noise while she sang loudly to Barbara Streisand. She'd tear the threads with her teeth, always sacrificing herself. And all this time I thought I'd been the only one making the sacrifices, giving up my childhood to her, giving her my time. I'd only done it in imitation.

She is a mother, and a mother is just a woman who gives up a part of herself for another. She'd taken me in and raised me and taught me maybe the best she could as she herself struggled through her own hell. In essence, who am I to judge her? At twenty, I can begin to see that adulthood is not all it looks like from a child's point of view. A parent is just a person in charge of younger people. A parent is not the all-knowing, all-loving entity we want them to be when we look up at them, fearing them. And what about my own biological mother, who hadn't even given it a try? Where was she when I needed her? My mother in Wisconsin would always be my mother. I know that now. As much as she lacked, she lacked only because I'd been her fiercest judge.

I stare out at the scenery whizzing by and am surprised by warm tears dropping from my eyes, which are quickly whisked away in the wind. I let them fall and keep my head turned away from Claudia. I would not have been able to explain my weeping.

We turn onto a dirt road and off the exit we've taken that reads, "Maricopa Indian Reservation," as the jeep jostles us in our seats and pulls us over rocks and stones that have gathered along the path.

"We're almost there." Claudia raises her eyebrows over the top of her sunglasses in anticipation, and I return her look of excitement the best I can, dabbing casually at the moisture under my eyes with the sleeve of my jacket. I could have said the wind made my eyes water. I exhale slowly, surrendering to the sweet weightlessness. The wind has blown the self-pity away and the battle within stands still for a moment. It isn't as terrible as it has been. It doesn't have to be anymore.

A dark-skinned young man stands at a makeshift gate and waves us through when he sees Claudia. "That's Tommy Twotree," she says, with a smile of familiarity.

"Tommy Twotree?"

"Yes. Did you see his legs? He's so tall and skinny, his legs look like two trees."

"That's kind of mean, isn't it?" I pull my eyebrows together in a quizzical knot, still feeling quiet inside and a bit sad in having to break the peace.

"Not really. He's proud of his Indian name." She looks over at me and winks in an effort to make light of what I am taking too seriously.

We park next to a long, wooden structure, press the tabs to let our seatbelts go reeling back in place, and open the doors to the jeep to let our aching bones stretch. I step down onto the earthy soil in my soft boots and feel as light as a woman on the moon. I breathe in a deep, cleansing breath, as if I've arrived at an important destination. We leave the top down and the windows loose.

I grab my backpack from the back seat and follow Claudia, who has been bombarded by small, dark children with big, bright eyes and dirty hands. She shakes their tiny paws with one hand and with the other pulls me through to the other side of the building where the sun has found an audience of a single, elderly woman sitting in a colorful lawn chair. In her lap is a half-finished tapestry woven with threads of turquoise blue, golden yellow, and burnt orange. She works on a small loom with her fingers doing all the work and her eyes none of it.

"Grandma Em." Claudia's voice, like warm honey, drops into the ears of this old woman and her head turns toward her granddaughter and away from the sun.

"Claudia." Her small brown eyes peer out of her sun-lined face and into that of the one who stands before her as she lifts her crooked and wrinkled hands to welcome her visitor. "Claudia." She repeats herself and motions to several small, wooden benches. Claudia pulls one of these closer to her grandmother and sits down. I follow her example, looking closely at this woman my friend reveres. She is clothed in brown cotton pants and a soft, cream-colored, long sleeved shirt that is hidden mostly by a large, beige and white striped poncho. Her hair hangs down thin and wavy on either side of her face, graduating from white and gray roots down to black ends. Around her neck, she wears a beaded decoration that seems to give her aging face power. In the center of the necklace, a black circle provides the background for a red and white phoenix that sits in the middle and stretches its wings outward.

"Grandma Em, I've brought someone with me. This is my friend, Rachel. Rachel, Grandma Emeline."

"It's very good to meet you." I mean every word. I am overcome with an immediate respect for this woman. There is an energy in her hesitation as she holds Claudia's hands and begins talking with her in slow, solid sentences.

"I dreamt of two birds this morning. They had come to bring me wonderful news." Grandma Emeline speaks deliberately and with a soft cracking in her voice so that we stay very still to hear her. "The birds are the same, one older, one younger, but the same."

"What did the birds say, Gram?" Claudia looks over at me trying to read how I am reacting.

"Now child. They didn't say anything. They were birds. And this kind of bird didn't speak." She blinks the small openings of her eyes several times and continues the tapestry as her gaze takes turns between the sun and her granddaughter.

"You need to use the bathroom, Rachel?"

"Yeah." I speak quietly remembering how badly I did. I'd been too involved in the delicate moment to request such a thing.

"Come with me." We walk along a dirt path to a smaller building. "In here."

"Thanks for bringing me with you, Claudia." We are in stalls next to each other, and although I always feel uncomfortable talking and peeing at the same time, I need to say this.

"She's amazing, isn't she?" We zip up and flush.

"She is." We stand at the sink, soaping up our hands and drying them on our jeans. There aren't any paper towels in the white container on the wall.

For several hours, we sit outside as the earth turns slightly, bringing its only light down to rest more comfortably across the horizon. Claudia does most of the talking, telling about Emma and how she is doing in school. She explains how I am a model and when we'd first met at her home. She reminisces about the shots we did in the snow and about the ones we'd just finished doing in the desert. Claudia attempts to fill the silence with animated stories and her grandmother attempts to stay focused on them as her eyelids drop occasionally during a pause in the one-sided conversation.

I listen and watch the old woman's fingers work the small loom, pulling vivid colors into place and pattern. And then I glance down at my own hands, still untouched by age, but creasing slightly here and there more than they had before. Claudia's hands rise in the air as she gesticulates the story she is telling.

After awhile, the old woman stands up and begins walking out into the open field in front of us and toward the dropping rays of the sun. We follow on either side of her. Claudia's arm is wrapped in her grandmother's as we stare into the light and distant, rocky hills.

"Rachel." It is the first time she's spoken directly to me.

"Yes?" I turn quickly to face her as she slowly and carefully pulls her hands around to the back of her neck. Claudia steps nearer to us both.

"I want you to have this." Her hands stretch out to me, shaking slightly. I offer mine to her and she gently lays her necklace in them.

"I can't take this from you." I start to shake my head. Who am I?

"You will take it, honey. Be strong now. Remember there are no coincidences in life. All is for a reason and a purpose."

I stand there holding the necklace in my hands, humbly baffled. Am I supposed to put it on right now? Claudia reads my confusion and steps in back of me, taking the necklace and fastening it underneath my messy braid as I hold it up for her.

"It is a bird of great beauty and a symbol of strength."

"Thank you for this." I touch the soft leather backing and look over at Claudia, who seems pleased now.

"You are very welcome. Come back and see me any time." She blinks several times quickly, glancing sharply into my soul.

"I really like it here. I'd love to come back." I say this timidly and truthfully as Grandma Emeline turns and begins walking slowly in the direction of the sun. I place my hands in the pockets of my jeans jacket and follow these two amazing women as we continue our journey across the golden field.

28

UNRAVELING

Running, running, running as fast as I can possibly go across streets, through yards, in through the back doors and out through the fronts of all the houses in my path. I am good at this. The momentum of the race heightens all my senses and I become the bionic woman, normal looking with normal fear, but with a great deal of extra speed and strength. I am super human, powerful, crazy with endurance. I have to be. I am being chased, and the race has gone on for hours and will continue until my capture. As long as I keep moving, watching what is ahead of me and planning my route accordingly, I will make it. I will be okay if I just keep moving.

Across the street, I see my old house, square and brick. It sits on the corner, vulnerable and available for all to see. Billy is riding his big wheel on the sidewalk. I am running too fast to stop, but glance quickly over at the empty swing set in the backyard. It is too small for me now. The yellow plastic seats would cave underneath me. I'd get stuck trying to slide down the slide. I am longer than the slide now. She would have to yell that I am too big, that I'd break it. Then I see her with a clothespin in her mouth, hanging the laundry on the line, concentrating on pulling each flowered towel straight, using one clothespin to hang two corners together, conserving the clothespins, making them last, doing it right. The look on her face is a mix of irritation and determination, and it is not the right time to visit. My heart goes out to Billy as I speed by without either of them seeing me. I am too fast for them now. I've escaped and the journey is now my own, and my own problem. I don't belong to them. Maybe I never have.

I round the corner, nearly running into the lilac bush she'd trimmed so many times. Then up the street and out of sight. I sigh, almost losing steam. I feel him come closer, and speed up. This is my neighborhood. This is my town. I know what will come before it appears, and I use this to my advantage, dodging him as I cruise into an alley way. Up ahead is my grandmother's house, and although there is a sense of comfort there, I know it will not last. It is nowhere I can stay, so why go at all?

I decide to take State Street all the way down past the grocery store and through the park. It is wild how everything is exactly how it has always been. A creepy feeling penetrates my body when I realize nothing at all has changed. The vacuum store still displays the same broken sign and the True Value parking lot remains an eyesore, taking up too much space. Why do they need so much space?

I race down the hill, knowing my high school is near, right past Woolworth's and 31 Flavors. All of these places are places I no longer need to go. I had been here and there. I'd walked the streets, I'd shopped the stores. No more. No reason to. All of it had stayed the same while I'd moved on what seems like so long ago. I need to get out. I am suffocating from the lack of change, from the permanence of each street sign I'd walked past ten thousand times. I need a new street sign.

Sweat pours into my eyes as I reach the park. I stop for just a minute and let my shaking hands fall to the tops of my thighs where I stand bent over, breathing heavily. Maybe I have lost him. I turn around.

No! Horror creeps up inside my chest. It can't be! There he is, just a few blocks away, flying straight toward me. His wings are spread wide and his one glass eye looks right at me, taunting me, possessing me. I know he isn't flying as fast as he can. He glories in the chase. It is what he does, and I am giving it to him, playing his game. But what other option do I have? I turn around to concentrate and steady myself. I reach my arms out in front of me and close my eyes as I bend my knees and slowly push myself off the ground just as I feel him nip at my butt with his beak.

"Ow!" At this, I hear him cackle in a deep, wicked voice. I push my arms out even further to ensure a steady, solid flight. I can't let him distract me or I will fall. If I fall, it will be over. At the same time, I need to stay near the ground, just in case. I don't feel confident enough to fly high. I can only fly ten feet off the ground at most. I stay above State Street, following the train tracks into a part of the city with which I am not very familiar.

The tracks lead into a grayer part of the city, and where before the sky had been blue it is now dark and cloudy. The sweat on my face and shirt dries in the wind as I begin to pursue a place of refuge. But I am out of my element now and scared.

"Caw, caw." His eerie call almost makes me fall. I look back and see his light, glassy eye peering at me with grotesque delight. I won't be able to keep this up much longer. I am going to have to land somewhere and hide. But it scares me even to pre-think my plans. I know he can read my mind.

Ahead are factories and office buildings and smoke pouring out of them, mingling with the thick clouds all around. I am lost. None of this is familiar to me anymore.

My strength is waning. I turn sharply to the right, but I can still feel him on my tail. The air becomes humid and a light drizzle begins its decent, pulling down on me as the moisture adds heaviness to my hair and clothes. Soon I can't see two feet in front of me and am forced to slow in my pace. My entire face squints into the distance, and I fear this might be the end.

Like a wild animal, he senses my trepidation and moves in closer. He begins to bite me on the thighs, first nibbling and pecking lightly, then drawing blood after I kick at his feathered head. His laughter provokes me and invites me further into the fight. Soon I am bleeding heavily and watch as my blood mixes with the now pouring rain. Blood and water stream down into the invisible ground below. We are surrounded by the fog, and I am certain we've flown much higher in it.

The bites on my legs are burning in pain, and even though I kick at him each time, it doesn't seem to deter this incessant torture. I can't stand it any longer. I know what I am doing before I do it. I am risking death by giving up my flight. I drop my arms and begin falling through the thick clouds, spinning and dropping as the familiar and terrifying feeling of fright rises up through the insides of my torso and out through my upper chest. I feel that I might die from the fright. But I am quiet. Screaming won't accomplish a thing. I just endure the fall, endure the pain and the terror as I give up the chase. I have lost.

* * *

Waking up now, I look around slowly and rub my eyes, opening them to a pale pink room filled with pink pillows of all shapes and shades. Hot pink hearts, rosy pink circles, and large, soft pink square pillows are gathered underneath me and all around me. The one window in the room shows the storm has cleared, and the sun has returned from its absence.

Remembering my flight, I quickly feel for the bites on my legs. They are gone, and my bare legs feel amazingly smooth. The room has a warm glow to it, and I feel comforted and safe. I stand up slowly, kneeling on several pillows as I do so, and realize with a curious sense of panic that I have no shirt on and am dressed only in ripped denim shorts and no shoes. I pull my hand up to the top of my collarbone and touch the soft leather backing and tiny beads of the necklace Grandma Em had given me. Quite suddenly, I decide I am cold and need to find a shirt. But the room I am in provides no clothes or closet.

I open the door of the pink room and venture out into the hallway cautiously. The navy blue carpeting feels thin beneath my feet. I know where I am. I'm in the hotel. I look to either side, to where the room numbers should be, but the doors are blank, so I keep walking, wishing I could remember where Claudia's room is. She'd have a shirt for me. She could help me.

My hair falls lightly on my bare shoulders and back as I walk down the hallway that seems to go on forever. I had seen these hallways before, in scary movies where the pursued run screaming or run in place, never finding a safe destination until it's too late, until the black-masked man with the knife comes slicing down with his shiny, silver blade, down into the heart from the back, and then over and over again. Why not? The victim is caught and dying a sure death. Might as well make it worth the trip.

So that's it, I think. I'm still dreaming. I woke up inside my dream to dream another dream. But it is a flickering thought, and I find myself more concerned with finding a shirt. To find a shirt, I need to find Claudia. She has to be around here somewhere. A door creaks open to my left. I turn to face it.

"Rachel. There you are. I've been looking for you." The door opens further and his scarred face gawks at me. I shake my head and my hair covers my chest. I look down the never-ending hall and stand petrified, wanting to run.

"Rachel, running isn't going to get you anywhere. You'd think you'd know that by now. Such a smart girl. It's a shame. Why don't you come in? I have some friends here you might like to see." His voice, so familiar, so taunting. It is a voice I have to obey, isn't it?

The door squeaks as he pulls it open for me, and I walk hypnotically past him. He slaps me on the behind, which makes me jump. He laughs.

"Girls, look who's here!" He crosses his arms casually, grinning his cigarette-stained grin. Behind me, he bolts the door. This is my hotel room. Immediately I notice Sam lying on the bed closest to the window with her hands tied above her head and fastened to the headboard. Her feet are also secured together with a rope. A white washcloth has been shoved into her mouth as a gag. We exchange glances, hers being much more apathetic than mine. Straight ahead and sitting at the table is Eliza, who has been bound by similar rope. Both her hands and feet are tied to the chair as she sits at the tiny round table. They are naked except that each of them wear flowered satin panties exactly like Yvonne's. Eliza's breasts hang down in front of her and wiggle back and forth as she tries to free her hands.

"Eliza." I begin walking toward her. How could he have done this to her?

"Rachel, I'm scared."

I fully intend on untying the knot, but as I approach the back of the chair, Alex appears and pushes me back and onto the bed next to Sam.

"It's not your responsibility to take care of my models, Rachel. That might be how it is with Michael, but not here. You should know better than to hide Samantha in your apartment. And you, too, Eliza. After everything I've done for you, giving you a free ride all the way. This is how you show your gratitude?" He stands next to Eliza, sneering at her as his right hand, so dark and creased, molds itself around Eliza's smooth, white flesh.

"Leave her alone!" I stand up again.

"Well, look at you, so feisty. Have you decided to take my advice about what we discussed?" He drifts slowly toward me as I back up against the wall. I can see Eliza behind him, frozen with fear.

"Eliza, it's just a dream. Don't worry."

"Just a dream?" Her face crunches in anxious perplexity.

"Is this a dream?" He takes the rough tips of his stained fingers and slides my hair over my shoulders, exposing my chest to him. I look down at my small breasts.

"Yes." It is. I can wake up if I want to. So why don't I?

"Well then, let's see what we can do in this dreamland of yours." His liquid voice is mesmerizing as he works his large hands up from my waist and over my ribs to cover my undersized mounds. He pushes me harder against the wall and surrounds me with his body. On the opposite side of the room, I can see the back of his black, silk robe and graying hair in the mirror as he firmly massages my chest. In my dreaming mind, this is inexcusably demeaning and yet I allow him to continue out of pure intrigue.

A minute later, he steps back from me. "Voila." I immediately catch my reflection in the mirror. My boobs have tripled their size. I look and feel entirely different. I turn from side to side admiring their shape and form. Then I realize with a cold shudder that he has done this. I've allowed him to do it. I am naked and ashamed. I try to cover my chest with my hair, but it's harder now. It looks silly. He simply stands there, leering at me, which makes me shiver again. Little bumps pop up all over my skin. My nipples tighten.

"Beautiful, yes?" Smiles from the artist, the creator, the conspirator, the captor.

Yes, I suppose. But this is not the point. And it's not me. I'm quickly annoyed by their size as I begin searching the room, my room, for some clothes. They bounce and are in the way, skin against skin. Annoying foreign flesh dangling from my chest. I want my body back. This is not my body. This is *his* body. All I want to do is cover them up, put them away, out of sight. They have done nothing to make me feel better about myself. I know this now. They are not for me, they're for all the others ogling, paying for the possibility of sensuality, of sex. Cleavage does little for the one wearing it. It is simply there to draw attention. And attention such as this, I do not require.

"What are you looking for, darling?"

Darling? My suitcases are gone.

"Did you think this was your room?"

His voice fills me with terror again as chills run through my body. I wrap my arms around myself and notice out of the corner of my eye that Eliza has freed her hands from the ropes. She gives me the look of someone who needs to communicate her entire plan of escape through the muscles on her face. Her dark, wavy hair hangs in small ringlets over her eyes. She looks desperate. Together we can get out of here. But as I look back at Alex, he looks over at her and advances unhurriedly in her direction, subsequently securing the knots back in place.

"You girls. So clever. Do you think I am going to let you go? You can't get away from me." He bends down next to the chair as Eliza yells for him to leave her alone.

I grab a pillow off the other bed and hold it in both arms, looking from Eliza to Sam, trying to figure out how I can free them. I sit down next to Sam while he seems preoccupied with silencing Eliza.

Sam peers blankly up at me while I lean back against the bed to get a look at the knots. But again, he senses my intentions and rises from his position behind the chair, stepping angrily toward the bed.

"I told you she's not your problem. Give me that." He darts at me, snatching the pillow from my grasp. My body begins to shake involuntarily. "You leave Samantha alone. She's just a no good whore, aren't you, my little cupcake?" His tone is devilish and smooth as he pulls a single finger down Sam's body from her neck to her satin underpants.

"You beat her until her face was black and blue!" I turn to him in defiance, staring straight into his scarred face and glassy eye. My arms cross in front of me, my hands tuck into my armpits. I am sick of him and of the control he has over us, even in a dream.

"Is that what she told you now?" He turns his dark, wrinkled face toward Sam. "You wicked, wicked girl. How could you say that?" He stands over her and pulls his black, silk robe firmly around his square waist. "You really are wearing me out lately, Samantha. I should have sent you back to your brother months ago, but you begged me not to, remember?" He plucks a cigarette from the pack on the table and lights it with a gold lighter from his pocket, cupping his withered hands and peering at Sam from above them.

"Here." He pulls out the gag and inserts the cigarette into Sam's mouth. She takes a long drag, turns her face in his direction, and spits at him.

"Fucking asshole."

His large palm responds with a shuddering slap across her face, and he reinserts the washcloth, resting the cigarette in his mouth as he does so. "Ungracious little wench." I can tell his spirits have been affected by what Sam has done, as if he was the father of a disobedient daughter, distraught as to what to do with her. But the moment doesn't last.

"Sam's had her turn with me. Who will be next?" His crinkled neck turns slowly back and forth like a teacher trying to choose whom to call upon when all the students know the answer. He keeps an eye on all of us as he pulls each turn of tar into his lungs, casually flicking the ashes onto the carpet.

The hum from the air conditioner kicks in and a chill runs across my bare flesh, bringing his attention to me. One leg up over the other one as he sits at the edge of the bed, and then I notice his feet. But they aren't feet at all; they're claws, and I realize now, remembering the first dream. My nightmare seems alive, and I wonder as to my power within it. Is it that I am not confident enough to set myself free? What is holding me here, topless, a victim in my own room, in my own dream?

"Rachel. Are you there? Rachel!" A woman's voice calls from the other side of the door. I glance in that direction as Alex rises from the bed to come to me. At first I can't speak. I open my mouth, but nothing is there. And the more I try, the harder it is to make a sound. I am paralyzed within my sleep. I feel ready to wake up, but it's as if not being able to scream is preventing me from the control I thought I had. The next thing I feel is his black silk robe engulfing me, drawing me in as his body presses against my enlarged breasts. I am numb. Where is my voice? Who am I to allow this? This is not me!

"Help!"

His strong right hand swoops up and clamps itself across my mouth.

"Rachel!" She is on the other side of the door. I crane my neck to find Eliza, but she's no longer there, and Sam is asleep, knocked out, drugged. I am alone with this beast and frozen within the dream.

"Rachel, are you there? Open the door!"

But I can't. His grotesque body is heavy as he pushes me down onto the bed with a thud, immediately securing my hands to the headboard with rope. With his right hand cupped firmly over my mouth, he takes the other and begins to unbutton my shorts. I kick my legs vehemently until he decides to sit on them, which brings an awkward smile to his wicked face. He knows he has me now. He's won. He has me how and where he wants me, and there's not a thing I can do about it. Is there? In all the movies, isn't there just that one second before the final deed takes place that everything could just stop and move in an entirely different direction? The rape, the murder, the jumping off a tall building, the teetering on the edge of it. This is my second, my one chance, and although it's just a dream, it is as real as any reality seems.

He sneers down at me, needing to hate me just a little to do what he is about to do. His body sinks closer to mine as he studies my new breasts, fondling them with one hand. With his attention distracted, I find the power within my legs to jolt my knees up into his stomach. His hand breaks free from my mouth, and I scream with all the rage I've ever allowed myself to experience.

"Claudia!"

"Rachel, open the door!"

I'm stumbling to the door and feeling my tiny breasts even before I slide the chain to one side to let her in.

"My God, are you okay?"

Her face is beautiful, like an angel's, and I check the room behind me quickly to make sure the devil has vanished.

"Thank you." I step quickly back to the bed and sit down, feeling as if I might fall otherwise.

"Thank you for what?" She is stroking my hair, pulling the tiny beads of sweat into it, patting it down, patting me back into the present moment.

"For waking me up."

"Bad dream, huh?"

"Maybe the worst one ever."

Claudia sits down across from me, on Sam's bed, probably to peer in at me, to counsel me. A counselor needs a little distance, more than a friend needs. I wonder if I can trust her now. To whom we decide to tell the truth makes all the difference. If we unveil our secrets to an inappropriate person, the secrets begin to lose their flavor, their importance. Perhaps this isn't a terrible thing, but not all the secrets are mine. Is it my place to share now? After all, it'd only been a dream. But in a sense it is real, and the reality of it could go on for years unless something is done. I had tasted in a dream what some had tasted in truth. I couldn't live with it any longer.

"You okay now?" Her womanly form is hidden inside her white overalls, drawing all attention to her earthly complexion and almond eyes. Her hair has been prepared for her flight in a French braid. I am impressed with her skill. "I wanted to say goodbye. My flight leaves in a couple hours." She takes my hands in hers, and I find sweet comfort there. My morning face glances into hers for a silent answer.

"I need to tell you something. I have to tell somebody." That's all it takes for the river of tears to begin to flow. Before I know it, I'm sniffling and shaking my head back and forth as clear mucous begins to gather in my nose and throat. Claudia walks swiftly to the bathroom. I hear the tissues being pulled from the container on the wall. She brings me three or four of them, depositing them in my palm.

"What is it, Rachel? Tell me."

But who is she to tell? Who is there to tell? What is there to report? A man in Paris takes his job too far? An agent in another country may or may not have raped some girls. Hearsay, gossip, lies, and dreams. But Alex is not a lie. He is a pervert, and he is getting away with it.

"It's not really my business." That's what I am supposed to say, as a lead-in, something to distance myself from what I am about to say even though I can still feel his presence in the room, his heavy flesh on mine.

"You can trust me, Rachel." And then she glances at her watch and for a moment, I think I'll just forget about it. What can be done anyway? But then I look over at her as she is sitting on the edge of the bed and I see Sam. I see her bruised face and broken spirit. I picture myself in the apartment, Alex looming toward me, groping, sneering, intimidating. I remember Yvonne. I cringe at what Susan must have gone through.

"It's just that I don't know what can be done or that I could make it any better."

"We don't know until we try." Her tone is comforting, like that of a mother.

"That's true." Still I hang my head between my shoulders, looking down at a stain on the thin carpet beneath my naked feet. Maybe it was coffee or tea. It'd been there awhile, probably. Some stains never come out.

"Rachel, look at me." I do.

"I am here for you." She looks me directly in the eye and deeper than anyone had ever dared prior, and this makes me lose sight of myself.

"It's our agent in Paris. He abuses some of the models there. I think he rapes some of them." I don't realize I've said this out loud until I catch her reaction. It's not at all what I expect. Claudia's serene demeanor vanishes as my words escape my mouth, and I quickly feel the need to console her somehow.

"His name."

"What?" I'm confused.

"His name, Rachel."

"His name?" As if this will make a difference in all of this. And then I forget his name and for the life of me can't think of it at all in my desperate attempt to remember it for her.

"Rachel!"

"Alex. His name is Alex."

"Oh, my God!" Her hands reach for her face, as if she'll find some comfort there as her body lifts from the bed involuntarily.

"Has he hurt you?" Her tone is desperate. She begins to pace back and forth at the foot of the beds, darting glances over at me with her questions. "Did he hurt you?"

"Not really. No."

"Is it not really or no?" She's becoming more impatient with me than I feel comfortable with, and I decide to get off the bed and help her pace.

"No. I mean he's made a couple moves on me, but I stayed away from him, you know?"

"Oh, Rachel. Darling. Come here." And with that she pulls my messy-haired head onto her shoulder and hugs me desperately.

"He's hurt some of my friends. That's what I was talking about. When I left, this girl Samantha was all beaten up, and she said he did it." It isn't me who needs the consoling. I am seeking help for another.

"Where is Samantha now? Is she all right?" Claudia steps back from me, still holding my head in her hands. She is crying.

"Are you okay?"

"I'm fine." She wipes her tears on the back of her hand. "Listen to me." She sniffs in and takes me by the shoulders. "Stay away from him." I want to get her a tissue, but her posture insists I stay and listen.

"I try to." I look from side to side wondering what dream I might be in now. "Do you know him or something?"

"He has a scar."

"Through his eye." I finish for her.

"Oh, God."

"What is it?" It is my turn to beg the secret.

"Just stay away from him."

29

HOME

I am not sure what to expect as the taxi pulls onto Rue de Saussure. Paris seems at once colder and grayer, the tiny streets bleaker. I am returning home, but home for me is only a dwelling, not the peaceful, restful haven the word is meant to entail. I feel restless and agitated as I take the small elevator up to the sixth floor. The squeak it makes annoys me.

Everything is backwards. Somehow my progress feels stunted in my return to France. Something happened when I left. The world got bigger and smaller and more confusing. Coming back to Paris feels redundant. I have already done this. It is over for me, like a relationship gone sour. Besides, Christmas is right around the corner. What will I do in Paris for Christmas?

I know I am here because of Michael. Because this is where I am supposed to be now, to bring home European tear sheets of myself from the magazines. Home.

The door is unlocked as I turn the handle quietly. The offensive smell of cigarette smoke greets my nostrils, and I blink my eyes to see in the gray air that matches my mood. Eliza stands at her easel with a joint in one hand and her paintbrush in the other. Sam sits curled up tight on the floor, holding her legs, puffing greedily on a cigarette. My dream creases my brain, and I am doubly grateful to see them both.

"Rachel!" Eliza notices me at the door. "Rachel!" She seems very excited to see me. I remember our friendship and set my suitcase and backpack on the floor so I can give her a hug. "God, look at you! We've missed you so much." She is giddy. High. Emotions run extra strong on drugs. Sometimes it's a very lovely thing.

"Oh, Eliza." If she only knew what she'd been through the night before.

"You okay?" She steps back from me to see me closer. "Here, take a hit." She holds the joint out to me and I take it, inhaling deeply. When in Rome.

"The place is so…" I only have to squint into the air to make my point. But I'm not really complaining. When you smoke pot with someone all conversation, positive or negative, is perfectly interesting and acceptable.

"Smokey. I know. Sorry." She puffs on the joint again, looking guilty, and turns to Sam for an answer.

"It's me." Sam stretches her small body as she stands up to say hello, although she never says it.

"You look much better." The bruise on her eye leaves only a light, purple hint under her pale skin. It is covered with makeup and from a short distance, barely visible.

"Thanks." She squashes her cigarette into a small ceramic bowl on the counter next to me. In it are lipstick-stained remnants of hours worth of lung damage. In my apartment. Luckily, someone closed my bedroom door.

"I'm so tired." I am, and the pot reaffirms it and makes it okay. It takes me into a place of comfortable fatigue.

"Um, Rachel?" It is Eliza. She looks cute with her hair on the top of her head. Paint stains sweep over her shirt and sweatpants.

"Yeah?" All I want to do is lie down.

"Sam's been sleeping in there. Hope you don't mind." She wants it to be cool. She wants me to understand, as she shares the joint, that the comfort of the all or anyone takes precedence over the privacy and boundaries of the individual. And if this were the case, no one would be homeless and no one could ever call anything "mine." We would all look out for the all, keeping close the idea that we are all one anyway, one in spirit, one in energy. We would pick up each other's trash. No one would ever stand on the corner with a cardboard sign begging for food. That would be an atrocity. It would be an embarrassment to the race. Imagine the aliens coming to visit and seeing people dirty and hungry hanging out inches from the immaculately groomed! Inconceivable.

I hold out my hand. Give me more of the drug that makes all of this not only conceivable, but necessary. It is the drug, that, if one allows it, can open the mind to the importance of putting the all before the I. I want this. I feel that. I know it is time to begin the journey of the all.

"That's cool." Of course it takes me awhile to get out the words. Maybe it is the first time I am able to be this allowing. If I don't start somewhere, I'll never get where I want to go.

"Let me get my stuff." Sam must have felt the pocket of energy open up, because all of a sudden her tone is just the tiniest bit brighter as she trots into the room to pull out several duffle bags and her giant purse while I stand by breathing in the pot and the second hand smoke.

"C'mon." Eliza motions to me to follow her and the roach that is left. I take it and burn the tips of my fingers as we make our way to her room. Solace. Not necessarily home, but refuge. We close her door behind us and melt into familiarity as Eliza lights a candle on her dresser.

"This apartment smells like a bar."

"I know. I'm so sorry." I can tell she is. "I didn't know what to do. It's too cold to keep the windows open. When I'm stoned it doesn't smell so bad." She speaks quickly with a worried expression.

"Don't get paranoid now. It's cool." I smile at her and we share red-eyed glances. I am feeling the high of my high, and it may as well be enjoyable.

"I think I'll roll one more. In honor of you coming back to be with us."

I nod my approval with a quizzical look.

"Where else would I go?" This is said with a sentiment deeper than humor. And now my head turns side to side as I contemplate this very thing.

"Dylan's gone."

"Where'd he go?" She takes the crispest franc she has in her wallet and wraps it around the new joint, rubbing the tips of her fingers back and forth to pack it tight.

"Who taught you that?" My mind is distracted by the buzz running through my legs and chest and brain, and it feels like talking about rolling one might be a tad more entertaining than discussing old boyfriends.

"Sam."

"Nowhere." He's out of my life, I guess. I guess I want it that way.

"Ty's gone nowhere, too."

"No."

"Yes."

"What happened?" And then a pause as Eliza lights the next one. Anticipation.

"What happened is that I'm not there. You can't expect a relationship to flourish without all the key participants."

"This is true." We both feel wise, and our tones reflect this self-image.

"It was some slut over Thanksgiving."

"What?"

"He fucked me over. I guess that's another way to put it." She looks over at me, apologetic that she'd broken the positive spell.

"Shit." And then I know what I've always known. Dylan has never been honest about what he does when I am away. And how can I expect him to? Eliza is right. The long-distance relationship idea is just that. It is a theory that we can somehow be larger spirits than our smaller human bodies seem to permit. We can visualize such a loyalty, devotion, and self-control, but in essence we need to take advantage of all the energy that comes our way, at least in the beginning. In this fashion, we come to understand our true nature so we can begin to celebrate that. Who we are is often how we see ourselves in the presence of others. If we limit this so drastically in our early lives, how can we know what we could know? "Maybe it's a sign or something."

"A sign?" She needs more than that for complete consoling.

"A sign that there's more out there for you."

"I know, Rache. I know. It's how I feel, too. Of course it completely pisses me off, but what the hell was I thinking?"

"Dylan's got his own thing going, too. We both do. We have to."

"So you guys broke up then?"

"Yeah. I think he could have gone either way. That's what makes me believe I did the right thing."

"Totally."

"It's not so bad, being on our own."

"No. It's kind of wild, actually."

The second joint dwindles into a pile of ash as Eliza smashes it face first into one corner of a small tin box she uses to store pot.

"Speaking of wild. Our houseguest? How long?" I don't want to say a whole sentence about it. I whisper.

"I don't know. She went and got her stuff a day or so after you left. I never asked her about it. We don't talk about Alex. I think it's better that way. Alex has such a hold over her somehow." We are crouched together sitting with our backs against the side of the bed. The one window in the room is cracked an inch. Nina Simone sings in the background. It's nearly dark outside, but Eliza hasn't turned on a light yet.

"Sometimes you have to talk about Alex." I stare straight at the wall ahead of me where several new paintings hang. I admire them without speaking.

"Rachel?" Meaning, *What are you saying, Rachel?*

"I met up with someone I worked with before. A makeup artist."

347

"In Arizona."

"Yeah. I worked with her in Connecticut. At her house."

"Wow. That's a coincidence."

"Yes it is."

"So?"

"So we got to know each other. I like her a lot. She took me to meet her grandmother. Amazing women, Eliza."

"Wow."

"I told her about Alex."

"Told who?"

"Claudia. The makeup artist." I am getting very hungry. I want to take a shower. But none of this matters as I sit with Eliza in the dark, with the flickering candle, and conspire against the man who holds us all in his grasp.

"What did you say?"

"I didn't have to say much. Seems like his reputation spreads farther than we know."

"She's heard of him?"

"Apparently. Enough to cry about it before she left. First I was crying about this dream I had, which you were in, by the way, and about what Alex did to Sam and everything, and then she starts crying when I mention his name."

"Shit."

"I know."

"What are we going to do?"

"It depends on what she does, I guess."

"How old is she?" Sometimes age plays a vital role, like how serious people can get about situations that are simply non-kosher.

"I don't know. Somewhere between thirty and forty maybe. She's beautiful. I miss her already."

"Can you get a hold of her?"

"I have her number. She gave me three of them, actually. Her home, cell, and boyfriend's."

"Huh." We sit there with new information digesting like food.

"He's a piece of shit, you know." Eliza takes the hair band out of her hair and shakes her soft curls loose.

"I know."

"I don't think what he does is right."

"It isn't." And then we both look at each other without having to share the details.

"I don't know what we could do though, about it. I mean who are we? This isn't even our country. And God knows Sam won't be saying anything."

"I can't picture it."

"Me neither."

"So what?"

"So we get the hell out of here."

I look over at her with the gratitude that there truly is someone to come home to.

"Out of here to where?"

"Anywhere. Here or there. Rachel, I have something for you." She gets up then and switches on the lamp by her bed. My joints crack as I lift myself from the space on the floor.

"What?" I'm immediately concerned that I didn't pick up something for her in Arizona. I need to start thinking more of others.

"You'll never guess." She's a kid, six years old, and we're on the playground. Bubblegum and jump ropes, boys in striped shirts with balls. She has a secret, and I'll never guess and she won't tell me until I at least try to guess.

"I don't know. You found my parents?"

"Your parents? No, but that would have been a good one." She pauses for a moment, then smiles again.

"Here. I thought you might like these." And there they are between her thumb and index finger, and then into my thumb and index finger. Two tickets to the Grateful Dead New Year's Eve. Bill Graham presents Grateful Dead, Oakland Coliseum Arena. I read the tickets in disbelief.

"I can't believe it."

"Believe it." She smiles, assured. My lack of a proper thank you pleases her.

"How did you get them?"

"California connections. It's not that hard. I have a couple as well. Will you come?"

"Will I come? Are you joking? Where in the world else would I rather be?" It's true. It is. I have quietly become a grateful fan of the Dead. Their music pleases my soul more than any other, and I always thought I'd end up at a concert with Dylan sooner than later. Thing is, the thought of seeing them despite the breakup is intensely liberating. A life without a boyfriend! Can it be?

"All you have to do is fly out there. You can stay with us, with my mom."

"Are you serious?"

"Yes."

"This is so cool, Eliza."

"We're gonna have fun."

* * *

As the blood in my body rises to the surface after a very long and very warm shower, I enter my room to dress quickly; I'd left the window open and the door closed. The chilly air closes my pores and seeps into my lungs, clearing out the spider webs of smoke. I breathe it in lovingly, making the final touches on my room, which is starting to feel like mine again. Mine. For now, I need a small space to call my own, my home. I know home is going to be wherever I dine, wherever I place my weary head at night. I know for now it is no longer a destination, an ultimate place where a family awaits. It will never be that for me. I don't need it to be.

The slightly yellowed white comforter covers the bed where I will sleep tonight. It invites me to forget about everything while the sun is away. But before I do, I decide to say good day to the night, to the Parisian night outside my window where the Eifel Tower shines in the distance.

With my tennis shoes securely tied, I venture out my window and crawl onto the roof to greet the sky and the early stars and to utter a short prayer of thanks for what is, for what I've done so far, for what I am beginning to understand. My mind is still swimming with THC, but my thoughts are crystal clear, like the night. I have to get out of here and make myself home somewhere else.

30

THE THREE OF US

Jim Morrison's dark and sultry voice serenades us from Eliza's boom box into the bathroom, where I am applying a rare coat of mascara to my upper eyelashes. It is hard to keep still. After I peer closely to make sure no clumps reveal too carelessly the mask I've painted on my bare and natural face, I gaze straight ahead into the mirror, letting the black goop dry while my body begins to rock.

"How about these?" Eliza holds up some silver hoops for me to view and contemplate.

"Perfect."

She places them in the palm of my hand, and I insert them into my holes while checking out the chick in front of me. "You look good." It is a small concession. A person confident with their own appearance easily admires that of another.

"Thanks." She is in faded jeans and a snug, black lace shirt. Her hair shows an unusual amount of volume, and of course her makeup is done to perfection. It's easy to do something when you watch it being done over and over by a professional. We are working on the finishing touches now, feeling the blood circulate in our bodies, preparing, but remaining in the sweet moment of it. So often it's the getting ready that beats the whatever you're getting ready for.

"Sam's got a bowl ready if you wanna come out."

353

"I'll be right there." I draw an outline around the edge of my mouth and fill it in with the same lipstick Eliza has on. It is called "Toast of the Town" and is a reddish brown that, once applied, graduates my look from plain and wholesome to bold and finished. I rarely wear lipstick on purpose, but tonight is probably the last night the three of us will be together, and it seems appropriate. Eliza has decided to fly back to California as soon as she can make the arrangements. She's invited me to go with her, but I have a two-day booking with French *Elle* next week, so I can't commit. Not yet. I can picture it, just Sam and me, which will feel like just me with smoky air. There's no way you can ask a smoker to stop smoking somewhere they've been smoking. I am not looking forward to this. I even consider canceling the booking.

Jim is chanting to himself, "Break on through to the other side, break on through, break on through." I settle into the living room, melt into the carpet in my tight jeans.

"He died here you know."

"Who?"

"Morrison." Sam is dressed all in black. Her lips are painted dark purple. Her look has an evil edge to it. She passes me the monster head pipe. It is grotesque, like a gargoyle, and I turn it quickly around so as not to meet it face to face.

"That's right. He died here, in Paris." Eliza brings me a second glass of Merlot, steadying it with both hands as she makes her way to our intended circle on the floor.

"It was over for him, you know? He'd done what he came here to do, and it was over. He knew it." Sam looks at nobody and nothing as she speaks in her spooky, hesitant way, as if life is truly this dramatic.

"You mean to Paris?" Eliza dares to make this a conversation.

"No, to earth." Sam is disturbed that she has to clarify.

"He was only twenty-seven or something when he died, right?" Eliza pushes, with help from the wine.

"You think that's young?" It is a challenge. I'm pleased I've stayed out of it this far.

"Don't you?"

"I think twenty-seven is old, don't you?" She's mocking Eliza now and enjoying herself.

"Not old enough to die." Eliza looks at me for help. I look back at her, shrug lightly, and swallow another mouthful of wine, feeling it sting my throat and coat my insides with a buzzing warmth.

"Death comes when it comes. It doesn't give a shit how old you are." And that is the end of Sam. She fills the bowl again and lights it up strong, inhaling deeply, exhaling through her nostrils. She never flinches. She never coughs. She is silent now; our conversation is not challenging enough. It doesn't deserve her attention. At once we both feel inadequate somehow, although we're not sure how it happened. We smoke the pipe and are quiet with Sam.

After spending a good deal of time around her, Eliza and I both know Sam's way of controlling, of sucking our energy into her own. As long as Sam remains even slightly mysterious and aloof, there will always be someone looking in at her, trying to figure her out. I play along, feeding her because I pity her. Deep down inside her tiny body I know there must be a very lost and frightened soul. Keeping this in mind is the only way I feel I can put up with the way she treats us. She never helps around the apartment or chips in for food. Of course she never asks for anything either, but it is obvious she doesn't have any money. So we always leave enough for her of anything we make. And then we leave her alone as well. Otherwise she won't eat it; like a finicky cat she watches us out of the corner of her eye until we're out of sight, then nibbles away in solitude. She is our pet. She knows it and we know it, but no one discusses it. Not ever. We allow her to keep what dignity she has left after all she's been through. What we receive in turn is bits and pieces of strange conversation, blank stares, and plenty of marijuana. No one ever asks where she gets it.

"Shit, two glasses and I'm gone." Eliza's lipstick sits on the outside of her empty mug. Sam taps the monster pipe into the plastic bowl, knocking out the weightless brains of the beast.

"Let's go." Sam rises onto her petite frame as she lights another cigarette and heads for the door, leaving her glass and ashtray on the floor. I pick them both up and take them to the kitchen.

"I have to pee first. I'll be right there." Eliza walks to the bathroom, steadying herself in her high-heeled boots. None of us had eaten much of a dinner, and the alcohol is doubling its effect on us, tripling if we count the mixing of marijuana. It is Sam who decides that going out is better if we went out already halfway there.

Between the three of us, we don't have enough on to keep one of us warm, but for some reason this is the furthest thing from our minds as we step off the elevator and through the doors to the outside world, where everything is possible and the future lies in wait, unknown to the conscious part of us.

Going out at night all dressed up and made up, looking for nothing in particular and expecting the most, is perhaps a dangerous thing to do for three young women. That's how my mother would look at it. We are young women, and the way we are dressed can only mean we are out looking for trouble. And we will get it if we don't watch out.

I stride down the street in my black cowboy boots feeling my favorite Levi's hug my body, my sisters on either side of me. I am determined never to become a young woman. Never to become a woman. A woman is an all grown up feminine person who is identified by her sex and judged by it. A woman carries a purse and talks to other women about womanly things. I don't need boobs or a purse or such a title as woman. I want to keep the androgyny I've experienced; to me, it is a feeling of balanced wholeness. I feel complete without ever growing up to become the woman titles of wife, mother, ex-wife, and grandmother. Once one enters such a race, there's no turning around. I want to stay in my boots and Levi's, breathe in the cool French air, and allow life to remain a mystery as I continue to become a little bit of everyone.

I am Dylan and Michael and Claudia and Eliza. I am Meryl Streep in *Out of Africa,* dressing in delicate and fashionable white cloth, telling stories by the fire, working on the farm with bare hands, and waiting for my man, patiently. Waiting and watching for weeks to enjoy that one evening sunset, that one dinner. And I am Robert Redford, too, going on safari, holding back emotion, falling in love. I am Kevin Costner in *Dances With Wolves,* alone on the wide open prairie, innocent with the natives, giving up one life for another with the rare courage that character possesses. And I am Julie Andrews, running from the confines of orthodox religion to search for the music and the freedom of escape. I am all whom I've ever admired, both real and imagined. I am Don Quixote and Laura Ingles and Jack Kerouac. There is plenty of room for all of them.

But I am also my mom. Even though I try not to sound like her or act like her, I am still her, for who else had been there through all the years? But now, when her voice and presence enter the stage in my mind, I have a variety of other characters there to add or delete, to argue in favor of or in opposition to what she is saying. In the end, I feel I can make a balanced decision about almost anything, thanks to the best of both sexes and all characters present.

"Should we grab a taxi?" Eliza pulls her thin jacket around her and glances at Sam.

"It's just a few more blocks." Sam continues straight ahead, smoking the end of her cigarette nonchalantly, then flicking it into the distance without a pause. She is in charge now, the leader. She makes the calls. She'll treat us however she decides. It is payback for how we probably make her feel when we set our leftovers on the counter.

Several cars slow down to watch us walk. The guys roll down their windows, peek their heads out to make some sort of gesture while speaking beautiful and broken English to us. Eliza and I check them out casually, keeping our strut at an equal and confident pace. If we act like we don't want them, they'll want us more. It is a game. The winner is whoever comes out the most wanted. It's an easy contest for the female sex.

"Here." Sam turns right at the corner and we follow down a

dark, semi-deserted street. It seems as if we've suddenly entered a poorer neighborhood. Wet newspapers cling to the curb where we walk, and the buildings look in need of maintenance.

"In here."

I am trying to imagine how anyone could have a successful business on such a lonely looking street when Sam pulls my hand and leads me through a heavy black door and into the club, where purple lighting and blaring music greet the three of us. Sam's dropped my hand by now, but Eliza still holds onto my other arm as we glance shyly at the bouncer who stands at the entrance, nodding us in. Immediately Eliza and I begin screaming into each other's ears, hearing nothing but the heavy beat of what I can only describe as heavy punk. The dance floor is packed solid with several hundred sweaty rockers working the grinding rhythm.

"Look at that!" Eliza tugs on my jean jacket and points to our left. A large screen projects naked bodies in all sorts of sordid positions, focusing on one not longer than a second or two. There are large boobs pressed against what looks like a back, swinging buttocks, vertical flesh, horizontal flesh, lesbians and tongues. We can't keep our eyes off of it.

"Where's Sam?" I scream. A shrug of Eliza's shoulders is a practical response. I peer into the blinking, dancing lights in search of a tiny, black figure. I feel lost without her. I don't feel bold enough to confront a bartender on my own, although I know that's what I'm supposed to do at a bar—order a drink, tip the bartender, order another, get drunk. It just seems like too much of a hassle even to begin.

"Bonsoir ladies. How do you do?"

Eliza and I look from the screen to a black-haired man in his mid-thirties or so, dressed in a leather jacket and tight-legged jeans. He is the kind of guy who has "one night stand" etched into his forehead. We just stare at him. Girls don't have to respond in this type of situation.

"May I buy you each a drink? What is your pleasure?" The music ceases for the several seconds he stands there, but starts up again as we turn to each other in an effort to respond. He motions for us to follow him to the bar, so we do. Over near the bar, the air is thicker with smoke and I have to stand back while Eliza yells in his ear that we'd like red wine. He seems pleased. But once we each have a glass in our hands, he is ready for the next step.

"You like to dance?"

Eliza and I look to one another for an answer. I wonder how he expects us to dance with glasses of red wine.

"You." He touches Eliza's elbow, pulling her over to the dance floor with his eyes. She just stares back at me with a silly, confused look on her made-up face. She holds up her drink as they enter the dance floor to prevent it from spilling. Soon they are disguised by the crowd as the massive group works their bodies in and out, up and down, side to side. It isn't the type of music I consider danceable. It is the kind of noise that shakes the walls and makes one deaf with a beat that never climaxes or comes to any resolution. It just goes on and on into a nameless, faceless, repetitious land of robotic monotony. I sip at my wine and despise the sounds that shatter my insides as I wait for Eliza to return safely to my side.

But she doesn't come back for a long time. So I begin to push my way through the crowds of people to find her, keeping my eye open for Sam as well. My head is buzzing and my heart is pounding to the beat as I search for my friends among the dead. The faces that stare back at me are faces of evil. Their makeup is white and black, their hair purple and scarce. Silver rings pierce their noses and eyebrows and lips. I can't tell if some of them are boys or girls. Androgyny gone awry. Some look at me with desire, others with hatred as I patiently pour through the masses in pursuit of Sam and Eliza. Where are they? I begin to panic. I no longer care about having a good time. The mascara and lipstick are in vain. These people don't deserve the effort.

"Rachel!" It's Eliza. I can hear her. I see her hand, then her head. Being tall has many perks. We push through the crowd toward one another, and I feel a surge of relief rising through my body. Everything is okay again. Hell is behind me. "Rachel, I've been looking for you everywhere!"

"Same here!" I nod in the direction of the door and she leads the way. We walk swiftly up to the bouncer, who opens the door to let us out. I feel badly leaving in such a hurry like that. I was supposed to be enjoying myself.

"Jesus."

"I know." Eliza and I walk a couple steps down the block when she turns around. "What about Sam?"

"Who knows." The cold wind feels like heaven, and I breathe it in deeply.

"Should we try and find her?"

"This is her scene." I glance around at the littered street and vacant alley ways knowing that she doesn't care whether or not we wait for her.

"You're right. Sorry about not coming back, by the way."

"What happened?" I pulled my jacket collar up around my neck and push my fists into my pockets as we began to walk against the wind back from where we came.

"At first we were just dancing. I didn't really get it, you know?"

"You mean the music?"

"Yeah. What the hell is the fascination?"

"I don't know. Maybe the beats and sounds are just the backdrops rather than the focus." I'd spent some time considering this as I waited for Eliza.

"Possibly." She looks at me, amused. "Anyway, I couldn't do much with a drink in my hand, so I tried to make small talk or something out there in the middle of all of it. He was kind of cute, don't you think?"

"He was okay."

"I thought so, too, until he starts moving in on me like he's going to do it right there in the middle of the club."

"Ick."

"I know. And that's not even the worst of it." We turn back onto a familiar street, and the wind begins to whip at us from the side now.

"What?"

"This other guy starts working at me from behind. And there I am, my drink in the air, and two guys zooming in on both ends. I nearly freaked out."

"What did you do?"

"Said I had to pee."

"Good call."

"Totally. So I begin working my way to the bathroom. I never did get there. The line was insane. It seems like I was looking for you for a long time."

"Me too." And here we are. Connected by a false night, the loss of a friend, our heads buzzing with wine against the cold wind. We are young and growing older, naive and growing more aware, drunk and getting sober. We are living the life, and it is all up to us.

31

ESCAPE

"Is it up to us?"

"I don't know." I am cleaning the bathroom, scrubbing the toilet and the sides of the tub with cleanser trying to make everything good again. Clean again is a start.

"Should we call someone?" Eliza is pacing in back of me. I would like it better if she picked up a broom or something to help. We are preparing to leave Paris promptly, but neither of us knows where Sam is, and this is why we haven't booked a flight yet, although we've made some calls. We both have just enough cash for a flight to California, but that's about it. Of course we have money coming to us from recent bookings, but it might take a month or more to find us. I ponder another month in France as I finish wiping up the floor, and consider it an eternity.

I am feeling absolutely relieved about not having to be perfectly thin for the moment when Valerie calls to verify my booking with French *Elle*.

"Oui. Next Tuesday and Wednesday. Dis is okay vith you, Rachel?"

"I guess." I stand there, my hair matted into a two-day rat's nest with a yellow rubber glove on one hand and spots of a white sulfur mask in three areas on my face where I feel I am breaking out. I can feel the pain under one pimple as I press on it and wonder if I can squeeze the stuff out and have enough time for the area to heal before Tuesday. Why can't I just say no? No. I don't want to be a model anymore. Please release me from this obviously impossible existence as a picture of perfection. The illusion is exhausting and involves energy I'd rather exude someplace else. I want exclamation marks at the end of each thought, but they're not available, lost instead in someone else's dream of modeling in Paris, at such a chance as this. Please! What am I complaining about? "Valerie?"

"Yes, darling?" Always doling out the tenderness when I possess what gives them reason to go to work each day. If she knew I was about to take off into the real world of accepting cellulite on my thighs and not caring too deeply if the ends of my hair are splitting, would I still be a darling?

"Have you seen Sam around lately?"

"Little Samantha? Is she not vith Alex?"

"Is she?" I take off my other glove and set it on the counter, wondering what I am getting myself into.

"But of course, Rachel. She lives there, no?"

"I guess." What does Valerie know? Probably more than she lets on. Pretty blondes seem to so easily conceal what they choose not to reveal. Is society, myself included, so quick to dismiss them, excuse them from the dirt reality brings with it? Did Marilyn Monroe suffer from one too many quick dismissals? Why is it that all Bo Derek needs to do is smile gently, bringing her cheekbones into full form, and we're good to go, thanks for the show. Don't open your mouth; you might spoil the effect.

Listening to Valerie sigh in French, I begin to understand the attraction we all have to perfect beauty. It is simple. It is good. It is quiet. It's comforting, in a world of chaos and illness, of war and conflict, of stress and dissatisfaction to view the human in near perfect form. Perhaps it gives one hope or a sense of control. Alex's daily task simply involves the epitome of society's desire for such perfection. His focus is the embodiment of the search for surface beauty and the quick buzz it gives us all. Only because he'd found himself in such a position of control, he took it a step further, like any good addict will. His drug is possessing what he will never be, which is beautiful. I quickly try to imagine growing up with a cut running through my eye and down the side of my face. Male or female, this would cost something. Self-esteem shattered at each turn in front of the mirror. Snide remarks from children on the playground, disappointment seeping from every visit with the relatives, horror from the opposite sex as he begins wanting to date.

I want Alex to be the enemy. I need him to be so I can have a reason to run again. But all of a sudden, as I set the receiver down, gaining absolutely no new information whatsoever, all I think of doing is returning to his place with the plush red carpet and the gilded-edged mirrors in search of something even more than Sam. I want to look at him without fear this time. I need to see him once more.

"I'm going over there." I am splashing my face with the warmest water that will come from our ancient faucet.

"Over where?" Eliza slides in her white, slouchy socks on the wooden floor to where I can see her.

"To Alex's."

"Are you crazy?"

"Maybe." I pat my face with a white, cotton towel, still feeling the zit, but not really caring about it. After next Wednesday, I'll be free from the confines of beauty on demand. And for some reason, this decided freedom is offering me a power and new sense of self I might describe as epiphanous, although I am not sure this is a word.

"Are you going right now?" Actually, I hadn't thought of that, but it did seem like a good idea. Go before I sabotage my epiphany, before I think about it all too long. But no, it will have to wait until tomorrow. "To find Sam?"

"Sam. Right." I am not thinking of her at the moment.

"You want me to go with you?" I consider my mission as warrior, as rescuer. I will go to rescue the sense of self he'd stolen, albeit briefly. I will go as warrior to wage against what he does to the innocents he lures into his web of promises and lies. It seems like a singular trip. Another might spoil the intensity.

"No. I'll go alone."

Eliza looks relieved. I pull a fresh white shirt over my head and consider my plan.

"We're getting out of here, right?"

"Of course."

"I heard you on the phone…"

"I know. One last booking next week, then we'll make our escape."

* * *

The next morning, however, I am not so sure about any of it. In the dark hours of doubt, when everything seems so completely unreal and nothing makes sense, between dreams and trips to the bathroom, I lose my courage. Maybe it is the wicked light on my face at 3:00 am when I decide to pop the zit. Blood comes oozing out, and I look grotesque to myself. I wonder what it is in me that I can't have left the thing alone, letting it gradually release by itself in a professional manner, putting a light touch of makeup on it until it just drained on its own in the shower or something, without me ever having control over it. Is it self-hatred, self-loathing, or the feeling of lost control as painful bumps rise up on the most important area of the human form without the slightest invitation? How can I not feel totally freaked out by this when I am getting paid to look perfect?

I lie in bed counting the hours before dawn, feeling the bump as it subsides, trying not to touch it, then touching it simply because I know I shouldn't. Then I wonder who I am to face the man of my nightmare. What change can I bring about for either of us? It is true—I wish to change his behavior, to save further model-wanna-bees from the tyrannical hold he seems to have over all of us. I want to hold the mirror to *his* face, to show him what he is, believing in the innate good within all of us and that it will conquer in the end.

But mainly I want to show him his grasp on me is no longer valid. His exterior view of me is ridiculous. I will say this casually as I explain what is real and what is not, mentioning something cliché about inner beauty. And yet all I can think of is this monster-ugly red zit and that I can never face him with my face like this. Even with makeup, he'd see right through it, right through me—to the me that is just as superficial as he is. All the while we'd be talking, I'd only be looking at him looking at me and all my imperfections, adding them up and subtracting them from my overall importance.

It isn't Alex that needs to change. It is me. If I don't get out of this business and this city where my reason for being is superficial perfection, I will end up like Alex, in a never-ending search for what simply doesn't exist with myself or with anyone else. The pages of magazines are fraudulent with the photographer's perfect lighting and the stylist's tucks and pins, the makeup artist's cover sticks and tricks and the model's complete permission to become an image to sell to a consumer who is consumed with a belief that such a picture is possible. For a moment, for a flick of the switch on the camera when the fan is blowing just right and the umbrella lights shine in unison, when the model, for a brief second in between blinking her eyes and breathing, buys into the clothes she is wearing and the smile she is smiling, maybe. For a moment maybe. And that's the picture, air-brushed and printed on glossy paper and copied a hundred thousand times to make it feel as if this image is all around us and yet completely unreachable—until we reach out and grab it from the stands as we are making our way to the check-out counter with our chocolate ice cream bars and frozen pizza.

I am already berating myself for a zit, as if I can do a thing about it. What will be next? I am already only eating food with less than 5 grams of fat per serving, pounding my body on hard pavement six days a week, and living exclusively to be accepted and recognized, or not, by a beast such as Alex. And I am only twenty. Years of fighting fat and aging and looking in the mirror loom ahead of me. Will I ever be able to shake the damage already done?

I need to change me. I need to get back to who I was before I was this. The terrifying thing is that I can no longer remember who that is.

32

I FIND THEM IN PARIS

"Rachel, you awake? Rachel!"
It truly takes me awhile to remember that's me. My morning dreams are deep and engaging, and the new day seems like a thousand years from yesterday. I am happy for the elapse in time. It helped put a light scab over the facial wound.

"What?" Don't mess with me so early in the morning! Don't you know I had a rough night while we were asleep?

"Someone's here for you." The wild tone in her voice helps me pull the soft cover from my body.

"Who?" I demand more information if I am not in prepared mode post shower, proper clothing, and certainly a dot of tinted Clearasil. Who needs to see my zit so soon in the day? But she doesn't need to answer, for the person makes herself known in my doorway, like a silent angel whose presence is complete without sound.

"It's you." I can't even speak her name.

"It's me." And the look in her almond eyes look into mine to say there's something more, something so much more. I let her do this for a second or two and then my conscious self takes over, and I beg them both to let me dress and make myself a bit more presentable. My two closest friends acquiesce, and I make a dash for the bathroom with my jeans under my arm. After all, I am only in my underwear and my cellulite is showing.

In the bathroom, I pee and try to prepare myself for this absolutely unexpected visit. If she has work here, this is beginning to be more than a coincidence, I decide.

In the mirror, I try to make peace with my new look. I brush my hair upside down, tuck my tee shirt into my jeans, and slide on a little lip gloss. I figure one spot of red isn't enough for full makeup, but covering just that will show I am bothered by it being there. If I am going to change, I need to begin today. I wonder what normal people do when they have a zit.

I hear Eliza's choice of morning tunes, and feel them appropriate. Joni Mitchell. Blue. It's music perfect for a chilly European morning with an unexpected guest in casual overalls. It's perfectly fine music for the zit. Nevertheless, I decide that a light covering of foundation will make *me* feel better, given that my makeup artist is certainly not here to work on me. I would have been notified if this were the case, right?

"I am on a lonely road and I am traveling, traveling, traveling, traveling; looking for something, what can it be?" Joni sings gently with strength, with casual power. The mellow sounds fill the apartment, fill the lack of conviction I feel at the moment early in this day.

I know there are days that are so unpredictable, so undeniably life-altering, that one could never have guessed what turn of events might have been scheduled by destiny or fate by the time our precious, natural light decides to wink and nod itself away again. This will be one of those days, I think, as I turn the handle on the bathroom door to bask in the morning light with my sisters, to enjoy a bit of Joni and a cup of tea perhaps.

Eliza reads my mind. Peppermint tea steam billows from three mismatched mugs, and I take a seat on the floor to get a proper and humble look at her.

"You're here."

"I am." She comes and sits next to me, and I am home, like the home one feels in a worn pair of Levi's or the smell of freshly cut grass or the taste of hot chocolate as it slides down chilled insides. Joni's quick lyrics stumble over each other beneath her sweet, soprano voice, and Eliza makes a grimace as if to ask when she's going to be let in on a secret. I shrug under my morning hair and look at Claudia's profile and her pretty olive skin.

"I have something to tell you." She places her ring-less hand on my Indian-style bent knee as she looks carefully at me and then briefly at Eliza, as if to ask my permission for the latter's continued presence. I nod around the room easily as if to communicate that all is well, that nothing could be more to my liking—not figuring in the darkened patch on my chin I'd attempted to cover and feel slightly awkward about in the company of a professional.

Claudia turns then, to face me more directly, and I quickly wonder if I should toss her an extra pillow for added comfort upon our hard floor.

At this, Eliza takes a silent cue and excuses herself to take a shower. And although I miss her instantly, I am grateful for her tact.

"I didn't want to tell you this until I knew for sure, Rachel."

"Yes?" Anxiety now, even between Joni's easy guitar and harmonious humming.

"Twenty years ago, I gave birth to a baby girl. I was just seventeen, then. The baby was the result of a rape, and my mother and father strongly encouraged me to give the baby up for adoption. I thought it was the best decision at the time, Rachel. I thought I had done the right thing until I met you again in Arizona." Her almond eyes swirl into my own—into my past, my present, and my future all at the same time. Suddenly a hot sensation seeps through the folds in my jeans and through to my knee. I set my mug on the floor next to me and try to breathe. What?

"What?" It's all I can think of to utter, a one-word reply of disbelief. Claudia is my friend, a makeup artist, a woman in the business....

"I guess you could call me your birth mother, Rachel." She is timid in her tone and placement of her hands as they shake slightly near mine. I want to hug her or hit her.

"Are you sure?" More questioning seems appropriate, as I attempt to digest this most unbelievable turn of events. My birth mother? She is someone who, by this point, could never exist in my life. She is a fantasy, an enigma, an illusion placed appropriately in my existence never to come alive. If it did, if there really was human flesh out there who I could connect to, then what? Everything would change. And the person that I finally think I am, is this the person that I am then?

"I am absolutely sure..."

But I don't give her more time to explain. My mind races like a bright bolt of lightning across the deepest darkness of the night sky. I wait for the sound of thunder to hit. My next question needs a prompt response and my stomach begins to churn with only sips of peppermint tea and apprehension in there.

"Who raped you?" The question is so bold, so personal, so horrible. I am sick to hear myself ask this, terrified of being the outcome of such a thing. I try to stand in my wet jeans, feeling faint. Claudia gets up and holds my arm. I need to be moving. She holds off answering for what seems like forever, for what is about ten seconds. We both walk over to the window to look out at what seems like an immensity of space in contrast to the claustrophobia I am experiencing. I open the window with all the strength I have left in me. Claudia's tears are not requiring a tissue. We both let them drop.

"Alex." That name. It may have well been the name of the devil. I fall to the floor, my back against the wall as I make myself as small as possible. Claudia is right there next to me, and our tears are the only thing required to continue our communication. What is there to say?

"Does Alex know?" We tend to want to hold onto something when everything else seems to be disintegrating around us. Like when we find out someone has died, we ask, "How did it happen?" as if the answer to this might ease the suffering or make it all a little more understandable.

"No."

No. That is something. It is a little innocence left to hold onto.

"He doesn't need to know." But then as soon as I say this, I want to track him down, wherever he might be lurking, and stand in his face as his "daughter." I turn to face Claudia, finally, as she blots her face with the back of her hand. It is the first time I see someone else besides this sweet woman and my friend. I see me. It's the way her nose and mouth appear in profile. The lower half of her face extends out in a pout exactly the way I've seen mine in numerous photographs. My tears and my embrace match up with hers as well as we huddle together on the floor—female victims, blood warriors, sisters.

"But we will tell him anyway." Claudia breaks the silence and I sniff in response as I stand up to get some tissues. My head rushes, and I feel absolutely faint for the second time. I hold onto the wall for a moment and realize my entire life is not what I thought it was.

"We will?" If I just continue on with this insane conversation, maybe something real will kick in and I will be able to seriously grasp the effect this information is going to have upon me.

"He has to know what he's done."

"What he is doing." I look over at her, forget myself, and feel more centered.

"I know." Claudia stands up. We both realize Eliza is finished with her shower and will be joining us soon. "All I have been doing since you left is figuring out the truth of who you are and making plans to be with you as soon as possible. Oh, Rachel, my sweet baby girl." Her hands place themselves on either side of my face as she peers into my eyes like a mother. Like a mother I never knew could be. A mother I should have had all along. I step back.

"You don't know what you did when you gave me up." Now the tears are wickedly deep, coming from my throat in regretful pain.

"Tell me." She moves toward me.

"No.... I can't." The past twenty years of my life whip in front of me as I fast forward all events, frustration, pain, and confusion until the moment where I am blowing my nose in front of the person who allowed it all.

"In time, then." And her soft words caress my broken heart as Joni's voice sings its last note of her album, "Blue."

"Hey, you guys!" Eliza's post-shower greeting is premature and startling.

"Hi." I turn to face her and in turn change the shape of her face.

"Rachel, you okay?" And suddenly I feel that I just might be exactly that.

"Eliza, this is my mom." I step aside for my friend to view the tear-stained face that matches mine.

"Oh my God, are you kidding?" She is ecstatic with her joyful surprise. "Rachel, Oh my God!"

"I know." Soon I, too, am dancing around a little bit with Eliza. It's sort of a jumping, hugging type of dance where the spirit does not know what to do with the body. Claudia looks on at us and for a small second, I feel like her daughter, like a daughter who is allowed to have happiness because the mother is strong enough in her own happiness.

* * *

My new mom and I spend the next couple hours crying and smiling hopefully in front of our audience of one. We manage to consume a couple bran muffins between the three of us, enough sustenance just to get us through what we intend on doing, which is facing Alex.

"He's got Sam. I know it." Eliza speaks excitedly, like one of Charlie's Angels on a mission to seek justice.

"Of course he does." Claudia wipes bran muffin crumbs from the counter into our little plastic waste basket. The sun sends a few rays through our open window, making it feel like a regular type of day, when it is exactly the opposite of this.

"How do you know for sure?" A huge part of me wants nothing

to do with the red carpet and the gilded mirrors and the scarred eye. What if I see myself in him as well? Then who will I be? I shudder and excuse myself to pee out some of the peppermint tea. In the mirror I am much older now, with streaks of dried foundation down each cheek. I try to see Claudia and Alex in the mirror and the longer I stare in there, the more unsure I am about myself. Because of this, I touch the scab, press at it, and consider reapplying the foundation all over again. How can I look at Alex today?

"Rachel, you okay in there?" It's my mom.

"I'm fine." Isn't that what you are supposed to say?

"You sure?" She's so sweet. And then I think about what Alex did to her. What he's doing to Sam. I gently wash my face of all tears and makeup and open the bathroom door with grave determination.

"Let's go."

* * *

In the taxi on the way, all three of us are quiet. We are gaining our power with our quiet breath, in and out, in and out through the narrow streets of Paris while the scruffy driver repeats the name of the street several times, breaking into our concentration, reminding us of the final destination, of the place of which we are each individually terrified. Together, however, the possibilities seem endless. We have history and secrets and blood. We have information and journeys behind us all leading up to this day. It is a day of reckoning, of reclaiming our spirits, our bodies, our peace. That a man could take these things away and that a woman would allow him to are the perplexities that boggle my mind as we make our way through streaks of sun and drops of rain.

"Je me suis egare."

"Pardon?" Claudia sits forward from the back seat with us to address the driver, who is apparently lost as he rattles the map around on the passenger's seat. I secretly wonder, while the two of them find the street on the map, if this isn't a sign we should not go.

But I know it is only my cowardice kicking in because it's been given a little extra time. Eliza sits to my left and nudges me.

"Are you scared?"

"Yes." I look into my lap at my hands and wonder if they are Alex's hands. I wonder about his feet and the way his ears curve. Do I have the genes of evil in me running through my DNA? Eliza puts her arm around me.

In a flash, it seems, we are pouring out of the backseat and gathering ourselves in the street, peering up at the door. Break on through to the other side of my life, of who I will now be. I will no longer be just the girl from Wisconsin with no connection to family. My mother now stands next to me.

"Come on, girls."

"I suppose we should knock?" Eliza stands frozen in place. She is right. It doesn't really feel like a knocking occasion. We are here to free the prisoner, to confront the jailer, to expose the rapist.

"Just see if it's open."

My mother is daring. I guess years of wondering where your first child might be gives one determination. I press at the door and am immediately confronted by the sick, stale aroma of cigarettes and dust and misery lurking from the corners, both afraid and possibly encouraged by the light and fresh air being brought in by the open door.

"Hello?" The place is darker than I remember. The faceless man who greeted me last time does not seem to be around. We inch into the living area and find ourselves among heaps of newspapers, magazines, and ashtrays brimming with crushed ends of cigarette butts. "Anyone here?" Claudia is brave with her words as she stumbles over a large bag of garbage to get into the next room. Eliza and I move around quietly, cautiously. The house looks as if it has not been tended to in weeks, and at the moment I am not quite certain what we are doing here.

"She used to sleep in there." I whisper and point and hope that either one of them will be brave enough to follow the direction of my finger so that I won't have to.

"It's so dark. Should we turn on a light?" Eliza looks up at us and snaps on a living room lamp without waiting for an answer. At once we all see the first evidence of what we came looking for—a pervert. On the coffee table are open portfolios of models. But the pictures are naked and grotesque—girls are photographed while sleeping, some of them chained to the bed with handcuffs, legs spread wide. With a detective's curiosity, Claudia flips through a few pages, touching just the bottom corner of each one. We gaze, shocked and sickened by who this man must be. I see Susan's creamy face and large breasts in one of the photos and remember her nightmares.

When we've all had enough, we use our new disgust to press into the back bedrooms, walking ever so carefully so as not to trip over dirty laundry or trash, which seems to have taken over the apartment.

At the end of the hallway there is a dim, red light streaming from underneath the door. Claudia is in the lead, as she should be, as my mother, as the eldest, as the one done the most wrong and for the longest time, perhaps. She is fearless now as twenty years shrink away between the two of us and we forge ahead for justice's sake. She knocks twice at the door, lightly, as if to say that even though we've broken in we still have enough decency to announce ourselves. There is no response.

That we are all here, all three of us, multiplied by our anticipation and curiosity and determination, makes Claudia's decision to try the handle on the door much easier. She doesn't even flinch as she goes for it, gives it a little turn and shake only to realize that it is locked.

"Now what?" Eliza asks, but the answer is evident. We didn't come this far to turn around and duck out. Claudia puts her ear to the door.

"Quiet. I think I hear something."

Eliza and I stand there in absolute obedience. "Sounds like someone is throwing up." We all inch closer and remain silent. Now that we know someone is actually in there, our mission begins to take on a very real feel. We are trespassing. We are trespassing at the devil's door—red light and grotesque noises seeping from the slice of space between the door and the floor.

I look at Claudia with widened eyes, as if to express the growing intensity of the situation. She looks numbly at what is keeping us from the finality of our fears and grants me the permission to go for it.

"Sam." I am nearly screaming. I am not dreaming. "Sam! Are you in there?" And then all three of us take a baby step backwards as we hear the rattle of the handle. The heavy, wooden door creeks open to reveal our small, gothic friend dressed in dark bodily bruises; smudged, red lips; and black leather bra and panties. Her eyes are wild and frightened and disgusted and vacant all at the same time as she looks from us to the bed and back again.

"A few minutes earlier and you might have been able to save him. Seriously." The room is engulfed in the dim, red light, in dust and garbage and magazines and clothes that are scattered all over the floor. There is no clear space to stand, and I imagine we must appear quite silly huddled together as we witness the room before us. "I just couldn't take it anymore, the way he flailed around like a retard, like an imbecile who has no control over his own bodily functions." And she motions with a sly gesture of body and face toward her villain, her victim, who is handcuffed to the headboard, legs spread revealing his nakedness, the black robe at his sides. His ankles are tied to the bed posts; his scarred face stares up at the ceiling.

"Jesus." Eliza utters this two-syllable word saved for sex and stress and death and fakes like she can't look at what we were all seeing.

"Yep. Only Jesus can save him now," Sam sneers, as she wipes a few chunks of whatever she had been throwing up onto the back of her hand. "Heart attack, I am guessing. Although who knows after all those pills. Could have been anything, but I am guessing heart attack the way he was wrenching around on that bed for so long. I couldn't take the noise anymore. You guys didn't hear it? Shit. It was horrible. The screams of a child. What an ass."

She begins to move around like a maid tidying up a room in a hotel with no respect for personal space. The job is almost done, just a few things and she will move on to the next one.

"Should we call someone?" It hits me hard that my father is lying on the bed, dead and naked. Sam shoots me a glance of disbelief.

"Who exactly are you going to call?" She prods with her newly acquired taste for revenge and death and justice for all. "The police?"

"I don't know. Someone."

"You think you are going to call the police on me now?" Her nonchalance tightens as she begins to realize the situation she is in. Claudia moves even closer to me and takes my hand in hers. You and me against the world.

"You think he didn't deserve this shit? Fuck. Who are we all kidding here? Who is grateful this perverted fuck lies dead on his own bed? Raise your hand." She looks at each one of us as her pulse begins to visibly race with a renewed hate. "Do you have any idea what this sick asshole has done to the girls he brings here? No? No, how could you. He feeds them pills and fucking rapes them while they are out. He feeds them with lies and ties them up like this and photographs them and tells them more lies when they wake up. All for what? So some little priss from Alabama or whatever can be a Paris model. Serves them right, these stupid glamour-hungry girls. Oh, they all want to be models so bad. They'll do just about anything, won't they? They sulk around here and wait to become famous. He gets bored with them. What is a sick fuck like him supposed to do? Play little sex games. No one gets hurt, right? Until someone fucking does."

At this, all the blood leaves the surface of her skin and she goes blank and pale as she attempts to button a large oxford shirt around her body in a weary hope to be taken more seriously, perhaps. And just like that, she drops into a tiny heap on the floor.

Claudia is the first one to move. She sweeps our Sam up off the dirty floor and begins to carry her down the hallway and into the living room. "Rachel. Call an ambulance." Eliza pushes all the magazines and trash off the couch for Sam as Claudia attempts to bring her back into consciousness with soft talk as she gently clears strands of hair from her face.

During this time, I feel struck dumb and numb. I won't go back into the bedroom. I can't. But I want to. I want to face him. I want to stare at him in the face, but I am too late. He's gone, and I know in some twisted way it's for the best. Should I cover him? But if I do, I would have to untie him as well and I just can't think of this. It would be best for the police to deal with the whole scene untouched.

Eliza and I exchange grave looks of horror and disbelief at the scene in front of us. "She's not breathing very well," I hear Claudia say, as she looks up at me. "Who knows what she's taken." There are little orange bottles of prescription medication sitting on the table, and we attempt to read some of the names. But they are in French and so all we can do is shake them and look back over at Sam, who seems as lifeless as a rag doll.

"I think I hear an ambulance. Is that what they sound like here?" I am asking no one in particular.

"I think so." Eliza tries to help.

"They better get here soon. I don't know if she's going to make it. Rachel, go to the door so they can see you, okay?"

"Okay." And I walk toward the entrance of my father's house and open the door, exposing his sins to the world, letting the sun shine in upon the dark life of a man I will never really know.

33

NEW YEAR'S EVE

Oakland Coliseum is burning with color and sweet earth aromas as Eliza and I make our way through the crowds of kids spinning and smiling and smoking and simply celebrating the life. We are sufficiently baked and seemingly lost as we hold hands on the way to where the bathroom is supposed to be. The show has not yet started.

"We should eat them now."

"You sure?" I can't imagine feeling any better than I do now.

"That way we'll peak during the first set and probably won't start coming down 'til the end. It'll be perfect."

"There it is." The bathroom offers us a long line of happy Heads all decked out in the most fantastic garb one would have thought went out of fashion in the early 70s, and yet here it is, so beautifully redone on some of the most gorgeous, young Americans I ever laid eyes on. Pink, perfect cheeks, blazing eyes that seemed to know the truth, wild hair, uncombed and glorious, clothes of all the colors mixed and matched and layered and always the dedication to the Dead wherever we look. Flowers in braids, old Converse tennis shoes, socks and skirts and patched jeans jackets, dancing bears and dancing skeletons, red roses and all the colors growing 'round and 'round in swirls of circles that have no end and no beginning. The sweet smells of pot and incense and homegrown foods greet us as we slink out into the parking lot where the festivities of a pre-show party are well under way.

We decide to pee over by the side of the building behind a small gathering of trees. Even if anyone sees us, they won't care. The rock and rhythm of this place is that it's all good. Here we all are, every one of us all the same, where dancing is the only work to be done and love and pot and food are shared as needed.

"Hold up the back of your skirt."

"Shit."

"Here, I'll do it." And I bend down to rescue the bottom of Eliza's light, flowered dress she wears over some leggings and under a Dead sweatshirt. It is then, as I am squatting next to her in the midst of the anticipation of the music to come that I realize I have made a very true friend.

For the past several weeks, I have been staying with Eliza and her mom as a much needed reprieve from the chaos my world has become. In California, I am nothing except whoever I want to be in the moment. I am not a model, which is an hourly thrill for me now as I begin to eat like a normal person. I am not some lost girl seeking her parents. They are now found, and thinking about how it all came to be takes up a good deal of my time while I am currently and officially homeless and jobless. With Eliza and her mom, I am a guest and a young woman who simply needs some time to contemplate what to do next. The Dead shows, of which there were several leading up to this one, stand as the zenith of my visit. Tonight's show will be our third in a row, and we saved the shrooms for this night. They are supposed to be good.

"So, ready?"

"I guess."

"Wanna get one of those organic veggie wraps and put them in there?"

"Excellent idea." Eliza and I move over to one of the many decked out van small business stands in the parking lot. Large tie-dye sheets hang to provide privacy for the Dead families who travel from show to show. A square folding table is the perfect spot to offer their homemade tacos for $3.00. A thin, bearded hippie man in a worn-out grey Henley shirt grins in our direction as we come to shop.

"Hey there, little school girls. I'm Jack Straw from Wichita. What can I get you this fine eve of the new year?" From his van, a live version of "Fire On The Mountain" plays, and Jack never misses a beat with his entire body. The music feeds his soul as the food feeds his body. He needs the music to breathe. It is his life. There is no other "real" life out there waiting for him. His glassy eyes blaze as he serves up two tacos wrapped in paper towels. We give him six bucks and bow slightly in appreciation of providing not only awesome nourishment right on cue, but the perfect hiding places for some very dry mushrooms. We are giggling.

"Over there?"

"Sure." It looks private enough, even amidst all the craziness of the pre-party parking lot show. A small, cement slab is where we decide to plant ourselves in order to partake. Dead tunes from all over play as dancing Heads jive in wild anticipation of the real thing, of the arrival of the mythological God of music, Father Jerry and of Bobby and Phil and the whole dedicated family who have been touring in shows where the music never ends.

"It's cold."

"Yep." We are shivering together and looking around to see if anyone is watching as Eliza takes the plastic baggie of shrooms from her oversized purse. The air has turned chilly as the non-existent sun hangs low in the sky. Light moisture mist drops onto our hair and cheeks, adding some weight to our layers of clothes, keeping us grounded in our endeavors to take our high even higher.

"It's been quite the year, huh?"

"Like no other." I drape my body around Eliza and our psychedelic sandwiches as she finishes dividing and inserting the illegal drugs in her lap.

"It's so incredible about Sam." Eliza and I realize that this moment is one of those moments we will never forget, a moment in time where space stands still to allow us the fullness of life, and if we die this very hour there would be no regret because here and now is all there is and all there ever was meant to be.

"She's due in the summer. July, I think." I am of course speaking with Claudia on a near daily basis. Our relationship is something I never thought I would experience, but here it is right in front of me and all around me; this woman I can call my own, this person who loves me because of me. And a new little sister to think about. Actually, I can't wait to get back East to be with all of them, even Sam.

"It's so cool she's keeping it. I mean, I don't know if I would."

"I know. Claudia has been her savior. She's been through it and then found me and how could she counsel Sam in any other way?"

"Sam really seems to trust her."

"Claudia took her in and says it's been an incredibly healing experience for them both." We chew our taco wraps in silence for a moment, thinking. All around us are signs of a brand new year pulsating through the clouds and crowds of people as we munch down our dinner, grateful. I breathe between bites and think of Sam, pregnant with my sibling. It's a very strange thought to think before a trip, and I have to calm myself with a few more breaths of cool, Northern California air. My long braided hair blows into my food, and I have to pull it out of my mouth before taking another bite.

"You're beautiful, Rachel." Eliza grins over at me as she wipes her mouth with the back of her hand.

"I am?"

"Uh, huh."

"Cool not to have to be though, right?"

"Right." And we both rise from our places on the ground and reach out in an impromptu embrace as a few tears mix with the mist.

"I love you, girl." I am entrenched with love right now.

"I love you, too."

"Let's ramble." I take her hand.

"Ramble on, baby." She holds mine.

"Settle down easy." We walk together into the coliseum, into the pleasure dome, our home for the night to say goodbye to the day, the year, tonight. We dance into a welcoming circle of brilliant, colored spirits who simply want to rock and roll and hold this moment of living in gratitude of what life can be when you let it be.